THE
NUMBERS

BOOKS BY NICK PIROG

NICK PIROG

THE
NUMBERS

**BLACK
STONE**
PUBLISHING

Copyright © 2023 by Nick Pirog
Lyrics to "Baby" by Justin Bieber reprinted by
kind permission of the copyright holder.
Published in 2023 by Blackstone Publishing
Cover and book design by Luis Alejandro Cruz Castillo

The characters and events in this book are fictitious.
Any similarity to real persons, living or dead, is coincidental
and not intended by the author.

Printed in the United States of America

First edition: 2023
ISBN 978-1-9826-7392-5
Fiction / Thrillers / Suspense

Version 1

CIP data for this book is available
from the Library of Congress

Blackstone Publishing
31 Mistletoe Rd.
Ashland, OR 97520

www.BlackstonePublishing.com

PROLOGUE

The second *B* in the Blockbuster sign flickered, the bright yellow fading, then just as quickly springing back to life.

Lew wondered if the assistant manager—the one he'd been watching for the past several days—was aware the sign needed fixing. Though in the grand scheme of things, it didn't matter. The man would be dead within the hour.

Lew pulled up the sleeve of his jacket and checked his watch. Seventeen minutes until closing time. He crossed the street, making his way into the seldom-used alley behind the store. The building opposite Blockbuster was two stories of gray brick. It was an accounting firm, and Lew had watched the last of the employees depart hours earlier.

A green dumpster was nestled next to the back entrance of the Blockbuster. It had rained the night before, and there were a few standing puddles of oily, black water. With a gloved hand, Lew lifted the lid on the dumpster and peeked inside. It was brimming with garbage bags and a half dozen empty pizza boxes.

Lew shook his head. He didn't understand how people could put that stuff in their bodies.

Wasted calories.

One of the pizza boxes quivered, then a well-fed brown rat scurried out. It gazed up at Lew predatorily, then thought better of it and disappeared under a garbage bag. Lew's stomach tightened. If there was anything he despised, it was rats.

Several days after Lew's dad had gone missing, a construction worker had found his dead body stuffed in a sewer drain. When Lew and his mother went to identify the body at the morgue, he could see where rats had feasted on his father's corpse.

Lew crouched on the far side of the dumpster and tried to conjure up a better memory. He pulled a switchblade from his pocket and flicked it open. His dad had given him the knife on his fourteenth birthday. He fingered its hard white ivory hilt. Well, *imitation* ivory. His father would have never bought anything made from a harmed animal.

No, his father was the ultimate protector.

At least, he had been.

Fifteen minutes passed, and then, just like the previous days, the back door opened. The assistant manager emerged. He was slightly overweight, with a bushy mustache dyed unnaturally dark, and he was clad in a blue Blockbuster polo with a name badge that read "Gene." Large black headphones covered his ears, and the cord snaked down to a small radio clipped to his khakis. He rocked his head side to side to the beat.

If the bumper sticker on Gene's silver 2004 Honda Civic was any indication, he was listening to 102.9 MGK—Philadelphia Classic Rock.

As Gene lifted the lid on the dumpster and tossed in the trash bag, Lew sprang from his hiding spot. He snaked his arm around the assistant manager's head and clamped his hand over his mouth. Lew was close enough that he could hear a song pouring from the headphones. It was "Superstition" by Stevie Wonder.

How fitting.

With his opposite hand, Lew plunged his switchblade between the man's ribs. Gene let out a muffled cry and dropped to his knees. Lew pulled out the knife, then sank it into the dying man's flesh again and again.

Lew's pulse pounded. It had been too long since he last killed. Far too long.

When Gene finally succumbed to his injuries, Lew lowered him to the ground. The corpse was laid out flat on his back, staring vacantly into the night sky. After straddling his victim, Lew touched the blade of the knife to the man's forehead, eliciting a droplet of blood. It took ninety seconds to meticulously carve the three numbers.

When he was finished, Lew stood and surveyed his handiwork.

He grinned.

Game on.

1

Each fall, in preparation for the dropping temperatures, the city of Philadelphia drained the water from the fountain in Love Park. In doing so, they unintentionally transformed the thirty-foot-wide fountain into one of the most iconic skateboarding spots in the entire world.

Sadly, the city had outlawed skateboarding at the park in the 1990s, and if the skaters wanted to take a crack at Love Gap—a fifteen-foot launch from the granite walkway to the bottom of the fountain—they had to do so with their head on a swivel. Philly cops were notorious for handing out expensive tickets and hauling kids off to jail.

But for the past week, the cops had turned a blind eye to the skaters—most likely because they were spread thin with the protests downtown. Occupy Wall Street first began in New York City in mid-September, then it spread like wildfire, making its way down the Northeast Corridor to Philadelphia three weeks later on October 6.

Each day, more and more protesters turned up. The marchers and activists were like gremlins, only it wasn't water that made them multiply—it was posters and megaphones. Hundreds of demonstrators gathered at Love Park each day, but most of the protests were actually taking place across the street at city hall. A tent city had erupted, and the marble walkways were swarming with tents, encampments, and meeting areas.

For the past several days, my Starbucks cup and I had been plopping down on one of the benches in Love Park to watch the skateboarders. It was overcast—the sky filled with pewter clouds—and the temperature hovered in the midfifties. Half the leaves in the park had fallen, and several were strewn on the fountain's exposed turquoise bottom.

"Ron-nie! Ron-nie!" the nearby crowd of skaters chanted. Many held out their phones, ready to record the action to come.

Ronnie was decked out in jeans, a T-shirt, and a backward cap. He pedaled on his board out of sight, disappearing behind the stacked red letters of the thirteen-foot-tall aluminum *LOVE* sculpture. A few seconds later, he skated back into view, pedaling swiftly toward the edge of the fountain. He ollied up a foot, the top of his board glued to the bottom of his sneakers. He sailed through the air—five feet, then ten feet—then smacked down to the fountain's bottom with a loud *clap*.

His board shot out from beneath his feet, sending him careening forward. He hit the ground and rolled onto his shoulder, stopping just two feet short of the fountain's concrete base.

I shuffled through my signs. Three days earlier, I'd found two discarded pieces of blank poster board and a black Sharpie lying on the ground. I'd decided to put them to good use.

I found the sign I wanted and held it up.

"A six?" Ronnie asked, getting to his feet and gazing at my rating. "A friggin' six?"

"You want something higher, you have to land it," I said, grinning. "Or you have to break something. And not a hairline fracture—I want to see bone."

He laughed.

The next two skaters didn't even come close to landing the trick. I gave them a two and a three, respectively. Following them was clearly a crowd favorite; she was young, maybe fifteen, and her black hair was twisted in a tight braid. This was her third attempt in the hour I'd been here.

My stomach tightened as she disappeared behind the *LOVE* sculpture. The other skaters knelt and pounded the front wheels of their boards against the ground.

Bang, bang, bang!

Bang, bang, bang!

"Come on, Braid," I muttered under my breath. "You got this."

She shot into view, ollied high, and flew through the air. Initially it looked like a perfect landing, but after hitting the ground, her board slid out to the right. She fell backward but somehow stayed on her feet.

There was a collective groan.

So close.

She glanced in my direction.

I held up an eight.

She shrugged and smiled.

Ronnie was up again next. When he was halfway through the air, I knew it was destined to end badly. The board had left his feet, and he was at the mercy of gravity and physics. He fell, one foot hitting the bottom of the fountain, the other hitting the edge of the last stair. The sound of an ankle shattering echoed through the still autumn air.

Before reaching for his ankle, he rolled over and looked at me.

I held up a ten.

He gave me a thumbs-up.

After Ronnie's injury, there was a lull in the action. A young boy was sitting with his mom to my left, and he'd been observing and enjoying my judging. I handed him my stack of numbers and said, "You're in charge now."

He took the signs with wide eyes and nodded solemnly. You would have thought I'd just knighted him.

I heard chanting coming from across the street and headed in that direction. As I walked to the corner of JFK Boulevard and Fifteenth, I could hear a large group chanting, "*O-C-C-U-P-Y, what's that spell? Occupy!*"

Catchy.

I crossed the street and approached a group of protesters. Most were in their late teens or early twenties, and there was a healthy assortment of Black, brown, and beige bodies. Many were likely college students playing hooky from their Tuesday classes at one of the universities—Temple, Drexel, or Penn— within a two-mile radius.

A handful of protesters appraised me.

In gray running sweats and a red zippered hoodie, it would be impossible for them to know I was the enemy: a one-percenter.

Granted, the millions of dollars in my sister's and my joint bank account was our inheritance from our parents. Four years ago, they'd died in a plane crash. I was twenty-six at the time and the youngest homicide detective in Seattle Police Department history. My sister, Lacy, who is eight and a half years younger, had been a senior in high school.

After graduating, Lacy headed to Drexel on a swimming scholarship. As for me, well, I'd just recently been fired from the SPD—smashing my partner's face into a locker was the last straw—and I'd decided to tag along to Philly.

A young man with his hair tied in a man bun and holding a sign that read "We Are the 99%" nodded at the Starbucks in my hand and said, "Big corporations are ruining America."

"You wouldn't say that if you'd ever tried a pumpkin spice

latte." Just the dregs of the tasty drink remained, and I offered him the cup. "Go ahead, give it a whirl. It's like your first kiss, but pumpkin-ier."

Man Bun smacked the cup from my hand.

"Now, why did you have to go and do that?" I shot my hand out and grabbed his sign. After tearing the poster board in three, I tossed two of the pieces over my shoulder. I handed him the remaining piece and said, "Now you are the thirty-three percent."

He stared at me like I'd just stolen his lucky hacky sack.

The tents started up twenty feet beyond, erected along the marble walkways leading to the towering city hall. The building was old and Gothic, its exterior proliferated with columns and pillars. Topping the building was an impressive clock tower and topping the clock tower was a twenty-seven-ton statue of William Penn. Evidently, he was the founder of the province of Pennsylvania, though I just thought of him as the Quaker Oats guy.

In the span of fifty feet, I counted thirty tents. Most were two- and three-person camping tents, but there was a smattering of the larger canopy tents, the kind you might see at a farmers' market.

There was an enormous gathering on the far western edge of the plaza, and even from a football field away, I could hear them chanting, "*Banks got bailed out! We got sold out!*"

I was heading to join the fun, when I heard a startled cry and turned. A small group of protesters was gathered around a blue tent. Two young women standing next to it were holding each other and crying.

I approached and asked, "What's wrong?"

"It's Brooke!" shouted one of the young women, pointing to the tent. "She won't wake up!"

As I pushed through the group, a young man said, "We need to wait for the police."

"I am the police," I said, edging past him.

It was a half-truth. I hadn't been officially employed since being canned from the Seattle Police Department three years earlier, but in the past eighteen months, I'd consulted on a number of cold cases with the Philly PD.

I kicked off my shoes, pulled my hands into the sleeves of my sweatshirt, then crawled into the tent. My nose twitched on entering. There was a faint aroma of something antiseptic.

It was a two-person tent, four and a half feet wide, with a depth of about seven feet. Centering the tent was a white megaphone sitting atop an unzipped green sleeping bag. Off to the right was a young woman—Brooke, presumably—lying on her back.

I crawled two more feet until I was directly over her body. She was dressed in a gray-and-blue University of Pennsylvania hooded sweatshirt and dark jeans. Her blond hair was splayed out around her head. Her eyes were open, which was never a good sign.

Enough residual light was sneaking through the front flap that I could see the whites of her eyes were dotted with petechial hemorrhages—broken blood vessels that are often a sign of death by asphyxiation.

With the sleeve of my sweatshirt, I gently pulled down the neck of her hoodie. Her throat was a cascading purple.

Brooke had been strangled.

2

I poked around for another minute, then heard sounds of the approaching cavalry.

"Back up!" a stern voice shouted. "Everybody needs to back up!"

A moment later, the beam of a flashlight whipped around the tent, then came to rest on my face.

"Prescott?" the figure barked.

I shielded the blinding light with my hand. "Present."

"What the hell are you doing?" I recognized the nasal voice of Officer Kip Hufley.

"I'm helping this young lady study for her philosophy quiz tomorrow." I smiled, then added, "Nietzsche."

"Get out of there!"

"Coming."

I exited the tent.

Kip Hufley and I were the same age (thirty), the same height (six feet), and roughly the same weight (a hundred and seventy pounds), but that's where the similarities stopped. I was lean and muscular with medium-length cinnamon-brown hair and, I would like to think, the easygoing affability of a sea otter.

Meanwhile, Kip was doughy, with curly black hair that always looked damp, and the prickliness of a sixth-century tax collector.

He was in full uniform and slipped his flashlight back into his utility belt. He shook his head. "I don't give a shit if you are Folch's golden child. You can't just trample all over a crime scene."

Jim Folch was captain of the Ninth District. After I helped solve a cold case that had stymied the Philadelphia Police Department for over a decade, he'd reached out to me on several occasions to consult on an active case. I wouldn't say I was his golden child—more like a bronzed third cousin.

"I didn't trample anything." I nodded at my shoes on the ground. "I'm not an idiot."

"Fooled me."

"Said the guy who failed his detective exam four times."

He didn't have a comeback for that, and he stood there with his mouth agape, revealing teeth more crowded than Woodstock. I clapped him on the shoulder and said, "Well, I better be going. Good luck with the investigation, *Hufflepuff.*"

Several other officers had pushed the crowd back thirty feet and began stringing crime scene tape.

I picked up my shoes, ducked under the tape, then walked to a wooden bench on the outskirts of the pulsing onlookers. As I was pulling on my shoes, two detectives approached: Mike Gallow and Desiree Moore.

I first met Gallow at a cheesesteak place three months after moving to Philly. I pegged him as a detective the moment I got in line behind him; he wore a green Philadelphia Eagles jersey, and I could see the outline of his off-duty piece on his hip. He ended up inviting me to play pickup basketball with a bunch of other cops at Capitolo Playground each Sunday morning, which is where I first met Captain Folch and the aforementioned Kip "Hufflepuff" Hufley.

Gallow was five foot eight and built like a minivan. He was in his midthirties, with a receding melon head and an Irish complexion. He and his wife of eleven years had one daughter, Ainsley, who according to Gallow, was causing her preschool teacher to contemplate early retirement.

Desiree Moore was his partner. Though I didn't know her exact age, I guessed she was a few years older than Gallow. Her skin was a warm brown, and her dark hair was styled in short ringlets. She was going on six months pregnant, and her belly pushed out through her open suit jacket.

I pointed to the far side of the plaza. "If you guys are looking to invoke your First Amendment rights, the protest is over there."

They both cracked smiles, Gallow's taking up the entirety of his wide face, and Moore's tight and compact.

"Damn," Moore said. "I left my megaphone in the car."

I chuckled.

Nodding at her stomach, I asked, "How are you feeling?"

"Like the Hindenburg."

"You got a name yet?"

"Names," she corrected. "Plural."

"Really?"

"Yep, twins."

"Congrats."

"The perks of IVF."

"How about you?" I nodded at Gallow's ever-growing paunch.

"Just the one." He pulled his dark-blue tie to the side and gave his stomach two light pats.

"You got a name?"

He didn't hesitate: "Geno."

After spending an entire life in Philadelphia sampling its

myriad of cheesesteak offerings, Gallow had declared Geno's
Steaks his favorite. He ate there four days a week.

"Makes sense."

"How's Carmen?" he asked.

Carmen was Gallow's half sister, and she was eleven years
his junior. I'd met her six weeks earlier at Gallow's Labor Day
barbecue, and we'd been seeing each other casually ever since.
There was only one problem: she was batshit crazy. She played
drums in a punk rock band, she rode a Harley, and she'd served
eight months' hard time for hacking her college transcripts and
making herself salutatorian. Not to mention that she routinely
clawed my back to the point you would think I'd stolen an egg
from a velociraptor.

I bit the inside of my lip at the mention of his half sister.
"Actually, I'm thinking of ending things."

"Can I have a key to your condo?" Gallow asked.

"Why?"

"I want to turn it into my man cave after Carmen murders
you and dumps your body in the Delaware."

"You don't think she'll take it well?"

Gallow and Moore locked eyes.

"The last guy who broke up with Carmen got his identity
stolen three times in one year," Moore said. "And the guy before
that? He was audited by the IRS, and they found a couple of
hidden accounts he had in the Caymans."

Never date a hacker.

Gallow was hunched over in laughter. He straightened, his
hands on his hips, his eyes wet with tears.

"I'm glad you think it's funny," I said. "Considering you
were the one who set us up."

He wiped his eyes with his forearm. "That's what makes it
even better."

Deciding small talk was over, Moore nodded at the tent and asked, "What can you tell us about the victim?"

I wasn't sure how they knew I'd looked at the body, but I guessed Hufflepuff had called Captain Folch to complain about me, and Folch had communicated this to the two homicide detectives.

"Twenty-year-old woman," I said. "Heavy bruising around the neck and moderate petechiae."

"Anything else?" she asked.

"This is going to be an absolute shit show."

"Why is that?"

After examining the young woman's body, I'd crawled to the rear of the tent, where there was a combination phone-wallet. The victim's driver's license was visible on the back of the phone.

I said, "The girl is Brooke Wexley."

Gallow leaned his head back and sighed. Then both he and Moore turned a half circle and gazed at the skyscrapers a block away on Arch Street. The second-tallest building, a glass mono- lith, was Wexlund Tower. Possibly right at this moment, sitting in his office on the top floor of the edifice, was Nicholas Wexley, the richest man in Philadelphia.

Brooke's father.

3

I made my way through the bustling Daskalakis Athletic Center, then pushed through a revolving door that led to a swimming pool and a diving pool. I took a deep inhale and let the distinctive tang of chlorine wash through me. I'd been dropping by Lacy's swim practices since she was ten, and the smell always brought a smile to my face.

It was a quarter after three, which meant Lacy and the other young women were just finishing their standard thousand-yard warm-up.

Twenty-odd girls splashed through six lanes. Lacy was easy to spot in the third one—clad in her favorite teal swim cap with flamingos on the side—gliding through the water with an effortless freestyle.

Three coaches stood near the starting blocks, each sporting a navy-blue Drexel University T-shirt and a whistle around their neck.

I gave a quick wave of acknowledgment, then found a seat in the metal bleachers. They were empty, save for a single young man—most likely one of the girls' boyfriends—who had an open book in his lap and a pencil in his mouth.

As I watched them swim, I couldn't help but think about Brooke Wexley. She was the same age as these young women—just seven months younger than Lacy. Alive one moment, her life extinguished the next.

After chatting with Gallow and Moore, I'd stuck around city hall for another hour to give my statement to one of the patrol officers and answer questions. It didn't take long for the news crews—many of whom were already on location, covering the protests—to get wind that a young woman had been murdered and flock to the edge of the police barricade. It was only a matter of time before it leaked that the victim was Brooke Wexley, at which point a hot local story would become sizzling national news.

I didn't know much about Brooke's father, but a year earlier I'd been considering taking some of Lacy's and my inheritance out of the conservative money market account where it was invested and putting it elsewhere. In my research, I'd come across several articles about Nicholas Wexley and Wexlund Capital. The hedge fund had been one of the top-performing investment funds in the US for six of the last eight years. They took a big hit during the financial crisis of 2008, but—unlike Bear Stearns, Lehman Brothers, and several other firms—Wexlund hadn't been heavily invested in the bundled mortgages at the center of that fiasco. The previous year, 2010, Wexlund had a 14 percent return, which was more than twice the industry standard.

I imagined Nicholas Wexley sitting behind his desk in an opulent high-rise office and his cell phone ringing, then getting the worst news a parent could hear.

Hopefully, Gallow and Moore would be able to get to the bottom of who killed his daughter. The next twenty-four hours would be critical.

Speaking of Gallow, my cell chirped. It was a text from his nutty sister—my soon-to-be ex.

CARMEN: You coming over tonight?

I texted back: "Only if you wear gloves."

CARMEN: You're such a pansy
ME: I'm going through a bottle of hydrogen peroxide a
    week
CARMEN: Ugh. Just come over. I'll be gentle
ME: You said that last time and I had to use our safe word
CARMEN: Don't remind me. I'll never look at HUMMUS
    the same

I took a deep breath, and before I could second-guess myself,
I typed, "Actually, I was hoping we could meet up somewhere
to talk."
I watched the screen.
Ten seconds passed.
Then twenty.
She replied: "Are you breaking up with me?"
We weren't boyfriend and girlfriend, but we'd hung out
enough that I didn't feel comfortable breaking up with her over
text message. Nor did I want to incur her wrath by doing so. I
was trying to figure out how to word my reply, when I received
another message.

CARMEN: Because it's okay if you are. We weren't
    serious

That was unexpected.
I responded: "I just think we'd be better off as friends."

CARMEN: Sounds good. Thanks for the laughs. See you around

After two more texts, it was done.

I considered texting Gallow to tell him how maturely Carmen had handled the breakup, but I didn't want to interrupt his work on the Wexley case. Plus, it would be satisfying to tell him in person.

When I set my phone down, the swimmers were wrapping up their warm-up. Lacy was fourth to finish. She hit the wall, stood, then pulled up her goggles. It took her two seconds to spot me. Her mouth opened wide, and she waved to me with both hands.

I stuck my tongue out to the side and crossed my eyes.

She giggled.

Once all the girls finished warming up, their coaches chatted with them for several minutes. A few girls switched lanes, then they started in on a serious workout.

I knew I'd have a couple hours to kill, so I'd made a quick pit stop at my condo beforehand to grab the book I was reading: *The Hunger Games.*

The dystopian YA novel had been published three years earlier, right about the time Lacy and I were uprooting from the West Coast to the East Coast. Lacy, who was an avid reader, had her head buried in the book for much of the forty-three-hour cross-country drive, leaving me to play slug-a-bug with myself. The movie adaptation was coming out in March, and Lacy demanded I read the book in preparation. I'm glad she did. It was a rollicking good read, and I only had a hundred pages left.

I was so immersed in the novel that I didn't notice Lacy until she was hovering over me. She wore her favorite yellow Drexel sweats and a white, long-sleeve T-shirt. Her blond hair was damp and had a greenish tint.

"So, what do you think?" she asked.

"About your hair turning into lime Jell-O . . . or the book?"

She pulled a strand of hair in front of her face. Lacy had never cared much about "swimmer's hair," and after a sigh, she said, "The book, you moron."

"It's awesome."

"Told you." She grinned. "Are you Team Peeta or Team Gale?"

"Team Gale all the way."

"Let me guess," she said in a dopey singsong voice. "Because he reminds you so much of yourself."

"Well, now that you mention it."

She rolled slate-blue eyes that were nearly identical to my own, then said, "Let's go."

Once outside, Lacy leaned in and hugged me. She was five inches shorter than me, and the scent of chlorine wafted from her head. She asked, "So, is there a reason you came to watch your baby sister swim laps, or did you just miss me that much?"

"I don't need a reason to walk my sister home from practice."

"But I know you have one."

I hesitated, and she asked, "Does this have anything to do with the girl who was killed at the protest?" Lacy told me she'd seen a Facebook post about the murder right before she put her phone away in her swim locker.

"I saw the body," I said.

She slapped my shoulder. "Bullshit."

"No, seriously, I did." I recounted my afternoon.

"Brooke Wexley!" she blurted, then covered her mouth with her hand. When she took her hand away, she said, "Oh my God!"

I wasn't aware Lacy knew of her, but I supposed, considering they attended neighboring colleges and Brooke's relative fame, it was more likely than not. "Did you know her?"

"I've never met her, but Dawn Marie—one of the freshman girls—went to high school with her. Even though Brooke came from one of the richest families on earth, Dawn Marie said that she was pretty unassuming. She kind of kept to herself."

I suppose even the ultrarich can be introverts. And it wasn't Brooke's money. It was her daddy's.

"Have you gone to any of the protests?" I asked.

"Me? Come on." With a full load of classes and two hours of swim practice each day, Lacy didn't have the time or energy for much extracurricular activity. "But Maya went a few nights ago."

Maya was Lacy's assigned roommate in the dorms for freshman year, and the two had instantly become best friends. Now they shared an apartment seven blocks off campus.

Lacy added, "She just wanted to go because the guy she's got a crush on was going."

"Well, tell her to be careful if she goes there again. And tell her not to spend the night."

"I'll pass that along."

We were two blocks from her apartment when I asked, "So, what else is going on? Are *you* crushing on any boys?"

"There's this guy who sits next to me in art history. All he does is doodle horses in his notebook during class. I might love him."

I laughed.

When we reached Lacy's apartment complex, I hugged her goodbye and told her I'd be at her swim meet on Saturday. I watched as she walked up the exterior staircase to the second story and disappeared through her door.

I was pondering what to do with the rest of my afternoon, when my phone buzzed in my pocket. I pulled it out and saw it was Captain Folch.

"Let me guess," I said. "You require my expertise with the Wexley investigation?"

"No, not that," Folch replied. "But holy hell, is that thing already ruining my life. In the last hour, I've gotten two calls from the chief, one from the mayor, and one from the governor. I won't be surprised if Obama himself calls me by day's end."

"Or, at the very least, Malia."

He laughed.

"What can I help you with?" I asked.

"So far, we've done a good job of keeping it under wraps, but it looks like we have a serial killer on our hands. He's killed three people in the past two weeks."

"I haven't heard anything about it on the news."

"And you won't—at least not for another day or two. Especially not with this Wexley thing taking over the news cycle. Anyhow, the department is spread pretty thin between the protests and this Wexley investigation, so I recommended you for the task force. You're a civilian, but they'll bring you on as a consultant." He paused, then asked, "So, what do you say? Do you want to help track down this asshole?"

My heart started to hammer. "Yes, I do."

4

The William J. Green Federal Building at 600 Arch Street, which housed the Philadelphia FBI headquarters, was ten stories of alternating dark glass and brown stucco. Out front was an expensive-looking fountain surrounded by circular green picnic tables. A number of people—most likely federal employees who'd just clocked out from their nine-to-fives—were scattered among the tables, enjoying the last half hour of sunlight.

I'd had a handful of run-ins with the Feds during my tenure at the Seattle Police Department—notably, when a senior agent informed me that my personality made him "queasy"—so I was a tad apprehensive as I walked through a metal detector just inside the front entrance.

A temporary day pass awaited me at the information desk, and after pulling the lanyard over my head, I was directed to a conference room on the eighth floor.

Exiting the elevator, I heard murmuring coming from a heavy door propped open six inches. I slipped through the door and into a dimly lit room with five rows of seats. Upward of twenty individuals were focused on a man at the front.

The man—whom I assumed from talking with Captain

Folch to be the special agent in charge (SAC), Scott Joyce—was all eyebrows and creases. He stood in front of a large projection screen. Off to the right was a dry-erase board with "Area Code Killer" scribbled at the top in thick black marker.

Agent Joyce stopped talking as I entered, and I gave a half wave. His heavy brows narrowed, and he asked, "Who are you?"

"Prescott."

"Oh, right," he said, nodding. "Sorry, lots of bodies coming through here today." He swept his hand at the filled seats. "Welcome to the task force."

Based on the attire, five law enforcement organizations were represented: the Philadelphia Police Department, the Philadelphia Sheriff's Office, the Pennsylvania State Police, the Camden County Police Department, and the FBI. It was mostly male and White, but there were four women and a sprinkling of Black and brown faces.

Several individuals cut their eyes at me, and I couldn't be sure if it was because of my dashing good looks or because I was still wearing the sweatsuit I'd bought with "Kohl's Cash."

I recognized one of the cops and extended my right pointer finger and raised my thumb. I shot him in the chest with a soft *pew-pew*. "Hey there, Hufflepuff."

Everyone turned and looked at Kip. A few people snickered. Even Joyce up front stifled a laugh.

I found an open seat in the back row as Agent Joyce continued, "Like I was saying, the first body was found on October third. Gene Kirovec, age fifty-two. Assistant manager at the Blockbuster on Thirty-Third and Aramingo. He was found in the alley behind the store. He'd been stabbed six times in the back."

Joyce walked over to a laptop and tapped a button. The projection screen filled with an image of a man lying on his stomach near a green dumpster. Blood soaked through the back of his blue polo. A pair of black headphones was lying next to him.

After clicking through images of the body, a close-up of the man's head filled the screen. He had gray hair, a wide nose, and a dark mustache. His face was stained red with blood.

"It wasn't until we cleaned away the blood that we saw what was carved into the victim's forehead," Joyce said.

The headshot image was replaced by another close-up, most likely taken on the autopsy table. Knife marks on the corpse's forehead stood in deep contrast to glacier-blue skin. The marks formed a number.

503.

Folch hadn't told me much about the case, only that the killer was targeting victims who were born in specific area codes. Hailing from the Pacific Northwest, I knew 503 as the area code for Portland, Oregon.

Hence, "Area Code Killer."

"The investigators didn't come up with any leads. There were no witnesses, no surveillance footage, and very little forensic evidence," Joyce continued. "Kirovec was closing up the store for the night, taking out the trash, when our perp attacked him in the back alley."

"His cell phone was still on him," said a man in the second row. "Kirovec hadn't made or taken a call in two days. Other than the numbers carved into the guy's head, we got bupkis." The man introduced himself as Lyle Willis, a detective out of the Twenty-Sixth District, where Kirovec's body had been found. Willis spent the next several minutes detailing their investigation and explaining that at first they'd firmly believed the stabbing to be a one-off.

"Until this happened," Joyce interrupted him, bringing up another photograph on the screen. It was of a woman.

"Constance Yul, age thirty-nine. She was found in her car in West Philly on October eighth, three blocks from where she worked.

"She was born in Portland, stayed there for most of her life, then moved to Philly in 2005. This is when we first linked the numbers to specific area codes." Yul's autopsy photo was similar to Kirovec's; the placid skin of Constance's forehead was intersected by deep, black carvings. This time, the numbers read 914.

Joyce said, "After Ms. Yul's murder and recognizing another area code, we knew we had an active serial killer."

I wasn't familiar with the area code 914, but my inquiry was preempted by Joyce, who said, "9-1-4 is the area code for Westchester County, New York, birthplace of our third victim, Peter Boland."

A female detective from the Camden County Police Department told the rest of us, "Peter was born in White Plains—in Westchester County—but moved to Jersey a few years ago. His body was found yesterday near the shore of the Delaware River in Wiggins Waterfront Park."

That explained why the FBI was spearheading this task force. A killer crossing state lines fell under their authority.

Next on the screen, Joyce showed us the image of Peter Boland. He had 386 carved into his forehead. The curves of each of the three numbers were smooth and precise.

"Where is area code 3-8-6?" I asked.

"Daytona Beach," Kip chimed.

"Is Hufflepuff right?" I asked Joyce, achieving my desired effect and making Kip's cheeks redden.

"Yeah, Hufflepu—" He caught himself, "I mean Hufley, is correct."

I bit the inside of my lip and processed what I'd learned over the past twenty minutes: On October 3, Gene Kirovec was killed, the lead domino. He had 503 (a Portland area code) carved into his forehead. Then Constance Yul, who was born in Portland, was found murdered five days later. She had 914 (which is the area code for Westchester County, New York) carved into her forehead. Then yesterday they had found Peter Boland, born in Westchester County. He has 386 carved into his forehead—the area code for Daytona Beach.

I said, "So you're assuming the killer's next victim will have been born in Daytona?"

"That's correct," Joyce said. "Or in one of the other communities covered by the same code."

A moment later, he introduced FBI profiler Susan Mallory from the Behavior Analysis Unit. Mallory strode to the front of the room and began her own slideshow. I half listened as she broke down the socioeconomic and environmental factors at play. She was explaining the outcome of her detailed profile algorithm—to no one's surprise, a White male in his thirties—when I coughed into my hand twice and blurted, "You guys are wrong."

All heads turned in my direction.

"What do you mean?" Agent Joyce asked. "The profile's incorrect?"

"No. I mean, odds are it *is* a Cody or a Tanner. But you're wrong about the area codes."

"In what way?"

It was too early to know what the killer's motivation was, but the murders didn't scream out to me *recreational*. Too much care was put into the carving of the numbers. The killer took his time. His victims' foreheads might as well have been the Sistine Chapel. No, these murders were *functional*.

"This guy has something to say," I said. "These numbers are his story."

"Yes," Kip said, standing up. "And his story is that he's targeting people born in specific area codes."

I cut my eyes at him. "That seems like something you could have said sitting down."

No one laughed, and I realized for the first time in a long time, Thomas Dergen Prescott—voted "Most Likely to Own a Car Dealership" in high school—was the butt of the joke. These people thought I was off my rocker.

I let out a sigh. "At least tell me that you considered the numbers might mean something else?"

"Like what?" Joyce asked.

I said the first thing that popped into my head. "I don't know, maybe it has something to do with the victims' weights."

I've only had instant regret a few times in my life: when I was six and I stuck my tongue to a frozen pole, when I was thirteen (with a mouthful of braces) and went in for my first kiss after eating an entire jumbo bucket of popcorn, when I was twenty-four and someone dared me to eat a Carolina Reaper pepper, and then this moment.

"Their weights?" Joyce's head moved back two inches. "I mean, Gene Kirovec was a big guy, but he was not five hundred and three pounds." He pulled up the picture of Constance Yul, a petite Asian American. "And maybe it's just me, but she doesn't look like she weighs nine hundred and fourteen pounds."

I glanced over at Kip. He was grinning so hard that I could hear his molars grind together.

Joyce flashed me one last look of annoyance before instructing Mallory to wrap up her last thoughts.

When she finished, Joyce spent the next fifteen minutes laying out an action plan and everyone's marching orders. Most of the task force were going to pore over these three murders:

reinterviewing witnesses, knocking on doors, talking to family, and double-checking the forensic evidence.

I waited for Joyce to give me an assignment, but it never came. Maybe my weight theory was so harebrained that he didn't want me within a thousand miles of this case.

The meeting ended, and the task force members exited.

I swallowed two bites of pride, walked up to the front, and asked Joyce, "Where do you want me, Coach?"

He faked a laugh. "I can't have you doing anything until you fill out some paperwork and we do a background check. Then we'll hire you on as a consultant."

Whatever Captain Folch told him about me—probably something along the lines of Sherlock Holmes meets a mischievous raccoon—must have overshadowed my earlier outburst.

Anyhow, I was looking forward to diving into the case head-first and asked, "Can I start off with copies of the murder books on the three victims?"

"I wish I could give them to you, but until we get your credentials, you're going to have to sit on the sidelines." He patted me on the shoulder. "Just lie low for a couple days."

"Gotcha," I said.

I'll lie low.

5

For my thirtieth birthday, Lacy bought me one of those four-slice toaster. It might not seem like the greatest of presents, but outside of an old letter opener of my father's, it was my most prized possession.

I opened a fresh box of chocolate chip waffles and popped three down in the toaster. When they were golden brown, I slathered them with peanut butter and covered them in maple syrup. I set my plate on the kitchen table next to my protein smoothie and grabbed my laptop.

Agent Joyce may not have given me access to the murder books, but that didn't mean I couldn't do research on my own. I flipped open the laptop and launched Google. The moment I did this, my computer flashed red three times and "SHITHEAD" began dancing across the screen.

I'd either been hacked by Anonymous or Carmen hadn't taken the breakup so well after all.

I restarted my computer, hoping whatever virus or malware Carmen uploaded into my system had disappeared. When my computer started back up, the screen flashed brown, this time reading, "NICE TRY SHITHEAD."

A huge poop emoji bounced on-screen and started pooping out a bunch of little poop emojis, all with my face on them.

"Looking forward to the IRS audit," I told my Eggos.

I finished eating, threw on a pair of jeans and a tan Henley, then walked to the Walnut Street West Library. Several computer terminals were available, and I plopped into one of the seats. I pulled up the *Philadelphia Inquirer* website and was unsurprised to see the leading headline was about Brooke Wexley's murder. I skimmed the article, which divulged little info. Learning nothing of any consequence, I turned my attention to Gene Kirovec, Constance Yul, and Peter Boland.

Joyce hadn't been kidding about keeping this story under wraps. There was no mention of Gene Kirovec's murder in either of the two major papers. The *Philadelphia Tribune* ran an obituary for Constance Yul, but there was no indication that her death was part of an ongoing murder investigation. Peter Boland's body had been found less than forty-eight hours earlier, and as yet, his murder hadn't garnered any press attention.

No one had connected the three murders. This would change if the media got wind of a multiagency task force working out of the FBI building. Or maybe their focus would stay on Brooke Wexley. So who knows, the serial killer case could slip through the cracks.

I googled "Area Code Killer."

Most of the results concerned the Zodiac Killer, who'd killed several people in San Francisco in the late 1960s. It came up because *code* was in the search criteria, and the Zodiac Killer had sent a bunch of ciphers to newspapers that had to be decoded. That killer had never been found, and it would be a stretch to think he was involved in these new murders.

Next, I searched "three number combinations."

I read about "Combinations vs. Permutations," and I started to get PTSD palm sweats from seventh-grade math.

Letting out a frustrated sigh, I searched "503 meaning."

I learned about "angel numbers." It was spiritual numerology stuff. 503 signified *New Beginnings*. 914 meant *Determination*. 386 meant *New Opportunities*.

I scoffed. "These are just fortune cookies."

Hitting a dead end, I scrolled down the results page for the number 503. On the third page, I came to an article from the *Detroit Free Press*. It read, "Local Woman Hits Big on 503."

I clicked the link.

The article was about the Pick 3 lottery in Detroit. A woman had played the number 503 for $100, and she'd won $50,000.

Could the murders be connected to the lottery?

I edged forward in my seat and searched "three number lottery."

The first four pages of results were from different state lottery websites, but on the fifth page there was a Wikipedia entry for "The Numbers."

I clicked on the link and began reading:

> The Numbers, also known as the Numbers Racket, the Street Numbers, or the Daily Number, is a form of illegal lottery played mostly in poor and working-class neighborhoods in the United States wherein a bettor attempts to pick three digits to match those randomly drawn the following day. Gamblers place bets with a Numbers runner at a tavern, bar, barber shop, social club, or any other illegal betting parlor. Runners carry the money and betting slips between the betting parlors and the headquarters, called a Numbers bank.

I'd heard of the Numbers racket—most of my knowledge was from movies like *The Godfather* or *Goodfellas*—but I wasn't aware the concept was based on a three-digit number.

As interesting as this was, the Numbers racket was a long time ago.

I was getting ready to click out of the link, when I noticed an image on the right side of the page. It was a photo of a tattered book: *Old Aunt Dinah's Dream Book of Numbers*. The cover was a cartoon sketch of a mystically dressed African American woman running a hand over an open book filled with numbers. Captioned below the book was, "One of the first dream books."

A dream book? I'd never heard of such a thing.

There was a link to a dream book entry. I clicked on it and began reading:

A dream book is a guide that interprets dreams and converts them into three-digit numbers that can be backed for wagering. The first one was published in 1862, and by the mid-1950s there were over three dozen in circulation. Each of the competing dream books has different numbers assigned to a wide range of symbols (things, names, places, feelings, experiences, even days of the week) that might show up in a dream. Where one book might have *Bicycle* playing for 452 another book would have *Bicycle* playing for 863.

I thought back on the three murders. Initially, the location of the numbers seemed arbitrary, but maybe carving the numbers into the victims' foreheads was significant.

Maybe the numbers were *dreams*.

≈

"I'm looking for dream books," I told the librarian.

She smiled warmly and said, "Let's see what we can find."

She clicked away on her keyboard for several seconds before glancing up. "All our dream books are checked out. I can put you on the waiting list if you'd like."

"That's okay." I thanked her and was getting set to leave, when I turned back. "Do you, by chance, have any books about the old Numbers lottery?"

She tapped away on her keyboard. "Looks like I do."

A few minutes later, I exited the library, having checked out *The Numbers Game: The History of the Lottery*.

A Barnes & Noble was a half mile away, and I jogged in that direction. Once there, I asked an employee about dream books for the lottery. He directed me to an aisle in the nonfiction section and said, "If we have anything like that, it will be with the dream-interpretation stuff."

The shelf was filled almost entirely with books on numerology and psychological dream interpretation. I rifled through the titles until I came to a thin orange book titled *The Lucky Star Dream Book*.

I flipped it open. It was alphabetized, and I found a list of dreams beginning with the letter *E*:

Egg – 086
Elbow – 633
Electrocution – 287
Elephant – 864
Elevator – 139

I ran my fingers down the list of numbers, page after page, until I located 503. I don't know what I expected, maybe *Murder* or *Killer* or *Death*.

Certainly not *Hedgehog*.

The print was small and there were fifty entries to a page,

which meant there were likely more than a thousand entries; ergo, there were likely additional 503s. I found the number three more times: *Knitting*, *Sister-in-law*, and *Wig*.

Still, this was only one book. According to the internet, there were over thirty different varieties.

I pulled out my phone and called Desiree Moore.

She answered on the second ring, and I asked, "How's the Wexley case coming?"

"I wouldn't know."

"What do you mean?"

"An hour after you left, I went into false labor."

"You're kidding."

"I wish. Scared the hell out of me."

"Is everything okay?"

"I spent the night at the hospital. I have something called preeclampsia. Not uncommon in IVF."

"Did the doctor put you on bed rest?"

"That punk-ass sure did."

I laughed, then said, "So, I have an odd question for you."

"Hit me."

"Do you know where I can get my hands on some dream books?"

"Dream books? Like for the lottery?"

"Yeah."

"They sell them mostly at newsstands and gas stations."

I kicked myself. Of course they sold them at gas stations—that's where most people played the lottery.

I was thanking her when she said, "Actually, if you can believe it, I'm looking at a bunch of them right this second."

"Dream books?"

"Yup. I'm staying at my mom's, and her bookshelf is packed full of the things. Got to be at least fifty of them."

"Is there any way I can come over and look through them?"

"Of course. What's this about?"

"I'll tell you when I get there."

"Sounds good," she said, then added, "Can you pick me up something on the way?"

6

Moore's mother's house was in a neighborhood in the northeast section of Philly called Kensington. It was a two-story row house with gray brick and light-green trim.

I walked up the front stoop's six steep stairs and knocked. The door was pulled open by a petite woman who I guessed to be in her early seventies. She had soft brown skin, curly gray hair, large red glasses, and a complicated set of dangling gold earrings.

"You must be Mrs. Moore," I said.

She put her hand up. "Please call me Ms. Ruby."

"Ms. Ruby it is."

"That's better." She flashed the same tight smile as her daughter. "And you must be Thomas."

"That I am."

"What a handsome man you are."

I was getting ready to thank her for the compliment, when from somewhere inside the house, her daughter shouted, "Stop flirting, and let him inside!"

Ms. Ruby covered her mouth and whispered, "She's been a little crabby today."

"Good to know."

She nodded at the paper bag in my hand. "Hopefully, that will calm her down."

"One can hope."

I followed her inside to find Moore lying on the couch, propped up by a large white pillow. She wore black stretchy pants and a T-shirt. Three inches of her very pregnant belly were visible. "Give it here," she said, waving me over.

I passed her the bag with "Miller's Twist" printed on the side. She snapped it open, pulled out the chewy pretzel, and without hesitation, ripped off an enormous chunk and stuffed it in her mouth. Her eyes closed and she let out a satisfied sigh.

When Moore first told me she was craving a pretzel from Miller's Twist, I hadn't thought much of it, as the bakery's soft pretzels are amazing. It was the second part of her request that I found troubling.

"I'm not going to lie," I told her now. "The guy behind the counter looked insulted when I asked him to dip one of their world-famous sausage pretzels in cheese, then roll it in cinnamon and cover it in sprinkles."

"*Soooo-gooooooodd*," she garbled.

Ms. Ruby had disappeared into the kitchen and returned with a large glass of lemonade. "Don't you choke on that now," she said, offering the glass to her daughter. "Small bites."

Moore rolled her eyes. "I know how to eat a pretzel, Mom."

"Of course you do, honey."

Ms. Ruby turned to me. "Can I get you something? Coffee?"

"That lemonade looks good."

"Freshly squeezed." She gave my elbow a light pat before heading back to the kitchen.

When Ms. Ruby was out of earshot, Moore ripped off another gigantic piece of pretzel, stuffed it in her mouth, and mumbled, "It's been less than a day, and she's already driving me crazy. She's been checking on me every eight minutes."

"Only three more months."

She groaned.

"If you don't want her, I'll take her."

She paused, as if to consider it, then swallowed. "No, she's mine."

Ms. Ruby returned with my lemonade, then directed me to a tan Barcalounger. She took a seat next to Moore, lifting her daughter's bare feet and laying them across her lap.

"Tell me about yourself," Ms. Ruby said to me with a smile. "Where did you grow up?"

I zipped through my thirty-year history. When I reached the part about my parents dying, Ms. Ruby shook her head and said, "Lordy, Lordy. I'm so sad to hear that."

"It was tough," I said, "but I had my little sister to take care of, so I had to push through."

"And your sister—where is she now?"

"She swims for Drexel. That's why we moved to Philadelphia."

"How fantastic," she said, clapping her hands.

After gushing about Lacy, I said, "But enough about me. How did you end up here?" I knew from previous conversations with Moore that her parents had migrated north from one of the Carolinas.

Before Ms. Ruby could reply, Moore said, "You might want to lay that chair back and kick your feet up."

Ms. Ruby swatted at one of her daughter's feet playfully, then said, "I'll just give you the highlights."

I was eager to take a gander at the collection of dream books that I'd already spotted on the bookshelf against the back wall, but I also wanted to hear Ms. Ruby's story. "I've got all day. Give me the unabridged version."

"Well, I was born in Asheville, North Carolina, in 1933. I was the middle child of nine."

"Nine? Wow!"

"Yeah, it was a darned circus. Kids everywhere. My daddy was a sharecropper, which was a tough way to make a living, and my momma helped out where she could. We had good years and we had lean years, but we always made it through." She told a quick story about growing up, then said, "I met my Clarence when I was twelve years old; he was one of my older brother's friends. We were high school sweethearts and got married the year after graduation.

"Two years after that, I got pregnant with Desiree's oldest brother, Clarence Jr. It was a terrible time for Black folks in the South, and a lot of people were migrating north in hopes of a better life. Clarence had an uncle in Philadelphia who said he could help him find work. In 1954, after CJ—that's what everybody calls Clarence Jr.—was born, we moved here and got ourselves a little apartment in North Philly."

Ms. Ruby narrated how her husband found work at a textile mill and after popping out Desiree's second brother, Terrance, she got her teaching license. She began teaching sixth-grade English in 1958 and then got pregnant with Desiree's youngest brother, Martin, in 1962.

"That little apartment was already cramped with the four of us, so we started looking for a house." She gazed around the living room. "The moment I first laid eyes on this place, I knew it had to be ours. But it was hard for Black folks to get a loan back then, especially for a house that wasn't in one of the redlined districts."

My mother had been a history buff, and from conversations with her, I knew about redlining. It was a program started in the 1930s by the federal government designed to increase and segregate America's housing stock. It was abolished in 1968 with the signing of the Fair Housing Act, but in 1962 it would've made it near impossible for Ms. Ruby and Clarence to buy a house in Kensington, which like a lot of Philly in the 1950s and 1960s was a predominantly White neighborhood.

"So, how did you get the house?" I asked.

"Since we couldn't get a loan from the bank, we had to buy the house on contract."

I cringed, knowing that buying on contract meant a predatory business arrangement that combined the responsibilities of home ownership with the disadvantages of renting. Essentially, the seller owned the home until the house was fully paid for, and if the buyer missed a single monthly payment, the owner could legally take back the property.

This arrangement must have worked out for Ms. Ruby and Clarence, but plenty of people had been swindled out of their life savings.

I bit the inside of my cheek. "Do I even want to ask what interest rate you had to pay?"

"Thirteen percent."

"That's criminal."

"Not only that, but the seller asked for a big down payment. Thirty percent of the sixteen-thousand-dollar asking price."

That was roughly $5,000. A hefty sum of money in 1962. "Did you have that much saved?"

"Half of it. We took out a loan for the other half."

"I thought you said you couldn't get a loan from a bank."

"We didn't. We got a loan from a *banker*."

I was confused and must have looked it.

"A Numbers banker," Ms. Ruby explained.

I felt my eyebrows lift. "Did that happen a lot?"

"Oh, yes. A lot of the big bankers—or Numbers kings and

queens, as they liked to be called—did wonderful things for the community. They gave out low-interest loans, seeded capital for all sorts of small businesses, and gave large donations to the NAACP and the Urban League."

"That's amazing."

"Of course, not all of them were so philanthropic, and some were downright rotten—refused to pay you when you made a hit or would simply disappear after taking a heavy day—but the ones I've dealt with over the years have been quite generous."

The Numbers was the reason for my visit, and I was tempted to transition to the topic then and there, but first I wanted to listen to the rest of Ms. Ruby's memoir.

I prodded her to continue, and she said, "Starting around 1964, Clarence and I got pretty involved in the civil rights movement." She reached out and took a quick sip of her daughter's lemonade, then set it back down on the coffee table. "Have you heard of Girard College?"

"I know of it." Only because it wasn't a college; it was a preparatory boarding school on College Avenue two miles north of city hall.

"In 1965, the school was still segregated, and Clarence and I joined the protests starting in May of that year. We marched on the school nearly every day that summer, and then in early August Dr. King came and spoke."

"As in, Dr. Martin Luther King Jr.?" I moved to the edge of the Barcalounger.

"Yep. He urged us to remain peaceful and to stay the course. And we did, though it would take another three years in court before Girard College finally admitted African American students. Sadly, Dr. King had been assassinated a few months earlier and didn't live to see it."

After a silent beat, I nodded at Moore and asked, "When does this one come into the picture?"

Ms. Ruby smiled wide and gave one of Moore's feet a rub. "You mean my oopsie-baby?"

"Mom!" Moore shouted. "Don't call me that!"

"Well, I didn't plan on getting pregnant when I was thirty-eight years old." She glanced at her very pregnant thirty-eight-*ish* daughter. "Though at least we did it the old-fashioned way."

Moore groaned. "Please. Not this again."

"I wish you could have found a nice man to marry." She reached forward and put one of her hands on Moore's belly. "But I'm going to love them science babies just the same."

Science babies!

"Quit calling them that!" Moore shouted, though she had a twinge of a smile clinging to her lips.

The three of us had a healthy laugh before Ms. Ruby sped through the rest of her biography. She'd taught English at the same inner-city school for thirty-five years. Clarence lost his job at the textile mill in the early '80s and bounced around other jobs until retiring in the mid-'90s. Sadly, he'd passed away two years earlier from a stroke.

"I'm sorry to hear that," I said.

"He had a good life," Ms. Ruby said, her eyes dancing. "He got to watch all four of his children graduate from college. He got to meet six grandchildren. And he got to see a Black man become president of the United States."

Moore's face tightened, and her eyes moistened.

Ms. Ruby said, "He would have loved them science babies too."

"Yeah, he would have," Moore said, holding her mother's hand.

I excused myself to go to the restroom, letting them have

their moment. When I returned to the living room, I pulled one of the many dream books from the bookshelf. "Okay, let's talk Numbers."

≈

Ms. Ruby had been introduced to the Numbers while growing up in Asheville.

"My mama used to play for a nickel," she said, "but only once or twice a week."

"Who did she bet with?" I asked.

"A runner named Clay. He'd do his rounds, coming by the farm every day to take bets."

"Did your mom ever win?"

"You mean *hit*? Only twice that I can remember."

"How did she choose her numbers?"

"Oh, she only played her pet number—her and my daddy's wedding anniversary: August tenth."

"So, she'd only play 8-1-0?"

"That's right."

"What about you? When did you first start playing?"

"I was saving every penny for the move to Philadelphia, so I never played while living in Asheville. But when we first moved to the North Philly apartment, one of our neighbors was a runner. Almost every day, he'd ask me if I wanted to play. I held off for a good while, but then one night I had a dream about running through a big field of peppermint. I didn't own a dream book at the time, so I went and bought one. Looked up *Peppermint*, and there it was."

"And you played it?"

"Yup, played it for a dime."

"And let me guess, you hit?"

"Wish it were that easy. No, those numbers are darn hard to hit. But it was so exciting. We were still scraping to get by, but I started playing once a week. Every Wednesday."

"When did you first hit?"

"November sixth, 1958."

"Don't tell me you remember the number you played?"

"Sure do. I had that same dream about the field of peppermint. Bought a different dream book, *Three Wise Men*, and played 4-3-8 for a whole dollar."

"How much did you win?"

"Six hundred dollars."

So a *hit* paid out 600 to 1.

"That's when we first started saving for the house," Ms. Ruby chimed.

"Have you hit many times since?"

"A handful." She pointed over her shoulder. "You see that nice dining room table? 5-4-3 paid for that." She pointed to a beautiful watercolor painting of wild horses on the far wall. "8-6-1 paid for that, plus some new curtains."

"Did you get all your numbers from dreams?"

"Most of them, but every once in a while, I'd see a number while I was out and about and get one of my hunches." She paused, then added, "Do you know about hunches?"

Her question had context with it. Do *White people* know about hunches?

"Of course, he knows about hunches, Mom," Moore said with another roll of her eyes. "He's a detective!"

"I do know a good bit about hunches," I said. "And mine have rarely steered me wrong. Actually, a hunch brings me here today."

"About the dream books?" Ms. Ruby asked.

"I think they might be connected to a string of murders."

I told them about the task force, the three murders, the numbers carved into the victims' foreheads, and the overwhelming theory that the numbers were area codes.

"It sounds like the area codes fit," Moore said. "What makes you think it's something else?"

"My problem with the area codes is that they aren't even considering any other explanation. I'm putting myself in the killer's shoes. He's going through all this trouble to carve these numbers into the victims' foreheads. I just have a feeling he's trying to tell a specific story. And it's not that he's going to kill someone born in Daytona Beach next."

Ms. Ruby said, "So, you think it's just a coincidence that the first two numbers matched up with the area code where the next victim was born?"

"No, it's too spot-on to be a coincidence. The killer meant to do it. It's part of his game—maybe a diversion. It's a long shot, but I have the nagging feeling that these numbers carved into victims' foreheads are connected to the old Numbers lottery." I told them about the research I'd done at the library and how I'd come across the article about dream books.

Moore said, "And because this creep carves numbers into the victims' foreheads, you think they're meant to signify dreams?"

"Precisely."

"So, what are you waiting for?" Ms. Ruby pushed her daughter's leg off her lap. "Let's get to work."

≈

"I've got 5-0-3 here," Ms. Ruby said.

"Which book?" Moore asked.

"*Raven's Lucky Numbers.*"

Moore typed the name of the dream book into the Excel

spreadsheet on her laptop that was balanced on her belly. "Alright, hit me."

"*Mule.*"

"5-0-3, *Mule,*" Moore muttered as her fingers clicked down the keys.

We'd been going at it for the past hour, Ms. Ruby and I painstakingly making our way through each of the forty-three different dream books—seventeen of which were different yearly editions of *Three Wise Men*—searching for entries for 503, 914, and 386. In a single book, you were likely to find each of the numbers between two and four times.

"I've got one," I said. "9-1-4, *Grandpa's Numbers Guide.*"

A moment later, Moore said, "Go ahead."

"*Pigeon.*"

"Got it."

"Like the bird," I said.

"Yep."

"Not the language—you know, pidgin."

"Uh-huh."

"As in, 'Hey look, a pigeon.'"

"Gotcha."

"P-I-G-E-O-N."

Moore glanced up from her laptop and said, "Can you not?" I laughed.

After another hour, and having gone through two-thirds of the dream books, I asked Moore, "Is there anything that's jumping out at you yet?"

"Not really," she said, shaking her head. "*Aero Dream Book* has 3-8-6 as *Saturday* and 9-1-4 as *Miriam*, but that's the only thing that could be something specific. Everything else is super vague: *Wrist, Kerosene, Chimney, Annoy, Yawn, Visit, Collar, Salt,*

Drunk, Mosquito, Comrade, Ford a Stream, Swelling, Pebble, Toes, Unbuckle, Guitar . . ."

After she finished reading through a list of more than a hundred words, I blew out a breath. "This is a waste of time."

"We just have the *Three Wise Men* books left," Ms. Ruby said. "Why don't I whip us up some lunch and you two keep at it?"

"What are you making?" Moore asked.

"Why? What are you craving?"

Desiree rubbed her belly with one of her hands. "Thanksgiving dinner."

Ms. Ruby slapped Moore's foot with a dream book. "Okay, just give me fourteen hours."

"What about a grilled cheese?" asked her daughter.

"That I can do." Ms. Ruby turned to me and raised her eyebrows.

I said, "Yes, please."

Fifteen minutes later, Ms. Ruby delivered us plates filled with diagonally cut grilled cheese sandwiches, heaping piles of potato chips, and pickle spears. She said she was going to do some gardening in the backyard and to holler if we needed anything. She kissed the top of Moore's head and gave my hair a ruffle as she walked past.

There's just something about a sandwich made by someone else's mom that warms your belly as it goes down. I savored a few bites, then picked up the *Three Wise Men* dream book from 1958.

An hour later, after calling out the last entry in the 1975 edition of *Three Wise Men*, I said, "Okay, let's hear them all one more time."

Moore spent ten minutes reading the entries. At no point did any combination of three words from any one specific book jump out at me.

After reading the last entry, Moore asked, "So, what do you think?"

I pondered her question. "I think what your parents had to go through to get this house is absolute horseshit. I think that was the best damn grilled cheese I've ever eaten. I think you should name your twins Max and Lou regardless of gender." I tossed the dream book in my hand atop the pile of forty-two others and lay back on the carpet. "And I think some poor sap from Daytona Beach is about to get fucking murdered."

7

I stepped out of the shower and checked my phone. Special Agent Scott Joyce still hadn't called me back. I'd called him twice yesterday evening and again earlier that morning.

"Come on, dickhead," I said. "Call me bac—"

My phone rang and the caller ID lit up.

"Finally," I muttered, flipping the phone open.

"Hey, Prescott," Joyce said. "Sorry I'm just now getting back to you."

"No problem. I'm ready to get to work." I didn't mention that I'd spent the entire previous day going down a rabbit hole of the old Numbers lottery.

"Well, there's a slight problem."

"What do you mean?"

"You didn't pass your background check."

"That's crazy. What could I possibly have on my record?"

"No, your record is clean. It was the conversations I had with a couple of your fellow officers at the Seattle PD that's the problem."

"Who did you talk to?"

"Kates and Millard."

Ethan Kates had been my partner for the two years that I worked homicide, and Sergeant Dan Millard was my direct superior. Neither would have many complimentary words to say about me.

Joyce said, "The words rogue, cowboy, and asshole came up a lot."

"In what context?"

"In the context that Kates called you a 'rogue cowboy asshole.'"

"I see."

"Did you really smash Kates's face into his locker?"

"Not exactly."

"What do you mean?"

"I smashed his face into *my* locker."

He was silent for a moment, then asked, "What happened?"

"Kates was a prick. He needed someone to smash his face into a locker twenty years ago."

"Okay, but what led to you doing it?"

"He used my deodorant."

It was a long time coming. My parents had died six months earlier, I'd just finished working a terrible case with a murdered child, and then Kates used my Old Spice.

"What did Millard say?" I asked.

"He said that you had the highest solve rate in the department, but you also had the lowest conviction rate. He said they had to throw out evidence in over half your cases because you didn't do things by the book."

This was my biggest regret. Fifteen guys weren't locked up right now because I colored outside the lines.

"I learned my lesson."

"Maybe, but he also mentioned the city of Seattle is being sued for seven million dollars by a suspect you beat the shit out of."

Daniel Proctor.

I'd do it again.

"Did you talk to my old captain, Dwight Stully?"

Stully knew how talented I was, and he'd campaigned for me to serve a six-month suspension instead of being fired. But the police chief said that with the looming Proctor lawsuit, they had to cut ties.

"He never got back to me. But it doesn't matter. You're just too big of a liability to have on the task force."

"I get it," I said, hanging up.

≈

Having been thrown off the task force, I had little on my plate for the rest of the day. I considered heading to the park to play pickup ball with the local kids. Or I could go grocery shopping. I mean, I only had seven boxes of waffles left. Or I could watch *The Price Is Right*.

I threw on clothes and plopped down on the couch.

"Higher!" I shouted at the screen. "It's higher!"

"So, what do you think, Gabe?" Drew Carey asked on-screen. He'd taken over the job from Bob Barker four years earlier, and I was still getting used to him and his enormous glasses.

Gabe said, "I'm going to go with . . . *lower!*"

Carey flipped down the flap under the blender, revealing the actual price ($42.99) was lower than the listed price ($44.99).

This day was going from bad to worse.

I watched Gabe play Plinko, spin a 70, opt out of a second spin, then lose the Showcase Showdown.

"No all-expenses-paid trip to Tahiti for you, Gabe!" I said, my mood swinging upward. "Have fun with your cheap blender."

I turned the TV off and pushed up from the couch. Needing

exercise, I grabbed my basketball shoes and went to the parking garage. I tossed my shoes into the back seat of my Range Rover, then headed toward Capitolo Playground in South Philly.

Halfway there, it started to sprinkle.

"Can't play basketball in the rain," I said, flipping a U-turn.

The universe had spoken.

I'd rent a movie instead.

≈

Netflix and Redbox had pretty much put Blockbuster out of business, and the movie rental Goliath had filed for bankruptcy the previous year. They'd closed most of their stores in Philly, but a few remained. Three, to be exact.

The parking lot at the Blockbuster on Thirty-Third and Aramingo was deserted, which went for the inside of the store as well.

A big guy with shoulder-length hair that desperately needed a good scrubbing was behind the checkout counter. His name was Dennis, and he was currently decimating their inventory of Whoppers.

"How's it going?" he said, Whopper dust flying from his mouth.

"Pretty good," I replied.

"Anything I can help you find?"

I had no intention of renting a movie and said, "I was hoping to ask you a few questions about Gene Kirovec."

Without access to the murder books, I didn't know the exact locations where Constance Yul and Peter Boland were killed. If I wanted to touch the actual crime scene, Gene Kirovec's murder was my only option.

"Aw, shit." Dennis dug one of his rotund fingers into the

Whoppers box and fished around for any stragglers at the
bottom. "I still can't believe that happened to Gene."

"Did you work that night?"

"I didn't. *The Thing* came out in the theaters at midnight,
so I'd requested the night off three months in advance. Me and
my friend Xavier got in line early, like two in the afternoon."

"When did you hear about Gene?"

"The next morning, I got a text from Missy."

"Who's Missy?"

"A girl who works here. She was coming to open the store
and saw a bunch of cop cars."

"Were you and Gene friends?"

"He was a lot older than me—I think he was like fifty-four
or something. We had completely different tastes in movies."

"Was he married?"

Dennis laughed. "Nope."

"Why is that so funny?"

"Just is. I never saw him show any interest in a woman.
Even when a hot chick would come in, he wouldn't bat an eye."

"Did he have any enemies?"

"Not that I know of."

There was a soft jingle as a woman entered.

I thanked Dennis, exited, then walked to the alley behind
the store. The dumpster was half-filled and pushed up against
the back of the building. I crouched down and fingered the
asphalt, splicing the picture I'd seen at the task force meeting
with the brick-and-mortar reality around me.

I said, "Taking out the trash, listening to some tunes, then
whack."

Stabbed six times in the back. He probably fell to his knees
after the first blow. Depending on the location of the next five
strikes, he could have lived another couple minutes or mere

seconds. Once he's dead, the killer carves 503 into his forehead, then rolls him over on his stomach. Then he flees.

My phone rang in my pocket, and I pulled it out.

It was Moore.

"What's up?" I answered.

"I've got something with the dream books."

"Let's hear it."

"So, I couldn't sleep last night—my babies' biological father must be Irish because I swear those babies were doing the Riverdance—and I went through all the books again. You and my mom did a pretty good job, but you guys missed a few entries."

"How many?"

"Thirteen entries across the forty-three books."

"I didn't miss any."

"Wow, way to throw Mom under the bus," she said with a laugh. "And not that it matters, but you were the one going through all the *Three Wise Men* books, and you missed eight."

I went quiet for a moment, and Moore asked, "Thomas?"

"I'm here. I'm just mentally flagellating myself."

"Don't feel too bad. You were going through them pretty fast."

I mentally gave myself the last of eight lashings, then I said, "Okay, keep going."

"Yeah, so I went over every book twice, double-checking that I found every entry for each of the three numbers. Once I had them all in my Excel spreadsheet, I started looking for any correlation between the numbers in a specific book. Nothing jumped out until I got to the listings from *The E.K. Dream Book*."

"I don't think I went through that one."

"Yeah, I think it was my mom. It was one of the smaller books. There was just one edition printed. It came out in 1954. Only fifty pages and roughly thirty entries per page, so about fifteen hundred entries in total. Most of the numbers are used once, and none are used more than twice."

I felt the hair lift off my arms. If the killer was using one of the dream books, it made sense to use a book with a limited number of entries and a standardized single edition.

"Anyhow," Moore continued, "My mom missed one entry— *Boston*."

"The city?"

"Yeah, it was one of two entries for 9-1-4. And get this, the only entry for 5-0-3 was *Hill* and the only entry for 3-8-6 was *War*."

"*Boston*, *Hill*, and *War*?" It took me a moment to make the connection. "The Battle of Bunker Hill."

"Exactly!" she shouted. "And get this, *Battle* is an entry in the book."

"But our killer used *War*." It took a moment for the signif-icance to wash over me. "Let me guess, the number that came up for *Battle* wasn't an area code."

"Nope. It was 4-2-7, which isn't an active area code."

"So the killer went to the next best word, which was *War*, which had a number that was an active area code." It had to be an area code to be part of whatever game or diversion the killer was playing.

Something else occurred to me.

"Thomas?" Moore said through the phone.

"Gimme a sec." I spun on my heel and headed back into the Blockbuster.

Dennis was behind the register and the woman who'd entered earlier was sliding a movie across the counter. She was clad in red leggings and the giant purse on her shoulder was overflowing with clipped coupons.

"Hey, Dennis," I said. "Quick question."

"Wait your turn," the woman snapped.

I picked up the DVD she was renting: *Primal Fear*. It was a movie with Edward Norton that had come out fifteen years earlier. "This is a great one," I said. "Edward Norton fakes a split personality the entire movie, but he's the killer. You never see it coming."

Her heavily mascaraed eyes opened wide. "Asshole," she said, then turned to go pick out a different movie.

"That's against movie code," Dennis said.

I ignored him. "Do you know what Gene's real name was?"

"You just spoiled the end—"

"I will jump over this counter and jam Whoppers down your throat until you suffocate."

He put his hands up.

"What was Gene's legal first name?" I had a good feeling I knew the answer, but I had to confirm it.

"Um, Eugene, I think."

I shook my head.

Our killer had tipped his hand.

"Moore?" I shouted into the phone, crashing through the exit. "You said the book was *The E.K. Dream Book*?"

Moore must have heard Dennis and my conversation through the phone. She said, "The first victim was Eugene Kirovec."

"Yep," I said. "*E.K.*"

8

I stopped by Ms. Ruby's, raced back to my condo, took a taxi to the Thirtieth Street Station, and barely caught the 1:32 p.m. Acela Express to Boston. I paid the extra twenty dollars for the quiet car and settled in for the five-hour-fourteen-minute ride.

The car was half-filled, and the seat next to me was empty. My destination was the Bunker Hill Monument, built in 1842 to commemorate the Revolutionary War battle. I was almost certain it would be the next stop for our serial killer.

Ms. Ruby had kept all of Moore's old backpacks and loaned me a purple JanSport, which I'd loaded with *The E.K. Dream Book*, the book I checked out from the library (*The Numbers Game: The Origins of the Street Lottery*), and a sack lunch Ms. Ruby had prepared.

As the train pulled away from the station, I cracked the library book open and lost myself in the history of the lottery.

Games of chance went as far back as the Chinese Han dynasty, but it wasn't until around the seventeenth century in Genoa, Italy, that the modern lottery was created.

Every six months, the Genoans would change out the members of their Great Council. They put all the council members' names in a hat and citizens would bet on which names were drawn. Thing is, these degenerates didn't want to wait another six months for another drawing, so they decided, Hey, let's swap out *Bartholomeus de Maglanis* and *Apollinaris de Cremona* for *6* and *19*.

This type of gambling was called "lotto."

Fast-forward to the early 1800s, and there were over two hundred officially sanctioned lotteries in the United States. But African Americans were barred from participating. The result was an illegal lottery called "Policy" that was played alongside the legal lotteries, wherein a bettor "insured" or "took a policy" on a number with a banker—effectively, making a side wager on one of the legal lotteries.

In the 1860s, there was a shift of thought in society. Almost overnight it became morally reprehensible to gamble. With all but three states passing anti-lottery laws, combined with President Lincoln's Emancipation Proclamation, illegal lotteries such as Policy grew even more popular. No longer slaves but finding themselves in grim financial circumstances, many Black Americans were seduced by the idea of turning a small amount of money into a windfall.

By 1894, all states had abolished lotteries. Policy continued to thrive, but without the legal lotteries to give credibility to the drawings' results, it became much easier for the Policy bankers— the bigwigs cashing in on the illegal lottery—to fix the results.

People desperately wanted a lottery that was fair, random, and with decent odds. But that didn't come until 1921.

Enter Casper Holstein.

"Great name," I said aloud.

A woman in the seat across from me glanced over. She was fortyish with glasses, and she was reading on one of those new electronic devices.

"Casper Holstein," I said. "Great name, huh?"

She stared at me vacantly, then said, "This is the quiet car."

"So that's why they took away my tambourine."

She huffed and turned back to her book.

I did the same.

Casper Holstein was from the Danish West Indies, which, I remembered from my eleventh-grade geography class, were islands somewhere in the Caribbean. His parents immigrated to Harlem when he was young, and after high school, Holstein worked as a porter at a store on Fifth Avenue. Legend has it he was sitting in a janitor's closet going through a large stack of saved newspapers when he began studying the Clearing House totals printed in the paper each day. The Clearing House was a financial institution that facilitated the daily exchanges and settlements of money among New York City's banks.

Holstein realized that each day's total was different—and most importantly, random. His moneymaking scheme was simple: every day, he used the Clearing House total to generate a winning three-digit number. (If the total was $1,656,876, the winning number would be 876.) Bettors then picked a number between 000 and 999 and hoped to match that day's number. When they did, it paid out 600 to 1. And since the chance of winning was 1 in 1,000, this system generated a nice take for Holstein.

It was straightforward, elegant: everyone had access to the winning number, and the source was unimpeachable. The game—now known simply as "the Numbers"—became a craze.

From Harlem it spread to Boston, Detroit, Chicago, Cleveland, DC, Philadelphia, and beyond. The money was rolling in for big bankers like Casper Holstein, and it wasn't long before people started referring to them as Numbers kings. But they weren't the only ones making money. Number runners—men and women who ran around the city taking people's bets six days a week—were paid 25 percent of whatever bets they brought in. Many Number runners were making upward of twenty-five dollars a day, a lot of money in the 1920s.

The scheme nearly fell apart in 1931 when the Clearing House—sick of people trying to bribe workers for the totals before they were officially released—stopped publishing their daily statistics. A new reliable number source had to be found. Bankers began generating numbers from the daily balance of the United States Treasury, from the number of shares traded on the New York Stock Exchange, or most commonly from a particular racetrack. None of these sources ever attained the "unfixable" cachet of the Clearing House, but they sufficed.

The next chapter of the book detailed how bettors came up with their numbers. Just like Ms. Ruby, whose pet number was her wedding anniversary, many bettors derived their numbers from birthdays, anniversaries, birth times, birth weights, death dates, historical dates, bible verses, flight numbers, even numbers from popular movies. Evidently, 007 became popular after the first James Bond movie came out in 1963.

"Prescott, Thomas Prescott," I muttered under my breath so as not to get scolded by E-Reader a second time. I was about to start the next chapter, when I glanced out the window and saw the train was nearing New York.

I took a quick bathroom break and retook my seat just as the train began slicing through Manhattan. I opened my sack lunch and ate the peanut butter and jelly sandwich, chips, and vanilla pudding cup. Once I'd licked the pudding cup clean, I got tired.

I pulled the hood of my sweatshirt up and leaned my head against the wall. A few minutes later, I was asleep.

≈

It was a little after 4:00 p.m. when I woke up, which put the
train somewhere in Connecticut. I wiped my eyes and grasped
at the vapors of a dream, but they evaporated before I could
catch them.

After cracking my back on both sides, then my knuckles—
which drew a passive-aggressive harrumph from E-Reader—I
picked up my book. I was hoping to finish the last half before
we reached Boston.

By the mid-1930s, the Numbers was booming across the
country. Although the game was played by a potpourri of back-
grounds—Jewish, Irish, Polish, Italian, Greek, Puerto Rican,
other immigrants, and Whites—it was most popular in the African American communities, and nearly all the Numbers kings
were Black. But with the Numbers grossing over $300,000 a
day (that's $80 million a year) in New York City alone, it was
only a matter of time until the Italian Mafia took notice.

With Prohibition ending in 1933, the Mob's bootlegging
profits were decimated, and they were in desperate need of a
new revenue stream. They found it with the Numbers. Over the
next several decades, there was an ongoing clash between Italian mobsters and African American bankers, but ultimately the
game proved popular enough for both sides to make money—
that is, until the government decided they wanted back in.

The first state to legalize a lottery was New Hampshire in
1963, and New York followed in 1967. New York brought in
over $54 million in revenue its first year, and other states took
notice. By 1970, twelve more states had legalized lotteries.

The Numbers bankers felt the impact. More trouble arrived
in the mid-1970s when several states announced they would be
offering Pick 3 daily lotteries—an exact rip-off of the Numbers.
Year by year, the state lotteries offered more games, more drawings,
and by the mid-1980s, the Numbers game was in deep trouble.

I expected the book to say the Numbers went the way of the woolly mammoth, but evidently, the Numbers went the way of the Sumatran rhino. It wasn't extinct, but it wasn't easy to find. In plenty of urban neighborhoods throughout America, a bet could still be placed.

Ten minutes later, we reached Boston's North Station. I glanced out the window. The sun had set a half hour earlier, and the aging city was draped in the fading orange of dusk.

It was time to catch a killer.

9

The Bunker Hill Monument was a mile from the train terminal. I jog-walked through Paul Revere Landing Park to Warren Street and to Monument Avenue. Even from two blocks away you could see the 221-foot granite obelisk rising into the heavens.

The monument closed at 5:00 p.m., but I didn't see any fences or gates around the area. Several streetlamps filled the square-block-sized park, and a light at the base of the towering pillar made it look like an enormous glowing crystal. In front of the monument was a silver statue, and directly behind, loomed an aging stone lodge.

I stepped closer to the silver statue. An inscription at its stone base read, "Colonel William Prescott." Wearing militia attire, with his left hand out and a sword held low in his right hand, Colonel Prescott looked like he was ready to duel.

I held up my hands. "Grandpappy?"

He didn't respond.

I inspected the statue for markings, numbers, or hidden messages, but didn't see any. Turning my attention to the monument, I examined it from all angles. Nothing looked askew or out of place. There was a door on one side, and I presumed you could go inside and find stairs leading to the top.

I tried the door.

Locked.

The stone lodge behind the monument was surrounded by low wrought-iron fencing, and I eased my way over it. I scanned every edge of the building's gray stone exterior. I tried the door, but again, it was locked.

"Hey!"

I turned.

A man in security blues, with a flashlight pointed at the ground, nodded toward me and said, "You can't be back there."

"Oh, right," I said. "Sorry."

I climbed back over the fence and hopped down. I half expected the man to approach me with his baton wagging or to write me a ticket for trespassing, but he was probably in his late fifties and didn't look overly eager for a confrontation.

"Monument closes at five," he said. "Be open tomorrow at ten a.m."

"Great, thanks."

He tipped his security cap at me. "Have a good evening."

He started to walk away, and I called out, "Can I ask you a question?"

"Sure thing," he said, turning around.

"Have you noticed any markings or graffiti at the monument in the past couple of days?"

He glanced upward and rubbed his jowls. "Not recently. But we had some about a year ago."

A year was a long time. Still, it could be something. "Mind if I ask what it was?"

"Big ol' penis." He pointed to the tapering granite pillar. "Went forty feet up. Biggest dick I ever saw."

I fought back a smile and thanked him.

He was turning to leave a second time and I asked, "You haven't by chance seen the numbers 503, 914, or 386 anywhere around town?"

"I haven't."

I sighed.

"But funny thing, now that you mention it," he said, "my friend Patrick saw numbers graffitied just last night."

I felt my eyebrows jump. "Where?"

"The cemetery just up the street: Bunker Hill Burying Ground."

≈

The security guard gave me directions. The cemetery was three blocks away, but he warned me it was closed, and you had to call and make an appointment twenty-four hours in advance if you wanted to visit. I told him I would do just that.

Five minutes later, I approached the black wrought-iron fence surrounding the graveyard. Minimal light from the nearby streetlights illuminated the surrounding bushes and trees.

Across the street was a convenience store, the Bunker Hill Market. I headed inside and searched the aisles for a flashlight, but there were none. Luckily, at the counter I spied an assortment of keychains, some with small flashlights. I grabbed a green one and added it to a Snickers and blue Powerade.

Once I'd jumped the cemetery fence, I pulled the mini flashlight from my front pocket and clicked it on. It illuminated a four-foot swatch of ground, and I scanned the light up the closest gravestone.

"Gladys Beaker," I said. "1732 to 1783."

Underneath it read, "Died Making Butter."

Just kidding. It said, "Mother, Daughter, and Wife."

Gladys Beaker was clear, and I moved on to Nate Wilhelm.

Over the next hour and a half, I went methodically from gravestone to gravestone. I inspected 148 of them and found no graffiti or any evidence of graffiti that had recently been power-washed away.

I checked my watch. It was a little after nine.

I pulled the Snickers from my pocket and tore into it. I finished it in three bites, swished it down with half the blue Powerade, then started in on the second half of the graves.

Twenty minutes later, the tiny flashlight's beam landed on Edith Montgomery's grave. I moved the flashlight up the gravestone, then walked around to its back.

"Bingo!"

Etched in black spray paint was a three-digit number.

772.

I pulled *The E.K. Dream Book* out of the backpack. The cover was light blue and tattered. It was fifty-three pages long and was bound with two thick staples. Centering the cover was a drawing of a Black woman holding her hands to a crystal ball. Written perpendicular to the woman was, "Beware of imitations. Only the original *E.K. Dream Book* bears this signature: Prof. Uriah DuBauer." According to my library book, Professor Uriah DuBauer was the pseudonym of the author, Ephraim Gladstone Kearns, hence *E.K.*

I flipped the book open and, with the flashlight in my mouth, I began running my finger down the entries. I made it through the A's, the B's, the C's, and halfway through the D's when my finger stopped.

772.

Digging.

10

Desecrating a grave isn't something I took lightly, but I figured Edith had been resting comfortably for going on two hundred years. Maybe she could do with a bit of excitement.

I walked to the far end of the cemetery, where there was a compact maintenance shack. I hoped to find a series of shovels leaning up against the side, whereby I could choose my favorite make and model—I'm a Fiskars 9668 type of guy—but alas, there were no shovels. The door was locked and after scouring the area for a shovel, I came up empty.

It was after nine thirty, and all the hardware stores in the area would be closed. I had no other option but to borrow a shovel from one of the surrounding homes.

I walked the perimeter of the cemetery, peeking over the fencing. At one point, I spotted a shovel lying in the dirt of a dying flower bed. I pulled myself over the fence, grabbed the shovel, then scrambled back over.

Once back at Edith's grave, I examined the ground. The grass was yellowing, and perpendicular lines of dirt were visible. From working as a landscaper for a year after dropping out of college, I knew the lines were a result of unprofessionally laid sod.

I dug the shovel into the grass and lifted up a few inches. The roots of the grass were still in their infancy. I guessed the sod had been laid three or four weeks earlier. Which meant that whatever I was meant to uncover had been done before Eugene Kirovec's murder.

What was the killer playing at?

There was only one way to find out.

I sank the shovel into the ground, pressed down hard with my foot, then heaved a sizable chunk of grass and dirt to the side.

It would take the average person between four to five hours to dig a grave, but I wasn't your average person. And I hoped that two hundred years ago they didn't dig down quite as deep. With luck, Edith would be resting comfortably *two* feet under.

She wasn't.

By midnight, I'd dug down three feet. My hands were covered in blisters, I was hungry, I was thirsty, and my back felt like I'd gone to a chiropractor licensed by the KGB.

"Keep going," I murmured, digging the shovel back into the dirt.

Another hour passed—my blisters now with blisters of their own—when I heard the soft echo of a casket.

"Good morning, Edith."

It took another thirty minutes to uncover the entire casket. I expected to find numbers etched somewhere in the wood, but there was nothing.

At least, there was nothing on top.

I was widening the hole around the casket, when I noticed a faint light in the distance. I turned. A man with a flashlight was approaching.

The security guard was even older than the security guard at the monument. He had white hair, thick glasses, and a beer belly hanging an inch over his belt. He engulfed me in the beam of his flashlight. "Hey, fella," he said. "Why don't you come on out of there?"

I pulled myself out.

He lowered the flashlight. "What exactly is going on here?"

"I'm Jason Calloway with GDE."

"What's GDE?"

"Grave Digger Express. Out of Cambridge." Cambridge was the only other town in Massachusetts I could think of.

The man wrinkled his forehead. "What the hell are you doing out here at one in the morning?"

"Edith's great-grandchildren just bought her a new casket. A stainless-steel number with a red leather interior." I whistled. "A real beauty. They're switching her out bright and early tomorrow morning. Got to get this done beforehand."

The guy cocked his head to the side. "The people at Bunker usually give me a heads-up if there's going to be anybody out here. They didn't tell me anything about you or . . . What was the name of your outfit again?"

"Grave Digger Express. You've probably heard our ad on the radio." In a singsong voice, I said, *"When Grandpa keels over and dies, don't you stress. Just pick up the phone and call Grave Digger Express."*

He stared at me. He looked like he was in the midst of a brain bleed. After a moment, he said, "This sounds a little fishy."

You think?

I said, "Well, it's all there in the work order."

Again, he just stared at me. "You, um, you didn't give me anything."

"Oh, right, I must have left it in the car. I can email it to you when I'm finished up here. What's your email?"

"Um, it's uh, it's Big Jack at—" Apparently realizing people don't just buy new caskets for loved ones and switch them out, he stopped and brought a radio to his mouth. "Yeah, dispatch, I'm going to need backup."

≈

"For the last time," I said to the two cops now surrounding me. "Grave Digger Express." I smiled. "You know our slogan: *The next time Meemaw gets that pain in her chest, just pick up the phone and call Grave Digger Express.*"

Officer Lyle Cantby, who was about the same age as me, said, "I think I have heard that."

Officer Allison Harris, obviously much sharper than her counterpart and in no mood for my games, said, "Desecrating a grave is a class B felony in the State of Massachusetts. Now be straight with us and maybe we can get this sorted out. Why are you digging up Edith Montgomery's grave?"

I considered the possible repercussions of impersonating a federal agent, and said, "I'm FBI. I'm working a case out of Philadelphia."

"You?" Harris said, scoffing. "You're FBI? Where's your badge?"

"I don't have one yet."

"You don't have one yet?"

"That's what I just said."

"What, the laminator is broken?"

I ignored her jab. "Just call someone from the local FBI and get them down here."

"I'm not getting the FBI involved in this bullshit. You're going to the station, and we're booking you for grave desecration."

"Look at the back of Edith's grave."

Big Jack and both deputies walked around to the back of Edith's gravestone.

"Seven hundred and seventy-two," Cantby chimed.

"What does a little graffiti have to do with anything?" Harris asked.

"You're just going to have to trust me." I pulled *The E.K. Dream Book* out of my backpack and handed it to Big Jack. "See what number is listed under *Digging*."

Big Jack thumbed through the book. A moment later, he said, "He's telling the truth. *Digging* is 7-7-2."

I said, "Now unless you want to impede a federal investigation, I advise calling someone from the local FBI field office."

Harris pulled out her cell phone and made the call.

≈

"Special Agent Wade Gleason, Boston Field office," the FBI agent said. He was a dark-skinned African American who I guessed to be in his early forties. He towered over me by five inches, and I was eye level with his well-groomed goatee. "Now, do you want to explain to me why I'm in the middle of a cemetery at two thirty in the morning?"

I gave him the short version, showing him the listings for *Boston*, *Hill*, *War*, and *Digging* in the dream book. Oddly enough, Gleason had spent most of his early life in Philadelphia, and he'd heard rumblings about Agent Joyce's task force. When I finished, Agent Gleason said, "So, you come up here, see the 7-7-2 on the back of the grave, and decide to *dig* up the coffin?"

"That's the gist of it," I replied.

"What did you expect to find inside?"

"I was more looking for something on the *outside* of the coffin."

"More numbers?"

"Exactly. Something that pointed toward the killer's next victim."

"But you didn't find any?"

"None on top. I was widening the hole when Big Jack here approached."

Big Jack, who looked happy to be involved in something so exciting, grinned, and said, "That's when he gave me his whole song and dance about Grave Digger Express."

"But Big Jack saw right through that."

"Not at first," he admitted.

"Okay, Big Jack eventually saw right through that."

He nodded.

Harris, who seemed relieved I was no longer her personal hemorrhoid, said, "I guess we could widen around the casket and look for numbers, but I don't think we should open it."

Gleason agreed.

"I would love to dig some more"—I showed everyone my hands—"but I don't think I'll be able to hold a *kitten* for a few weeks."

The beam of Big Jack's flashlight illuminated my hands. He squinted and asked, "Are those—?"

"Yes, I believe those are my tendons."

Officer Cantby offered to shovel, and he jumped down in the grave. It took him ten minutes to widen the hole around the casket enough to see the entire left side. There were no markings. Over the next hour, we inspected the other three sides and found nothing.

Big Jack asked, "What about the bottom?"

"That would be a lot of work," Harris said. "The killer would have had to pull the casket all the way out, write a number on the bottom, and then put it back in."

"I'm pretty sure there's nothing on the bottom," I said, then added, "but we have to look inside."

"We can't."

"There could be a number in there that leads to the next victim or worse yet, the next victim could be inside."

"You need a warrant to open it. Next of kin need to sign off on any sort of exhuming. I'm not having any part of this."

"You don't have to worry about anything coming back on you guys," Gleason said to Harris. He turned to me and asked, "How positive are you that there's another number or a body in there?"

I leaned my head back. "Sixty-three percent."

Gleason was quiet for a few seconds, playing out his ass-ripping, demotion, and possible firing if the only thing in the casket was dear-old-Edith.

Finally, he said, "Open the casket."

"You sure?" Cantby asked.

"Open it."

Cantby unclasped the two clasps, then dusted dirt off the handle. "Here goes."

He flipped the top of the casket open with a loud creak. Big Jack and Harris both shined their flashlights down through the wafting cloud of dust.

When it cleared, Harris said, "Holy shit."

Edith wasn't alone.

≈

If you want to get technical, there were three bodies in the coffin. Edith was nothing more than a skeleton, and the other two were crammed on top of her. Both of those corpses were still clad in clothes, though the fabrics were beginning to decompose. If there had been numbers carved into the victims' foreheads at one point, it was impossible to tell. Their skin had mummified into something resembling beef jerky.

Gleason said, "Those bodies aren't fresh."

"They certainly are not," I said.

This threw me for a loop. I expected the victim to have been killed in the past month.

"Are those platform shoes?" Cantby asked.

I leaned down on my haunches and inspected the shoes. They were black with a large two-inch heel.

"Tony Manero," Big Jack said.

"Who?" Harris asked.

"Tony Manero—John Travolta's character from *Saturday Night Fever*."

"What about him?" I asked.

"Those are the shoes that those guys wore. Hell, I had a pair myself."

Gleason put on a pair of gloves, and he ran his hand over the victims' pants and heavy collared shirts. "He's right," he said, glancing up, "these two guys are dressed for the disco."

A bell went off in my head and my eyes must have lit up. Gleason cocked his head at me and said, "What?"

This serial killer was playing a different game entirely.

Big Jack, Cantby, Harris, and Gleason all had their eyes trained on me.

"The killer isn't using the numbers to tell us where he's going—" I paused dramatically. "—he's using the numbers to tell us where he's *been*."

11

After I made a phone call to Agent Joyce that could be summed up in the three-word phrase "YOU DID *WHAT!*" the coroner and crime scene techs arrived. A half hour later, I said farewell to my new friends and joined Wade Gleason—now officially part of the task force—in his blue Ford Taurus.

Gleason merged onto I-90 westbound, and I got to know my new *partner*. I asked, "When was the last time you were back in Philly?"

"Last Thanksgiving."

"You still have family there?"

"My parents, my nana, plus a few aunts, uncles, and cousins."

"How did you end up in Boston?"

"It was pretty competitive after I finished up at Quantico. My first job was in the Minneapolis field office, doing white-collar crime. After three years in the cold— and by cold, I mean, *freeze-your-pecker-off*—I applied for a Violent Crime position in Boston. Been here for just over a decade now. What about you?" he asked. "What's your story?"

"Grew up in Seattle. I was with the Seattle Police Department from the age of twenty-one until twenty-seven. Homicide for the last two."

"That's pretty young."

"Youngest detective in SPD history."

"Then what?"

"Then my little sister got a scholarship to Drexel, and about the same time I got sacked."

"For what?"

"My partner and I had a few differences of opinion."

He didn't pry, leaving it at that, then asked, "How did you end up with the FBI?"

"I'm not with the FBI officially. I was recommended by someone at the Philly PD and the Feds are bringing me on as a consultant." Though after the tongue-lashing Joyce had given me, they might be bringing me on as a window washer.

"How did you end up hooking up with the Philly PD?"

"I was at Geno's and I—"

"Geno's?" he said, shaking his head. "Come on now."

"Let me guess: you're a Pat's guy?" Pat's was a rival cheese-steak place across the street from Geno's. Both shops had been there for ages, and most Philadelphians had an allegiance to one or the other.

"Through and through," Gleason said, licking his lips. "Geno's doesn't even come close."

I was of the minority who enjoyed both places equally, and I listened for the next few minutes as Gleason ticked off the many reasons Pat's made the superior sandwich. After he finished his lecture, I recounted how after meeting Gallow at Geno's, he invited me to play pickup ball with him and a few other cops.

"Sunday mornings at Capitolo?" Gleason asked.

"You been?"

"Been?" He scoffed. "I used to own that park. Played there almost every day when I was growing up."

"I knew I liked you."

He laughed, then asked, "Are you any good?"

"I can hold my own. I walked on at the University of Washington my freshman year."

"Really?"

"Yeah, but three practices after making the team, I was late, and the coach made me run sprints."

"And you told him to piss off."

"Wow, it's like you were there."

We laughed, then he said, "Alright, so you meet this detective, and you start playing ball—"

"And he asked if I wanted to take a look at a couple cold cases he was working. I solved one of them and it got me in the good graces of Gallow's captain."

"Which district?"

"Ninth."

"Folch?"

"You know him?"

"He's ten years older than me, but I remember watching him play a couple times. He was a legend."

"Could he shoot back then?" Folch was one of the best pure shooters I'd come across. At fifty-five, he wasn't the quickest guy, but he only needed a few inches of open space to get off his shot.

"He was deadly."

"He still is." I told a quick anecdote about how he made twelve shots in a row during a game a month back, then I steered us back to the case. "So, what do you know about the Numbers?"

"Like most working-class Black folks in the fifties and sixties, my parents played it weekly."

"Do you remember any runners coming to your house?"

"Not to take numbers. My parents would just phone those in. But I remember runners coming to the house at the end of each week to collect money."

"Did your parents ever win?"

"I don't remember my dad winning, but my mom hit a few times. She'd only play for a quarter, a dollar at most."

"Was she into the whole dream book thing?"

"Oh, yeah. Black folks love their dream books."

"So I've heard." I told him about Ms. Ruby and her vast collection.

"My nana wasn't much different. She had an entire library of the damn things."

He told a quick story about his ninety-seven-year-old nana who was still "fit as a fiddle." When he finished, he let out a yawn.

A quarter mile later, he pulled the car over to the shoulder of the interstate, opened the door, and got out.

Looked like I was driving the rest of the way.

≈

It was just after eight thirty when the ring of my cellphone startled Gleason awake. I pulled my phone out of my pocket and looked at the caller ID.

Gallow.

I flipped the phone open. "Yo."

"I hear you've been digging up old revolutionary women."

"You hear correctly."

I gave him a quick rundown, then asked, "What's going on with the Brooke Wexley case?"

Gleason raised his eyebrows and said, "Put it on speaker."

I put the phone on speaker and set it on the center console.

Gallow and Gleason said a quick hello, then Gallow was off to the races. "The autopsy report came back yesterday, and it corroborated what we already knew. Death by asphyxiation. There was severe structural damage to her omohyoid and ster-nohyoid muscles. Her larynx was basically crushed."

Meaning the killer was most likely male or your stronger-than-average female.

"No signs of sexual trauma," Gallow continued, "though they did find traces of semen. But that could have come from days prior. Coroner estimated time of death somewhere between midnight and three a.m. on Tuesday morning."

"What about forensics?" I asked. "Those guys find anything?"

"Not a whole lot. The killer swabbed Brooke's neck and the entire tent with disinfectant."

I thought I'd smelled something antiseptic upon entering. "What kind?"

"Dimethyl benzyl ammonium chloride."

This was the active ingredient in both Clorox and Lysol wipes.

I asked, "Any fingerprints on the outside of the tent other than Brooke's?"

"The nylon doesn't hold oil very well, but we found a couple partials that didn't belong to Brooke. So far, no hits in the database."

"Witnesses?" Gleason asked.

"We interviewed everyone in the surrounding tents, plus another hundred kids who were there at some point that night. No one saw much. One witness says he was sitting on a bench, smoking, and saw Brooke exit her tent around 1:30 a.m. We checked with her university, and they have her card-swiping in at her dorm—Rodin College House—at 1:51 a.m."

"Any surveillance footage there?"

"No, but there's a traffic cam on the Market Street Bridge that picked her up headed back toward city hall at 2:07 a.m. She was carrying a laptop under her arm. We can assume Brooke arrived back at her tent a few minutes after the bridge footage, and we can assume soon thereafter our perp entered, strangled her, wiped down the evidence, then took her computer."

"Why take her computer and not her cell phone?" I asked.

"Yeah, if it was just a burglary gone wrong, that's odd. But these new phones have tight security. A lot of them are useless if you steal them."

"Anything else missing?" Gleason asked.

"We couldn't locate her school ID card or a set of keys."

I said, "So if it was a theft gone bad, the perp might have planned on breaking into her dorm room and stealing more stuff."

"We don't think he did. Nothing from her dorm room was missing. Anyhow, they've already had the locks changed and deactivated her ID card."

"Did you sit down with the family yet?" Gleason asked.

"Yeah, late Wednesday night, we met with Nicholas Wexley, his wife, and their two other kids at their Spring Garden condo. It was painful, as always."

"They have solid alibis?"

Even in a case as bizarre as this one, you had to look at family and friends first.

"The wife and youngest daughter were home. The son— he's a senior at Penn—was at his fraternity. Bunch of witnesses put him there."

"What about Nicholas Wexley?"

"He was at his office until around one a.m., then went to their condo. He said he worked out for an hour and a half, then went to bed at around three."

"Any evidence to back this up?"

"Surveillance footage has him leaving Wexlund Tower at 1:03 a.m. CCTV has him coming into the parking garage at the condo ten minutes later. There are cameras in the condo lobby, and they have him checking for a package at the front desk at 1:17. Then he's on video in the fitness center starting at 1:38, working out until right around three in the morning."

That's a lot of time on camera. A skeptic might even speculate a little too much.

"How did he act in the interview?" I asked.

"He was gutted. No red flags."

"What about boyfriends for Brooke?" Gleason asked.

"According to her roommates—she lived in a sophomore quad on the twenty-third floor—she didn't have a boyfriend. There were a couple text exchanges with two guys on her phone, but she wasn't in any sort of relationship."

"You talk to those guys?"

"We did. Both gave DNA samples voluntarily, and both said they were interested in Brooke, but she wouldn't give them the time of day."

"Roommates check out?"

"Yeah, three girls. All nice enough. Though I got the feeling one of them might be holding something back. Might take another crack at her in the next day or so."

"Find anything interesting in her room?"

"Just one thing—a vial of GHB."

Gamma-hydroxybutyric acid was a club drug, but it could also be used to incapacitate someone.

I wondered aloud, "Did Brooke Wexley have any in her system?"

"No, her tox screen came back clean."

"What about social media?" Gleason asked.

"Almost entirely Occupy Wall Street posts since it first began. A couple of trolls left some comments about how she was from one of the richest families in the United States. Some vulgar stuff. We're still trying to track a few of those creeps down."

"Are you feeling the heat?" I asked.

"Oh yeah. I'm in the cauldron. Folch has already had calls from both the mayor and the governor. This is top priority."

We were about to hit Philly city limits and I said, "Alright, good luck, brother."

"Yeah, you guys too."

12

Two miles later, Gleason's cell phone rang.

He answered the call, his eyebrows shooting upward after several seconds.

"What?" I asked.

"It's one of the forensics guys," he said, covering the phone with his hand. "They found three numbers written on the back of Edith Montgomery's skull in black Sharpie. Preliminary chemical analysis has the ink less than a month old."

My mind was whirring, and I nearly rear-ended the Prius in front of me. The murders might have happened over thirty years ago, but the staging of the bodies and the writing on Edith's skull happened within the last month.

"What are the numbers?" I asked.

"8-0-7, 3-9-4, and 6-1-1."

I committed the three numbers to memory, then reached my hand into the back seat where *The E.K. Dream Book* was sitting. I snagged it with my fingers and then riffled it open, holding the book to the steering wheel.

Two cars honked their horns—evidently, I was driving in

two different lanes—and Gleason yanked the steering wheel to the right.

"You're going to get us killed!" he shouted.

I tossed him the book. "We need to find those entries."

"What's the big hurry? The last numbers pointed to a murder that happened thirty years ago."

He was right, of course. But for some reason, I felt a sense of urgency. It probably stemmed from a history of watching killers run free because law enforcement deemed them predictable.

"Just find them," I said.

It took Gleason seven minutes to locate the entries for the three numbers. 807 was listed twice: once under *Kettle* and again under *Delaware*. 394 was also listed twice: *Exodus* and *Dock*. 611 was only listed once: *Boat*.

"I think we can rule out *Kettle* and *Exodus*," Gleason said.

I nodded in agreement. "So, *Delaware*, *Dock*, and *Boat*."

"That's a needle in a haystack. Delaware has four hundred miles of coastline. That's hundreds of docks."

Which translated to thousands of boats.

I pulled out my phone and dialed Agent Joyce.

He picked up on the first ring, and I relayed the information. "You need to check all the marinas. Start with the Delaware City Marina and move outward." The marina was fifty miles south of Philadelphia.

"I'll run that up the chain," he said, which was odd, considering he *was* the chain. "Most of the task force is filtering in right now, and we'll go through everything we know and decide how to best proceed."

That's the problem with a task force comprising twenty-plus individuals. It was lethargic. It moved like a kid with mono. To catch a serial killer, you need to move quickly and decisively.

"Fine. We'll be there in ten minutes."

I flipped the phone shut and set it in my lap.

I turned to Gleason and asked, "Why are these three clues so much vaguer than his first three?"

"Maybe he wants us to have to work for it."

"I disagree. He's been waiting thirty-odd years to tell whatever story he's trying to tell. I think he wants to make up for lost time."

"Maybe there will be another number, or even another set of numbers, they'll find when they do the autopsies."

He was right. Edith's grave-mates might also have numbers carved into their foreheads. "Could the medical examiner decipher numbers carved into the victims from thirty years ago?"

"I doubt there will be any traces on what's left of the victims' skin, but if the blade penetrated to the bone, it might be possible."

I touched my forehead with three of my fingers. The frontal bone was flush with the skin. The blade wouldn't have to penetrate very deep for there to be markings in the bone. Still, I had a hard time believing the killer would bank on an autopsy revealing this.

From my experience, most serial killers are control freaks.

"That's too big of a risk for the killer," I said, thinking out loud again. "What if they don't find any markings? Or the numbers aren't clear? Where else could we find numbers?"

I snapped my fingers and shouted, "Edith's gravestone!"

The killer had three hundred graves to choose from. Why pick Edith Montgomery? Was it by chance or had he picked her for a reason? So far, the killer's MO had been leaving clues on the victims. Would he switch it up?

Gleason nodded, then asked, "Do you remember the dates?"

I closed my eyes and pulled up the image from the Thomas Prescott Super Detective Database. "1732 to 1814."

Gleason flipped back open the dream book. "Let's try 7-3-2 . . . found it, *Peckish* . . . here it is again, *Muscovado*. What the hell is muscovado?"

"It's a type of sugar. Now check for 8-1-4."

He did. It only came up once: *Geranium*.

Obviously, none of these made any sense.

The exit for Central Philadelphia was a half mile away, and I eased my way into an exit lane. I closed my eyes. The dates from Edith's gravestone were still there, blinking neon orange.

1732 to 1814.

I recalled when I'd first seen the dates and thought, *Wow, that's a long life.* The average lifespan back then couldn't have been much higher than forty or fifty.

"Oh, shit!" I screamed, ripping the steering wheel to the left and narrowly missing a collection of orange crash barrels. The tires screeched, and Gleason's body rammed into mine.

"What the hell, Prescott?" Gleason shouted as I attempted to bring the car under control.

"It's not the dates! It's the time between the dates!"

"What do you mean?"

"It's how long Edith was alive."

He did the math in his head. I let him, hoping to corroborate my math.

"Eighty-two years," he said.

"Right."

He couldn't piece it together on his own and I explained, "The Delaware River. Another name for a dock. And one big-ass boat."

After a long second, he blurted, "Pier Eighty-Two!"

"Yep."

It wasn't exactly a boat—it was a *ship*. And it was docked on Pier 82 on the Delaware River.

The SS *United States*.

≈

We drove three more miles, then exited the interstate for the Port of Philadelphia. A few minutes later, we screeched to a halt near the entrance to Pier 82.

There was an eight-foot chain link fence topped with barbed wire and the enormous rust bucket that was the SS *United States* could be seen in the background.

I didn't know much about the ship other than the fact it had been a popular ocean liner in the 1950s and had been docked in Philly on the Delaware River for the past fifteen years.

"How do we get past the gate?" Gleason asked.

Unlike the port's many other piers, which were stacked with shipping containers and permeated with workers, Pier 82 was empty and abandoned.

I parked the car parallel to the fence, nestling it close enough that I could barely squeeze out of the driver's-side door.

"What are you doing?" Gleason asked, jumping out of the car.

"Give me your jacket."

"My jacket?" He ran his hand over one lapel. "Hell no!"

I stared at him.

After a loud sigh, he stripped off his jacket and handed it to me.

I hopped on the hood of the car and then crawled onto the roof. It sounded like the crushing of a soda can as my weight dimpled the blue steel paneling.

"You're paying to get those dings out!" Gleason yelled from behind me.

I ignored him.

I folded Gleason's suit jacket in half, then draped it over the two rows of barbed wire. I pushed the jacket down with my hands, swung my legs over, then climbed down the opposite side.

"You coming?" I asked, glancing backward through the fence.

"Nope."

"Okay. Call Joyce and tell him to get down here. And get port authority to open that gate."

He said he would.

I turned and ran toward the ship. It was eight stories high and over three football fields long. Most of the paint on the sides was stripped away and everything that was metal was either a rusted brown or a mildewy green. At the midpoint of the ship was a removable aluminum bridge leading into an opening in the hull.

I clanked across the ten feet and into the belly of the ship. Instantly I was taken aback. The morning sun shone through the many small circular windows, revealing that the interior of the ship had been gutted. All that remained was the bare floor, the yellow steel frame of the walls, and a plethora of exposed electrical wires.

It should have been called the SS *Skeleton*.

I spent several minutes making my way through the bottom two levels of the ship. I'd never been on a cruise ship—I prefer to have my explosive diarrhea on land—so I had a hard time imagining what the interior might have looked like in the ship's golden years.

I ducked my head through an opening and saw what at one point could have been a casino, then discovered another room with a sloping floor that might have been a theater. The staterooms began on the third level; each was at least a hundred and fifty square feet, and the corner suites double that.

A brief cry echoed through the ship.

I cast my gaze upward. The noise had come from the level above me.

I turned on my heel and backtracked to a metal staircase. I needed a weapon. The aluminum stair railing was connected in several two-foot sections, and I shook it. It rattled loudly. After three hard shakes, I pried away one of the sections. It was a hollow pole, two and a half inches in diameter.

The pole in hand, I cautiously climbed the stairs, then emerged on the fourth level. Written in blue chalk on one of the yellow steel walls was "C Deck."

To the right were more staterooms. To the left was an open doorway leading to a room.

I went left.

"Hello!" I shouted, making my way toward the room. My words bounced off the steel walls, echoing throughout the ship.

I waited for a response. None came.

I entered a large square room with an impressive indoor swimming pool. Two metal swim ladders led down into the empty pool. I took three steps forward and gazed down. Sprawled at the bottom of the pool was a man with a beard and long hair matted with blood.

I whipped my head back and forth.

The killer must still be close.

I exited the room, pulling my phone open as I started back to the stairs. Gleason answered on the first ring.

"He's here!" I shouted. "Victim is in the interior pool on the east side of C deck."

I snapped the phone closed before Gleason could reply. When I reached the stairs, I paused and listened for footsteps. Several soft thumps echoed from above.

I stormed up the stairs and exited on the fifth level. At the end of the corridor, a hundred feet away, was a person dressed in jeans, boots, a dark sweatshirt, gloves, and a ski mask. Ballpark height: five foot ten; ballpark weight: a hundred and sixty pounds.

I only glimpsed the back of his head as he disappeared from view.

It took me six seconds to sprint to the end of the corridor. A door led outside, and it hadn't fully shut. I pushed through the door into the daylight and ran along the outside railing. The floor had a green tinge, and you could still make out the faint lines from the decades-old shuffleboard court.

I glanced over the edge of the railing. I was on the north side of the ship. The Delaware River was fifty feet below, its slow-moving waters a cascading midnight blue. A hundred yards of open water separated the ship from the next pier.

I climbed a ladder to the deck above and, at the top, scanned the area. It was the lido deck—a term I wasn't sure why I knew—which referred to the deck with the outdoor swimming pool.

The killer was nowhere to be seen.

Splash.

I hopped down from the ladder and sprinted toward the back deck of the ship, where I was certain the splash had originated.

I raced past a giant propeller—old, rusted, the blades deeply fissured, and secured to the back deck with thick chain—and to the back railing. Fifty feet below, ripples of whitewater churned outward in growing concentric circles.

"Shit!" I screamed.

The killer had jumped.

13

"This was one of the first iterations of safety glass," Marty Inaba said, knocking his knuckles against one of the many portholes lining the C deck hull.

Over the past half hour, Lew had feigned interest as Inaba chronicled the ship's sixty-year history, from its 1952 maiden voyage—where it broke the eastbound transatlantic speed record—to its decommissioning in 1969, and on to finding its home at Pier 82 in 1996.

Inaba was in his forties with an unkempt beard and blond hair tied back in a ponytail. He wore jeans and a black long-sleeve shirt that read, "SS *United States* Conservancy." The ship wasn't open to the public, and it had taken Lew several weeks trading emails with Inaba to book a private tour.

"Let's head this way, Roger," Inaba said, nodding his head toward one of the remaining enclosed spaces.

Lew's alias at the moment was Roger Horton, a software engineer from Cleveland, who was in town on business.

"This was considered the finest indoor pool of its kind," Inaba said, waving his hands over the empty rectangular pool centering the room. "It was only accessible to first-class passengers."

Inaba's feet were less than a foot from the edge of the pool drop-off.

Lew fought down a grin as he eased himself behind his tour guide. He pulled his switchblade from his jacket pocket and flicked it open. The snap of the knife echoed through the room.

Inaba started to turn around just as Lew plunged the knife into his back an inch below where the man's ponytail ended. Lew felt the blade sink through muscle and tissue and then slide into the man's lung.

Lew pulled out the blade and gave Inaba a soft push. Inaba let out a mangled cry as he plummeted eight feet to the tiled bottom of the pool.

Lew took leather gloves out of his pocket and pulled them on. He'd been careful not to touch any surface while he was taking his "tour." He climbed down the metal swim ladder and dropped the last two feet to the bottom of the pool.

Inaba was barely conscious, his torso rising slightly with each wheezing breath. Lew dropped to his knees and rammed the knife into the man's back four times.

When Inaba stopped breathing, Lew rolled him over. There was a gash above the man's left ear where he must have struck the bottom of the pool, and his hair was matted with blood. Lew had just touched the tip of the blade to the man's forehead, when he heard a faint rattling.

Someone was on the ship!

Lew had packed a ski mask for just such an emergency. He pulled it from his jacket pocket and slipped it over his head. After adjusting the eyeholes, he climbed up the swim ladder. As he exited the room and hustled down the hallway, feet clanked up the stairs.

A door to the exterior of the ship was locked. Lew backtracked, peeking around the edge of one of the yellow steel walls.

A man bolted from the indoor pool doorway. He had a phone to his ear and shouted, "He's here!"

Lew had a dossier on everyone on the FBI task force searching for him.

Thomas Prescott.

Prescott had been the one to figure out that the numbers on the three victims weren't area codes—which had been an artful misdirect on Lew's part—but were instead numbers corresponding to entries in *The E.K. Dream Book*.

Prescott had also been the one to unearth the two bodies in the grave in Boston less than twelve hours earlier.

That hadn't been easy for Lew to set up.

A month earlier, through an intermediary, Lew had paid some kids to ride their dirt bikes through the Bunker Hill Burying Ground. They'd destroyed the grass so badly that the cemetery had been forced to resod the entire grounds.

A few days later, while every able-bodied Bostonian was glued to their TV watching the Red Sox lose the wild card to the Orioles, Lew went to work. He recovered the two bodies—which had been remarkably well preserved by the thick plastic sheeting they were wrapped in—from the woods where they'd been buried since 1976. Then he drove to the Bunker Hill Burying Ground. He didn't see another person for the next five hours as he removed the freshly laid sod, dug up Edith Montgomery's grave, added the two bodies, then wrote the numbers on the back of Edith's skull.

Then, on October 19—just two days earlier—Lew had paid one of the same kids to spray-paint 772 on the back of Edith's grave.

Lew hadn't anticipated anyone piecing together the second set of clues for at least a couple more hours. But he'd underestimated the task force.

Or at least Mr. Prescott.

"Victim is in the interior pool on the east side of C deck!"

Lew overheard Prescott shout into his phone.

Lew couldn't risk being cornered and darted across an open hallway. He was momentarily exposed while heading toward an exterior exit. He was relieved when he found the door to be unlocked and he pushed into sunlight. Running toward the back of the ship, he glimpsed an enormous rusted propeller fastened to the deck with thick chain.

Lew intended to head up to the next level but changed his mind when he spied a large two-foot-long metal oval nestled near the railing. It was corroded, the galvanized steel oxidized to a burnt orange. Lew assumed it was an old link from the ship's anchor chain that was on display. He hefted it up—the link must have weighed close to ninety pounds—and heaved it over the side. He heard the splash as he darted to the nearest door, where he entered and waited, watching from its porthole.

Five seconds later, Prescott rushed past, then uttered a loud "Shit!"

Prescott assumed his prey had jumped.

Lew's ruse had worked. Though if Prescott opened the door and peeked inside, he was cooked.

Lew held his breath.

Prescott's shadow flitted over the porthole as he raced back the way he'd come.

Lew exhaled, then chuckled.

Maybe the young man wasn't so clever after all.

Lew cracked open the door. The coast was clear. He made his way back to the propeller. With his switchblade, he etched two numbers on the underside of one of the giant blades.

When he finished, he glanced over the side of the ship.

He couldn't escape via the Delaware River as planned. They'd soon be searching the water, pier, and banks for him.

Lew would have to find another way off the ship.

14

After realizing the killer had jumped fifty feet into the Delaware River, I considered jumping myself and giving chase. Thankfully, before I did my reverse two and a half pike, I decided the best play was to alert the proper authorities.

I whipped out my phone and dialed Gleason. "He jumped off the ship!" I shouted.

"From where?"

"Back of the ship." I peered over the edge of the railing. "I don't see him anywhere in the water. He could have swum under the ship, or on the off chance he could hold his breath for a couple minutes, he might have made it to the opposite pier."

"I've got port authority on the other line. I'll tell them to be on the lookout for our perp in the water." He disconnected.

I jogged the length of the ship, searching the water below for any sign of the killer. After several minutes, I gave up and headed back inside. As I was descending the steps to the fourth floor, I was startled by a man in a port authority uniform. He was rectangular, with short hair, and a thick neck.

"Hands in the air!" he shouted, his gun aimed at my sternum.

I put my hands up.

"On your knees!"

His arms were shaking, and I worried he was one tremor away from giving me some unwanted lead jewelry.

I followed his instructions.

"My partner, Agent Gleason, is the one who called the murder in," I stated calmly.

His arms lowered at the sound of Gleason's name. "You got any ID?"

"I'm going to reach into my back pocket."

"Slowly."

I pulled out my wallet and flung it toward him. He picked it up, inspected my license, then lowered his gun. "Sorry about that," he said, returning my wallet.

He introduced himself as Officer Billups.

"Any sign of our perp in the water?" I asked.

"No one's spotted anything yet. But we got hundreds of people on the lookout. If he's in the Delaware, we'll find him."

I led him to the interior pool.

"Holy shit!" Billups said, gazing down at the victim.

"Do you recognize him?"

"No, but I recognize his shirt. He must work for the conservancy."

"What conservancy?"

"The SS *United States* Conservancy. The old tub was headed for the scrapyard when they bought it earlier this year. They sometimes give private tours."

If the killer had set up one of these tours, there would be a paper or electronic trail. Even if the killer took precautions—used an alias, an untraceable email, or even a burner phone—he may have made a mistake.

All it takes is one.

I lowered myself to the ground and scooted toward the edge of the pool.

"What are you doing?" Billups asked.

I ignored him, lowering myself to the bottom. Ski Mask might have used the pool ladder, and I didn't want to risk compromising any fingerprint evidence. But I also wanted to get a look at the latest murder victim up close.

The pool's floor was slanted, and rivulets of blood ran from the body toward the deep end. I sidestepped the blood, crouching over the victim's head. On the man's forehead was a single drop of dried blood.

"Any numbers?"

I glanced up.

Billups was gone and in his place was Special Agent Joyce. From below, his eyebrows resembled two mating caterpillars.

"Nope," I said, shaking my head. "Looks like he started, but I must have spooked him."

I inspected the body for another thirty seconds, then climbed out of the pool. Joyce offered me a hand, helping me to my feet.

"Where's Gleason?" I asked.

"He's down on the pier with the others, trying to control the frenzy," Joyce said. "Gonna be hard to keep this one from the looky-loos and the media."

You could see Pier 82 from the highway, and I'm sure with all the flashing lights it was starting to look like Christmas in October.

Joyce looked over my shoulder at the corpse, then said, "Well, Prescott, you are one lucky son of a bitch." After a slight pause, he added, "But good work."

He pulled an envelope out of his pocket and handed it to me.

Inside was a card that read, "Federal Bureau of Investigation," with the FBI seal on the far left. Under my name it read, "Special Contract Agent."

He clapped one of his hands on my shoulder. "Don't make me regret this."

I think we both knew that he would.

≈

Ten minutes after Agent Joyce showed up, C deck started to get crowded: task force members, CSIs, port authority police, and a slew of other law enforcement.

I gave a quick summary of Gleason's and my actions to the task force, plus my vague description of the killer, then headed out. I'd been awake for over twenty-four hours and smelled like a post-rave teenager.

After taking a taxi to my condo, I ate some cereal, had a protein shake, decided to forgo a shower, then lay down in bed. I closed my eyes. I was exhausted and desperately needed sleep. There was only one problem: I couldn't shake the image of the dead body. Not the dude at the bottom of the pool. No, Brooke Wexley was the ghost in my cerebrum.

My eyes shot open.

Gallow had mentioned that when he was interviewing Brooke's roommates, he'd gotten the feeling one of them was holding back.

Brooke's dorm was less than a mile from my condo. I ran a stick of deodorant under each arm, bandaged up the blisters on my hands, and headed in that direction.

Rodin College House was five blocks west of campus, a high-rise tower, half the building gray, the other half brown, with hundreds of windows reflecting the day's overcast sky. A granite sign in the courtyard had been turned into a memorial to Brooke Wexley. There were piles of flower bouquets, a handful of flickering candles, and five or six pictures of Brooke.

I waited near the entrance for someone to exit the locked door, then hustled through into the foyer. A few kids strolled the halls of the twenty-third floor, but I didn't need to ask them which room was Brooke's. Another memorial had been erected near her door.

After I knocked, a tall girl with brown hair opened the door. She was wearing pajama bottoms, and her eyes were red and puffy. Her name was Rachel.

I introduced myself solely by name, omitting that I was simply a nosy civilian. I only wanted to use my still hot-off-the-printer FBI badge as a last resort.

I said, "I have some follow-up questions about Brooke." She assumed I was a detective investigating the case and motioned me inside.

The quad was basically a small apartment. A coffee table near a red fabric sectional was topped with two empty bottles of cheap wine and a bowl containing the remnants of macaroni and cheese.

"Are your other roommates around?" I asked.

"Lauren is, but Julie's in class."

Rachel went to grab her roommate, and the two returned a moment later. Lauren was short, with a nest of brown hair pulled back in a ponytail. Much like Rachel, she was clad in pajama bottoms and a tank top. She held an enormous purple water bottle in her hand.

She took a drink from the bottle and said, "We already told the detectives everything we know."

At this, Rachel's body tensed, her toes curling into the shag carpet.

"You know what, I just have a few routine follow-up

questions." I nodded at the young woman who I was almost certain was the squirmy one Gallow had been referring to, and said, "I think Rachel here will be able to answer them."

Without a word, Lauren spun on her heel and left.

"Uh, are you sure?" Rachel muttered. "You don't need Lauren? I mean, I don't know much."

"I'm sure." I motioned toward the kitchen table. "Can we sit?" We did.

I asked, "How long had you known Brooke?"

"I met her at orientation. We were at the cafeteria and both getting ice cream for breakfast." Her eyes turned glassy at the memory.

"Did you know she was from a prominent family?"

She shook her head. "I'm from Arizona. I'd never heard of the Wexleys before."

"When did you find out?"

"It was the second week of school. Brooke and I were hanging out in my dorm room, and a guy from across the hall came in. He took one look at Brooke and said, 'Not another Wexley.' I thought maybe he was doing a bit from Harry Potter—you know, a play on the whole Weasley thing—but he wasn't. Then he called her Richie Rich or something."

"How did Brooke react when he said that?"

"To be honest, she seemed ashamed."

Rachel walked me through how she and Brooke became closer friends over the course of the year. Brooke had visited her for a month that summer in Phoenix, and they'd moved into the sophomore quad together earlier this year.

"But when Occupy Wall Street started, Brooke totally changed," she said. "It's all she wanted to talk about. She took the train up to New York twice to go to marches there. She was one of the first people to start the protests down here."

"What about the rest of you guys? Did you ever go down and protest?"

"Julie and Lauren never did. I went there once, just to see what it was all about, and, you know, to support Brooke."

"Was she still attending her classes?"

"I think so. But school wasn't her priority. I know she had a big paper due, and she totally blew it off."

"What class?"

"Some sociology class she was taking."

"Was that her major?"

"Brooke hadn't declared her major yet. She was interested in philosophy, psychology, sociology, women's studies."

"Did she have interests outside of school?"

"She used to go to one of those rock-climbing gyms with her little sister. She spent a lot of time by herself. She'd go hiking up in the Poconos. She read a lot."

I thought about the vial of GHB found in her room. "Did she ever go clubbing?"

"Never. She hardly drank."

I waited a beat. "Brooke was beautiful. She had to have boys chasing her."

I didn't need to look under the table to know her toes were again curling into the carpet. Her entire body was one big toe curled into the carpet.

"Of course boys chased her," she said. "Brooke was, like, stunning. But she always gave them the brush-off."

"But there had to be someone."

"Oh my gosh, how rude of me." Rachel pushed up from the table. "I never even offered you water."

"Please, sit back down."

She sat.

"Tell me about him."

"I don't know what you're—"

"I saw Brooke's dead body."

Her eyes widened.

"I saw the bruises around her neck where somebody strangled her."

She sucked air in through her teeth.

"I know you think you're protecting her, maybe protecting her image, maybe something she wouldn't have wanted to get out—but you're not. You are protecting this guy." I reached out and held her hand. "Now tell me who he is."

She leaned her head back and said, "She never told me his name."

"What did she tell you?"

"Just that she really liked him and that she'd been seeing him for the past few weeks."

"Did she describe him?"

"No, though she mentioned he had a cool tattoo on his arm." She smiled meekly. "Brooke loved tattoos. She wanted to get one, but her dad forbade it."

Forbade.

I skipped over this. "Did she say what his tattoo was of?"

"I think it was a tattoo of a dragon."

"Why wouldn't Brooke just tell you about him? Why keep it a secret?"

She closed her eyes, then opened them. "Because he was a professor."

≈

Rachel gave me a copy of Brooke's class schedule, which I perused as I walked the path from Rodin House to campus.

Brooke was taking five classes, four of which were on

Mondays, Wednesdays, and Fridays. I'd missed her 9:00 a.m. class, but she had back-to-back-to-back classes starting at noon.

I arrived at the bustling University of Pennsylvania campus at 11:43 a.m. The university was established in 1740, and many of the buildings were Victorian. Red brick, gray brick, tan brick. Spires, fountains, gardens galore. It was without a doubt, the most beautiful campus I'd ever set foot on.

I was plotting my course on a large campus directory map when I noticed that within the renowned Wharton School of Business complex was the Wexley Conference Center.

I could only imagine how much money Wexley had donated to his alma mater for the distinction. I'd never met the man in person, but from his public persona, I would guess his donation was rooted less in philanthropy than in hubris.

It took me ten minutes to walk to the building where Brooke's noon class, Intro to Women's Studies, met.

The class was large, easily over a hundred students, and I slipped into a seat in the back of the auditorium. A few students nearby shot me curious glances, but I wasn't sure if it was because my deodorant wasn't strong enough to mask my stench, that the blisters on my hands were covered in fourteen Snoopy Band-Aids, or simply because I didn't have a laptop in front of me.

The professor arrived a moment later. She was a woman in her sixties with gray hair in a tight bun. Whatever her preferences, I couldn't picture youthful Brooke lusting after this frumpy woman.

Strike one.

I exited the class, then walked to the commons, where I found the bookstore and bought the second book in the Hunger Games trilogy: *Catching Fire*. I spent twenty minutes reading while I indulged in a Double Western Bacon Cheeseburger at the Hardee's.

Brooke's 1:10 p.m. class was a second-level sociology course. Professor Cartwright was in his midforties, and he was two-thirds of the way to a bald head. He wore a wedding band on his finger, and he probably had two and a half kids and a golden retriever at home. I'd been wrong before, but Brooke didn't exactly strike me as a home-wrecker.

Strike two.

I crossed him off my suspect list, went back to the commons, then read for another half an hour and ate four freshly baked chocolate chip cookies. I was well on my way to packing on the "freshman fifteen."

A little before two, I entered Brooke's 2:10 class: Comparative Literature. About seventy students had already taken seats, and I found a spot near the classroom's back row. The professor was already there. He was young, maybe late thirties, and with his blue sweater and wire-frame glasses he could have been cast in a rom-com as Handsome Young Professor.

The girl next to me had a book out next to her laptop. It was titled *My Uncle Napoleon*.

Professor McDreamy began teaching, and within two minutes my eyelids turned into anvils. My twenty-eight hours awake combined with my Double Western Bacon Cheeseburger and four cookies were inducing a coma.

I jerked my head up.

Had I just fallen asleep?

I tuned to the professor—". . . now what Pezeshkzad was trying to get across was . . ."—but my eyes were so . . .

"Wake up!"

I pulled my head off the desk and squinted upward. I could feel drool running down the side of my cheek.

Professor McDreamy stood over me.

"Am I boring you?" he asked.

"Ummmm."

He picked up the bestselling novel in front of me. "Would you prefer we discuss Miss Katniss Everdeen?"

"As long as you don't spoil the ending."

He chuckled to himself, then he walked down the stairs and resumed his spot at the front of the class. He was still holding my book and he said, "Show of hands! Who here has read *The Hunger Games*?"

Half the class threw their hands in the air.

"Since I have officially bored some of you to sleep"—he glanced in my direction—"let's switch things up here." He shook *Catching Fire* in his hand, leaned his head back in thought, and then said, "Okay, here's a question: In what ways was Panem complicit in the horrors of the Hunger Games?"

Twenty hands shot up.

Professor McDreamy looked around the room, then settled his eyes on me. "Let's hear from Sleepy Sleeperton."

Most of the students laughed, and all eyes swiveled to me.

"Me?" I asked, pointing to my chest. After he nodded, I stood up—which from the three people around me fighting down smiles, did not appear to be the normal routine when answering a question. But I'd look even stupider if I sat, and I stammered, "Well, the people of Panam—"

"Panem," McDreamy corrected. "Pan Am is an old airline."

"Right," I said, then cleared my throat. "Panem is complicit because they, um, they—" *Come on, Thomas, think! You got this!* "—because they were the ones who ultimately, um, decided, that the, that the Hunger Games should be—" *Brain? Hello, Brain, are you there? Anybody home?* "So, take Peeta for example, he, um, his family makes bread, and bread is made from wheat—" *Did you just say bread is made from wheat?* "—and wheat can only grow if there's proper sunshine—" *Welp, we've really gotten off track now.* "What matters is that the people of Panem, much like the Greeks—" *The Greeks? The fucking Greeks?* "The bottom line is, society is a mirror, and Katniss, by offering to take her sister's spot, reflects—that's right, *reflects*—" *Really backed yourself into a corner now.* "Did I say *reflect*? I meant *deflect*. It deflects—" *How is that any better?* "Here's all I know: like my dad used to say, you can't catch a rabbit in Velcro shoes—" *First, your dad never said that. No one has ever said that. And second, things have really spiraled out of control here, let's wrap it up, buddy.* "—case closed."

The room was quiet. Everyone who was staring at me earlier couldn't bear to look at me now. Professor McDreamy had his head angled and his forehead looked like it was trying to switch places with his chin.

After a long moment, McDreamy nodded and said, "That's an interesting response."

I wish I could say it was an act, that I'd answered like a babbling fool to set him at ease when I questioned him later, but it wasn't. I was delirious from lack of sleep. My brain, which had up until now been a staunch ally, had flipped me the bird and gone off-line.

I sat and closed my eyes.

"That's going to be hard to follow," McDreamy said. "But does anyone else have any thoughts?"

My fellow literary scholars were still in shock—some appeared concerned I might need medical attention—but several raised their hands. McDreamy called on a young woman in the fourth row.

She said, "Though the Capitol runs the Games, the entire society of Panem showed its support by refusing to boycott them. Though capable of rebellion—they revolted once before— the population of Panem lacks the strength to question and challenge their system, instead allowing themselves to be led through spectacle."

Exactly what I said!

A few more students shared their thoughts, then McDreamy dismissed the class. After the room emptied, I went to his desk, where he was waiting for me.

He handed me back the book and said, "If you were actually a real student in my class, I wouldn't have tried to embarrass you."

"I think I did that all on my own," I said, with a laugh. "I'm comfortable with public speaking but, man, my brain just flatlined."

"It happens to the best of us." He shuffled through some papers on his desk. "Now, might I ask what you're doing in my class?"

"I'm investigating the Brooke Wexley murder."

He nodded. "I've already spoken with a couple different detectives, but I have a few minutes. What do you want to know?"

I asked him routine questions: Was Brooke a good student? Did she come to class? Did she participate? Were there any guys that appeared to pay her special attention? He answered thoughtfully and seemed at ease, which is a good barometer for when the questions became a tad more invasive, like when I asked him, "Did you ever see her outside of class?"

"Can't say I did." He bit his bottom lip. "Although, I suppose I did see her a few times at the gym. We might have said hello but nothing more."

His pupils didn't dilate, his hands didn't fidget, and I'd guess his heart rate didn't rise above sixty.

Still, I pushed. "She was pretty."

"That she was."

"You're a young, handsome professor. Did she maybe have a thing for you?"

"If she did, I wasn't aware."

Nothing about the guy was raising my hackles, but I wanted to ask him one more question before I left. "Where do you get your tattoos done?"

"I don't have any tattoos."

I believed him.

Strike three.

15

I'm surrounded by all types of bread: sourdough, rye, pumper-
nickel, ciabatta, brioche, focaccia. Loaves and loaves.

"We're going to need more flour," someone says.

I turn around, expecting to see Lacy. But it's not her. It's
a young man. He's short, with blond hair, and he's wearing
an apron. Though the movie doesn't come out until March, I
saw the preview six months earlier when I went to see *Captain
America*.

"Peeta?" I ask. "What are you doing here?"

"Making bread," he says with a straight face. "It's what we
do every day."

"We?" I look down at my hands. They are covered in flour.

"Well, the three of us." He nods over my shoulder.

I turn.

Standing behind me, juggling three crescent rolls, is an enormous woman with a terrible haircut. I haven't seen the woman
in eighteen years, not since I graduated middle school.

"Principal Daly?"

She stops juggling, and the rolls fall to the floor. "You need to
start making bread, Thomas. Don't make me call your mother."

"Yes, ma'am," I mutter, then I turn to Peeta and ask, "Where's the flour?"

"It's out in the shed."

I exit the bakery and find myself at the bottom of a large hill. A bunch of merchants are hawking their wares. Thirty yards away from me is a shed. I walk there and pull open its door. The shed is filled with flour but not bags. Just a giant pile of flour. There is a bucket on the floor, and I take the bucket and fill it. That's when I hear the screaming.

I duck out of the shed.

Several people run past me, and I ask, "What's going on?"

One of them turns and points to the top of the hill.

I look up.

At the top of the hill is an enormous rolling pin. It's the length of a football field and as tall as a four-story building. It has large eyes that are narrowed in menace, and from its mouth it laughs maniacally.

"Run!" someone screams as they fly past. "Save yourself."

The Rolling Pin Monster begins to roll down the hill. It flattens huge trees in its path like pancakes.

I run back to the bakery. I have to save Peeta and Principal Daly.

"A gigantic rolling pin is coming!" I yell.

When the three of us run out the door, the rolling pin is halfway down the hill, leaving carnage in its path.

"What are we going to do?" Mrs. Daly cries.

"I have an idea." I point at the sudden appearance of a hot-air balloon.

The three of us run to the balloon and climb into the basket. I release the ropes and the balloon rises five feet, then ten, then stops.

"We're too heavy!" Peeta yells.

Both Peeta and I turn and look at Principal Daly.

"No," she says, shaking her head. "Please, no."

"It's the only way," Peeta says.

"Please, Thomas," Principal Daly begs. "I'll never call your mother again. Even if you keep stealing strawberry milk from the cafeteria."

I turn and see that the rolling pin is only a hundred feet away. It's reached the bottom of the hill and is rolling over the merchants' tents and the merchants themselves, destroying everything in its path.

"Sorry," I tell Principal Daly.

Peeta and I both grab her by one of her legs and tip her up over the basket. We push her and she falls to the ground with a loud splat.

The hot-air balloon rises twenty feet, then thirty, then forty, then a hundred feet.

We are safe.

Peeta and I glance down.

Mrs. Daly has made her way to her feet, and she is fleeing in panic from the fast-approaching rolling pin.

It reaches her and flattens her like a steamroller, then continues on.

Beep, beep, beep.

Beep, beep, beep.

Beep, beep, beep.

≈

I cracked open my eyes and reached for my phone on the nightstand. I silenced the alarm and looked at the time: 8:30 a.m.

It'd been fifteen hours since I'd gotten home from Penn campus—after spending another two hours there asking students if they knew of any professors with a dragon tattoo—taken a shower, and then crawled into bed.

I pushed myself up, walked to the bathroom, and was midstream when my dream came rushing back. I saw everything perfectly: Peeta, Principal Daly, the village, the merchants, the gigantic Rolling Pin Monster.

I went to the living room and found Moore's purple JanSport. I'd studied *The E.K. Dream Book* judiciously for an hour while Gleason had been driving us back to Philadelphia, and I vaguely remembered seeing the entry.

I flipped the book open, fanned pages until I reached the R's, and then moved my finger down the column: *Road, Roaring, Roasting, Robbers, Rocking Chair, Rods, Roller* . . . then finally . . . *Rolling Pin.*

618.

≈

"Are you nervous?" I asked Lacy.

We were near the diving pool at the back of the Daskalakis Center. Lacy was clad in her yellow and blue Drexel warm-ups. She put one of her arms behind her head and stretched out her triceps. "Not yet," she said. "I will be when it gets closer to my race."

The first swim meet of the season, against the La Salle Explorers, kicked off in fifteen minutes, but Lacy's 100 Fly wasn't slated until 1:40 p.m.

Lacy looked at me and asked, "Why? Are *you* nervous?"

"If by 'nervous' you mean my stomach feels like I just ate a carton of Panda Express that was sitting in the sun for a week."

She rolled her eyes.

In all seriousness, few things made me more anxious than

watching Lacy swim. I was competitive to a fault—when I was eight, I stabbed a kid in the arm after losing a game of Pick-Up Sticks—but when it came to Lacy, I went full John McEnroe.

"Please try not to get kicked out of this meet," she said with a tilt of her head. "I don't want to have to explain away another incident to the coach."

"I'm telling you, that girl was on steroids. She had a goatee!"

Lacy was about to roll her eyes once more, when her gaze darted over my shoulder. She gave a quick wave. "Come on," she said, giving my arm a light tug. "I want you to meet my art professor."

We made our way to the bleachers and Lacy introduced me to Jennifer Peppers. Lacy had spoken of her previously, saying how funny and smart the art history professor was, but she'd neglected to mention that she was a bona fide knockout. She was in her midthirties, with dirty blond hair, hazel eyes, and a small beauty mark a half inch to the right of quite possibly the cutest nose ever constructed.

She had a stack of papers on her lap and a red pen in her hand. "You must be Thomas," she said, grinning. "Lacy was telling me about you just yesterday."

I looked at Lacy. "Oh, were you now?"

Lacy nodded. "We were talking about impressionism, and I told them about the time you were in elementary school and your class took a field trip to the art museum."

"You didn't!"

When I was in third grade, we went to the art museum. I got bored with the tour and went off on my own. Long story short, an hour later a guard found me running around naked in the impressionist wing.

Jennifer grinned and asked, "Why did you take your clothes off?"

"I'm not sure. But even to this day, if I see a Monet or a Van Gogh, I get the urge to drop my trousers."

She laughed, her face creasing and somehow making her another incredible click more attractive.

I asked, "How did Lacy trick you into coming to watch her swim?"

"Don't tell this to anyone." She cuffed her hand around her mouth. "But your sister is my favorite student."

Lacy winked at me.

A horn sounded and Lacy said, "I gotta go."

"Crush 'em," I told her. "No mercy."

We watched Lacy skip down the bleachers.

"Well, I'll leave you to it," I said, nodding at the paper on Jennifer's lap. "Nice to meet you."

"You're more than welcome to join me," she said, scooting over a few inches. "These can wait until tomorrow."

"I would love to, but I get a little carried away when Lacy swims. I wouldn't want you to get the wrong first—or I suppose, after Lacy's story, *second*—impression of me."

She smiled.

Roughly two hundred people were in attendance—which is a good turnout for a collegiate swim meet—and I found a spot at the opposite end of the bleachers.

I spent the next thirty minutes halfheartedly cheering on the other Drexel swimmers and keeping an eye on Lacy in the warm-up pool.

Finally, at 1:46 p.m. they announced her race.

Lacy walked to lane four and took the block. She swung her arms back and forth, slapping them against her body.

The announcer introduced each swimmer. When he said, "In lane four, Lacy Prescott," I stuck two fingers in my mouth and whistled.

A moment later, the horn blew.

Lacy was notoriously slow off the blocks, and she was the second to last one in the water.

"Shit," I mumbled.

The race was four lengths of the twenty-five-yard pool. Lacy made up ground the first length, and she was the fourth of the six girls to hit the first wall. Her turns were her bread and butter, and when she reappeared, she was in third place.

The lead swimmer was ahead by a body length, but by half-way through the third length, Lacy had cut the lead in half.

My hands were balled into fists.

"Come on," I said, no longer whispering. "Get a good turn."

I held my breath as the lead swimmer and Lacy both disappeared underwater. When they emerged, Lacy trailed by only half a stroke.

"Yessss!" I screamed.

Without noticing, I'd stood up.

"You got her!"

People around me were staring.

I didn't care.

"Dig! Dig! Dig!"

Lacy and the lead swimmer both flew through the water, their arms up and crashing, up and crashing. It was going to be a photo finish.

"Finish strong!"

Both Lacy and the girl next to her reached out for the wall.

I looked up at the scoreboard. Lacy had lost by less than two-tenths of a second.

Of course, I wanted Lacy to win, but second place in her first race of the season was still great.

"Way to go, Lace!" I yelled, clapping wildly.

She pulled herself out of the pool, looked my direction,

and shrugged. I gazed over at Jennifer Peppers. She gave me a thumbs-up.

I swept my hand over my forehead and let out a long exhale. *Whew!*

She laughed.

I looked back at the scoreboard, committing Lacy's swim time to memory. At the top of the scoreboard it read, "Drexel Dragons."

That's when it first hit me.

It was a tattoo of a dragon.

Brooke was dating a professor—just not one from her school.

16

Lacy's second race was the 200 Back. She finished fifth, though her time was one of her best. She was getting ready to swim in the 400 Medley Relay, but my attention was elsewhere. I couldn't stop thinking about *The Professor with the Dragon Tattoo*.

Could he be a professor at Drexel?

Lots of people got tattoos of the mascot from the school they attended. Was it farfetched that a professor might do the same?

I stood and made my way over to Jennifer Peppers. As I took the open seat next to her, she turned and smiled.

"Lacy swam great!" she said.

"Yeah, she's a stud."

We made small talk until Lacy's race was announced. Lacy swam her leg of the race great, but the last girl struggled, and they placed fifth.

When it was over, I asked Jennifer, "Can I ask you a weird question?"

"I love weird questions."

I laughed, and then I asked, "Do you know of any Drexel professors who have a tattoo of a dragon?"

She eyed me suspiciously, but she didn't press me on why I wanted to know. She did say, "Seven."

"Seven?"

"Yeah, I know seven professors with dragon tattoos. Let's see," she started ticking her fingers back, "there's Howard in the Philosophy Department. Big-ass dragon. Then there's Gwen in the Communications Department. Huge fricking dragon."

I laughed and said, "I can see why Lacy likes you so much." She had the same wavelength of silliness.

She grinned, and then her eyes sprang open. "You know what? All kidding aside, there actually is a guy with a dragon tattoo on his forearm."

"Really?" I couldn't tell if she was still messing with me. If she was, then *forearm* was one hell of a lucky guess.

"Yes, really." She tilted her head to the side. "I want to say his name is Hutchings. Something Hutchings. I remember him telling me how he went to Drexel for undergrad, grad school, and now he teaches here."

"Do you remember what he teaches?"

"Finan—no, economics."

"What's he look like?"

"Tall, fit, generally handsome."

"Age?"

"Midthirties."

I could see how a tall, handsome, young, economics professor might be alluring to Brooke Wexley.

"What's this about?" she asked, her curiosity getting the better of her.

"I'll tell you another time."

"Over lobster, please." She smiled with her mouth wide open.

With the Carmen debacle still fresh, I wasn't sure if I was

ready to get back in the saddle just yet. Still, I was intrigued. I laughed and said, "That could be arranged."

I thanked her, told her I looked forward to seeing her at Lacy's next swim meet, then got up and left.

The Drexel library was across the street from the athletic center. I hopped onto the faculty page of the Drexel University website, found an email for Matthew Hutchings, then sent him a message, detailing that I was a production assistant for NBC and we were interested in interviewing him for a segment on Occupy Philadelphia.

I twiddled my thumbs for ten minutes, then checked my inbox. He'd already replied with his cell phone number.

After a quick phone call, we set up a meeting.

≈

"How long have you worked for NBC?" Matthew Hutchings asked. He was six foot three, with brown hair and several days of stubble. He could have passed for the fourth Hemsworth brother.

We were at a Whole Foods a mile from Drexel. Half the tables were occupied with people eating or sipping beverages from the coffee and tea bar.

I wiped a raspberry Danish crumb from my lips. "Five years now," I lied. "I started at the morning show, and now I'm a segment producer for the nightly news."

"That's awesome." Hutchings bounced his tea bag several times in his cup of hot water. The cuffs of his shirt were rolled up, and several inches of the red, orange, and green dragon on his forearm were visible. "I've never been on TV."

"You were made for TV."

He laughed.

"What can you tell me about the protests?" I asked.

"What do you want to know?"

I didn't know many specifics about the whole Occupy Wall Street movement and asked, "For starters, what exactly are they protesting?"

"They're protesting four major things." He held up four fingers. "Income inequality, the growing disparity in wealth, the undue influence of corporations on government, and the absence of legal repercussions behind the recent global financial crisis."

"Do you think their causes are legitimate?"

"Have you heard of the Pareto principle?"

"Was she at Montview Elementary?"

"Not that kind of principal," he said, laughing. "The Pareto principle states that eighty percent of the results are produced by twenty percent of the causes. For example, eighty percent of traffic accidents are committed by twenty percent of the drivers. Or at a retail store, eighty percent of the sales are accounted for by twenty percent of its employees."

He gave me an inquisitive nod, and I said, "I'm with you so far."

"The Pareto principle is especially true in American economics. The richest twenty percent of Americans own eighty-four percent of the nation's total wealth. And after the financial crisis of 2008, that number went up from eighty-four percent to eighty-seven percent."

"So, when shit hit the fan, the rich got richer."

"Precisely."

"Like Nicholas Wexley, for example?"

"Uh," he stammered. "I guess so."

I took the last bite of my Danish, then wiped my mouth with a napkin. "I don't work for NBC."

He didn't respond.

"I'm a retired homicide detective. I'm helping out with the Brooke Wexley murder investigation."

I watched Hutchings closely. *Homicide detective* hit him with a left jab, *Brooke Wexley* followed up with a stiff right, and then *murder investigation* took a samurai sword off the wall and stuck it in his gut.

"Were you sleeping with Brooke Wexley?" I asked.

"Of course not!" he said, shaking his head. "I've never even met her."

"Do you know that traces of semen can stay in the vagina for five days?"

His hand shook around his cup of tea. Terror will do that to you.

"I'll bet my life that when they take a DNA swab from your cheek, it's going to match the semen found in Brooke Wexley."

He closed his eyes a half second, then opened them. "Yes, I was sleeping with her."

Boom.

"How long had this been going on?"

"Since the start of the semester."

"Where did you meet her?"

"I live on the opposite side of Penn, and sometimes I walk to class. The chain had fallen off her bike, and she was struggling with it. I stopped to help, and she asked me what class I was coming from. She thought I was a grad student. I told her I was an economics professor at Drexel."

"When was this?"

"It was the week of September nineteenth, maybe that Thursday."

"Did you know who she was?"

"I had no idea, I just thought she was super hot."

"Did you guys go for coffee or something, or did she just give you her phone number?"

"She wouldn't give me her number," he said, shaking his head. "She made me write down my number and give it to her."

Brooke probably couldn't go a full day without a guy asking for her number. Most guys she would rebuff, but at some point, she'd meet a guy who she'd want to go out with. By taking their number, she had the power, and she wouldn't be bombarded with messages. Or worse yet, dick pics.

"When did you guys connect?" I asked.

"She texted me the next day."

"And where did you go?"

"She didn't want to go anywhere around here, and neither did I, so that night we went to a spot in West Philly."

"Where?"

"A tapas bar. I don't remember the name, but I can find it out."

"Did she go home with you?"

"No."

"Did she tell you about her family?"

"Yeah, halfway through dinner."

"What did she tell you about being the daughter of the wealthiest man in Philadelphia?"

"It was this scarlet letter she had to wear. Brooke said that if we kept seeing each other, I would have to keep it a secret."

There was nothing illicit about a student dating a professor from a different school. Sure, the age gap might raise eyebrows, but there were countless twenty-year-old women sleeping with men far older than Matthew Hutchings.

"Why did it have to be a secret?"

"Brooke's dad." His face stiffened. "She said that if he found out she was sleeping with a professor at Drexel, he'd disown her."

That seemed overdramatic. Why would her dad care?

Hutchings could tell I wasn't buying this and said, "Seriously, that's why she wouldn't give me her phone number. Her dad reads her text messages. She got a burner phone, and that's the number she'd contact me with."

That explained why Hutchings hadn't been on Gallow's radar. Her text messages and phone calls to him were stored on a burner phone.

I stated the obvious: "So you agreed to keep it a secret. At what point did you sleep together?"

"Brooke came over to my place a couple of days later."

"Did you use protection?"

"She was on the pill."

"And how did things proceed after that?"

"She'd come over to my apartment a few times a week."

"Did you fall in love with her?"

He shook his head. "No, it was pretty casual. She was fun at the beginning. I mean, she was super attractive, but she was really serious—too serious for someone her age. She always wanted to discuss economics, the pay gap, the racial divide. Occupy Wall Street was consuming her. At the end of September, she asked me to go to the protests in New York with her."

"You didn't go?"

"I'm not looking to get tear-gassed and arrested. Plus, I'm an economics professor. Even if I support the protests, I can't be seen holding signs and chanting. That could cost me my job."

I hit Fast-Forward: "So, when was the last time you slept with her?"

"Three days before she was killed."

"You sure?"

"Positive. It was the fifteenth. She was in a real state when she came over. She didn't even want to talk. She just wanted to screw, then she left."

The time had come for the all-important question. "Where were you the night she was killed?"

"Asleep."

"Can anybody vouch for this?"

"No." He put his head in his hands, then looked up. "That's why I didn't come forward and tell the police. I know they always think it's the boyfriend. And with us keeping it a secret, it looks even sketchier. And I don't have an alibi. I guess I was just scared the cops would pin it on me."

"Bullshit."

He was scared, but not of being arrested for murder. He was a good-looking White man. The system was built for him.

I said, "You're scared, but not of the police."

He didn't need to respond.

"Her dad?"

He nodded. "From what Brooke told me, he sounds crazy. I didn't know what he'd do if it got out I was sleeping with his daughter. The rich and powerful are rich and powerful."

More than likely, Nicholas Wexley would make a few well-placed phone calls, and Professor Matthew Hutchings, whom I presume was several years from tenure, wouldn't find another job teaching in the Milky Way.

I said, "I'm guessing you deleted all the messages from Brooke on your phone."

"Yeah."

"I need the number of her burner phone."

Hutchings had it memorized, and he rattled it off. I typed it into my phone.

"Did you ever see Brooke's burner phone?" I asked.

"Yeah, it was a blue and gray Nokia."

"Do you know what network she bought it through?"

He didn't.

There wasn't much more I could do, and I said, "You need to go to the Ninth District station. Do you know where that is?"

"Yeah. I'll take a taxi there now."

"Just tell them the truth, and you should be fine."

I exited Whole Foods, then called Gallow. I gave him a quick recap of what I'd learned, relayed the burner phone number, and told him to expect Matthew Hutchings in the next half an hour.

Twenty seconds after ending the call, my phone buzzed.

It was Gleason.

"The SS *United States*," he said.

"What about it?"

"They found numbers."

17

I poured myself a cup of coffee from the carafe on the table, added two creamers and two packets of sugar, then joined Wade Gleason at the back of the task force headquarters. There were a few open seats but, like me, Gleason preferred to stand.

I sipped the coffee and cringed.

"What's wrong?" Gleason asked.

"This stuff is garbage."

Gleason took a sip of his own cup. "Tastes fine to me." He licked his lips. "You know, some of us working folk can't afford your four-dollar-a-day latte lifestyle."

"Eight dollars a day," I corrected. "Sometimes I get two."

"My apologies, Your Caffeinated Highness."

I chuckled. "King Thomas the Magnificent."

Gleason and I made small talk for the next few minutes about how we would rule our respective kingdoms. Gleason would be a man of the people, whereas I would rule with an iron fist.

The meeting kicked off, and Agent Joyce made his way to the front of the room. Written in big bold letters on the dry-erase board next to him was "The Numbers Killer."

"Here's what we know so far," Agent Joyce said, pulling up

an image of the victim at the bottom of the pool. "Marty Inaba was a part-time employee with the SS *United States* Conservancy. He gave private tours a couple times a week. According to his email, he'd been meeting with a Roger Horton for a private tour yesterday at nine a.m. The two had been communicating for the better part of—"

Joyce was interrupted by some asshole's cell phone going off. Or to be more accurate, he was interrupted by the sound of *my* cell phone.

As I frantically dug into my pocket, two things struck me as odd. Like any decent member of society, before going to a restaurant, a movie, a funeral, or say, an important FBI task force meeting, I'd set my phone to vibrate. And two, my phone was not playing "La Cucaracha" like usual.

From my pants pocket, it blared:

> *And I'm like*
> *Baby, baby, baby oooh*
> *Like baby, baby, baby nooo*

I pulled out my phone and wasn't surprised to see the caller ID: *Carmen*. She'd hacked into my phone and switched my ringer to a song by a teen heartthrob who Lacy had a poster of on her wall: Justin Bieber.

The eyes of every task member glared at me as the song boomed from the tiny phone speaker. These were not fans of the Beebs.

> *Like baby, baby, baby oooh*
> *I thought you'd always be mine*

I flipped the phone open and closed.

"Sorry about that. I'm not sure how that happened." I toggled the phone to Silent and slipped it back into my pocket.

All eyes swiveled back to Joyce. He continued: "Like I said, the two had been comm—"

> *And I'm like*
> *Baby, baby, baby oooh*
> *Like baby, baby, baby nooo*

All eyes swung back my way.

I ripped my cell phone back out of my pocket and powered it off.

"I am so sorry," I said.

Wade Gleason moved several feet away from me, so as not to be associated with the selfish prick who refused to turn off his phone.

Joyce asked, "Do I need to take your phone away from you, Mr. Prescott?"

I shook my head. "Turned it off. We are good to go."

After a beat, he said, "They had been com—"

> *And I'm like*
> *Baby, baby, baby oooh*
> *Like baby, baby, baby nooo*

"What the hell, Prescott?" Joyce shouted. "Turn your phone off!"

I tried to slip my phone out of my pocket, but I was so flustered I couldn't get my hand out. The song played and played and played.

> *Oh, for you I would have done whatever*
> *And I just can't believe we ain't together*
> *And I wanna play it cool, but I'm losin' you*

I got the phone out and flipped it open. I snapped it in half, threw it on the ground. I stomped on it with my foot until it was in fifteen pieces.

Part of me wanted to explain that I'd dumped a malicious hacker, and she was methodically trying to ruin my life or, at the very least, turn my devices against me, but I didn't want to waste any more time. Since the room was filled with law enforcement officers, maybe by this point everyone had realized something more was going on than just a dolt who didn't know how to work his phone.

I tossed the pieces of the broken phone into the trash and said, "Sorry, sir. You were saying something about this Inaba and a Roger Horton?"

"Do you need to step outside for a second?" he asked, looking concerned about my mini meltdown.

"Nope. All good."

Agent Joyce let out a long huff and then said, "Like I was saying, our victim was communicating with this so-called Roger Horton for over a month. Horton's email and phone number both came up dead ends. Also, our killer stayed off the surveillance cameras that cover the pier. Our working theory is that he could have swum to the pier. Maybe packed a bag of dry clothes."

He clicked a fresh slide, the screen filling with rusted metal.

"This is the underside of one of the blades on the large propeller at the back of the ship. As you can see, our killer carved two numbers into the blade before he jumped into the water."

The numbers were 415 and 623.

Joyce nodded in my direction and said, "Thanks to Bieber Fever over there, we know our killer is using *The E.K. Dream Book* as his playbook."

A few people clapped.

I took a soft bow.

When I straightened, I noticed Kip out of the corner of my eye. I winked at him.

Agent Joyce continued, "Both of these numbers only have one corresponding entry."

He grabbed a black marker and on the dry-erase board, he wrote both numbers. Next to 415, he wrote *New Orleans*. Next to 623, he wrote *Church*.

"If our killer continues his trend, we theorize these numbers point to a murder that occurred decades earlier. The FBI field office in New Orleans has been notified, and they have temporarily closed over five hundred religious institutions. With the help of the local PDs, they're hoping to get a cadaver dog into every church in the next two days."

That was a whole lot of sniffing.

Joyce gave an update on the two victims from Boston. Autopsy reports revealed that both men crammed into old Edith's grave had been stabbed multiple times. There was no evidence of any numbers carved into their forehead tissue or anywhere else on their bodies. Based on the attire of the men and forensic dating, the medical examiner's best guess was that the men had been killed between 1973 and 1978. Boston authorities were going through missing-persons files from those years, but they'd yet to make any identification.

When the meeting wrapped up, Joyce called out assignments. He didn't give Gleason or me a specific task.

I was confused until Gleason grabbed my shoulder. "You're with me."

"Where are we going?"

"We're off to see the Queen."

18

It was starting to get dark when Gleason pulled his blue sedan out of the William J. Green Federal Building's parking garage.

I asked, "And who is this Queen?"

"Loretta Carroll," Gleason said, giving the steering wheel a couple light taps. "She was the biggest Numbers banker in North Philly for more than thirty years."

Ms. Ruby had mentioned that there were Numbers kings and *queens*, but for some reason I'd visualized all the big bankers as men. Obviously, I should have stayed for the entirety of Brooke's Intro to Feminism course.

"My aunt Deanna used to bet with her," Gleason said. "She would tell me all the stories." Gleason spent the rest of the drive recounting everything he knew about Queen Loretta.

Loretta Carroll had been born in the Bronx in the late 1920s. Her mother gave her up for adoption, and she spent most of her childhood in an orphanage. At fourteen, she ran away and began living on the streets. A little over a year later, she fell in love with a small-time crook. But when he attempted to pimp her out, she stabbed him in the eye with a fork. Loretta departed New York City on a bus headed for the City of Brotherly Love.

She fell in with a tough crowd in North Philly and began selling drugs and running numbers with her new boyfriend, Reggie. After four years, Loretta had saved $15,000 and told Reggie that she wanted to leave him. Reggie tried to strangle her, but she squirmed from his grip and gave him a shove. He fell, hit his head on a table, and died. Authorities called it self-defense.

In 1947, at the age of nineteen, Loretta began taking numbers herself. She succeeded in this male-dominated and cutthroat clandestine lottery by hiring ruthless enforcers, bribing cops, and taking risky bets that others refused. Her empire grew. By the mid-1950s, she was the biggest Numbers banker in North Philly. That was when she acquired the regal moniker "Queen Loretta."

She sat on her throne until 1981, when she was raided by the FBI and indicted on racketeering charges. After serving three years in a women's prison, Loretta returned to her North Philly home to live out the rest of her life in relative obscurity.

"Wow," I said when he finished. "That's a gangster story if I've ever heard one."

"Yeah, the Queen is something alright."

I went quiet for a moment, and Gleason asked, "What are you thinking about?"

"Just imagining all the people who I want to stab in the eye with a fork."

He laughed.

"Seriously, that has to be so satisfying," I said.

"Who would you stab first?"

"This guy named Doug."

"What'd he do to you?"

"He keeps messing up my order at Starbucks."

Gleason shook his head, and a moment later, steered the car left onto a side street. He slowed and parked in front of a narrow row house. On the front stoop, an old Black man held up a large green watering can, tending to several hanging flowerpots that looked ready for hospice care.

"That's Jumpy," Gleason said. "Back in the day, he was the Queen's enforcer."

Jumpy glanced up as Gleason and I exited the car.

"Hi there," Gleason said with a curt nod. "Is Queen Loretta in?"

Jumpy set the watering can on the stoop and squinted at the FBI agent.

"Tell her Deanna Parker's nephew wants to see her," Gleason added.

Jumpy stared ahead vacantly, then turned and entered the house. Thirty seconds later, he reappeared. "Come on up."

Gleason and I followed Jumpy through the front foyer into a small, elegantly decorated sitting room with two red sofas, a rocking chair, a coffee table, and a grandfather clock.

Loretta Carroll looked every one of her eighty-three years. Her skin was heavily wrinkled, her gray hair thin at the temples, and she looked tired, like a dried sponge found under the sink.

Sitting next to her on a tan leather sofa was an equally ancient-looking man, his skin a deep umber. He had bifocal glasses perched on his nose, and his left foot crossed over his right knee. He was introduced as Palmer.

"I can see a bit of your auntie in your face," Queen Loretta said to Gleason, her mouth spread in a wide, creaky smile. "I was so sorry to hear of her passing."

"Thank you," Gleason said, crossing the room to clasp her hand. "She was a wonderful woman."

"That she was. She loved to box them numbers. Every time I'd ask, she'd say, 'Why you even ask me that, Queenie, when you darned well know the answer?'"

Gleason chuckled.

We did a quick round of introductions. Jumpy sneered when Gleason mentioned we were part of an FBI task force, but neither the Queen—nor Palmer, who I assumed was her significant other—flinched.

Gleason said. "We're working on a homicide case that might be linked to the Numbers, and we're hoping you could answer a few questions for us about the way it works."

The Queen narrowed her gaze, her light-brown eyes scanning Gleason's face.

"You want me to show them the door?" Jumpy asked.

"No, no," the Queen said. "It's okay. Please, take a seat." She motioned to a love seat across from her.

After we sat—Gleason's right thigh nestled up against mine on the narrow couch—I said, "You'll have to forgive me. I'm new to this whole Numbers thing."

"You just ask your questions, honey," the Queen said.

"Okay, first off, when you were talking about Gleason's aunt, you said that she liked to 'box them numbers.' What does that mean?"

"A straight bet would be 1-2-3," the Queen explained. "*Boxing* means every combination of 1-2-3, so 1-3-2, 2-3-1, 3-2-1, and so on. Ends up being six different bets, so it pays out at 100 to 1 instead of 600 to 1."

"Gotcha." I put my hands on my knees, then asked, "How many bets would you get in any given day?"

"Well, let's see." She straightened her spine proudly. "By the mid-1950s, the operation was getting pretty big. I had over twenty runners on the payroll—plus Jumpy and a few of his friends. At one point, I was getting three thousand slips a day."

"How much money is that?"

"Anywhere between ten and twenty thousand dollars."

"And you had enough to cover the winnings?"

"I'd been cleaned out a few times when I was just getting going, but by the fifties, I'd accumulated a pretty healthy bank. And if betting one day was heavily favoring one number in particular, I'd cover that number with a competitor so I wouldn't get wiped out if that number hit."

I'd never considered this. It was a way to hedge your bets. I hadn't done much gambling in my life, but I'd heard that some of the sports books in Vegas would do this. If an especially lopsided bet came in, they would take the same bet with another casino to minimize the risk.

"What did you do with all the betting slips?" I asked. "Weren't you worried about getting busted?"

"There's always that risk, but I was paying a pretty penny in bribes to keep clear of any raids."

"Who were you paying off?"

"Police officers, judges, councilmen, councilwomen. Payoffs were my biggest expense. And my runners *still* got busted all the time."

"What would happen?"

"Usually, the runner could pay their way out of it. Give a cop a few hundred dollars, and he's likely to let you go. Every once in a while, a cop wouldn't budge, and they'd get arrested. Still, it was just a small fine. Rarely any jail time."

"What happened to those bets that had been placed with them?"

"Null and void. It's part of the risk when you're illegal."

I wondered how many times bettors had played the winning number only to be told their number runner had been picked up by the police. Seemed like an easy way to avoid paying out a sizable sum.

"What happened when they legalized the lottery in Pennsylvania?" I asked.

"That was 1972," the Queen said, shaking her head side to side. "Crazy year." She briefly made eye contact with Palmer and Jumpy. "That damn lottery cut my business by half."

"That much?" asked Gleason.

"At least. The first drawing was at the beginning of March, and within six months there were four one-million-dollar winners. A lot of folks eventually came back to the street Numbers, but by mid-1973 all of us were just trying to sur—" Her cell phone chirped on the table next to her.

The Queen picked it up, along with a notepad underneath it. "Hiya, Miss Jess," she answered. "3-2-6 straight for two dollars . . . 1-9-1 straight for three dollars . . . 8-1-6 boxed for a dollar . . . Okay, you tell those kiddos I got extra big Snickers for Halloween this year . . . Okay, bye now." She set the phone and pad down.

"Wait," I said, leaning backward a few inches, my mouth wide open. "You still take bets?"

"Sure do."

Gleason fidgeted in his seat next to me. Before I could inquire further, he said, "You were talking about what happened in 1973."

The Queen picked up where she left off: "With the state lottery coming out, outfits were looking to expand. The Capettas—who split South Philly with the Benussi family—started sending runners up this way. Started stealing business."

"What did you do about it?" I asked.

"We paid a visit to one of their lieutenants—Ugly Marky." For the briefest of moments her eyes flickered to Jumpy, who was leaning against the wall.

I wondered if "paid a visit" equated to thumping Ugly

Marky with a baseball bat or if it meant something more maca-
bre, a.k.a. a trip to the morgue.

"Did the Capettas get the message?"

"They did, and they retaliated."

"What'd they do?"

"They snatched three of my runners."

"Were they ever found?"

"Nope. I assume they were dumped somewhere in the Atlantic."

"And what did you do?"

"Nothing," Jumpy chimed in bitterly. "Not a damn thing."

I turned and saw the old enforcer had both of his fists
clenched, and he was staring at the Queen.

"We've been over this," the Queen said sternly. "If we'd gone
back at the Capettas, we'd all be dead. We played our hand,
they played theirs."

As big and powerful as her operation was, there was no
competing with the Italian Mafia.

"Plus," the Queen said, turning back to us, "the Capettas
and the Benussis started fighting over South Philly soon after,
and they stopped trying to get a foothold up north."

"How did you get busted?" I asked.

She blew out a breath. "One of my competitors got arrested
for federal tax evasion. In exchange for a lighter sentence, he
handed me over to the Feds on a silver platter. They put in a
wiretap, listened in to all my business—and I mean *all* my business!—for months. Then here they come, crashing through the
front door early one morning. Grabbed more than a million
dollars I had in the attic."

From her sly grin, I had no doubt they'd found only a sliver
of her fortune.

I moved from the past to the present, asking, "Do the
numbers 5-0-3, 9-1-4, 3-8-6 mean anything to you?"

"Not any more than any other numbers," she said.

It was a long shot. Still, we had to ask. I recited the rest of the numbers that the killer had left thus far.

None of them had any significance to the Queen.

"Where are you finding these numbers?" she asked.

Gleason and I looked at each other. Finally, he said, "They've come up in a murder investigation."

She wiggled her chin but said nothing.

There was a moment of silence.

I broke it: "Is there a certain dream book that you prefer?"

"Oh, I've used them all at one time or another. When I make bets for myself, I use *Sally's Number Book*."

I was surprised to hear that she bet herself and asked, "How often do you bet?"

"Every day. Heck, I still do."

"Who do you bet with?"

"That I'm not telling," she said with a calculated smile.

Gleason's and my laughter was interrupted by the loud chiming of the grandfather clock. After its sixth chime, Palmer leaned over and whispered something to the Queen. I read his lips: "News is coming on."

Gleason nudged me with his elbow.

I knew not to get between old people and their news, but I couldn't help myself. I asked, "Can I make a bet?"

Gleason's face blanched. You would have thought I'd just asked the Queen if I could take a quick bubble bath in her tub.

To both Gleason's and my surprise, the Queen grinned and grabbed her notepad. "Let's have it."

I thought back on my dream: *Rolling Pin*. "Can I get 6-1-8 straight for five bucks?"

She scribbled on her pad, then glanced at Gleason.

"Why not?" he said, with a shrug of his broad shoulders.

"Give me 5-7-3 boxed for five dollars and let's do a single—three for twenty dollars."

"What do you mean a single?" I asked.

"A single, one through ten," the Queen said.

Gleason explained that you could bet on the full three-digit number, or you could bet the two-digit number (called a "bolito") or the one-digit "single." If the winning number was 362, then 62 was the winning bolito (which paid out sixty to one) and 2 was the winning single (which paid out six to one).

"Okay, I want a single," I said. "Eight for twenty dollars."

The Queen scribbled it in her book.

"One last thing," Gleason said. "We don't know what this killer is up to. He's proven extremely unpredictable. I'll sleep a lot better if we could station an officer out front of your house for the next few days. Just until we can get a better handle on this thing."

The Queen looked at Jumpy. Her enforcer. He was thirty years removed from his prime.

I was surprised when he was the one to say, "Do it."

≈

"Mamma mia!" I said, pulling the bag of popcorn from the microwave and tossing it on the counter.

I ran my scalded fingers under the faucet for a few seconds, then grabbed my favorite red popcorn bowl and filled it up. After settling in on the couch, I flipped on the TV.

Gleason told me that Queen Loretta used the number from the Daily Pick 3 lottery drawing at 7:00 p.m., broadcast live on Channel 8.

I watched the last fifteen minutes of *Wheel of Fortune* and polished off half the bowl of popcorn. Once the news started, they cut to a man behind a machine of tumbling lottery balls.

"Our first number for the Daily Pick 3 . . ." the man shouted as a ball was sucked up, *". . . is EIGHT!"*

I pumped my fist—I'd hit the single!

"Hello, one hundred and twenty dollars!" I shouted.

The second ball was sucked up into the machine. *"Our second number is . . . ONE!"*

I lifted a few inches in my seat, sending a barrage of popcorn spilling from the bowl on my lap. I was one number away from hitting 6-1-8.

"Come on six!" I yelled. "Come on six!"

The last ball was sucked up.

It was a five.

I hadn't even realized I was holding my breath and exhaled. I'd been only one digit away from winning $3,000.

But it wasn't about the money. Now I understood the thrill. I could fully grasp why people bet day in and day out.

My new flip phone—which I'd picked up from a gas station on the way back from Queen Loretta's—chirped on the table.

It was a text from Gleason: "SO CLOSE."

19

I shut the passenger door of Wade Gleason's sedan and asked, "When's the last time you were here?"

"It's been ages," Gleason said.

We were at Capitolo Playground in South Philly: four acres with a large playground, a baseball diamond, and two basketball courts.

My gravedigging blisters had mostly healed, but my hands were still covered in sports tape. I dribbled the basketball I'd brought as Gleason and I started toward the caged courts. He put his hands up, and I passed him the ball. "How long has it been since you shot a basketball?" I asked.

"Good question." He gripped the ball in one of his enormous hands. "Got to be a few years."

"Well, at least you look good."

Gleason wore a throwback Philadelphia 76ers jersey (Charles Barkley), black shorts, and a pair of white Reebok pumps, circa 1989. "I can't believe my dad had a pair of these lying around." He leaned down and gave each shoe a couple of pumps.

We pushed through the caged door and into the courts. A local game was underway on the far court—predominantly young men—then twenty cops shot and warmed up on the near court.

Mike Gallow stood near the three-point line and nodded hello. He wore baggy red shorts, a sleeveless black T-shirt, and white high-tops. His pale bald head glistened in the afternoon sun.

"That's Gallow," I told Gleason.

Gallow clapped his hands twice, the international language for "Pass me the ball."

Gleason passed him the ball. Gallow took two dribbles, then chucked the ball at the hoop. The ball clanked off the top of the backboard.

"He's terrible," I whispered to Gleason, "but he plays hard."

Gleason laughed.

At the opposite hoop was a guy wearing goggles, a headband, two knee braces, and a white sleeve on his left arm. I nudged Gleason and asked, "Do you recognize that bozo?"

Gleason squinted. "Is that Hufflepuff?"

That Gleason was now referring to Kip as Hufflepuff made my heart swell. It's the little things.

"That's him."

"That's white bread if I've ever seen it."

"Yeah, he tries too hard. Sometimes, we play against the local kids, and they call him 'the Accountant' because he calls out the score fifty times a game."

He laughed. "And what do they call you?"

"Cooper."

"As in Bradley or Anderson?"

"They never specified."

Gallow heaved up an air ball, and Gleason asked, "Do the kids have a name for him?"

"Shrek."

"I can see it!" he said, barking a laugh.

"Hey, Prescott!" someone called from behind us.

I turned.

Captain Jim Folch was in his midfifties. He had a full head of gray-streaked brown hair, a neatly groomed gray mustache, and stood an inch shorter than my six feet. He was a seasoned triathlete, and his calves and arms were sinewy and vascular.

With Occupy Philly and the Wexley investigation both taking place in his district, I hadn't been sure if he would be able to join us today. It would be bad optics. If the press spotted him here, he'd have some explaining to do.

"I'm surprised you showed," I said.

"I can only stay for one game, then I have to get to a meeting with Stalnaker about how to handle these protests."

Bertram F. Stalnaker had been the mayor of Philadelphia since 2007. He was up for reelection in a few weeks, and the polls had him leading by a slight margin.

I introduced Wade Gleason.

After shaking hands, Gleason said, "I remember watching you play here when I was just a kid."

"Ah, my glory days," Folch said, chuckling.

A man in his midfifties opened the gated door and entered the court. "Over here!" Folch called, waving him over.

We made brief introductions.

Allen Collier was African American, with black-framed glasses. He was clad in a blue sweatsuit, and white ankle braces were visible poking out the top of his Nike high-tops.

The four of us joined Gallow, plus a handful of other cops, at the far hoop and started shooting around. After running down an errant rebound, then missing a jumper, I found myself next to Collier. On closer examination, he had sallow cheeks and dark rings under his eyes. He looked like he needed to sleep for a month straight. And maybe take some vitamins.

He nodded at the blue Drexel hat I was wearing backward and asked, "Are you a Drexel alum?"

"I'm not. My sister goes there now. She's on the swim team."

"Nice," Collier said. "I teach criminology there."

"What course?"

"Actually, I teach three courses: Freshman Seminar, Introduction to Criminal Justice, and Advanced Criminological Theorizing." Collier cocked his thumb at Folch, who was fifteen feet away and had just drained four straight baseline jumpers. "In the middle of November, Jim will be guest lecturing."

"Which class?"

"The intro-level course."

"I might have to drop in on that."

"You're more than welcome," he said, then asked, "Are you a detective?"

"I used to be." I gave him a recap of my short but illustrious career.

After we both took a shot and both missed, Collier asked, "Have you ever thought about teaching?"

I hadn't thought further ahead than the bristle strength of my next toothbrush. "I haven't."

"Might be something to look into."

Teaching? I'd never even considered it.

"Would you be interested in guest lecturing at some point?" Collier asked. "It would be a good way to see if it's up your alley."

"I'll think about it." And I would.

Folch finally missed a shot, then walked over and patted Collier on the back. "If you gentlemen will excuse us, we have to go do some stretching. It takes a while to get these old bodies ready for action these days."

Everybody laughed, and Collier and Folch meandered off. When they were out of earshot, I said to Gleason, "Don't

let Folch fool you. That old body of his just did the Ironman—
the real one that they do in Hawaii each year—two weeks ago.
He placed ninth in his age group. And in the triathlon that he
talked me into doing after I first met him, he won his age group."

"Damn," Gleason said, impressed. "How did you do?"

"Pretty good."

"You make the top fifty?"

"Oh, no, I didn't finish the race," I said, waving him off.
"But I did get the number of the cute paramedic who resusci-
tated me."

He thought I was kidding.

I wasn't. Her name was Monica.

At noon, we divided into four teams. My team was Gallow,
Gleason, plus two cops from the Twentieth District: Zlader and
Mullins, who was one of two women who came. We shot to see
who'd play first, and our representative, Zlader, missed his free
throw, which meant we had to wait our turn.

The first game was Hufflepuff, Folch, and Collier's team
versus a group from the Seventeenth District. The rules were
simple: play to 11; win by 2, or first team to 15. Games usually
took twenty minutes, and while we waited, Gleason, Gallow,
and I leaned back against the perimeter fencing.

Gleason asked Gallow, "Did you get your hands on the
transcripts for that burner phone yet?"

"Not yet," Gallow replied. "The provider wouldn't hand
them over, so we had to get a warrant. Hopefully, we'll get them
by the end of the day."

"Did Matthew Hutchings come by yesterday?" I asked.

"He did. I grilled him for about thirty minutes. Seems like
an okay dude. He offered to take a poly. Passed with flying
colors. I'd be surprised if he had anything to do with Brooke's
death."

"Still, he doesn't have a rock-solid alibi, so you can't rule him out completely."

"True."

On the court, Folch pulled up from behind the arc and drained a twenty-three-footer. On the next possession, a player on the opposing team whizzed by Collier and went in for an easy layup. Collier wasn't in as good shape as Folch, and he wheezed as he ran back up the court.

"Nicholas Wexley is holding a press conference tomorrow afternoon," Gallow said. "Two thirty, in front of their Spring Garden condo."

"I'm surprised it took this long," I said. "Any idea what he has planned?"

"None whatsoever."

On the court, Collier knocked down a shot from the baseline. He might not be in game shape, but he had a beautiful stroke.

Gallow asked, "So, what's going on with your guys' case?"

Gleason recounted the latest developments.

"*New Orleans* and *Church*?" Gallow said, his eyebrows knitted together.

Gleason nodded. "The New Orleans FBI is searching all the churches down there with cadaver dogs."

"A city the size of New Orleans? That's got to be at least a hundred churches to search. Maybe double that."

"Make that five hundred."

"*Geez.*"

On the court, Folch knocked down another bucket.

≈

I checked the ball to Hufflepuff, who'd insisted on guarding me. He was covered in a gallon of sweat, his goggles were half-fogged, and the sleeve on his arm was soaked through. He looked like he'd just been through a car wash.

"Game point," he said, flaunting a big goofy smile.

"Are you sure?" I asked, raising my eyebrows. "I thought it was tied."

"No, it's game point."

I glanced over at Gallow. "It's tied, right?"

He nodded. "Yeah, it's eight all."

"No," Kip said, "It's game point."

I shook my head. "Gleason, what score do you have?"

He put his finger to his chin. "Tied, eight-eight."

"*Nooooooo*," Kip said, rocking his head. "It's game point. Ten to five. I've been calling out the score every time."

"Cortez," I said. "What score do you got?"

Cortez was a Hispanic cop from the Seventh District. He and another cop had taken over Folch and Collier's spots after they'd left after the first game. Cortez smiled and said, "I thought you guys were up by one."

I fought back a smile. Even Kip's own teammates had turned on him.

Kip looked like he was on the cusp of a seizure, and I said, "We're just messing with you. Everyone knows it's ten-five."

Kip let out a thankful sigh.

He was getting ready to check the ball, when I asked, "You want to make a bet?"

He pulled the ball to his hip and straightened.

I said, "If we win, you have to play next Sunday in a onesie."

"And what if we win?"

"I'll wear one."

Gallow shook his head at me. I didn't blame him. Our chances of coming back and winning were negligible, especially with how Cortez was shooting.

"Deal," Kip said. Then to everyone's absolute dismay, he repeated, "Game point."

He checked the ball. I passed it to Gallow. I faked flaring to the left, then cut back to the top of the key. Gallow tossed the ball back to me, and I shot a long two. It sailed through the net.

"Ten-seven," Kip said.

Gleason and I made eye contact, and we trapped the player bringing up the ball. He tried to dribble around us, but the ball went off his leg.

A few seconds later, Sarah Mullins missed a shot, but Gallow got the rebound. He shot the ball to Gleason, who knocked down a short jumper.

"Ten-eight," Kip said.

They got the ball to Cortez, but I stuck to him like glue. He faked a shot, then went right. I stripped him clean and trotted to the opposite hoop for an uncontested layup.

I brought the ball back up and handed it to Kip.

"Ten-nine," he called out, a tad more reluctantly than previously.

Kip and his team worked the ball around. Zlader lost Kip, and he was wide open near the basket. Cortez threw Kip the ball. Kip's eyes grew wide as he caught the ball and then released what he thought was the game-winning shot. It hit the front of the rim, and Mullins pulled down the rebound. Mullins passed the ball to Gallow, who tossed the ball to me. I was posting up Kip on the baseline. Kip's breath was hot on my neck. I faked right, then turned left and drilled a turn-around fadeaway.

"Ten-ten," Kip said, his voice cracking.

I stuck to Cortez. He ran me into a pick, but I fought through it. Kip passed him the ball, but it was a lazy pass, and

I went for the steal. I was a half second late and only able to get one finger on the ball. The ball changed trajectory, but not enough, and Cortez caught it. He was wide open. He released the ball and it sailed through the hoop.

We lost.

≈

After playing and losing another two games, we headed for lunch. Pat's King of Steaks and Geno's Steaks were both across the street from the park, and Gallow and Gleason each lobbied for their favorite. Since I liked both equally, it was up to me to decide. I picked Geno's because the line looked shorter, to which Gleason remarked, "It's shorter for a reason."

Gleason and I sat at one of the outdoor tables. Gallow took our orders and went to stand in line.

"Do they even make adult onesies?" Gleason asked.

"They sure do."

"What sort of onesie would you have brought him?"

"I have it at home. It's a kangaroo."

"You already ordered it?"

"Yeah, I've been waiting to make this bet with him for weeks now."

He laughed. "If you don't mind my asking, What do you have against him?"

I leaned back in my chair. "It was my third time out here playing. I'd stopped on the way to the court and picked up a blue Powerade and I kept it next to my jacket. Between games, I saw Hufflepuff go up and take a big swig."

"Of your Powerade?"

"Yep."

"Did you say anything to him?"

"Nope."

"Instead you decided to wage a years-long campaign of tyranny and subjugation."

"More or less."

I was extremely gifted when it came to holding grudges. I still had one against Ben Honig from when he accused me of cheating at four square.

It's called a "cherry bomb," Ben. It's completely legal, Ben . . . No, I'm not going to the reunion, Ben.

A minute later, Gallow returned with our sandwiches and drinks. Both he and Gleason had opted for the traditional cheesesteak "whiz wit"—*whiz* meaning Cheez Whiz, and the *wit* denoting "with onions." My order was fancier, as I preferred provolone and extra peppers.

Gleason took his sandwich. "Thanks, Shrek."

Gallow glared at me. "You told him?"

"I did."

"I was wearing green that day!" he shouted.

We all laughed.

Little was said for the next five minutes as we devoured our sandwiches. When Gallow finished, he said, "I should pick one up for Moore and drop it off at her place."

I said, "Better get one for Ms. Ruby as well."

He nodded as if to say, "Good thinking," then stood and made his way back to the counter. He returned a moment later with a quizzical look on his face.

"What's up?" I asked. "Are they out of steak or something?" It had happened before on a busy Sunday.

"No," he said, waving me off. "I was thinking about Ms. Ruby's house. There's a street nearby that only runs for three blocks."

"What about it?"

"It's called East Orleans."

Gleason and I traded a glance.

But Gallow wasn't done. He added, "And there's a church on it."

20

Trinity United Church was brown brick with a white steeple. A giant cross hung above its entrance, and out front was a letter board reading "Jesus Saves."

In the two hours since Gallow's epiphany, a series of dominoes had fallen, and now half the task force was congregating on the church lawn.

"How much longer until the cadaver dog gets here?" I asked Agent Joyce.

"Any time now," he said.

It had taken a while to convince Joyce that even though it was a long shot, we had to investigate the grounds of the church, especially since it had already been searched.

Evidently, not every move the task force was taking was transparent, and someone else on the task force had made the connection to the church on East Orleans Street. Cadaver dogs had been brought in to do a sweep of it two days earlier, but they hadn't alerted on anything. Which was no surprise, as it was widely believed the entries (*Church* and *New Orleans*) pointed to an old murder that took place in the city of New Orleans. To that point, they'd checked more than half the churches in the

Big Easy and they'd discovered nothing more than one pastor was having an affair with the organ player.

"This is a waste of time," I heard Kip say from a couple feet behind me. He'd been cocky and smug since he arrived, no doubt still bolstered by winning our onesie bet.

I turned. "No, it's not."

He put his hands on his hips. "They already did a sweep of the church. There's nothing here."

"Yes, there is." I knew it in my bones.

"Wanna bet?"

"I don't bet on murder investigations." Under my breath, I added, "You nitwit."

Agent Joyce shot us both a look.

A K-9 Unit SUV pulled to the curb, and a compact woman got out and opened the back door. A German shepherd bounded out, hit the ground, and gave a quick shake of its body.

Officer Katie Wellish strode forward and introduced us to four-year-old Cassie, who sat back on her haunches and gazed up at us. Gleason said, "May I?"

Wellish smiled and nodded.

Gleason squatted and gave Cassie a few nice rubs.

"What are the oldest remains that Cassie here has alerted on?" I asked.

"She found the body of a boy who'd been missing for over four years." She paused then asked, "Why? How old are the remains we're looking for here? They didn't tell me much over the phone. Only that you needed the best cadaver dog in Philly."

"The last two bodies we found were from the mid-1970s."

"Thirty-five-year-old remains?"

"Maybe even older." Who knows how far back our killer went?

"Cassie's the best in the business," Wellish said, "but that's asking a lot."

"Is it possible?"

"Yeah, it's possible. It's happened before. There are a lot of variables: temperature, humidity, the softness of the earth. Decaying matter still needs to be present."

I nodded, then looked down at Cassie gazing up at me, eyes wide and wagging her tail. "Are you ready to do some smelling, girl?"

She stuck out her tongue and panted.

A young pastor from Trinity United, who introduced himself as Reginald, led us inside. Our small group watched as Wellish and Cassie sniffed every nook and cranny of the fifty-seven-year-old church.

Cassie didn't alert on anything in the rectory, and we moved outside to the church grounds. The sun was setting on our backs as the dog trampled through fallen leaves, her nose to the earth.

I held my breath as Cassie stopped, then thrust her hips forward.

"Did she find something?" I asked.

"Just taking a whiz," Wellish said with a grin. "You'll know if she alerts on something; she'll bark and start digging."

For the next forty-five minutes, Cassie did not bark and start digging. We walked around to the back, up to the fence of the neighboring house, then back to the front of the church.

I wasn't used to being wrong, and I bit the inside of my cheek. "I thought for certain this was where the killer was pointing us."

Gleason clapped me on the shoulder. "Can't win 'em all."

Kip glanced over and smirked.

I looked at Cassie, then pointed to Kip. "Attack!"

She didn't.

Several churchgoers started arriving for Trinity United's 6:30 evening service.

Pastor Reginald walked toward our group and asked, "Are you guys done in the rectory?"

"We sure are, Father," Agent Joyce said. "Have a nice service." He turned to me and said, "I called in a lot of favors to get that dog down here, Prescott."

He was waiting for me to apologize.

I didn't.

Because I wasn't wrong. There were bodies here somewhere. Maybe they were too old for Cassie to smell. Or maybe Cassie wasn't the best cadaver dog in Philadelphia. Maybe Cassie couldn't smell a freshly killed *T. rex*.

"There are bodies here," I said.

Gleason said, "Cassie would have—"

I cut him off. "We need to get a bunch of shovels."

"Will you listen to yourself?" Joyce said. "You want to dig up a bunch of holes in a church courtyard." He shook his head. "We brought a cadaver dog in twice. There's nothing here. Not all hunches pan out."

I almost said, "Maybe not all *your* hunches," but I didn't want to alienate him further. I might need him to bail me out of jail when I brought a small tractor here later tonight and dug up the entire yard.

Out of the corner of my eye, I noticed a petite woman walking toward us. She was dressed in her Sunday best: a light-blue dress and a large ivory hat. In the fading light, it took me a moment to realize it was Ms. Ruby.

I waved at her.

She squinted, waved back, then made her way over. I gave her a hug, then she turned to Gleason and asked, "And who is this beautiful man?"

Wade Gleason shook her hand. Ms. Ruby wiggled her body and fanned herself. When she was done swooning, she said, "Mikey said you guys might be over here at the church." She cocked her head to the side. "Did you find what you were looking for?"

"Unfortunately, we didn't." I nodded at Cassie. "She didn't alert on anything in the church or in the yard."

Ms. Ruby pointed to the fence to the right of the church. "Did anybody tell you about that house there?"

"No."

"Who from the church was helping you out?"

Gleason said, "Reginald."

"Oh, Reggie. What a nice man. Heart for Jesus. But he's young. A baby. He wouldn't have known." She paused for a breath, then said, "I've been coming to this church for close to fifty years. It's changed hands three times. Started out as Kensington First Baptist, then it became United First Baptist, then about twelve years ago, it became Trinity United."

My antennas were up and spinning. I asked, "What wouldn't Reggie have known?"

"The land that house is on"—again she pointed at the fence and neighboring house—"used to belong to the church." She explained how, when the church changed hands in the late 1970s, the new owner sold the extra lot to developers.

Gleason and I traded a glance. Gleason waved Joyce over and said, "You have to hear this."

Ms. Ruby told them what she'd told us. It would kill Kip if I was right, but even he said, "We have to get Cassie over there."

Joyce nodded. "We'll need a warrant."

"Not if they consent," Gleason said.

I asked Ms. Ruby, "Do you know who lives there?"

"Sure do. Gwen and Patton Johnson."

Five minutes later, Ms. Ruby knocked on the door and explained the situation to the Johnsons. They consented, and Wellish led Cassie through the gate to the backyard.

Our entire group stood on the porch and watched Cassie sniff her way through the yard. Near the back corner, not far from the fence, was a small birch tree clinging to the last of its leaves. Cassie stopped a couple feet shy of the tree, let out two loud barks, and started digging.

Two hours later, with several large halogen lamps erected, we uncovered the remains of four bodies.

21

The Numbers task force was at an impasse until the autopsy results on the four bodies came back—the church had been scoured, and no numbers had been found anywhere—so I decided to take in Nicholas Wexley's afternoon press conference.

Wexley's $7 million luxury penthouse condominium was in Spring Garden, a neighborhood a mile north of city hall. A dozen news vans and a crowd of more than a hundred people gathered out front of the twenty-two-story Springlight Building.

I joined the back of the group, searching the crowd for Gallow. I found him a moment later, leaning back against the bumper of a parked car and chatting with two uniformed officers. He noticed my gaze and gave a quick half salute.

A few feet behind me, a female reporter held a microphone with FOX 29 on the side. She gazed into a large camera on a tripod five feet from her and said, "That's right, Tina. I'm live outside the Wexleys' riverside condominium, where in just a few minutes Nicholas Wexley and his family are expected to have a press conference.

"Six days ago, on October eighteenth, the body of twenty-year-old Brooke Wexley was found in a tent outside

city hall. She had been one of hundreds of protesters camped
out, and police quickly ruled her death a homicide.

"In a statement released yesterday, Philadelphia Police Chief
Halson said they are following several different leads, but no
arrests have been made." The small crowd buzzed, and the
reporter said, "Here they come now."

I turned my attention to the darkened glass entrance to
the condo. The doors opened and several people stepped out.
I recognized Nicholas Wexley from the press coverage. He was
bald—what was left of his hair, buzzed short—and unseason-
ably tan, but the look suited him in a swarthy Billy Zane sort of
way. He wore a suit that cost more than my entire wardrobe, and
you could tell, even at fifty-two, he was rock-solid underneath.
His wife, Vera, who I'd seen pictures of on the internet—mostly
from her time as a stage actress—was a stunning brunette with
high cheekbones and green eyes. Even from thirty feet away, I
could see her chin quivering as she tried to remain stoic.

They were joined by their two children, who I'd seen
mentioned in several of the articles I'd read. Claire was seventeen, a senior in high school. She had dark-brown hair held
back in a ponytail and her eyes were puffy and nearly swollen
shut. She held a handkerchief in hand and dabbed at the creases
of her eyes. Evan was a twenty-one-year-old version of Nicholas. He was fraternity-boy handsome with wavy black hair and
his mother's cheekbones. Unlike his sister, his eyes were bright
and clear.

Bringing up the rear was Wexley's business partner, Steven
Eglund—who had a full head of gray hair and designer
wire-frame glasses. Beside him was an angular blond with short,
cropped hair, who I assumed was Eglund's spouse.

Vera Wexley walked to the black lectern, and the five others
fanned out behind her. She had blue tape wrapped around her

right wrist from what I guessed must have been a sprain, and she wiped her eyes. "Six days ago, my beautiful, vibrant, and intelligent daugh—" Her breath caught. Tears began streaming down her face. Her head began shaking. She muttered, "I can't do this."

Nicholas Wexley put his arms around her and guided her away from the lectern and into the arms of their son. He took her place behind the lectern.

After staring out at the crowd for two breaths, Wexley said, "This is every parent's worst nightmare." His voice was rugged and booming. "Getting a call that your daughter, your own flesh and blood, was murdered. I don't wish that on anybody." He worked his tongue back and forth over perfectly white veneers. "I've started a tip line, and I'm offering a reward for information that leads to the arrest of the coward who robbed me of my daughter." He paused, then added, "Ten million dollars."

Eyes popped, and mouths dropped.

I turned and looked at Gallow. He locked eyes with me, shaking his head back and forth.

I fought down a smile.

Mike Gallow's investigation had just gotten ten million times more difficult. Don't get me wrong, rewards work every once in a while. And maybe the person who killed Brooke Wexley got loose-lipped with some of his pals, and they might come forward for the dough. But odds are they would have come forward for a reward of $100,000. Offering a $10 million reward was the equivalent of building a bonfire to cook a single marshmallow.

Even though Nicholas Wexley had started an independent tip line, in the coming hours and days, the Philadelphia Police Department would be flooded with calls, emails, and "pop-ins." And it would take hundreds—perhaps thousands—of man-hours to separate the credible info from the crackpots' reports.

That said, I couldn't blame Wexley; in his world, there wasn't anything money couldn't buy—Bentley, mansion in the Hamptons, G5 jet . . . *justice*.

Ignoring an onslaught of questions from the surrounding press, the Wexleys and Eglunds retreated inside the condo. Another man, probably one of the hedge fund's lawyers, took over the lectern, answering questions and giving more details about the tip line and a website.

I pulled out my cell phone and saw I had five missed calls and several incoming text messages. All were from Lacy.

My heart fluttered.

She'd never called me five times in her life. And the calls had all come in the last half hour, when she should have been at swim practice. I opened her text messages:

I don't feel good. Can you come pick me up from practice?
Answer your phone, butthead.
Tommy!
Come pick me up!

I called her back. She picked up halfway into the first ring. "Finally."

"Are you okay?"

"Yeah, I called Jennifer, and she came and got me."

"Jennifer?"

"My art professor."

"Oh, okay. What's wrong?"

"We were finishing warm-ups, and I got dizzy. I thought it might just be low blood sugar or something, but I ate an energy bar and it didn't go away. Coach thinks I've been overtraining."

The knot in my stomach slowly unwound. "Do you want me to bring some food to your apartment?"

"I'm at the condo."

Seeing as how we'd paid for it with our shared inheritance, the condo was both mine and Lacy's. It was a two-bedroom, two-bath, and she usually stayed there a few nights a month.

"I'm a mile from home," I said. "Do you want me to pick up pizza from that place on Twenty-Third?"

"*Mmmmm.* Yes, please." I didn't need to see her to know that she was rubbing her belly while she said this.

"What kind do you want?"

"I just want cheese—" There was a moment of murmuring in the background, then she returned. "—and Jennifer wants pepperoni and mushroom."

"She's still there?"

"No. I'm going to mail it to her."

Right. Dumb question.

≈

"Four slices," I said. "That's pretty impressive."

"True confession," Jennifer said, licking pizza sauce off her thumb. "If you weren't here, I would eat at least two more."

"How very ladylike."

We'd been sitting at the kitchen table, eating and talking for the past half hour. After a slice of pizza, Lacy had felt dizzy again and excused herself to lie on the couch. It didn't take long for her to conk out. Every so often, one of her soft snores would waft into the kitchen.

"You can take that pizza with you," I said. "I don't like mushrooms."

Her face cringed at this apparent character defect.

"Sorry if I don't enjoy eating fungus."

She picked a mushroom off a slice and popped it in her mouth. "Yummy fungus!"

I laughed.

There was a deck of cards on the far edge of the table, and Jennifer reached over and grabbed them. "You a solitaire guy?" she asked, opening the box and sliding the cards out.

"I am a solitaire guy."

She closed one eye and cocked her head at an angle. "Yeah, you seem like a solitaire guy."

"Is that so?"

"You give off a lone-wolf vibe."

"I have lots of friends."

"Not according to your sister."

"What's she been telling you?"

"Just that you've lived in this building for three years and you don't even know most of your neighbors' names, let alone made any friends."

"That's not true. Alvin's on four, and then there's Simon on nine."

She raised an eyebrow. "And where does Theodore live?"

"Six."

She grinned.

Actually, I knew the name of every single person who lived in the building. All seventy-eight. But Lacy was right—I wasn't friends with any of them.

"I bet you have tons of friends," I said.

Jennifer was beautiful and bubbly, and you couldn't help but want to be inside her hula hoop.

"Five good friends. Abby, Janet, Chloe, Jeff." She glanced over her shoulder at the living room. "And now your sister."

We both stared at her for a couple of seconds, then I surprised myself and said, "I hope she feels better tomorrow."

Though it was just a little dizziness, it worried me. From the look on Lacy's face when she stood up to go to the living room, I saw it had her worried too. But then again, it was most likely just overtraining.

"She'll be fine," Jennifer said, reaching out and softly touching my hand.

I smiled at her.

She pulled her hand back, then expertly shuffled the cards. "So, you're an ex–homicide detective, huh?"

"I am."

"How'd you start down that road?"

"It's not that interesting."

"Indulge me."

I sighed, then said, "When I dropped out of college at twenty, I had no idea what I wanted to do with my life. I was staying with my folks, looking for a job. Just something temporary until I could figure out my next move.

"I ended up getting a job with the landscaping crew that took care of my parents' yard. One day, while we were working on this super-nice house, the cops showed up. The owner had called them, alleging that somebody had stolen tools out of his garage. Now, I didn't know the guys on the crew all that well, so I couldn't be sure none of them did it. But there was something about the asshole property owner that I didn't like. So, while the cops were busy chatting up the owner and interrogating the rest of the crew, I snuck into this prick's house through the back door.

"I made my way into his basement, and I found the tools the guy was talking about. I brought them out and dropped them in front of the owner. The look on his face—it was priceless. Then

he started backtracking, saying that maybe the medication he
was on was making him hallucinate. Utter bullshit."

"Did you ever find out why he made it up?"

"Turns out that his wife was having an affair with one of
the guys."

She laughed.

"I hadn't ever considered being a cop, but after that incident,
I looked into the police academy. Started a few months later.
Worked a beat for a couple years, then took the detective exam."

"Were you any good?"

"I was."

In all seriousness, I was better than good. You need "the
two I's" to thrive as a detective: *instinct* and *intuition*. One is
primal, the other learned. I had both. But sadly, I had a third I:
impulsiveness. That's why half my cases had to be thrown out.
And that's why I'd ultimately been shown the door. I didn't work
well within an organization, which is why I was having trouble
collaborating with anyone in the task force besides Gleason. I
worked well in a duet. Even better as a free agent.

I kept this to myself.

"What about you?" I asked. "How did you end up teaching art history?"

"Failed painter."

"No."

"Oh, yeah. I sucked. Your sister is ten times better than I
ever was."

Lacy had always been a good painter. If she hadn't had to
allocate so much energy to swimming, I had no doubt she could
have made it as an artist.

Jennifer went in for another slice of pizza, and she expounded
on her circuitous route to teaching. When she was finished, she
asked, "Do you know how to play rummy five hundred?"

"I do."

"Excellent, because I'm about to whoop your ass at it."

"Do your best."

She dealt the cards.

We played for the next three hours—she won two games and I won two games—and we talked about everything. And we talked about nothing.

Then she took her pizza and left.

22

When Lacy and I received our inheritance, we agreed to each splurge on one item. It was an easy decision for me. My parents had a Range Rover growing up—theirs was still parked in the garage at the house in Seattle—and I went and bought myself a brand-new one. For Lacy, the decision was more difficult. It wasn't until we'd been living in the Philadelphia condo going on six months that Lacy said, "I know what I want."

She had a mischievous grin eating up her face, and I remember asking, "Oh, do you now?"

"A bed."

I'd spent $50,000 on a brand-new car, so I expected her to say something more outlandish. "Come on," I said, "buy something crazy. A motorcycle or a diamond tiara. Or, like, Michael Phelps's blood."

But she wasn't having it. "Just wait until you see this bed," she kept saying.

Six weeks later, the bed arrived. I watched as twelve enormous cardboard boxes were carried into Lacy's room by three men who only spoke Lithuanian. Lacy closed the door to her room with a smile. After six hours, she opened the door and the three men left.

A moment later, she yelled, "Okay, you can come see it now."

I pushed the door to her room open and fell to my knees. "Oh my God!"

It was a four-poster bed fit for royalty. Each post was ornately carved out of what I would learn was African blackwood, the most expensive wood on the planet. Semitranslucent silk curtains hung around the bed, and once I made my way back to my feet, I pulled them aside. Lacy was curled up at the top of the mattress constructed of six thousand pocketed springs, fleece wool, and cashmere. She tossed me a gold-sequined throw pillow and said, "Check that out—twenty-four karat."

"How much did this cost?"

That's when I learned my sister had spent more on her bed than I had on my car.

Now, three years later, I pulled the curtains aside. Lacy was lying on her side with her eyes closed, but I could tell she was awake. I asked, "Did your fifty-six-thousand-four-hundred-and-thirty-three-dollar-bed heal you?"

"No," she said, opening one eye. "I should have gotten the one with the diamond inlay."

I laughed, then asked, "Seriously, how are you feeling?"

"I'm still dizzy, and now my vision is all blurry in my left eye." She pulled her legs out from under the covers. "Plus, I keep getting these weird spasms in my legs."

After a moment, her calf twitched, like a dimple flashing.

I looked at her silently for a few seconds, and then she said, "Stop worrying."

"I'm not."

"Yes, you are." She pulled one of the three gold-sequined

pillows to her chest. "One more night's sleep in Delilah here, and I'll be good as new."

Oh, I forgot to mention Lacy had named her bed Delilah.

"Do you want me to cook you up some breakfast?"

"Maybe an Eggo."

"Which kind?"

"Boo-berry," she said in a kiddy voice.

"Just one?"

"Two boo-berry Eggo waffles, please."

I fought back a smile. "Syrup or powdered sugar?"

"Two boo-berry Eggo waffles with powdered sugar, please."

This time, I was unable to stifle my laugh. A few minutes later, I delivered her waffles and orange juice and told her I'd be at a task force meeting for the next few hours but to text if she needed anything.

I had just reached her bedroom door, when my phone chirped.

I checked the message. It was from Lacy. It said, "Thanks, Big Bro."

≈

I arrived at the 12:30 p.m. task force meeting ten minutes early. As I plopped three dozen doughnuts and two large to-go carafes of Peruvian medium roast on the side table, I was greeted by my colleagues with thunderous applause. The doughnuts were from a local Amish bakery called Beiler's, and they were the best in Philly and maybe the entire East Coast.

I'd finished my coffee and a vanilla sprinkle doughnut on the drive over—to which both my shirt and jeans could attest—and I walked to the back of the room.

A minute later, Wade Gleason nestled up next to me. He

was holding a chocolate coconut doughnut, and I said, "And here I had you pegged for a Boston cream."

He laughed, then said, "Man, the Amish know their way around a doughnut."

"They sure do."

After Agent Joyce finished his doughnut, he dusted his hands off on his pants and said, "Alright, let's get started here."

Most everyone had taken a seat, but Gleason and I remained standing against the back wall.

The cool kids.

Agent Joyce spent the first few minutes recapping the investigation. The identities of the four present-day victims—Gene Kirovec, Constance Yul, Peter Boland, and Marty Inaba—had been investigated down to the quick. There were no ties between them. None of the four had any history with the Numbers, and it was believed they were mere cannon fodder in a much larger war. I had a hard time believing any of them were the killer's true target.

Boston authorities were closing in, but they still hadn't identified the two victims found in Edith's casket. They had to play a larger role in the killer's puzzle, but without their identities, it was like trying to play Clue with Colonel Mustard, Professor Plum, Miss Scarlet, plus the entire cast of *The Lord of the Rings*.

It was Elf #174 with the candle in the conservatory.

As for the four bodies found at the church—which were more skeletons than bodies—the FBI labs were currently running the mummies' DNA through CODIS, the federal government's Combined DNA Index System. The odds of getting a hit were slight.

That being said, autopsy results had come in.

"Like the two corpses buried in Boston," Agent Joyce said, "the four victims found near Trinity United were heavily decomposed. According to the biological profile, all four of them are male and aged between twenty-five and thirty-five. The coroner found evidence of knife wounds on the frontal bone of three of the four victims." He opened a folder and pulled a stack of photographs. "Pass these around."

It took a moment for one of the photographs to make its way back to us. It was an X-ray scan of a skull. The frontal bone was covered in jagged gray lines, dots, and dashes. The lines didn't create any obvious numbers, though if you connected several of the smaller dots and dashes, they could feasibly make a three.

Someone shouted, "This could be any number that has a three in the second or third digit."

That could be hundreds of numbers.

"I agree it would be difficult to glean anything from that picture alone," Joyce pulled another stack of pictures from the folder and handed them out, "but when you have all three images side by side, you start to see a pattern."

A second glossy image made its way back to us. It was divided into four quadrants, the top right quadrant blank. The X-ray of the skull we'd already seen was in the top left, and the bottom two quadrants were filled with X-rays of two other skulls.

"A pattern?" Gleason said, running his finger over the lines on each of the skulls. "This looks maybe like a seven."

I pointed to the third picture. "Is that a nine?"

I was trying to see a pattern, but nothing was jumping out. Were the numbers going up? Down? Up by ten? Down by fifteen? Was it something more complicated? Were they prime numbers? Was it a famous number pattern, like the Fibonacci sequence? Had we just stepped into *The Da Vinci Code*?

It was one of the sheriff's deputies that figured it out. He said, "It's the same number."

Gleason and I both squinted, moving our eyes over each image. There were unique marks on each of the images, but if you took all the marks from all the images and combined them . . .

"Seven ninety-three," I said.

Joyce had moved to the dry-erase board, and he wrote *793*.

"Three of the four Trinity United victims had the same number carved into their foreheads," Joyce said.

Everyone in the room collectively held their breath as Joyce wrote a single word after the number.

Queen.

23

Lew waited for a woman walking two German shepherds to disappear from view, then he stepped out of his rental car. The street was quiet, the residents of the middle-class row houses most likely parked in front of their TVs watching the nightly news or preparing for bed.

He pulled his ball cap down another half inch, then approached a black sedan parked on the street. The windows were tinted, and Lew could just make out the shadow of a body in the driver's seat.

After cinching his gloves tight, Lew rapped on the passenger-side window.

The window slid down halfway.

The police officer was in full uniform. He was in his midthirties with blond hair parted to the side. His silver nameplate read, "Clement." A bag of potato chips rested between Clement's legs, and there was an energy drink in the cup holder. A half-empty pack of Twizzlers rested on the passenger seat.

"How's your watch going?" Lew asked.

It was obvious that Officer Clement recognized Lew, and he replied, "Pretty good, sir."

Clement's deference was the exact reason that just a few days earlier, Lew had strolled off the SS *United States* without raising an eyebrow. Lew was a man of authority. No one questioned his presence.

"Do you mind if I keep you company for a bit?" Lew asked.

"Not at all," the officer replied, picking the pack of Twizzlers off the seat.

The window went back up, and Lew climbed into the car. Clement offered him a piece of licorice, but Lew declined. He wasn't one for sweets.

"Which house are you watching?" Lew asked.

Clement pointed to the house across the street. "The one with all of the hanging flowerpots out front."

"See anything suspicious?"

"Not in the least."

"How long have you been with the department?"

"Going on five yea—"

Clement's reply was interrupted by two quick coughs from the silencer attached to the barrel of a Beretta 92FS. Lew preferred using a knife, but he wasn't opposed to using a gun. He was anything but predictable.

The officer stared at the two holes in his chest, his eyes open wide in surprise. A moment later, his body went limp, his head collapsing to the side.

Ninety seconds later, Lew stood on the doorstep of the house across the street.

He knocked.

The door was opened by a Black man in his seventies. He went by the nickname Jumpy. Not as good as *Lew*, but pretty decent as far as nicknames go. Though, to be fair, *Lew* was more than a nickname. It was a doctrine. A way of life.

Before the man could utter a word, Lew pulled the Beretta

from his waist and shot Jumpy in the forehead. The out-of-practice enforcer tumbled backward onto the carpet. Lew stepped into the house, pulling the door closed behind him.

A second man came barreling around a corner. Loretta Carroll's longtime partner. "What's going on?" Palmer shouted.

Lew dispatched the man, sending three bullets into his chest. Palmer fell to his knees, then collapsed forward.

Lew stepped over Palmer and came clear of the hallway. Loretta Carroll had been washing dishes. She stood next to the sink, her hands dripping with suds, a dinner plate held in her left hand.

Part of her must have expected this moment for going on fifty years.

Lew shot her in the stomach.

He wanted her to suffer.

Twenty minutes later, when the Queen took her last breath, Lew pulled out his switchblade and got to work.

24

Gleason drove like a maniac, and we were the first ones from the task force to arrive at Queen Loretta's.

Local cops had been alerted, and the flashing lights of seven squad cars and three fire trucks shrieked under the overcast sky. A crowd of gawkers congregated at the edge of the crime scene tape, and dozens of residents stood on their compact stoops, trying to get a view of the action.

More eyeballs than you would expect on a chilly Tuesday afternoon.

We flashed our badges, signed in with the crime scene recorder, then ducked under the yellow tape.

A plainclothes detective stood in the center of the street, and it was evident he was calling the shots. He introduced himself as Detective Tarter. He looked to be in his late forties, with salt-and-pepper hair cut short, and oversized glasses. He'd already talked to Agent Joyce, and he'd been expecting us.

"What have we got?" Gleason asked him.

Tarter nodded at a black sedan parked on the side of the street. "One vic in the car. Officer Clement out of the Third District. Young guy looking for some overtime."

Gleason had been the one to initially request a car stationed out front of Queen Loretta's house. If he felt any guilt, he didn't show it. He was a pro.

"When did he last check in?" Gleason asked.

"His shift started at two p.m. yesterday," Tarter replied. "He last checked in at five p.m."

"Why didn't someone raise the flag when he missed his next check-in?"

"We're still trying to figure that out. They're interviewing the watch commander right now."

"What about inside the house?" I asked.

I knew it had to be bad. There were no ambulances.

"Three vics," Tarter said. "It's pretty ugly."

"Has anyone else been inside?"

"Nope. Just me. I was instructed not to let anybody in until you guys showed up."

Good boy.

I wanted to get a quick look at Clement's body before heading inside. The three of us walked to the patrol car.

After pulling on a pair of purple latex gloves, Tarter opened the passenger door. Officer Clement was crumpled in the driver's seat. There was a bag of chips between his legs, a can of soda in the cup holder, and a half-empty pack of Twizzlers sitting on the dash. Blood had poured from the two gunshots in his chest and soaked his jeans and the seat.

"What do you make of it?" Gleason asked.

"He was caught off guard," I said.

"No defensive wounds," Tarter quipped. "He didn't even have time to get his hands up."

Most likely, the killer had been sitting in the passenger seat when he plugged two shots into Clement's chest.

Out of the corner of my eye, I noticed a van turning onto the street.

I nodded at the news van and said, "Here comes Keith Morrison."

"Damn," Gleason said. "Though I'm surprised it's taken this long."

I think he was talking about the investigation as a whole. There had been a blip in the media after Marty Inaba's body had been found on the SS *United States*—even the phrase "possible serial killer" had been uttered—but miraculously, the details about the numbers in the victims' foreheads had yet to see print, air, or internet.

Three more cars turned onto the street, one I recognized as belonging to Agent Joyce. The rest of the task force had arrived, which meant we only had about ninety seconds if we wanted first dibs on the crime scene inside the house.

"Let's boogie," Gleason said.

We hustled across the street and walked up the same six steps we'd walked up three days earlier. Tarter had joined us, and after quickly pulling on booties and latex gloves from boxes outside the front door, we pushed inside.

Jumpy was on the ground just inside the foyer. He was on his side, and there was a hole in the center of his forehead. An eighteen-inch radius of carpet beneath him had been stained scarlet.

"How long do you figure they've been here?" Gleason asked.

Based on the smell of the body (pungent, but not yet putrid), the stage of rigor mortis (his fingers were stiff and unpliable), and his outfit (a wife-beater and pajama bottoms), I said, "I'm guessing twelve to fifteen hours. They were probably killed late last night."

I lifted Jumpy's shirt. There were no numbers on Jumpy's chest or back. I pulled down his pants. Again, no numbers.

Gleason was ten feet away, crouched over Palmer's body. Unlike Jumpy, he'd taken three in the chest.

"Does he have numbers?" I asked.

Gleason nodded. "5-9-1."

I made a mental note of the number for later, then walked around the corner and into the kitchen. The Queen was on the ground, lying near a small rug nestled beneath the sink. Pieces of a broken plate surrounded her. Needless to say, I would not be collecting my $120.

Tarter, who had already seen the body, said, "He shot her in the stomach."

Stomach wounds were notoriously painful.

Did the killer want the Queen to suffer?

"2-5-8," Tarter said. "That's the number carved into her forehead."

Tarter, and most likely the entire world would know the details of the case in the coming hours, so I didn't give it a second thought as I pulled *The E.K. Dream Book* from my back pocket.

I found 258 twice. "*Carriage* and *Whooping Cough.*"

"Are you sure?" Gleason asked. "Those are pretty odd."

Odd was an understatement. But I'd triple-checked; those were the entries.

Next, I looked for the number carved into Palmer's forehead—591. Again, the number was listed twice: *Fragrance* and *Soldier.*

Gleason ignored how vague the entries were, asking, "Why no numbers on Jumpy?"

I'd been wondering the same thing since examining Jumpy's body. Why carve numbers into Palmer's and the Queen's foreheads but not Jumpy's? Was it simply logistics? Was the killer forced to dispatch Jumpy with a shot to the forehead because the aging enforcer was so close to the door and he couldn't risk him screaming? And if not the forehead, then there was plenty of other canvas for him to carve numbers: chest, back, legs, arms. Or was it as simple as this: the killer only meant to leave two numbers?

He'd done it previously—etched into the propeller blade on the ship—but those numbers corresponded to obvious clues: *Church* and *New Orleans*.

But these four entries (*Carriage, Whooping Cough, Fragrance,* and *Soldier*) were ridiculous.

We heard footsteps and turned.

Agent Joyce stood at the edge of the kitchen linoleum. After Gleason and I gave him a quick rundown, he said, "Okay, let's clear this place out and let the crime scene techs take over."

We exited the house, and then, much like the rest of the task force, Gleason and I spent the next half an hour canvassing the neighborhood, seeking witnesses. No one we talked to remembered seeing or hearing anything suspicious the previous evening. Though, as Gleason pointed out, most of the people we talked to were of color and didn't particularly like talking to police. If they had seen anything, they might call in an anonymous tip in the coming days. Or they might take their information to the grave.

The news van from earlier had been joined by six of its cousins. As we headed back to Gleason's car, we were bombarded with questions from reporters. A quadruple homicide, one victim a cop and another Loretta Carroll, was headline news, and the entire investigation would be public knowledge within the next twenty-four hours.

After my seventeenth "No comment," I hopped back into the passenger seat of the blue Taurus.

"What do you think?" Gleason asked, cranking up the heat.

"No numbers on Clement, no numbers on Jumpy. And the two numbers our killer left don't make a lick of sense."

"Maybe he switched to a different dream book?"

"This late in the game?" I shook my head. "No way."

I held my hands to the heater, then said, "Think about what our killer did at the Bunker Hill Cemetery."

"You mean, the dates on Edith's grave?"

"Exactly. The killer feared that we wouldn't make the connection with the three entries alone, so he added a fourth breadcrumb to help narrow down the search." I pulled my hands away from the heater. "There has to be another number somewhere."

"Maybe they'll find something in the house or in the car."

I closed my eyes, tried to run the footage. But I came up blank.

I stared at the clock on the dash, silently watching it turn from 1:55 to 1:56 then to 1:57.

"I'm going back inside the house," I announced.

"You heard Joyce," Gleason said, shaking his head. "No one inside until the techs finish."

The techs wouldn't be done for another couple of hours. Swabbing and dusting, bagging and tagging—it takes time. It isn't something that can be rushed.

"Yeah, I heard him," I said, jumping out of the car.

I ducked back under the crime scene tape and jogged to Loretta's front door. A cop stood out front—Hufflepuff. His curly hair looked so wet you'd have thought he'd just fought a typhoon.

"I was wondering where you'd gotten off to," I said. He hadn't been at the task force meeting. In fact, he seemed to come and go as he pleased.

He ignored me, and I said, "I need to get in there."

"No one is allowed in until the techs finish up," Puff huffed. "Why can't you just follow orders like the rest of us?"

"Listen, numbnuts, there's a third or even fourth number in there somewhere. We need to find it. And now."

I took a step toward him.

He extended his hands to push me away. I sidestepped him, then used his momentum to propel him forward. He hit the porch railing and then continued over, flipping into the bushes below.

"Cowabunga," I muttered.

I stuffed the box of booties and gloves in the bushes that Kip was struggling to free himself from, which would hopefully buy me some time, then ducked under the crisscrossed yellow tape.

Two teams of crime scene techs were in the house. They were dressed in white jumpsuits, and they were busily collecting all the juicy forensic material that would theoretically lead us to a suspect. There was just one problem: this killer was too good. If he hadn't left any evidence at the first four crime scenes, he wasn't going to start now.

"Get out of here," one of the techs mumbled from behind his N95 mask and goggles.

"I will, I just have to take a quick piss first."

I ducked into the small dining room, scanning the walls. No numbers. From there, I went into a downstairs bedroom. No numbers. I was darting up the stairs, when the front door opened and someone shouted, "Prescott! Get your ass out here!"

It was Joyce.

I went into the bathroom. No numbers. Another bedroom, likely Jumpy's. No numbers. Then the master bedroom. I was examining the Queen's extravagant mirror, when feet began clamoring up the stairs.

Agent Joyce, Detective Tarter, Hufflepuff (who had a bunch of twigs in his hair), and two other uniformed cops entered the room. They all had booties on their feet and gloves on their hands. That's why it had taken them so long to come inside. Someone had to track down fresh boxes from one of their cars.

"I knew bringing you onto the task force was a bad idea," Joyce said.

"There's another number here," I said, backing away from them. "There has to be. Finding that number is top priority."

"No, top priority is letting the crime scene techs do their job and not contaminating the scene any more than we have to." To Hufflepuff and the other two uniformed cops, Joyce said, "Get him out of here."

Hufflepuff grabbed me by my biceps, which I should point out, is a trigger for me. (My high school basketball coach used to grab me by the biceps when he wanted to yell at me about something. Thankfully, coaches can't do that crap anymore.)

"Let go of my arm," I said, softly.

"Or what?" he said, grinning.

"Is this really necessary?" Detective Tarter asked.

Everyone ignored him, including me.

I stared Hufflepuff in the eye and said, very slowly, and very loudly, "LET–GO–OF–MY–ARM!"

Joyce nodded at him, and he released my arm, but not before giving it one last hard pinch.

It took everything in my willpower not to punch him in the throat.

"Now, we are all going to walk peacefully out of here," Joyce said. He nodded at me. "And I'll deal with you later, Prescott."

I knew when I was beaten, and I complied.

We marched down the stairs and were steps from the front door when I spotted one of the news vans through the window. Suddenly, my body felt detached, and I was overcome with déjà vu so intense that I stopped walking. Why did it feel like I'd lived this moment already?

My brain whirred.

News van.

News.

News.

And then, just like that, it clicked—Palmer whispering to Queen Loretta, "News is coming on."

"What time is it?" I asked.

No one answered, and I shouted, "What time is it?"

Detective Tarter, who had become my ally in the short time I'd known him, checked his watch and then said, "2:03 p.m."

I'd jumped out of Gleason's car at 1:57 p.m. Another minute dealing with Hufflepuff, in the house by 1:58. Now it was 2:03 p.m.

I should have heard it.

"The grandfather clock," I said. "It didn't chime at two p.m."

"So what?" Hufflepuff asked.

"So, when Gleason and I were here three days ago, it chimed exactly at six o'clock on the dot. Why didn't it chime a few minutes ago?"

Everyone swapped glances, but no one said anything.

"Where's the clock?" Detective Tarter asked, breaking the silence.

I pointed. "Over there, in the sitting room."

Tarter jogged to the room. A moment later, he called, "You might want to come see this."

The rest of us caravanned into the room.

"Shit!" Joyce said.

I'm not sure if he was more upset that I was right or that our killer was bending his own rules once again.

The grandfather clock hadn't chimed for a reason—someone had stopped it. The hour hand was pointed halfway between the four and five. The minute hand was pointed at the last tick before the seven.

"4-3-4," I said.

Both Joyce and Hufflepuff—who to his credit, knew when *he* was beaten—whipped out copies of *The E.K. Dream Book.*

Hufflepuff was the first to find the one and only entry for 434. He gulped loudly and then read, *"Mafia."*

25

"I don't want to go," Lacy said. "You can't make me."

"Either I take you or one of the trainers takes you," I said. "You decide."

"*Ugh.* Fine. I'll go."

Lacy had met with the Drexel team doctor yesterday afternoon. He still felt Lacy was most likely suffering symptoms from overtraining, but her prolonged dizziness and blurred vision were worrisome, and he wanted to run some routine blood work just in case. Everything came back normal except Lacy had a positive ANA test, which I learned stood for antinuclear antibody test, and can be an indication of autoimmune disease.

The team doctor had pulled some strings, and Lacy had a busy day ahead of her. First stop was the lab, to have more blood drawn, then we had appointments with a rheumatologist, a neurologist, and she was scheduled to get an MRI.

I was trying not to worry, but my intestines hadn't gotten the memo, and they were twisting themselves into a French braid.

"I'll take you for ice cream after," I said.

"Dairy Queen?"

"Sure."

She clapped her hands together. "I'm gonna get a Peanut Buster Parfait."

Lacy was clad in her Drexel sweats, and as we walked to the condo elevator, I noticed she held herself up against the wall and blinked her left eye closed.

Did I say *French braid*? Because I meant to say *dreadlocks*.

The elevator opened to the parking garage, and Lacy and I walked to my Range Rover. I hit the fob, unlocking the car, and climbed into the driver's seat.

"You might want to come see this," Lacy said, staring at me through the passenger window.

This was the second time I'd heard these exact words in the past twenty-four hours.

I exited the car and walked around to the other side.

The entirety of the passenger side was covered with white spray paint that read, "Honk for the Shithead."

I leaned my head back. "Dammit, Carmen!"

Lacy was in near hysterics, her laughter almost tipping her over at one point. Once composed, she asked, "How did I never get to meet this girl? She's awesome."

There's no doubt in my mind that Lacy and Carmen would have been fast friends. It was one of the reasons I'd never introduced them. It would have made it harder when I inevitably had to break up with "Coo-Coo-for-Cocoa-Puffs."

"What are you going to do?" Lacy asked.

"Nothing," I said, peering at my watch. "We're already running late."

Lacy hopped into the car, and we pulled out of the parking garage. It only took ten seconds before the first car honked its horn and then another three before the second car followed suit.

"This is going to be a fun day," I said.

Lacy giggled.

We made a quick stop by a Quest lab so they could, to quote Lacy, "suck her dry," and then we drove to Thomas Jefferson University Hospital, where Lacy's appointments and MRI were scheduled.

Lacy's appointment with the rheumatologist—a doctor who specialized in several autoimmune disorders—lasted fifteen minutes. Lacy didn't want me to go into the exam room with her—she said that my nerves made *her* even more nervous—and I was happy to sit in the waiting room and skim through old copies of *Good Housekeeping.*

When she finished and we were walking through the hospital corridors to the neurologist's office, I asked, "What'd he say?"

"*He* was a *she*, and she won't know a whole lot until the results come back on the three gallons of blood they took from me."

"What did she do in there?"

"She listened to my lungs, tested my reflexes, asked me a bunch of questions."

"But no diagnosis?"

"What did I just tell you? She wants to look at the results of my blood tests first."

"Okay." I paused. "*Sheesh.*"

She slapped my arm. "I'm sorry. I know you're just trying to help."

We stepped into the neurologist's office and Lacy signed in. They called her name a few minutes later, and I wished her luck.

I was just getting ready to take a quiz in *Cosmo*—"Which Sitcom Actor Are You?"—when my phone vibrated. A sign on the wall read, "No Cell Phones," so I exited the room and went into the hallway.

The caller was Mike Gallow. I answered, "Giddy up."

He wanted to know the latest on our Numbers investigation. I spent ten minutes bringing him up to date: After scouring

Loretta Carroll's house for a fourth number and coming up empty, we'd finally called it quits at 7:00 p.m. The task force spent the rest of the evening eating Thai food at the federal building and brainstorming where the killer was pointing us. The overwhelming theory was that *Soldier* (591) and *Mafia* (434) were connected, but we couldn't even begin to postulate where the entries of the third number (258), *Whooping Cough* and *Carriage*, factored in.

Maybe we were looking for a soldier with ties to the Mafia who loved playing *Oregon Trail*.

At any rate, Joyce was calling in agents from the Organized Crime Unit to assist with the investigation. Oh, and I was on such thin ice that if I—and this is a direct quote from Agent Joyce's lips—"so much as dropped a Tic Tac," I was off the task force.

Gallow chuckled, then asked, "Are you back at the federal building now?"

"No, I'm helping Lacy out with something today." I didn't get into specifics, and from the tone of my voice, Gallow decided not to pry.

"What's going on with the Wexley case?" I asked.

He let out a long sigh. He was overwhelmed with all the leads coming into the Philly PD, plus he was constantly being bombarded by the private investigation team that Wexley had hired. Led by some asshole named Rocklin. They had agreed to share information, but so far it was just a one-way street.

After complaining for another few minutes, Gallow said, "Actually, I've got one piece of good news. We got the text messages and GPS coordinates on Brooke's burner phone."

"Did anything jump out at you?" I asked.

"She was texting with Professor Matthew Hutchings plus one other guy."

"No name?"

"She was careful not to use one."

"Could you pull the call history and messages from the person she was talking with?"

"We did. It's another burner phone. Only calls are to Brooke, and only messages are to Brooke."

"What about GPS data?"

"On John Doe's phone, it has him mainly in a four-block radius of downtown Philly."

"What about Brooke's?"

"Mostly in and around Penn campus. A couple times it has her up in the Pocono mountains."

"Her roommate said she liked to go hiking up there."

I waited a beat and then asked, "Can you email me the messages and the GPS data?"

Part of me hoped he said no. That he would save me from myself.

But Gallow trusted my instincts, and he said, "Sure thing. I'll send you everything we've got so far. The more eyes, the better."

We ended the call, and then I went back into the waiting room. I'd just finished my quiz when Lacy came out. I knew better than to ask questions, and all she said was, "The doctor said he'll call me once he looks over my MRI."

As we wended through the hospital corridors to the MRI appointment, I said, "Guess what? I'm Elaine."

"What are you talking about?"

I explained how I took the "Which Sitcom Actor Are You?" quiz in *Cosmo*.

"And it said you were Elaine from *Seinfeld*?" she laughed, though I could tell it was forced. Any other day, she would have gotten a big kick out of this.

She definitely wasn't feeling herself.

The MRI took forty-five minutes, and afterward, Lacy

looked exhausted. She didn't even want to go to Dairy Queen; she just wanted to go home to bed.

I dropped her off at our condo.

I needed something to keep my mind off things, so I drove to the library and printed out the documents Gallow had emailed.

Ever since Lacy had mentioned DQ, I'd had a banana split on my mind. I went through the Dairy Queen drive-thru, then parked. I crushed the banana split in fifteen bites, licked the spoon clean, then turned to the stack of printed pages.

The top page was a scan of a Walmart receipt. It was time-stamped 6:35 p.m. on October 17, 2011. The night of Brooke Wexley's murder. She had bought a megaphone, a Lipton Iced Tea, a granola bar, and a roll of blue sports tape. The latter of which I assume she used to repair a hole or tear somewhere in her blue tent.

I flipped to the next batch of documents. They were the phone records from Brooke's iPhone 4. They went back two and a half months to the beginning of August.

Less than a hundred phone calls were made over the time period, but well over two thousand text messages. Most were between Brooke and her roommates. They were dense for two months. Then, starting the first week of September, the texts became more sporadic. School had just started; perhaps they were all buckling down. Also, with Occupy Wall Street kicking off, Brooke was, well, *pre*-occupied.

As for Brooke's family, she frequently texted with her little sister—listed as *Claire-Bear* in her contacts—who was a senior in high school. According to one of their conversations, Claire had been accepted to Penn early and was beyond thrilled to be join-ing her older sibling. She'd even thrown a big Quaker-themed party to celebrate.

Brooke texted every few days with *Dad*. Mostly just check-ing in, telling him her plans for the week. Lots of one-word answers: *yes, no, maybe, probably, okay.* But I suppose if Nicholas was reading all her text messages, he knew, or assumed he knew, what was going on in her life.

There was only one text from her brother Evan, listed as *Bro.* It came in mid-September, and it read, "No. Just no."

Brooke never replied.

The strangest thing was that Brooke had her mom listed as *Vera*, which stood in stark contrast to *Claire-Bear*, *Dad*, and *Bro.* I read a few exchanges between mother and daughter, mostly texts from Vera saying, "Call me," or more often, "Call me now!"

I checked the call records and noted that Brooke never called her mother after one of these texts. Not once. That relationship seemed strained, if not worse.

Next, I turned to the burner phone records.

There were calls and messages from only three different numbers. One was Matthew Hutchings. One was the John Doe that Gallow mentioned. And the third was Brooke herself. She texted herself twice, each time a number. The first was five digits: 07835. Three days later, she texted herself an eight-digit number: 27186491.

Nothing about the numbers jumped out at me, and I concentrated on the text exchanges between Brooke and Burner Phone.

The first text was from Brooke on September 14.

BROOK: Hey!

BURNER PHONE: Hey, Brooke. It was nice bumping into you.

BROOKE: Sure was. You want to meet up?

BURNER PHONE: Okay. Where?

BROOKE: Same place. In an hour.

BURNER PHONE: I'll be there.

A few days later, there was another quick exchange.

BROOKE: What are you doing?

BURNER PHONE: Shopping for new eyeglasses.

BROOKE: What's wrong with the ones you have?

They exchanged another dozen messages, and then Burner Phone texted, "Okay, I gotta go play ✎"

BROOKE: Lol. Have fun. Beat him good.

Carmen would frequently text me the eggplant emoji, and I knew it represented a penis. Which means this guy was comfortable enough with Brooke to tell her he was about to go jerk off. Kinky.

There was nothing else interesting until the first week of October, when Brooke texted, "Hey, Grandpa."

BURNER PHONE: I told you not to call me that.

BROOKE: Well, you are a grandpa . . . a HOT one!

So, Burner Phone wore glasses, and he was a grandpa—which put him at least in his forties.

I spent the next few minutes poring over the GPS data for both phones.

One variable narrowed the search considerably. Ninety-five percent of Burner Phone's text messages came between 1:00 and 2:00 p.m. and had pinged in a four-block radius of downtown Philly.

Burner Phone was a creature of habit.

It was now 1:27 p.m.

I turned on the car.

Maybe I could get lucky.

26

My first stop was the Warwick Rittenhouse Hotel. I parked and strode inside the landmark hotel, which had been around since the 1920s. There were three restaurants in the hotel, but the only one currently open was Bluestone Lane, an Australian-inspired café. It was just one of several places that Brooke's mysterious lover might frequent during his texting "window."

The hostess was a woman a few years older than me. She wore a black pantsuit, and her bangs were cut short.

"How many?" she asked.

"Just me. I'm just going to grab a coffee and maybe something to go."

She nodded at a barista behind a white wraparound bar. "Courtney will take care of you at the bar."

I bellied up to one of the open seats and perused the menu. I hadn't planned on eating, but the BLATE—bacon, arugula, avocado, tomato, fried egg, and garlic aioli on a brioche roll—sounded too amazing to pass up.

After delivering drinks to a couple to my left, a young woman with dark hair and two nose rings slid a glass of water in front of me.

"Hello, Courtney," I said.

"Hello." She tilted her head to the side. "I want to say, *Pete?*"

I made a buzzer sound.

"*Lance?*"

I shook my head.

"*Chad?*"

"How dare you."

She laughed, and I introduced myself. She took my order, and when she returned with my lemonade a moment later, I said, "Couple of quick questions for you."

"I'm gay."

"Not one of my questions, but good to know."

She laughed, then said, "Whatcha got?"

"How often do you work this shift?" I asked.

"I have a set schedule. I work Monday, Wednesday, Thursday, and Saturday."

"Do you have a lot of regulars?"

"A fair amount."

"Any single men between forty-five and sixty who wear glasses?"

She put her hands on her hips. "Why are you looking for this person?"

"I'm an assassin."

She got a kick out of this and said, "There's a guy named Marshall who comes in almost every day. He's in his early fifties, has glasses."

"What time does he usually come in?"

"Pretty early. Around ten thirty."

I shook my head. "Is there anybody who comes in between one and three?"

"Jeff comes in a few times a week for a late lunch." Her face fell. "But he got LASIK a couple of years ago, so he doesn't wear glasses anymore." She washed a glass, then added, "I'll keep thinking, but no one else comes to mind."

She didn't come up with any more names, and after devouring the sandwich, I left her a humongous tip and left.

I spent the next hour canvassing the four-block radius. I poked my head into a Starbucks on one corner, but none of the baristas could recall anyone who fit the profile. There were a handful of other restaurants, a rare-book bookstore, a salon, and two bars. I struck out at each.

I was heading back toward the hotel to pick up my car, but there was one last place I wanted to check out: Saint Mark's Church. The sprawling cathedral was part of the Philadelphia Archdiocese and took up the better part of a city block. The church was a great place to go if you wanted to send a clandestine text message. Hiding out in an empty pew. Maybe even in the confessional?

No, Father, I'm not texting.

I was heading in that direction when I peered to my right, down Sixteenth Street. Somehow in my less-than-methodical canvassing, I'd missed half a city block. Even from a hundred feet away, I could see the overhang for another of the city's landmark institutions: the Racquet Club of Philadelphia.

The texts.

I pulled the folded-up pages from my back pocket and shuffled until I found the exchange I was looking for.

BURNER PHONE: Gotta go play 🏑
BROOKE: Lol. Have fun. Beat him good.

I'd assumed the exchange was sexual. But maybe it wasn't. Maybe the guy was using the eggplant emoji as a play on words.

Maybe he wasn't going to go play with his dick. Maybe he was going to go play . . . *squash*.

≈

Walking toward the Racquet Club, I started second-guessing myself. Technically, eggplant isn't squash. It's a nightshade, in the same family as tomatoes, potatoes, and peppers. I knew this because my mom had been allergic to nightshades. But how many people knew that? And it's not like there's a separate squash emoji. And then there was the fact that some people, mostly southerners, called eggplant "guinea squash." I wasn't sure how I knew this useless fact, but it was implanted in my brain, probably an old clue from Trivial Pursuit, which Lacy and I still played at least once a month.

When the entrance to the club came into view, I stopped. Even if Burner Phone was sending those texts from the Racquet Club, how was I going to get inside a private club? You couldn't just stroll in and ask for a day pass. It was a long and expensive process to become a member.

I turned on my heel and started back the way I'd come. It took me five minutes to jog to the Bank of America ATM, withdraw $500, and jog back.

I wiped a bead of sweat from my brow as I pushed through the glistening glass doors of the club and walked to the front desk. There was a young man working—early twenties, with a name tag that read "Greg"—and I said, "I don't have my membership card with me."

"No problem," Greg said with a smile. "I'll just pull you up in the system."

"Here's my ID." I handed my driver's license to him, which had a hundred dollars tucked beneath it.

Greg expertly slid the money into his pocket and handed me a lock. "Have a good workout."

I gave him the softest of winks, then I walked to the small store. After several minutes, I exited with a squash racket, goggles, shorts, and a T-shirt.

The locker room was opulence at its finest, and I kept a lookout for Burner Phone as I changed into my new gear. The only two guys I saw were both old and naked, with the saggy balls I could look forward to someday.

Once dressed, I appraised myself in the mirror.

"Pretentious asshole?" I whispered. "Check and check."

I made my way to the courts. All five were occupied, and I walked up and down, scrutinizing the ten players. Eight of them were men, and each appeared over thirty. One set of men was well into their seventies, and I dismissed them. That left six. Burner Phone's only distinguishing trait was that he had glasses, but all these men wore sports goggles. These were specialty goggles that went over regular glasses, but they also made prescription goggles, so theoretically, any of the men could be glasses-wearers.

However, in the center court, there was one man wearing goggles over his designer glasses. He was a couple inches taller than me, with bulging calves, and from afar, I put him in his late forties.

I needed to figure out how to get the guy alone, and I came up with a mediocre plan that I decided had a 42 percent chance of succeeding.

I waited for the duo to finish up their point, then knocked on the glass. Both men turned. I pulled open the glass door and stuck my head inside. From the look on the two men's faces, I suspect I'd breached an unwritten rule of etiquette.

I said, "Sorry to interrupt your game."

Neither man responded.

"What kind of car do you guys drive?"

"Why?" scoffed Suspect's diminutive playing partner.

"Someone broke into a car."

Both men took a few steps toward me.

"Where?" Suspect asked.

Surrounding the club was street parking and two parking garages. If the club was anything like the fancy clubs my parents belonged to in Seattle, they offered members discount pricing at one or both garages. I could have picked one or the other, but then I was cutting my odds in half. I kept it vague: "The parking garage."

Shortstack's eyebrows rose. "Liberty?"

"Yep."

Before they could ask what kind of car was broken into, I preempted them with, "What kind of car do you guys drive?"

"White Tesla," Suspect said.

Tesla was an electric car company that had only been around for a few years. It was still a small niche group that bought electric, but I saw more and more of the cars each day.

Shortstack said, "Mercedes 7 series. Silver."

"That's the one," I said, with a double scoop of despair. "They busted out your passenger window."

"Ah, shit." He turned to Suspect. "Sorry, Jeff, I have to take care of this."

"Of course," Jeff replied.

"Next week though."

"You bet."

Shortstack thanked me for the heads-up, then left. I guessed I had a five-minute window until Shortstack found out his car hadn't been broken into and returned in a huff.

I asked Jeff, "Do you want to play?"

"Why not?" he said. "Are you any good?"

I'd played racquetball a handful of times when I was younger, and I picked it up faster than most. I knew squash had basically the same rules except that, unlike racquetball, the ceiling was out of bounds. "Not really. I've only been playing a month now."

"No worries."

"Can we warm up?"

We batted the ball back and forth against the wall. Jeff Urlock was fifty-one, he worked at a commercial real estate firm downtown, and he'd been playing squash for the past seven years.

"What about you?" Jeff asked. "What do you do for work?"

"I'm a homicide detective." I watched him closely to see if he'd flinch. He didn't.

"Oh, wow."

Our rally ended, and I picked up the ball. Before hitting it, I said, "I'm working the Brooke Wexley case right now."

"Tragic."

"Did you know her?"

"Her or her father?"

I didn't want to push it. "Either of them."

"I met Nick a few years back at a fundraiser. His daughter might have been there, but I don't remember meeting her." He nodded at the ball in my hand. "Let's go."

Jeff was either a gifted liar or he was telling the truth. I wouldn't know for certain unless I sat across from him in an interrogation room for a couple hours, but my gut told me that Jeff wasn't Burner Phone.

Back to square one.

We volleyed for another minute, and then the door opened. It was Shortstack. He was smiling and said, "Not my car!"

I shook hands with both guys and exited the court. As I

walked past the final squash court, I noticed the two old-timers had left, and two other men had taken their place.

The men were lined up for service and both had their backs to me. One man was bald, and the other man had a mane of gray hair. Halfway during their point, the gray-haired man turned around to play the ball off the back wall.

He didn't have glasses underneath his goggles, but he had been wearing glasses when I'd seen him two days earlier at Nicholas Wexley's press conference.

It was Wexley's business partner: Steven Eglund.

27

Apple had come out with the iPad in 2010, and I'd seen a sign at the front desk that you could check one out. I slipped Greg another couple twenties, and he handed me one of the sleek tablets.

Several plush chairs were situated opposite the squash courts, and I plopped into one. Keeping an eye on Steven Eglund—who appeared to be a seasoned squash player—I typed his name into the Google search bar and read up on the fifty-two-year-old billionaire.

Eglund was born in South Carolina in 1959 to middle-class parents. He graduated third in his class in high school and received a partial academic scholarship to the University of Pennsylvania. He pledged Alpha Tau Omega his freshman year, which is where he met fellow pledge Nicholas Wexley.

After graduating, Eglund got a job at a brokerage firm in Philly, and a year later he married his college sweetheart. Nicholas Wexley, who was working at a competing firm, was best man at his wedding. The couple gave birth to their son, Julian, eighteen months later.

At the age of twenty-seven, Eglund and Wexley started a

boutique private equity firm called Wexlund Capital. Over the next decade, the small firm grew into one of the wealthiest hedge funds in the United States.

In 1998, Eglund's wife, Christy, filed for divorce. It was a highly publicized split, and photos of Eglund cheating with a much younger woman had flooded the media. In the end, Christy took half of Eglund's fortune to the tune of $1.3 billion.

Eglund remarried six years later to Robin Cathaway, a waitress he'd met at a diner on a trip back to his small hometown in South Carolina. Currently, Eglund was the 878th richest person in the world, with a net worth of $3.7 billion. (Nicholas Wexley was 384th.)

After reading about Eglund for another ten minutes, I set down the iPad.

Could he really be Burner Phone?

A generous amount of circumstantial evidence suggested he was.

Eglund had a history of cheating with younger women. He'd obviously known Brooke. He was from South Carolina, which fit with his use of the eggplant emoji as "guinea squash." He wore glasses. There was no mention of his being a grandpa, but his son would have been twenty-eight by now, so it was more than likely. And perhaps the most telling: he was at the Racquet Club right this moment—smack-dab in the middle of the four-block radius where a vast majority of the phone calls and texts had pinged the cell towers.

Of course, there was a chance this was a big crazy coincidence. I mean, would this guy really sleep with his best friend's daughter?

I'd know soon enough.

I played *Tetris* on the iPad for the next thirty minutes, then finally the door to court 5 opened, and Eglund walked out. He placed his racket into his sports bag, then pulled out a glasses case and traded his sports goggles for designer wire-frames. His mane of gray hair was dripping with sweat, and his skin was shiny.

I walked past him and was pulling off my clothes in the locker room when he walked in and went to a locker one row away. Eglund took off his clothes and made his way to the shower.

I considered slipping into his shower and confronting him there, but that felt a little too *Shawshank Redemption*. I stepped into the stall opposite him and was getting ready to scrub with the most amazing-smelling coconut body wash, when Eglund exited the shower.

He wasn't showering, he was *rinsing*, which means he was headed for either the hot tub, the steam room, or the sauna.

I counted to thirty, wrapped myself in a towel, and then walked to the hot tub. There were two naked men sitting on the edge with just their legs in the water. I peered through the foggy glass of the steam room. A solitary man sat in the back corner, but it wasn't Eglund. By process of elimination, he was in the sauna.

I pulled the wooden door open and stepped inside. Eglund sat on the bottom ledge of the small room, a towel wrapped around his waist. He was wiping the sweat from his brow with a white washcloth.

He nodded at me.

"How's it going?" I asked.

"Good, good," he muttered, then took a deep inhale of the 165-degree air.

Tucked into the wall on the opposite side was the rock pit, with a water spigot and a ladle underneath.

"Do you mind if I add some water?" I asked.

"Go right ahead. The hotter, the better."

There was a loud hiss as I dumped a ladle of water over the rocks.

I found a spot a few feet away from Eglund. His glasses were off and sitting on the bench next to him. His eyes were closed.

"You were sleeping with Brooke Wexley," I said.

Eglund's eyes shot open, and he turned toward me. He grabbed for his glasses and slipped them on. "What did you just say?"

"You heard me."

"Who are you?"

"Just a concerned citizen."

"You're out of your mind."

"You bought Brooke a burner phone in the middle of September so you could communicate with her without her father knowing."

"I'm getting security."

I stood and blocked the door.

Eglund was fifty-two and starting to sag around the middle. Going through me wasn't an option. But he could yell. The sauna was airtight, but I doubted it was soundproof. I waited for him to scream, but he didn't.

"Did you kill her?" I asked.

"Who? *Brooke?* Of course not!"

"But you were sleeping with her."

"Never! She was like a daughter to me." He said it defiantly, and it was convincing.

Had I gotten this wrong?

"You're not even a member here, are you?" He stood. "Now get out of my way."

I didn't move.

"Seriously, if you don't move right now, I'm going to start shouting."

I punched him in the solar plexus, my hand sinking into the flesh above his soft stomach. The breath was knocked out of him, and he fell to his knees. I grabbed the wash-cloth that he'd been using to wipe his face and stuck it in his mouth.

"I'm going to ask you questions, and you are going to answer them. Nod for yes. Shake your head for no."

He stared up at me, wheezing against the towel in his mouth.

"Do you understand?"

He nodded.

"Did you kill Brooke Wexley?"

He whipped his head back and forth.

"Were you sleeping with Brooke Wexley?"

Again, he whipped his head back and forth.

I sighed. I was in too deep. If I couldn't get him to admit that he was Burner Phone, then I was going to jail.

"I didn't want to have to do this." I grabbed his arm and yanked him toward the far end of the sauna. He fought against me, but he was a rabbit fighting off a python. I pinned his body to the back wall and grabbed his right hand. I pulled it down toward the sizzling rocks.

"Were you sleeping with Brooke Wexley?"

"Nnnooooo!" he mumbled through the towel.

I pressed his hand down on the eight-hundred-degree rocks.

He screamed.

I lifted his hand up and turned to him. Our faces were six inches apart. His eyes were closed, and he was whimpering.

"Open your eyes!"

He did.

"If you don't tell me the truth, the next thing to touch those rocks will be your dick."

His eyes screamed open.

"Were you sleeping with Brooke Wexley?"

Tears welled in his eyes.

He nodded.

I pulled the washcloth out of his mouth. "How long were you sleeping with her?"

He gritted his teeth against the third-degree burn on his hand. "We fooled around a few times, but no sex."

I highlighted this in bright yellow, then asked, "When did it start?"

"The second week of September. I bumped into Brooke at a smoothie place."

"Which one?"

"Smoothie King. The one on Twenty-Fourth."

There was a Smoothie King in the University of Pennsylvania commons and another one four blocks away. Why go to the one so far away from her dorm? Was she at the location on Twenty-Fourth by circumstance? Or was it intentional?

Eglund was a creature of habit, and I wouldn't be surprised if he visited that particular Smoothie King daily. I'm sure he had a punch card in his wallet that could attest to this.

"What happened at Smoothie King?"

"Can I go run this under cold water?" He held his right hand gingerly in his left hand. "It's killing me."

I ignored him. "What happened at Smoothie King?"

"It's not what you think. I've known Brooke her entire life. I watched her grow up. I had no intention of making a pass at her." He grimaced, the pain in his hand must have been unbearable. "I hadn't seen her in over a year, and we just talked about her school, her plans for the future. Then she asked if I could help her get an internship next summer. She didn't want help from her dad. She didn't want him to know. I told her sure. But Nick is super protective, at least with his girls. He reads their text messages. Sees who they call. I told her to set up an anonymous email, and we could communicate that way." He shook his head. "But then she had me follow her to her car, and she handed me this cheapo burner phone."

Interesting—*Brooke* had been the one to buy the phones. Had she been the aggressor?

"Why did she say she had the burner phone?" I asked.

"She said she had a couple phones she used—so her dad couldn't track her every movement. I thought it was strange, but I took the phone. She said it was paid up through the year and that she'd text me on it the next day."

And she had.

I thought back to the text thread. How it all started.

BROOKE: Hey!

EGLUND: Hey, Brooke. It was nice bumping into you.

BROOKE: Sure was. You want to meet up?

There had been a two-minute break where Eglund must have realized that this wasn't about an internship. Maybe he flipped open his moral compass, saw it was broken, then texted back: "Okay. Where?"

BROOKE: Same place. In an hour.

EGLUND: I'll be there.

I didn't want Eglund to know I had access to their texts. I wanted to see if he'd tell the truth.

"Did she text you?" I asked.

"Yeah, the next day. She asked to meet up."

"And you did?"

"Yeah, in the Smoothie King parking lot. She told me to

jump in her car. She said she wanted to show me something.
She drove to this place in the woods and parked."

Wow, just like high school.

"Who made the first move?"

"I did."

I'm sure Brooke was in full Siren mode by this point, but
her intentions would have been too obvious if she made the
first move.

"How did it progress from there?"

"She'd text me every so often, and we'd meet."

"Where did you guys go?"

I'm not sure if the pain in his hand was getting to him,
but he paused a moment. Finally, he said, "At first we'd just
mess around in her car, but then we started going to different
hotels."

"You'd pay for the hotel and then sneak her up?"

"Yeah."

I didn't buy this. He'd already been caught cheating on one
wife, and it had cost him $1.3 billion. He'd be more careful the
second time around.

"Where were you the night that Brooke was killed?"

"I was at home . . . with my wife."

"You were there all night?"

"Yeah, we'd just started watching this new show on HBO.
Game of Thrones. It's in their On Demand catalog. We watched
like six episodes."

"Game of what?"

"*Thrones*. It's medieval fantasy stuff."

I'd never heard of it.

I asked, "When's the last time you saw Brooke?"

"October twelfth."

This fit with the text thread. There had been a few follow-up texts from Eglund after that date, but Brooke hadn't responded to any of them.

And maybe that was his motive.

The jilted lover.

"What did you guys do on October twelfth?"

"We went to our spot in the woods. She brought drugs. Ecstasy. I'd never tried it before. I don't remember much after that. Woke up in the back seat, feeling like shit."

I'm guessing that it wasn't Ecstasy. It was most likely the GHB they'd found in Brooke's bedroom.

Anyhow, I knew the general area of the woods, but I wanted to see what he said. "Where is this spot?"

"Not too far. Twenty minutes away."

Eglund was lying. On October 12, they weren't in the woods twenty minutes away. At least, not according to the GPS data from Brooke's burner phone.

On the twelfth, they were an hour and a half from the city.

In the Pocono Mountains.

28

While I filled up the gas tank of my graffitied Range Rover, I called Gleason.

After the second ring, he answered.

"How'd it go today?" I asked.

"The Organized Crime guys spent a few hours briefing us on the Capetta and Benussi organizations. Both are pretty active."

"Do they think one of them murdered the Queen?"

"I'm not sure. Seemed like they were holding out on some info. They've been investigating both families for several decades, and they have a handful of guys from each organization under surveillance. They've been trying to build a RICO case against Frank the Tank—the head of the Capetta family—for the past seven years."

"Is OC taking over the Numbers case?"

"Not officially, but there's not a whole lot that we can do until they report back."

"Were they able to identify the bodies at Trinity yet?"

"They were. At least two of them. They had dental records on file. Two brothers, Maurice and Lenny Jackson. They'd been running numbers for the Queen for three or four years. Then they went missing in seventy-three. One of the other bodies is presumed to be a guy by the name of Maxwell Yates, the other runner that went missing."

"What about the fourth body?"

"No positive ID, but they were able to run his DNA and it's coming back as mostly Eastern European."

"So, he's White?"

"Correct."

"That's odd." The other three were Black, he was White. The other three were stabbed, he was shot. The other three had numbers carved into their foreheads, he did not.

Where did John Doe fit into the picture?

Gleason said, "They were finally able to identify the two Boston vics."

"Let me guess: they were also number runners?"

"They were. After the positive ID on the Queen's missing runners, they narrowed the pool in Boston. Two number runners went missing in 1976. Jessie Dalwood and Clyde Landis."

"Who did they run for?"

"A small-time banker named Carter Von."

"Any connection to the Queen?"

"None on paper."

"Is he still around?"

"No, he died in 2007."

"Anything suspicious about his death?"

"Nope. Complications from diabetes. He was eighty-eight."

I'd been so distracted with Lacy's appointments and my hunt for Burner Phone that I hadn't checked the news. "What about the media?"

"There are ten news trucks in the federal building parking lot right now. The story is everywhere. Just turn on any radio news channel."

"Will do."

We chatted for another minute and then I dropped the f-bomb.

"A *favor?*" he repeated.

"Yeah."

"How big a favor are we talking here?"

"Bigger than asking you to help me move a refrigerator. Smaller than asking you to pick me up at the airport."

He was silent for a moment. "Proceed."

"Do you have anyone who could do a quick property scan for me?" I could have asked Gallow, but I didn't want to put him in an awkward position. What I planned to do was in a gray area legally. And when I say gray, I mean *midnight* gray.

"I might. Is this for the Wexley case?"

"The less you know, the better."

"Oh, it's going to be like that." He paused for a half second. "Yeah, I got a guy."

"Is it another Fed?"

"The less you know, the better."

"Gotcha."

"What's the location?"

"Let's do a property search for a five-mile radius around Lake Harmony and look for any red flags—anything owned by a multinational or something registered out of the Caymans or anywhere else suspicious. Nothing in town or immediately surrounding the lake."

He had me repeat the information, and I could hear him scribbling it down somewhere. When he was done, he said, "He doesn't work for free."

"Cover me, and I'll get you back double."

"I like the sound of that."

"The next two Pat's are on me if you can get back to me within the hour."

"I'll see what I can do."

We ended the call, and I replaced the nozzle on the pump. Ten minutes later, I merged onto the highway and headed north toward the Pocono mountains.

After finishing up my interrogation with Steven Eglund, I'd instructed him to soak his hand in cold water, then go to the CVS to buy gauze, then call his lawyer and come clean about his affair. As for his guilt or innocence, I couldn't yet make a judgment call. That Brooke had broken off their rendezvous didn't seem like enough of a motive.

There was more to the story.

≈

The drive to Lake Harmony was over an hour and a half. Half-way there, I turned on the news. Some of the broader details of the Numbers investigation had leaked, and for the most part, they'd gotten the big picture correct: someone was killing people and carving numbers into their foreheads, and it appeared to be tied to the old Numbers lottery.

My name didn't come up, which I was both thankful and a tad bitter about. None of the specific numbers were mentioned or that the numbers were tied to *The E.K. Dream Book*, which meant that no one from the task force had leaked anything to a reporter. There was a sound bite from Agent Joyce about how the FBI was cooperating with several different agencies and that the serial killer would soon be brought to justice.

When I entered the densely forested mountains, the radio signal waned, then devolved to static.

Thankfully, I still had a phone signal, and ten minutes later

Gleason called back. "Okay, so there are five hundred and thirteen properties in a five-mile radius of Lake Harmony. Four hundred and six of those are outside your parameters—meaning they're either in town or on the lake. Of the remaining properties, forty-two are owned by reputable rental agencies."

"So, that leaves sixty-five properties."

"Wow," he said, impressed by my number crunching. "I didn't know I was dealing with Rain Man here."

"You should see me do long division."

He chuckled, then continued, "My guy ran those sixty-five properties through a quick background check and three of them raised red flags. All cabins, all secluded."

"Nice work. Can you text me the addresses?"

"Yes, but I'm not finished."

"My apologies."

"I think we can narrow it down to one property owned by a corporation called Delair LLC."

"Isn't there a Delair Bridge somewhere just outside Philly?"

"There is. But get this, the LLC is registered in Singapore."

He texted me the address and I said, "I owe you big."

"How about Pat's for life?"

"How about Pat's for October?"

"Deal. I'm driving there now. I'll keep my receipt."

≈

I parked on the side of the road a hundred yards from the property. Walking back toward the cabin, I glanced over both shoulders. There hadn't been another car on the road for twenty minutes, and the closest house was a half mile away.

I eclipsed the last of the sprawling evergreens, and the property came into view. It would be a gross understatement to call it a cabin. It was a beautiful mountain house befitting a multi-billionaire the likes of Steven Eglund. The house was two stories with a small balcony accessed by sliding glass doors. Several four-foot-high white stakes girdled the asphalt driveway, which I guessed helped to maneuver a car when the winter snow arrived.

I wasn't sure what my intentions were, but I'd brought a screwdriver just in case I had to pry off a window or, you know, fight off a bear.

I walked up the steps to the front door and stopped.

"Interesting development," I said, taking in the digital keypad above the door handle.

It should have only taken me two seconds, but it took me closer to four to have the epiphany. I ran back to the car and grabbed the printout from Brooke's burner phone. I found the page with the two messages she'd sent herself and then sprinted back to the cabin.

The first number sequence Brooke had sent herself was 07835.

I tapped in the numbers.

The moment I tapped in the final digit, there was a soft click. *Well done, Gleason.*

I pulled the door open and stepped inside. "So, this is where you were four days before you died," I said to the high ceilings and impressively designed interior. "But what did you come up here for?"

I peered at the eight-digit code Brooke had sent herself three days after the first code. "And what did you open?"

I looked around for any video cameras, but if there were any, they were well camouflaged.

Next, I walked behind a white leather sofa and into the kitchen. The counters were marble, and the refrigerator was paneled in the same dark wood as the cabinets. I pulled it open.

There wasn't much: condiments, a jar of pickles, an unopened block of mild cheddar.

The second floor was covered in thick beige carpet, and there were two bedrooms. I started in the larger one. It didn't take me long to navigate to a large walk-in closet and see the three-foot-tall standing safe in the back corner.

I squatted and tapped in the eight-digit code.

It didn't work.

I tried it again making sure I put in each number correctly. 2-7-1-8-6-4-9-1.

Again, no luck.

There were several different explanations, but I thought the most likely was the existence of a second safe.

≈

I searched the house for another hour, but I came up empty. I was making a third sweep when I ran my hand over a panel in the guest room walk-in closet. It slid to the right, exposing a hidden door.

Voila!

I pushed the door inward, revealing a staircase. I walked down thirteen steps, then flipped a light switch, illuminating an impressive five-hundred-square-foot bunker.

Enough provisions were stacked against the far wall to last five years. Enormous bags of rice, beans, and other nonperishables. A pallet of MREs. Six enormous tanks filled with water. The back wall was loaded with two shotguns and an AR-15 assault rifle.

Eglund was a doomsday prepper!

I walked around the bunker, rifling through gas masks, candles, tanks of gasoline, an elliptical bike, and a shortwave radio. An old submarine door hatch was welded into the concrete, and I turned the crank. The door opened with a puff of dust. An escape tunnel led away from the bunker, and I guessed it led to another hatch somewhere in the forest.

Eglund must have spent a fortune having this place built.

A three-foot safe was tucked in the back corner. The safe was electronic, and I typed in the eight-digit code from memory.

After a soft whir, it opened.

Inside was a black Dopp kit—a toiletry bag men use for traveling—sitting on top of two thick folders. I pulled out the Dopp kit and unzipped it. There was a few hundred thousand in cash, a small felt baggie filled with diamonds, a stack of gold coins, and a fake passport in the name of Charlie Rondale.

This was what we in the business call a "bugout bag." If shit hit the fan, Steven Eglund could grab the bag, move to Mexico, and live out his life as Charlie Rondale. He might not have his billions at his disposal, but he'd have enough to survive.

Better than the death penalty, I suppose.

I set down the Dopp kit, then grabbed the top manila folder. It was a half inch thick, and I flipped it open. It was full of photographs of his current wife, Robin. The photographs seemed benign: her leaving a shopping center, filling up her car with gas, walking the dog, leaving a yoga studio. Then there were countless typed reports, presumably from a private investigator who Eglund had paid to follow his wife. He wasn't taking any chances getting burned a second time.

I had a feeling I knew what was in the second folder, and I had an even better feeling that its contents were what Brooke was after.

The second was thicker than the first. I flipped it open. The top sheet was a picture of Nicholas Wexley getting out of his car.

Eglund was also having his business partner followed.

I flipped to the second sheet of paper. It was blank. In fact, the next twenty-seven pages were blank.

I was guessing that Brooke found the second safe and had taken the file on her father. Then she'd replaced those pages with blank printer paper. She'd left the top photo in place so that if Eglund glanced at the file he'd assume that nothing had been disturbed.

"Brooke, you clever girl."

There was no doubt in my mind that whatever was contained in those pages had gotten Brooke Wexley killed.

29

Gleason pulled his blue sedan in front of my condo building, then rolled down the window. Today the special agent was
dressed smartly in a purple dress shirt under a blue sport coat.
He lifted a pair of Ray-Bans up onto what appeared to be a fresh
haircut and said, "If I get fired for this, I want two hundred
thousand dollars."

"Okay," I said with a shrug.

"I'm serious."

"I am too."

"Serious, serious."

I said, "Cross my heart and hope to die, stick a needle in
your eye."

"It's *my* eye."

"Exactly."

He let out a frustrated grunt, then said, "Get in."

I plopped into the passenger seat, then asked, "How do we
even know he's going to be there?"

"There's a barbershop across the street from the restaurant.
I went there yesterday after we talked. Apparently, the guy is at
his restaurant every day at lunch."

The guy in question was Francis "Frank the Tank" Capetta, the current boss of the largest Mafia organization in Philadelphia. He'd been promoted to head of the Capetta crime family in 1988 when his father was arrested on a slew of racketeering charges and sentenced to twenty-five years in jail.

The FBI had been building a case against Frank for the past decade, but after two prolonged trials, including one for second-degree murder, he'd kept the orange jumpsuit at bay.

The drive to South Philly took fifteen minutes, which Gleason used to gripe about the hotel the FBI had put him up in. Evidently, the lack of sourdough toast at the continental breakfast was a capital offense.

As we neared the restaurant, Gleason pointed out the barbershop he'd visited the previous day, Tyrone's, which had the archetypal rotating red, white, and blue pole out front.

"Have you ever been to a Black barbershop?" Gleason asked.

"I haven't."

"Let me guess: you go to a fancy salon and pay a hundred bucks every three weeks."

"I'll have you know I get my hair cut every two months, and I go to Chet, a very gay man, who lives in my building and cuts hair in his kitchen."

Gleason scoffed. "Just when I think I have you pegged."

We found a parking spot twenty yards from Frank Capetta's restaurant. Villa di Parma was narrow and glass-fronted, squashed between a dry cleaner and a butcher shop.

We stepped inside the restaurant and were greeted by the heavy red-sauce aroma of Italian cooking. A long bar ran along the room's left side, and two of its nine stools were occupied. One woman wearing business casual had a half-empty martini in front of her and a full one just inches behind it. An empty bowl was pushed off to her left with the remnants of what I guessed was eggplant Parmesan, and she clicked away on the laptop in front of her. Most likely, a working lunch that she'd bill to a client.

Five stools from her was a man in jeans and a windbreaker. He had a notebook in front of him and was holding a phone to his ear. He fit the decor perfectly—most likely, a bookie taking bets.

Across from the bar were eight small tables, each with a white tablecloth. A family of four filled one of them—one kid in a booster seat, the other in a highchair, both with small bowls of spaghetti in front of them—then there was a lone man sitting at the table near the back wall.

Strategically, it was the best seat in the house. He had his back to the wall, with a clear view of the only entrance and the wide glass front window.

This was my first look at Francis "Frank the Tank" Capetta. A more fitting nickname would be "Frank the Plank." He was skinny, like someone had put a robust Italian man into a trash compactor. At sixty-three, he still had a full head of gray-streaked black hair, which by some rule of Mafioso law, was slicked back and shiny. Olive skin wrapped around sharp cheekbones. His dark brows arched high as Gleason and I approached his table.

"What can I do for you gentlemen?" he asked, setting his pencil down on the *Philadelphia Inquirer* in front of him.

He didn't inquire if we were Feds, cops, or otherwise. I'm sure he had us pegged the moment we stepped inside the place.

"We just want to have a quick chat," I said.

"Regarding?"

"Loretta Carroll."

"Damn shame." He made the sign of the cross. "But I already had a nice talk with some folks about that just yesterday."

"Well, we need just a few more minutes."

"I'm very busy."

I glanced at the half-finished puzzle he was working on in the newspaper. "Eleven down is *King Henry the Fourteenth*, thirty-one across is *Gwen Stefani*, and forty-four down is *Ontario*."

He glared at me, looked down at the paper, glared back up at me. "This is a Sudoku."

I shrugged.

I supposed he found this amusing or he was curious just how stupid I really was. Either way, he turned the paper over and motioned for us to take seats across from him. He asked if we cared for anything to drink. Club soda with a lime for me and a Dr Pepper for Gleason. Capetta called our drinks out to the bartender, then turned his attention to us.

"I assume you have an alibi for the night the Queen was killed," Gleason said.

"That I do," Capetta replied. "I was in Atlantic City. At the craps table pretty much all night. Did pretty well too. Came up about forty-seven hundred."

If there was one place that had a lot of surveillance, it was casinos. Of course, we would verify this, but a seasoned criminal like Capetta wouldn't lie about something that was so easily checked. Which meant that Capetta personally didn't commit the murders. But as the current boss, he could easily have ordered the hit by one of his lieutenants or soldiers, so he wasn't out of the woods yet.

"Is it true there was a beef between you and the Queen?" I asked.

The bartender dropped our drinks off, setting a fresh iced tea in front of Capetta. He pulled four packets of Sweet'n Low from the condiment holder and piled a small mountain of the artificial sweetener atop the floating ice. He swirled the tea with his straw. "We had a few disputes a long time ago, but there's been no bad blood for the past several decades."

"But there was a feud at one point," Gleason said. "In the early seventies?"

"I suppose."

I said, "The Queen suspected that you had abducted and killed three of her runners in 1973."

"That wasn't us."

I glared at him.

"I was twenty-four and still working my way up," Capetta said. "Trust me, if anyone in our organization had snatched three of the Queen's runners, I would have been involved."

By "involved," I guessed he meant *pulled the trigger.*

"Why'd she think it was you guys?" Gleason asked.

"The Pennsylvania lottery came out the year before, and all of us lost a good chunk of our revenue overnight. Everyone was looking to expand their foothold."

"So, that's when you started sending your runners up north into the Queen's territory," I said.

He tilted his head slightly but didn't answer.

"Then Jumpy killed Ugly Marky and you retaliated, killing three of the Queen's number runners."

Capetta sat up two inches. "What are you talking about?"

Gleason recounted what Jumpy had told us about paying a visit to one of their lieutenants.

"Jumpy killed Ugly Marky?" Capetta pushed back in his seat. "We thought that was Tall Paul."

"Tall Paul?" I asked.

"The Benussi family enforcer."

"What happened to Tall Paul?"

Capetta didn't answer, but from the smirk buried in his cheek, I guessed Paul became fish bait.

Gleason said, "So, you have no reason these days to go after the Queen?"

"No."

"Know anyone who does?"

"No single person comes to mind."

Gleason and I traded a quick glance. It appeared Frank Capetta was not involved in the Queen's murder, but that had only been half the reason for our visit.

"The person that murdered the Queen," I said, "they might come after you next."

Capetta picked up his pencil and turned the eraser toward me. "What exactly do you mean by that?"

I was tempted to tell him about how *Mafia* had been one of the clues left by the killer, but that might jeopardize the case.

"Just watch your back," Gleason preempted me.

"I've been watching my back for my entire life." His eyes darted over my shoulder, and he craned his neck to the side. "Speaking of which, I've seen the same car drive by three times since you guys got here."

"What kind of car?" Gleason asked.

"White Explorer, scratch on the back left bumper."

This guy was observant. No wonder he was still alive.

Capetta asked, "Is he with you?"

"Not officially," I said, pushing up to my feet. "I'll be right back."

≈

The white Explorer was parked half a block from the restaurant. I walked nonchalantly toward the car, then knocked on the window.

Hufflepuff stared at me vacantly without moving.

I said, "I will break this window if I have to."

The window slid down halfway.

"What are you doing here?" I asked.

He feigned ignorance, leaning back a few inches from the window. "I'm, uh, just, uh, about to go get my haircut, at, uh, Tyrone's."

I swallowed a laugh. We both knew he was following us. Had Agent Joyce sent him or was he here of his own accord? I was tempted to ask, but instead, I said, "Well, don't let me stop you. Your hair definitely needs work."

"Uh, okay," he stammered.

The window went up, and he exited the car. I escorted him across the street to the barbershop. I pulled the door open for him and snuck a quick peek inside. It was a slow day, and there were no customers. Three barbers, each a different shade of brown, sat in chairs and chatted.

As Kip walked past me, I noticed his fingers fidgeting.

I walked back to Villa di Parma and joined Gleason. Capetta was absent, and I asked, "Where'd he go?"

"He went in the kitchen, says he wants us to sample a new dish they're working on." He paused for a moment and then asked, "Did you find out who was in the car?"

I told him.

"Why would Hufflepuff be tailing us? You think Joyce put him up to it?"

"Joyce seems like a straight shooter. I think if he knew we were here, we would have already gotten an ass-chewing."

He agreed, then asked, "Is Puff still there?"

Puff!

I fought back a grin. "No, he's currently getting his hair cut at Tyrone's."

"What?" he laughed. "That White boy is going in there?"

I nodded. "How would you feel about giving your guy Tyrone a quick text?"

"What are you thinking?"

I told him.

"You are evil," he said, his laugh doubling, then tripling. He pulled out his phone and sent my request.

Less than a minute later, Capetta returned and set a deliciously aromatic plate in the center of the table and said, "Clams baked and then stuffed with peppers, onions, mushrooms, and bacon." He slid a small saucer across the table. "We're thinking of calling it Clams Vegas. Let me know what you think."

As Capetta watched, Gleason and I dug in. The dish was excellent. I gave it a 9.2 out of 10. Gleason was even more impressed and gave it a 12.

After a busboy came by and cleaned up the dishes, I wiped my face with a napkin and looked up at Capetta. "What can you tell me about soldiers in your organization?"

"Soldiers are entry-level guys."

"That's it?"

"You want to know more, google it."

"Fair enough."

Gleason asked, "Were there any soldiers in your organization in 1973 that might have had a beef with Queen Loretta?"

"Now are we talking soldiers or soldier?"

"What do you mean?" I asked.

"There were plenty of soldiers back then. Hell, I was one of them. But there was only one *soldier*. My cousin Dominic 'the Soldier' DeSipio."

"That's what he went by?"

"Well, he mostly called himself that. It never really caught on."

Gleason did the math. "I'm guessing that he fought in Nam?"

He nodded. "Got drafted in sixty-seven. Got out in sixty-nine after taking a bunch of shrapnel in his right leg."

"You said he was your cousin."

"Yeah, my aunt Emilia's kid."

"Where's he now?" I asked.

He looked at us expectantly, as if we should have already pieced together his response. "Dominic was killed in 1973."

Gleason and I traded a look.

"How?" I asked.

"Two in the chest. At least, that's what I heard."

"What do you mean? You never saw the body at the funeral?" It was traditional for Italian Catholic families to have open caskets at the funeral. Mourners touched the body as they passed, and many even kissed the deceased.

"Closed casket."

"That's strange." I imagine if the deceased took a full round in the face, you might want to keep the lid shut, but why if the victim took two in the chest?

"I agree." Capetta nodded solemnly.

"Do you know who shot him?" Gleason asked.

"We figured Tall Paul for that one as well. He never did cop to it, even after a little, how do you say—"

"Persuasion," Gleason interrupted.

Capetta fought a grin.

"Someone had to see Dominic's body," I said. "Who found him?"

"My father."

Angelo Capetta, the aforementioned don of the Capetta family for forty years.

"And your father never mentioned anything strange about the body? Maybe something on Dominic's forehead?"

"Forehead?" Frank touched his forehead similarly to when he'd done the sign of the cross. "Not that I can remember."

"Where is your father now?"

"He's been at St. Michael's Nursing Home for the last four years."

"Do you think he'll talk to us?"

"You can try. But his brain is mush. The last time I was there, he thought I was his brother Carlito."

"Alzheimer's?"

"Dementia."

Another dead end.

Gleason glanced at me as if to say, "You ready to go?" but I had one more question. I asked, "Do you still take Numbers bets?"

"You think I'm stupid?" Frank scoffed. "The FBI has been trying to put me away for the last fifteen years. You think I'm going to tell two Feds that I'm running numbers?"

I'm not sure why, but I said, "The Queen was still taking numbers."

"I don't doubt it," he said, grinning. "You play with her?"

"Actually, I did."

He must have noticed the slight dip in my shoulders and said, "She died before you could collect." It wasn't a question. He leaned forward. "Now, this is in no way an admission that I am or have ever been associated with the Numbers racket, but it would be my honor to pay the Queen's debt."

I looked at Gleason to see how he reacted. *Was this a thing?* He shrugged.

Frank pulled a gold money clip out of his pocket. "I always respected her. She held her own in a man's world." I half expected him to mention her race, but he didn't. Maybe it didn't matter to him. Maybe he didn't care if she was Black, pink, or blue.

He respected power. And the Queen had it. And she'd wielded it expertly.

"How much did she owe you?" he asked.

"A hundred and twenty."

He began peeling off twenties, when I put my hand up and stopped him.

"What?" he asked.

"Is there any way I could get that paid in *pasta*?"

30

"Are you catering an event that you didn't tell me about?" Gleason asked, as I strategically placed the four large trays of pasta in the footwell of the back seat.

"Just trust me," I said, hopping into the passenger seat. I buckled up, then added, "I think we should still go see the old man at Shady Acres."

"One, it's called St. Michael's. And two, you heard what Capetta said. His old man doesn't remember anything."

"What if he's faking?"

"Faking?"

"Sure. Why not? I'll bet it helped get him out of prison earlier." I didn't know if this was true, but I didn't want to tell Gleason my actual plan. He'd think I was crazy. "Don't you think it's strange that DeSipio had a closed casket funeral? I suspect it's because there were numbers carved into Dominic's head. Old Man Dementia might be our only link."

He paused a beat to think. "Just to make sure we're on the same page, you want to drive to a nursing home to question a ninety-year-old man with dementia about a body he might have found forty years ago."

"Correct."

"I'm upping it to three hundred thousand dollars because I am three hundred thousand percent going to get fired from the bureau after this."

"Deal."

"Again, I'm not kidding."

"Again, neither am I."

He glared at me for a second. "How much money do you have?"

"Enough."

He made me shake on it, then swear on Michael Jackson's grave.

"What about Puff?" he asked, looking over his shoulder. "There's no way he doesn't rat us out to Joyce when we pull into the nursing home."

Gleason was right. Whether Kip was tailing us on his own or on Joyce's orders, the moment we pulled into St. Michael's, he'd know what we were up to.

"You let me take care of Puff," I assured him.

He rolled his eyes, then cranked the wheel, pulling away from the curb. I pointed fifty yards ahead. "Pull even with the white Explorer."

He came even with Kip's car, ostensibly blocking traffic, though there were no cars behind us. I grabbed one tray of pasta from the back seat and stepped out.

Kip's window was still up, though I could make out his profile behind the tinted windows. Holding the tray with one hand, I knocked on the window. It didn't go down. I knocked again. "I have a peace offering."

The window slid down three inches, then five, then ten.

If I hadn't been holding an eight-pound tray of linguine Alfredo, I would have thrown my hands up in surprise.

I'd asked Gleason to see if his barber could add a little pizazz to Hufflepuff's trim, but it appeared Tyrone had gone overboard.

"Don't say anything," Kip said through clenched teeth.

From my time playing basketball in high school and college, I was familiar with the lingo when it came to Black men's haircuts. Tyrone had given Hufflepuff what the brothers called a "hi-lo fade with a half-moon part."

Kip's curly locks were no more, shaved down nearly to the skin on the sides. The top was maybe a half inch, perfectly squared with a razor. Then there was a curved line that had been razored into his part.

It gets worse.

On the back of Kip's head—and perhaps taking my directive a bit too literally—Tyrone had used the clippers to etch *pizazz* into his hair.

"It, uh, suits you," I said.

He ran his hands over his hair, or lack thereof, and glanced in the rearview mirror. "You think?"

"Absolutely."

Tyrone must not have shown him the back of his head. Kip had no clue that it said "PIZAZZ" surrounded by three stars and a lightning bolt.

Holding back laughter, I said, "Here, I have something for you." I handed the tray of pasta to him. "It's from Frank Capetta. He sends his regards and says he knows a guy who can help fix that dent in your bumper."

"Sure, he did," Kip said, half sneering. He pulled the foil back on the pasta. "Is this Alfredo? You know I can't eat dairy."

He'd mentioned this once while playing basketball. I'd brought him a chocolate milkshake the next five Sundays in a row. "My mistake," I said. "I thought that was spaghetti."

I pulled another tray out from the back of the car and slid

it through to Kip. He pulled back the foil, rising steam escaping over twelve servings of spaghetti and meatballs.

He inhaled through his nose. "That smells amazing."

The tray of Alfredo was on the passenger seat. "Pass me that one."

He did.

I pulled the foil back. For a brief moment, Kip must have thought I was going to pour the contents onto his lap. And I'd be lying if I said I hadn't thought about it.

"Relax," I said.

Then I dumped the entire contents on the windshield of the Explorer.

"What in the hell, Prescott?" Puff-Diddy spat.

He turned on his wipers, hoping they would cut through the thick Alfredo covering the windshield, but the wipers got caught in the pasta, and smeared the sauce back and forth, dragging noodles with every swipe. After six sweeps, the windshield was completely opaque.

"Loved your last album," I called to Kip, then jumped back into Gleason's car. "Hit it!"

≈

As we pushed through the front entrance of St. Michael's, I turned to Gleason and whispered, "Smells like a preschool."

He raised his eyebrows but didn't reply.

The woman behind the front desk greeted us warmly as we approached.

"We're here to see Angelo Capetta," I said.

"Oh, how lovely," the woman replied. "He doesn't get many visitors."

I was surprised that we didn't have to show ID, but simply

sign a form. Gleason signed ahead of me (Mark Glacky), and I
signed just below him (Ernest Worrell).

"How do you guys know Mr. Capetta?" the woman asked.

I said, "Pickleball."

Her eyebrows rose, but she didn't ask a follow-up question.
She told us we could find Angelo outside, painting, and she
directed us to the courtyard.

We walked into a sunny courtyard that was a fifty-yard oval.
Two wide benches basked in the shade of a large maple tree and
a line of easels were set up in the grass. Standing behind several
of the easels were eight wrinkly dinosaurs.

"That's him," Gleason said, pointing. "The third one in."

Angelo Capetta was clad in a yellow sweater and gray
pants. He was four-fifths bald, what remained atop his head a
silvery white. He was jowly, with enough skin hanging down
to outsource another full neck.

Gleason and I made our way behind the painters. Each
of them was painting the tree in front of them. A few of their
efforts were decent enough, and you could at least make out
what they were attempting.

Angelo's painting looked like a sick giraffe. Rembrandt, he
was not.

A nursing home worker hovered nearby, going from person
to person, giving pointers and offering encouraging words. She
smiled when we told her we were there to see Angelo. She said
that he was having one of his good days, which was encouraging.

"Hi there, Mr. Capetta," I said as Gleason and I sidled up
next to him.

Dabbing his paintbrush into the orange paint, he stopped
and turned, running his eyes over the two of us. To Gleason,
he asked, "Are you Carl Lewis?" He had a thick Italian accent,
and the words came out soaked in pomodoro.

Gleason was not amused. "No, I'm not."

He then turned his attention to me. "Who da fuck are you?"

"I'm a friend of Frank's," I lied.

"Frank?"

"Francis. Your son."

"Oh."

I waited for him to expand or to ask me another question. He didn't. He did say, "Paint the trees."

"Yep, you're painting the trees."

"We all paint the trees."

I wasn't sure what he was getting at, but Gleason whispered, "I think he wants us to paint with him."

Gleason and I grabbed two unused easels and set them up to the right of Angelo. The nursing home worker came over thirty seconds later with a palette of paint, several brushes, and a rinse bucket for each of us.

I mixed green, red, yellow, white, and black until I had a nice deep brown that resembled the tree trunk twenty yards in front of us.

"How'd you do that?" Gleason said, impressed. He'd taken off his sport coat and rolled up the sleeves of his purple button-down.

"My sister is a talented painter, and I've spent a few hundred hours watching Bob Ross paint trees." Bob had said it best: *There's nothing wrong with having a tree as a friend.*

After coaching Gleason, then painting grass and sky, I turned to Angelo and said, "Do you remember your nephew, Dominic?"

Angelo stopped painting and turned to me. He stared my way for a second, then turned his gaze to my painting. "Your sky is too blue."

To my right, Gleason whispered, "You still think he's faking?"

"Nope." This guy's brain was applesauce.

"I have an idea." I set my paintbrush on the easel. "We need to *Notebook* him."

"What the hell are you talking about?" Gleason asked, his tree now taking up the entirety of his canvas.

"You know, the movie—*The Notebook*."

He shook his head. The guy had no idea what I was talking about.

"How have you never seen *The Notebook*?"

"For the same reason you've never seen *Madea's Big Happy Family*."

"Fair point."

I spent the next few minutes explaining to him the plot of the movie and my idea. After I finished, Gleason said, "So, you think he's just going to snap out of it?"

"Worth a try."

"One problem."

"What's that?"

"You don't have a journal."

This was, of course, a crucial element of my scheme. "We can just list a bunch of stuff that happened in 1973, and maybe that will do it."

"So, what happened in 1973?"

I racked my brain. "Vietnam."

"*And?*"

"Vietnam protests."

He scoffed.

"Oh, and you can do better?"

"No, I can't, because at the time I was five years old."

"Give me your phone."

He pulled out his iPhone and handed it to me. I googled "1973" and found a list of major historical events.

When I turned back to Angelo, he had a fresh canvas, and he was painting a series of triangles.

"Nineteen seventy-three," I said.

Angelo turned and stared blankly at me, then returned to his triangles.

"The first POWs are released from Vietnam."

He didn't so much as flinch.

"Tricky Dick is president."

Nothing.

"*The Godfather* wins the Academy Award."

Nothing.

I lifted my chin up a couple inches, and in my best Don Corleone, I said, "*I'm gonna make him an offer he can't refuse.*"

Nothing.

"Secretariat wins the Triple Crown."

Nothing.

This wasn't working. Time to step it up. I reached out and grabbed Angelo's right hand.

"What are you doing?" Gleason whisper-shouted.

I glanced over my shoulder at Gleason. "This is what he does in the movie."

"Ryan Gosling grabs an old man's hand?"

"No, were you not listening earlier? James Garner plays the old man, and he lays in bed next to his wife and grabs her hand."

I turned back to Angelo, who was staring down at our hands. He didn't pull away. He actually looked quite content.

"Nineteen seventy-three," I said to him. "The Vietnam War is coming to an end. Richard Nixon is caught up in the Watergate scandal. *The Godfather* wins the Oscar for Best Picture. Secretariat wins the Triple Crown."

He blinked a few times.

"And your nephew Dominic DeSipio is murdered."

He leaned back a few inches. I ran my free hand across my forehead. "When you found the body, there were numbers, weren't there? Dominic had numbers on his forehead."

He let go of my hand. Then he threw his paintbrush at me. Then Angelo Capetta jumped on my back and started screaming.

≈

"Remember what you said," Gleason remarked from the seat next to me. "Three hundred thousand dollars."

"You're not going to get fired."

He leaned his head back against the wall outside of Agent Joyce's office. Poor Gleason; I don't think he'd been called into the principal's office many times in his life. Lucky me; I'd been called into the principal's office so many times in middle school that Principal Daly had added a bronze plaque with my name on it to the chair in her office.

The door in front of us opened, and Kip Hufley exited and stormed past us. His eyes were downcast. I'm not sure if he was still depressed from his horrible haircut or if he'd been reprimanded by Joyce. Regardless, if he were a dog, his tail would be covering his testicles.

Agent Joyce appeared in the doorway. "Both of you. Inside!"

Gleason and I stepped into his office, then took seats across from his desk.

Joyce slammed down into his chair, then shouted, "It's bad enough that I'm getting stonewalled by these Organized Crime assholes, but now I have to deal with your bullshit."

"Sir," I said, "It was my idea—"

He waved off my words and stood. "Listen, I get you going to talk to Frank Capetta. Shit, I almost did the same." He threw his hands up. "But in what universe did you think it would be

okay to go to a nursing home, sign fake names, and then interrogate an old man who can't even wipe his own ass?"

I raised my hand.

Joyce glared at me, and I could feel him mentally lighting
my arm on fire.

I took my chances. "We have reason to believe that Capetta's nephew, Dominic DeSipio, may have had numbers carved
into his head. This case jumps back and forth in time. DeSipio's murder could have been the first one—how this all started."

"Dominic '*the Soldier*' DeSipio," Gleason added helpfully.

"*Soldier?*" Joyce took a seat. "The Organized Crime guys
never mentioned him."

"According to Frank Capetta, it was a nickname he gave
himself that didn't really catch on. I doubt many people outside
of his immediate family would have known."

I said, "And according to Frank, his dad, Angelo, found
Dominic's body." I explained about the closed casket.

Joyce grunted. "But Frank Capetta also informed you that
his dad suffers from dementia."

"He may have mentioned that, which is why I decided to
Notebook him."

In response to his quizzical expression, I said, "Like the
movie, you know? Ryan Gosling, Rachel McAda—"

"I know the damn movie!" He calmed himself, then asked,
"And how'd that strategy go?"

"It could have gone better."

"You beat up a ninety-four-year-old man!"

"I merely defended myself from an assault by a ninety-four-
year-old man and a few of his geriatric posse." I wasn't about
to admit to anything. Joyce didn't have proof of any misbehav-
ior on my part. All he had was the word of one cranky nursing
home worker.

Or so I thought.

Agent Joyce opened his laptop and turned it toward us. "One of the resident's daughters was visiting, and she recorded this on her cell phone. She uploaded it to YouTube thirty minutes ago."

The video was titled "Man Attacks Group of Old People," and it already had twenty-six thousand views.

Gleason put his head in his hands.

Joyce hit Play.

A shaky video began. A smiling old lady was in frame, and then I heard a loud scream. The video swept to the left, and I saw Angelo Capetta hanging off my back with his hands over my eyes. I couldn't see anything at the time, and I ran forward, knocking over my easel, then the easel of the old lady in front of me.

I'm spun, trying to rip Angelo's hands from my eyes, but he was an eighty-nine-pound gorilla. The woman whose painting I'd knocked over joined the fray and she was stabbing at my ribs with her paintbrush.

"My tree!" she shrieked. "My tree!"

I could be heard yelling back, "Your tree sucked!" as I stiff-armed her in the chest and knocked her down.

This upset the rest of the old-timers, and they converged on me.

In the background, I saw Gleason drop to his hands and knees and crawl through the grass, out of screen.

"You were a lot of help," I said, turning to him.

He gulped.

I turned back to the video, where I had finally pried Angelo's hands from over my eyes. I wrestled him off my back, and now I was swinging him by both his arms and spinning in a circle, using him as a weapon to knock down the rest of the approaching elderly zombies.

Angelo's legs whipped around, knocking each of them to the ground.

"My heart!" one man yelled.

When I released Angelo's arms, he went flying, landing in the grass and tumbling. He came to a halt and a soft groan could be heard.

The helpful videographer swiveled from Angelo back to me. I can be seen quickly checking the pulses of the eight elderly people on the ground, then running toward the perimeter fence and crawling over. My ignoble flight from the scene had been recorded for posterity.

The video ended, and Agent Joyce turns his laptop back around.

"You're lucky no one died," Joyce said.

"I was defending myself," I replied. "They had weapons."

"They had paintbrushes!" He let out whatever is one level above an exasperated sigh and said, "I should kick both of you off the task force right this second." He shook his head, then glared at me.

I almost said, "You guys would still be chasing your tails if it wasn't for me breaking this case wide open," but I thought if I uttered another syllable, Joyce might pull out his Glock and shoot me in the leg. He was getting ready to dish out whatever punishment he had decided on, when my cell phone buzzed in my pocket.

I pulled it out. If it were anyone else in the world, I wouldn't have answered it. But it was Lacy.

I flipped the phone open and listened for thirty seconds.

"I'm leaving now," I told Lacy, ending the call.

Gleason must have noticed all the blood drain from my face. "What's wrong?"

"My little sister," I said, my voice cracking. "She has multiple sclerosis."

31

Lacy has MS.

These three words played in my head over and over again like a stock market ticker at the bottom of the TV. No matter what else I tried to think about, there they were, scrolling through my brain—my *healthy* brain. Unlike Lacy's, which was under attack by a bunch of rogue antibodies.

I hadn't known much about MS when Lacy called me to tell me her diagnosis. Now, almost eighteen hours later, I knew everything Google could tell me. Multiple sclerosis is a disease in which the immune system attacks the protective covering of nerve cells in the brain, resulting in disrupted communication between brain and body. This causes a wide range of symptoms: loss of coordination, pain, fatigue, muscle spasms, dizziness, impaired vision, and even vision loss.

Sadly, there is no cure. But the disease can be mitigated by physical therapy and a slew of different medications that suppress the body's immune response. Of course, the meds come with risks of their own and a barrage of unpleasant side effects.

Multiple sclerosis might not kill my little sister—at least not any time soon—but it would forever change the course of her life. And it already had. Her coach had sidelined her for the remainder of the swimming season. She wasn't off the team, but she couldn't practice or compete. He wasn't allowing her back until her symptoms were under control and Lacy's neurologist gave her the okay.

After the phone call with her coach, Lacy was inconsolable. Her life had revolved around swimming since winning her first race when she was eight years old.

I remembered that day well. I'd been a junior in high school at the time, and the last thing I wanted to do was go watch my kid sister splash around in the pool on a Saturday morning. But that day I'd been grounded, and my parents made me a deal: if I watched Lacy swim, I could go out with my friends later that night.

I spent most of the swim meet glued to my Game Boy. It wasn't until halfway through Lacy's first race that I glanced up.

Lacy was so far out in front of the other girls that it looked like she'd had a ten-second head start. She was slicing through the water like she had fins. She was a four-foot-two-inch torpedo.

When she finished the race, she came running up to me. "Did you see me, Tommy? Did you see me?"

"Yeah, Lace, I saw you. You were awesome."

"Yeah, I was," she agreed.

For the next thirteen years, almost every day of her life, she'd be in the pool.

I knew her coach at Drexel had little choice in the matter, that he had to pull her off the active roster, but that didn't change the fact that I wanted to punch him in the face.

Lacy would be staying at the condo for the foreseeable future, so I went to Lacy's campus apartment to pack up a bunch of her stuff. After I tossed the last of her stuffed flamingos—she had four—into a cardboard box, I added several half-burned candles she had on her nightstand. I was putting the last of her unhealthy amount of yoga pants into the box when my phone chirped.

It was a text from Lacy. Well, *another* text from Lacy. She kept remembering things that she wanted me to retrieve for her.

LACY: Grab my journal . . . it's hidden under my dresser.

There was a small gap between the bottom of her dresser and the carpet, and I leaned down. I saw the outline of her journal, and I slipped it out.

Ten minutes later, I arrived back at the condo and found Lacy in bed. Her eyes were red and puffy. She asked, "Did you get Fred and Wilma?"

"Yes," I said, pulling two flamingos from the box and handing them to her. "And I got Pebbles and Bam-Bam too."

She took the two smaller flamingos, giving them both kisses on the head.

"Did you get my Bieber poster?" she asked.

"Of course." I pulled the rolled-up poster out of the box and hit her softly on the knee with it. "You know he's like sixteen years old."

"Yeah, a sixteen-year-old angel dropped from heaven."

"What does your roommate think about you having a poster of a *child* on your wall?"

"Maya has two posters of him. And a calendar."

I combed my hair forward with my hand so it covered my forehead. "I think I'm going to wear my hair like him."

She laughed.

I handed over her journal. "I only read fifty pages."

"Good stuff, huh?"

"Very graphic."

She laughed. "You didn't *really* read any."

"I wouldn't read that with a gun to my head. I don't want to know what you and Horse Doodler get up to." I pulled a few more things out of her box and put them on the dresser.

"Did you get it?" she asked.

Lacy had texted me one last time right as I was walking out of her apartment.

"Yeah, I got it."

"Give it to me."

I let out a sigh, then dug my hand into the second box and pulled it out from where I'd buried it.

I handed it over.

Lacy fingered the aging blue ribbon. The one she got when she was eight years old. The one I'd watched them give to her. The one she'd worn to school that Monday to show off to everyone else. The one she kept on her mirror.

Her face crumbled, and she turned over on her side.

"Lace—" I started to say, but I didn't have any words to follow it up. I couldn't just sit there in the house. I had to do something. That I couldn't help my little sister was a white-hot poker to my chest. But maybe I could help someone else.

Brooke.

"I'm going out," I said.

When I was reaching under the dresser to grab Lacy's journal, the ticker in my brain—*Lacy has MS*—turned off for a brief second.

I had remembered the file about her father that Brooke had stolen from Eglund. Maybe she hid another copy somewhere.

≈

I'd just picked up my daily pumpkin spice latte when Gallow called.

On the drive back from Eglund's cabin two days earlier, I'd called Gallow and informed him Steven Eglund was Burner Phone, and I'd recounted my trip to his cabin and the missing file on Nicholas Wexley. Gallow had called in Eglund for an interview yesterday afternoon, but I'd yet to hear back.

"How'd it go with Eglund?" I asked.

"He came clean about his relationship with Brooke," Gallow replied. "Corroborated everything you said."

"Did you ask Eglund about the file on Wexley?"

"Not specifically. I couldn't mention it without alerting him that someone had broken into his cabin."

"Can you get a warrant to search the property?"

"No way. Whoever set up the company that owns the cabin knew what they were doing. There's not an iota of evidence linking Eglund to the place. No judge is going to want anything to do with it."

He was right. A judge would have a hard time seeing probable cause for any ordinary muggle, let alone a multibillionaire. Careers have been ruined for less.

I asked, "Is Eglund sticking with his story about where he and Brooke went on October fourteen?"

"Yeah, he says they went to some place in the woods."

"Did you tell him Brooke's phone pinged in the Poconos?"

"I did, and Eglund didn't blink an eye. He said they were driving around for a few hours and chatting. He wasn't sure where they went, maybe they could have been somewhere near the Poconos at some point."

"Is he doubling down on his alibi for the night Brooke was killed?"

"Sure is. Watching *Game of Thrones* with his wife."

"Did she vouch for him?"

"She did. She said that they started watching at nine thirty that night. Started with episode five and couldn't stop. Watched six episodes that night, then went to sleep around four in the morning."

"And she said for a fact that it was Monday night into Tuesday morning?"

"She did. Supposedly, another couple told them about the show at a dinner they went to on Saturday night. They watched the first four episodes that Sunday, then the rest Monday night and into Tuesday morning."

"Seems fortuitous that, of all nights, they have specifics for that particular one."

"I agree. It's a better alibi than just saying you were asleep."

"Did you tell Mrs. Eglund about her husband's affair with Brooke?"

"Yeah, she was pretty disgusted."

I thought of the file that Eglund had on his wife, Robin. I hadn't flipped through it, but I surmised there was something in there that gave him as much leverage over her as she had over him.

"Did you tell Nicholas Wexley about Eglund?"

"I phoned him, but Eglund had already confessed everything."

"How did Wexley sound?"

"He did a good job holding back his rage. I wouldn't be surprised if Eglund shows up to work in a few days with a broken nose."

"Were you tempted to tell Wexley that Eglund has been keeping a file on him?"

"That file is just hypothetical right now."

"Oh, it's real. And it's what got Brooke killed." On that note, I asked, "How thoroughly did they go over Brooke's room? Are you certain there were no documents there?"

"I was there myself. We scoured the place pretty good. Why?

You don't think Brooke had the documents on her in the tent where she was killed?"

"I do, but I also think she made a backup copy and hid it somewhere." It's what I would have done.

Gallow mulled, then said, "I'll get someone back over to her dorm in the next day or so to perform another search."

I would have preferred him to send someone right away, but I wasn't going to press it. I guessed I'd just have to do it myself.

≈

It took fifteen minutes to walk to Rodin House. I knocked twice on Brooke's door, but no one answered.

The door to the room across the hall was open, and I stuck my head inside. Two guys sat on the bottom bunk, each with a video game controller in their hand.

"Do you guys know when the girls across the hall are going to be back?" I asked.

Without glancing up from the TV, one said, "No idea."

The other one eyed me in his peripheral vision and said, "I saw Lauren heading into the cafeteria ten minutes ago."

The guy had similar coloring to me, and I asked, "Can I borrow your ID card?"

He sneered. "Uh, no."

"How about you let me borrow your school ID to go eat in the cafeteria, and I won't tell your RA that you guys sold Brooke Wexley GHB two weeks before she died?" It was a Hail Mary, but I wanted to see how it played out.

They paused the game.

"Who are you?"

"Don't worry about it. Just let me borrow your ID real quick."

"We don't sell drugs."

"I don't care either way. I just need your ID card."

He thought about it for a moment, then said, "Piss off."

Duly noted.

I told the woman scanning IDs at the entrance of the cafeteria that I'd lost my ID card. She was immersed in a gossip magazine and waved me through.

I hadn't eaten since learning Lacy had MS, and at the sight of abundant offerings, my appetite came rushing back. I grabbed a red tray and loaded two plates with hard-boiled eggs, cottage cheese, a roast beef sandwich, yogurt, a bowl of Honey Smacks, and a strawberry milk.

I spotted Brooke's roommate Lauren sitting at a table by herself. Unlike the last time I'd seen her, her brown hair was down and she wore jeans and a thin jacket. Her nose was buried in a textbook and the remnants of her lunch were pushed off to the side.

I sat next to her and asked, "What are you studying?"

She pulled up the book to show me the cover.

Organic Chemistry.

"*Ouch.* I heard that's a tough one."

"I'm premed," Lauren said. "They're all tough."

I ate a hard-boiled egg in two bites, swallowed hard, and asked, "Is Brooke's stuff still in her room?"

Lauren grabbed several Honey Smacks from my bowl. "Yeah, no one has come by to get anything yet. I think the cops might have taken a couple things when they came, but for the most part, it's how she left it."

She closed her eyes for a moment, then reopened them. She ate one of the Honey Smacks and asked, "Why?"

"I need to look at her room."

"Okay."

I scarfed down the rest of my meal and listened to Lauren lay out her ten-year plan for me: undergrad, med school, residency, and then *boom*, at age thirty-two she's Dr. Lauren Gunday.

"You might want to change your last name," I mumbled with a mouthful of cottage cheese. "It sounds like 'gonna die' in Australian, which, I mean, isn't great for a heart surgeon."

I took another enormous bite of cottage cheese. "Maybe change it to Notgunday."

I left her to contemplate her future, returned my tray, and then grabbed an ice cream cone and topped it with four inches of vanilla-chocolate swirl.

≈

I spent thirty minutes going through every nook and cranny of Brooke's bedroom. If there were a stack of documents hidden there, they were invisible.

When I finished up, I found Lauren sitting on the couch, an ignored textbook in her lap.

"Gun-day," she mumbled under her breath in an Australian accent. "Gun-day. *Gonna die.*" She glanced up at me, wide-eyed. "How has no one ever told me this?"

I shrugged.

I was getting ready to leave when I asked, "Do you know if Brooke went anywhere special the days before she died?"

"Nowhere special that I know of," she said, snapping out of it. "That entire week before, she was mostly at the protests." She tilted her head to the left. "Though I heard from a guy a couple days ago that he'd seen her at Alpha Tau Omega three days before she was killed."

"A fraternity house? Why would she go there?"

"To see her brother."

32

OCTOBER 29, 2011
12:24 P.M.

"How are you feeling?" I asked, pulling apart the satin curtains on Lacy's bed.

She had earbuds in and slipped one out. "What?"

"How ya feeling?"

She squished her face together. "Queasy."

I'd picked up several medications for Lacy that morning. Her first regimen had been six different pills, and she'd have to take three more sets of pills by day's end. All in addition to the subcutaneous injection that required her to jab herself in the stomach.

"And depressed," Lacy added.

"Well, that can be a side effect." Depression was listed as a side effect on four of Lacy's medications.

"It's not the meds."

"What is it?"

"Lady Gaga and the Black Swan."

Lacy read my confusion and explained, "Those were going to be my Halloween costumes."

Now I understood. Lady Gaga was a female singer who'd gotten extremely popular in the last couple of years and *Black Swan* was a movie with Natalie Portman that had recently been released.

Halloween had always been Lacy's favorite holiday. She'd go all out, planning costumes months and sometimes even years in advance.

"Halloween is the best night of the year," Lacy said. "And in college, it's like the best three nights."

I'd only done a year at the University of Washington, but I remembered Halloween being amazing. I'd worn my same costume—*Ace Ventura: Pet Detective*—all three nights of my Halloween bender, but my female friends had a new costume for every night, each costume more revealing than the previous.

"Were you going to go as Slutty Lady Gaga and Slutty Black Swan?"

She rolled her eyes. "Of course I was!"

I chuckled, then said, "I'm going to head out for a bit."

"Okay, I'll just be here in my bed, hanging out with my MS."

I'd never known Lacy to throw herself a pity party, but these were uncharted waters. I left her comment alone and said, "I'll be back in an hour."

Ten minutes later, I was eating up the asphalt. The temperature was in the midforties and falling fast. I was clad in sweats, a hoodie, a beanie, and thin running gloves. Between the Numbers task force and my pro bono work on the Wexley case, I'd only run a handful of times in the past two weeks.

Halfway through a six-mile loop, I had my hoodie tied around my waist and I'd built up a nice sweat. I'd inadvertently made my way near Carmen's house. She'd uploaded a virus to my computer, hacked into my phone, and vandalized my car. It was in my best interest to apologize in person before she escalated to framing me for insider trading.

Carmen's house was the nicest one on the street, evidence of the mid-six-figure salary she earned as a white-hat hacker, helping companies find vulnerabilities in their cyber security.

Her beloved Harley was parked on the walkway leading up to her porch. It looked pristine, and I guessed she'd washed and waxed the bike just that morning. Sitting on her front stoop were two large pumpkins. One had "Fuck Off" carved into it. The second one read, "See First Pumpkin."

I'd only come across a few things in my life that truly frightened me: Australia's enormous huntsman spider, that four-patty hamburger from Wendy's, the movie *The Ring*, and Carmen Gallow.

I steeled my nerves and lightly knocked on the front door. No one answered.

"Come on, Carmen," I said. "I know you're in there." She never went anywhere without her bike. "I just want to tell you how sorry I am."

"So, tell me."

I turned.

Carmen emerged from the side of her house. Her hair was buzzed and dyed bleach blond. Her eyes were dark green, and she had three nose piercings, one in each nostril and then a small ring through her septum. She was clad in torn jeans and a black Mötley Crüe tank top. Her heavily tattooed arms were hidden behind her back.

"I'm sorry," I said.

"For what?"

"For breaking up with you by text."

"How sorry?"

"Very."

She shook her head. Evidently, she was looking for a higher level of contrition. She pulled her arms out from behind her back and revealed a gun. Well, a paintball gun.

The first paintball hit me in the chest, the next one in the neck, and the third right in the crotch.

"Carmen!" I yelled, covering my face in my hands.

The hits kept coming. I was under attack. I turned and ran, five more paintballs slamming into my back as I fled.

When I was a safe distance away, I gazed down at my shirt. I was covered in yellow blots of paint.

"That didn't go very well," I muttered.

≈

The second half of my run brought me to the Target on Chestnut Street. I washed as much of the paint off my neck and arms as possible in the bathroom, and then I went to the electronics section. I picked out an iPad like the one I'd used at the Racquet Club of Philadelphia, in hopes it would cheer Lacy up.

I was exiting the store with the tablet, when I noticed a group of people surrounding the back end of an old truck in the parking lot. Everyone was smiling and reaching into the truck bed.

I walked over and peeked down.

The truck bed was covered in blankets, and there were nine gray blobs darting around, vying for people's attention.

Puppies.

Pug puppies.

"Oh my God!" a young woman said next to me. "I want all of them." She picked one of the puggies up and held it up to her face. It squirmed and couldn't lick her nose fast enough.

A man opposite me leaned against the truck, watching with a wry grin on his face. He had gray hair under a trucker hat and several days' worth of stubble. He looked like a farmer, and I guessed he'd driven in from out of town.

"How old are they?" I asked him.

"Eight weeks."

"How much?"

"Fifteen hundred. Cash only."

"For a dog?" I assumed they'd be cheaper than the iPad.

It was a Saturday, and the banks were closed. The most I could get out of the ATM was a thousand dollars.

I pointed at a puppy in the corner who was lying belly up and fast asleep. "How much for the broken one?"

The man tilted his head to the side. "I could do twelve hundred."

"A thousand."

He shrugged. "Sure, why not?"

After stopping by the ATM inside Target and picking up everything a puppy would need (collar, leash, food, food dish, water dish, puppy pads), I went back to the truck and handed the man the money. I scooped up the little dog—who was still sleeping—and shook him. He remained comatose for three shakes, then opened his eyes. His little tongue darted in and out, and he snorted.

"I'm not your dad," I told him. "I'm just the delivery boy."

He didn't understand and instead fell in love with me.

It happens.

I cradled the little puppy in my arms for the fifteen blocks back to my apartment. I was stopped seven times by people wanting to pet and take pictures of the little guy.

When we made it to the door of our condo, I turned the gray blob around and explained, "Here are the house rules: no peeing, no pooping, no barking, no running, no jumping."

He gave no indication he agreed.

It took me a few minutes to wriggle on the dog Halloween costume that I'd bought, then I went to Lacy's room and eased open the door. She had her earbuds back in and was lying on her side with her back to the door.

I was about to set the tiny puppy down on her bed, when I realized he was asleep again. He was in a tiny Batman costume with a cape and a pointy black headband.

I shook him.

Nothing.

I shook him again.

Nothing.

I tickled his tummy.

His eyes opened.

I gently set him on Lacy's bed. The puppy made his way down to Lacy's feet—his tiny, curled tail wagging so violently I feared he might become airborne—and began sniffing. Lacy lifted one of her feet and scratched it.

I fought back a laugh.

The puppy began pawing at her legs. Lacy flipped around and saw him. She ripped out her earbuds and picked up Batpug. He squirmed in her arms and attacked her with kisses.

Lacy glanced up at me. She was crying.

"Happy Halloween," I said.

≈

My earlier conversation with Lacy about Halloween started me thinking about Evan Wexley. If I was going to get myself into his fraternity, there was no better time than tonight.

My computer still wasn't working but using the iPad I'd given Lacy, I logged onto the Alpha Tau Omega web page. I checked their calendar of events, and lo and behold, this evening they were throwing their annual Monster Mash.

The festivities began at 9:00 p.m.

It would look suspicious if I went alone, so I picked up my phone and sent a text: "Want to go to a party?"

≈

Jennifer Peppers opened the door to her apartment. She was unrecognizable. She wore slacks, a light-yellow button-up with a tie, and had on large wire-frame glasses.

Dwight from *The Office*.

"Hey, Dwight," I said.

"Hey, um, Mr. Kangaroo."

I had nothing to wear, so I'd put on the kangaroo onesie that I'd bought for Puff.

"Who's the kiddo?" she said, nodding at the joey resting in the front pouch.

"That's Rufus."

She laughed.

She asked about Lacy, and I gave her a quick update.

"I feel bad going out when she's just there at home all alone," she said.

"She's not alone," I said. "I bought her a dog."

"You bought her a dog?"

"Well, he looks like a little baked potato right now, but yeah, I think he'll become a dog at some point."

She texted Lacy, requesting a picture, then asked, "So, where are we going tonight?"

"A frat party at Penn."

"Really?"

"I have ulterior motives." I told her what I was after.

When I finished, she said, "So, you want me to go to a frat party with you, hang out with stupid college kids, act like your girlfriend, and help you get some douchebag wasted?"

"That's correct."

She smiled. "Best first date ever."

33

"What's your name?" Frankenstein asked. He sat on a stool outside the front entrance of the fraternity, holding a clipboard. On a stool next to him were two red cups. One was half-filled with beer, the second one empty, save for a sludge of red jungle juice at the bottom.

"Last name, Garoo," I said. "First name, Ken."

"Ken . . . Garoo," the kid repeated. "I'm not seeing it."

Next to me, Jennifer burst out laughing.

"Actually, we aren't on the list," I said. "I'm visiting from the University of Washington Alpha Tau Omega chapter." I reached out and took his hand, then did a series of complicated movements, ending with me slapping his hand to my cheek.

"What are you doing?"

"The secret handshake."

There was a line forming behind us, and Frankenstein— Frankenstein's monster, to be entirely accurate—had no time for my antics.

Thankfully, Jennifer stepped in. She reached into her pocket, extracted a small green baggy, and handed it to him. "Can you check the list again?"

His eyebrows lifted, and he slipped the bag into his pocket.

"Ah, here you are." He put a pink bracelet on both our wrists and sent us on our way.

When we'd crossed the threshold, I nudged Jennifer and whispered, "How much pot did you give him?"

"It's not pot. It's hemp."

Hemp is part of the cannabis family but doesn't contain enough THC to get you high.

"One of the other art professors buys hemp flowers in bulk to cook with," she said. "She gave me a bunch a couple months ago. I snagged a little bit on the way out, thinking it might come in handy on this little adventure of yours."

"Smart *and* beautiful."

She raised her eyebrows behind her large glasses.

"Did I fail to mention how hot you look? Even dressed as Dwight, you are totally smoking."

"You did not mention that. And thank you, kind sir, for the compliment."

A few steps later, we entered chaos.

A DJ in the back corner was blasting music, projected multi-colored lights crisscrossed the dance floor, and tables were set up where drunk kids were loudly playing beer pong.

Directly in front of us, a zombie was holding a box of Franzia, and Dracula was on his knees guzzling from the nozzle.

"Where do we get a drink?" I shouted.

Zombie turned and called out, "Kitchen!"

Jennifer grabbed my hand and pulled me through the thicket of bodies until we reached our destination. In the kitchen were five kegs and two large, exposed coolers filled with jungle juice.

"What's your poison?" I asked her.

"Well, I don't feel like getting roofied tonight, so I'll stick with beer."

"Good call."

It took another five minutes to work our way to the front of the line. The Hulk filled two red cups and handed them to us.

"Thanks, Bruce," I said.

He laughed.

As we made our way back to the main room, Jennifer said, "There he is."

I'd pulled up a picture of Evan Wexley on Jennifer's smartphone and told her to keep an eye out for him.

"Four o'clock," she said, nodding. "Hugh Hefner."

Evan wore black lounge pants and a red smoking jacket. A wooden pipe hung from the pocket of his jacket. He stood at the end of a table, a pyramid of red cups in front of him.

We weaved our way as close to the beer pong game as we could get. Evan (Hugh Hefner) and his partner (Werewolf) were winning. They had eight of their ten cups remaining, while their opponents (Jersey Shore and Tarzan) were down to their last cup.

When it was Evan's turn, he picked up the Ping-Pong ball, blew on it, then tossed it. The arcing shot landed in the last cup with a splash.

Hefner and Werewolf high-fived.

"We got next," I said.

Evan appraised me, then huffed, "Sorry, Kangaroo Boy, but Craig and Ted are next."

"First, I'm a Kangaroo *Man*. And second, I bet you a hundred bucks that me and Sexy Dwight Schrute here beat the shit out of you."

"Okay." He smirked. "You're on."

≈

Jennifer expertly filled our ten cups from a large beer pitcher.

I said, "Looks like you've done this before."

"I may have," she said with a sly grin.

"You were in a sorority, weren't you?"

"Maybe."

"You can outdrink me, can't you?"

"Without a doubt."

"Let's go!" Evan shouted from across the table.

Word of my challenge had spread through the party, and a thick crowd had formed around the table. Evan had insisted I put my hundred dollars on the table, and there were five twenties lying in a thin puddle of beer.

Jennifer finished filling our cups, and I noticed they were all full.

"Are you trying to kill us?" I whispered.

"You want this guy loaded, right?"

"Yeah."

"Okay then."

She tilted her cup toward Evan and Werewolf and said, "Full beers, *bitches.*"

Who was this chick?

Team Douchebag shared a look, and Werewolf grabbed their pitcher and began topping off their sixteen-ounce red party cups.

"You do know we basically have a full twelve-pack of beer sitting in front of us," I said.

"I'm aware."

I planned on getting Evan drunk, but I hadn't planned on blacking out in the process.

"Alright," Evan said, raising a cup overflowing with beer. "Let's do this."

Because Team Douchebag had won the last game, they got to go first. Evan drained his throw in the center cup to thunderous applause. Without skipping a beat, Jennifer picked up the cup and chugged.

Evan's eyes nearly popped out of his head at the speed in which Jennifer drained the beer.

"How'd you do that?" I asked.

She wiped her mouth with her arm and raised her eyebrows behind her glasses. "No gag reflex."

"I'll get us a cab."

She chuckled.

There was a soft splash. Werewolf had sunk his ball as well.

Jennifer picked up a cup and handed it to me. "You're up, Ken Garoo."

I took the cup and chugged. Or tried to. I'd never been able to drink fast, and it took me fifteen seconds to finish the entire cup. My eyes were watering as I set the beer on the table. To my utter dismay, it was still half-full.

Jennifer shook her head—in amusement or apathy, I couldn't be sure—and finished the rest.

"Sorry," I said.

She made a pouty face. "You tried your hardest."

"You sound like my dad after a track meet when I knocked down almost every hurdle."

"Give 'em back!" shouted Evan.

"What?"

"We both made our shots. We go again."

I'd forgotten this rule.

Jennifer and I bounced our Ping-Pong balls back over. Werewolf and Evan both shot at the same time. I watched in slow motion as Werewolf's Ping-Pong ball splashed in the top cup of the pyramid and, a millisecond later, Evan's ball splashed into the same cup.

The crowd went berserk.

This rule I remembered.

Death cup.

If one team shoots and both balls land in the same cup, the game is over.

"Drink up, bitches!" Evan said.

I looked at Jennifer.

She said, "Well, this backfired."

"You mean because Evan didn't have to drink at all and now, we have to drink eight more full cups."

"Like I said: *backfired*."

Evan slapped his hand down on the one hundred dollars and spat, "Thanks for playing."

"We don't have to drink them," Jennifer whispered. "It's not like we have anything to prove to these ninnies."

She was right, we didn't. But I still needed to have a chat with Evan, and if we didn't drink our beers, he wouldn't give me the time of day.

"We have to," I said.

With the crowd watching, Jennifer and I picked up the first of our remaining eight cups and touched them together.

"Down the hatch," she said.

"Down the hatch," I echoed.

34

I was queasy after chugging five beers in the span of ten minutes.

Jennifer and I stood on the fraternity's front lawn. It was packed with people smoking cigarettes or those who just wanted to escape the blazing heat and madness for a few minutes.

We found a small section near the side of the house that was more private. I had my hands on my hips and my eyes half-closed. Bile rose in my throat like molten lava, and my gums were sweating like they were crossing the Gobi Desert.

"What's the outlook?" Jennifer asked.

I dry swallowed. "All systems point toward expulsion."

"When's the last time you threw up?"

"May 17, 2007." Bad oysters.

My stomach fluttered and I leaned over. I drooled, but the tide held back. After thirty seconds, I straightened.

"You look better," she said. "Less Kermity."

I felt better. It appeared I was going to keep my ninety-six ounces of Keystone Light down after all.

She turned her phone toward me and said, "Look."

It was a picture of Lacy's puppy. Just like when I'd first seen him in the back of the truck bed, he was flat on his back, fast asleep.

"He sleeps a lot."

"All puppies do."

She was probably right. I'd never had a dog.

After sending Lacy back a quick text, she slipped her phone into her pocket and said, "Shall we resume the mission?"

"We shall."

Once inside, we walked back to the beer pong table. Evan and Werewolf had either been beaten or resigned their throne, and two girls dressed in red *Baywatch* one-piece swimsuits had taken their place.

"Good to know there are lifeguards on duty," I said.

In her elevated state, Jennifer found this amusing and giggled.

I stood on my tiptoes and scanned the room. I spotted Hef nestled in the back corner of the room with a scantily clad bumblebee.

"Target acquired," I told Jennifer. "Give me twenty minutes, and then I'll come find you."

"I'm going for the jungle juice," she said with a wide grin. She swayed slightly, indicating the alcohol had finally found its way into her petite 120-pound frame.

"How about you wait for me, and we have jungle juice together?"

"Promise?"

I nodded.

"Pinky swear."

I held up my pinky. She wrapped her pinky around it, then she kissed her thumb. I did the same. Without thinking, I pulled her hand away from her mouth and leaned in, giving her a quick kiss.

"First date smooches!" she said, pumping her fist in the air.

Oh, God.

She was plastered.

A young girl in a cow costume stood nearby, sipping awkwardly from a red cup. I gave the elbow of her costume a light tug and shouted over the blaring music, "Can you watch over Dwight here for twenty minutes?"

Cow looked happy to have something to do and said, "I can do that!"

Feeling slightly guilty for abandoning Jennifer—who'd gone from sober to sloshed in approximately ninety seconds—I started toward Evan and his bumblebee.

As I approached, they were full-on making out. When I drew closer, Blond Bumblebee broke away and turned. I did a double take. With her blond hair, light-brown eyes, and thin frame, for the briefest of moments, I'd thought it was Brooke.

"Sorry to interrupt," I said, shaking off the thought. "I just wanted to properly congratulate you for kicking the shit out of us."

Evan jutted out his chin. "That was an ass-kicking, alright."

I pulled a flask I had hidden in my shorts underneath the onesie and asked, "Can I buy you a drink?"

He took the flask.

"Evvvaaannn!" Bumblebee whined, throwing up her hands. "You said you were done drinking."

The way she said it, I assumed it had sexual context—i.e., *I don't want to have to bat around your limp dick in two hours.*

"It's Halloween!" Evan said. "Give me a break!"

She shook her head and departed.

"Don't mind her," he said with a wave. "She gets jealous every Halloween."

So maybe it wasn't about his limp dick. Maybe if he had too much to drink, he got a wandering eye.

"How long have you guys been together?" I asked.

"Two years." He unscrewed the top of the flask and took a drink. He crooked his neck to the side and blew out hard. "Damn! What was that?"

"Spiced rum." It was spiced rum, but not any ordinary spiced rum. It was Bacardi 151. Most hard liquor is 80 proof, meaning it's 40 percent alcohol by volume, but 151 is 151 proof, which equates to 75 percent alcohol. Technically, you could power a car with it.

He handed the flask back to me. I titled the flask and took a small drink, the liquid singeing my esophagus as it slid down.

I wiped my mouth with my arm, then asked, "How are you dealing with everything?"

He glared at me, and I thought he was going to tell me to get lost. Thankfully, he took the flask back. He tilted it and drank. One beat. Two beats. "Okay, I guess."

"When was the funeral?" I knew it had been two days earlier, but I didn't want him to know I was invested.

"Thursday."

He offered me back the flask. I could have pretended to take a drink, but I was feeling a nice buzz and was on autopilot. After a hearty swig, I handed it back to him.

He reached out for the wall to brace himself, evidence the 151 was working its magic. I asked, "When's the last time you saw her?"

"Who?"

"Brooke."

He was sufficiently inebriated that the question didn't raise any concerns.

"Three days before she was killed."

"Where did you see her?"

"Here at the frat. First time she ever set foot in the place."

"Why'd she come over?"

"Beats me. All she did was talk shit on our dad."

"What did she say?"

"Oh, you know, just all the crap they were saying in the news a few years back. That he's a crook and this and that. Spouting her Occupy bullshit, and that Dad ruined our lives."

"Did she give you anything?"

"Give me anything?" He cut his eyes at me. "Why would she give me anything?"

"Oh, no reason."

He gazed at me for two seconds, then unscrewed the top of the flask and finished off its contents.

"Did you guys talk down here?" I asked.

He tightened the lid on the flask and slid it into his own pocket. I guess it was his now. "Down here, and then she said she wanted to see my room."

"She was in your room?"

"Yeah, she's a freak, always playing jokes. She even locked me out for a few minutes."

I almost asked which room was his, but I could figure it out on my own.

≈

Jennifer and Cow were nowhere in sight as I made my way to the stairs, then slithered my way between sloppy collegiate bodies up to the frat house's second floor.

I guessed there were at least forty rooms split between the second and third floors. I knew from their website, that Evan was the treasurer of his frat, which meant he probably had one of the nicest rooms. I was guessing the most sought-after rooms were on the second floor, if for no other reason than you only had to get a girl to walk up fifteen steps.

I tried the first door I came to, but it was locked. A wise decision considering the frat's free-to-roam policy. The next door I tried opened. I dipped my head inside. Four guys and two girls sat in a circle around a tinted glass table. It was covered in powdery white lines.

"Want a bump?" asked Zombie, who I suspected was the same guy I'd seen walking around with the box of Franzia and just wanted everyone to have a good time.

"Thanks, but I'm good."

I was about to pull my head back, when I said, "Wexley wants me to plug in his phone. Which room is his?"

Zombie didn't hesitate. "Top floor, fifth, or sixth room on the right."

I thanked them, then headed up to the third floor and an empty hallway. You could hardly hear the music blaring from two stories below, though you could feel the bass rippling through the carpet. I passed three doors, then stopped at the opening to a large communal bathroom. I took two steps onto the tile and leaned in. Under the sound of a shower running, I could hear the soft moaning of young love.

Classy.

The fifth door was locked. I pulled out my wallet and slipped out a credit card. The lock was cheap, and within ten seconds I'd jimmied the door open.

I flipped the lights. Clothes were all over the floor, and it smelled like someone had spilled a gallon of maple syrup under the bed. I had a hard time believing this was the bedroom of straitlaced, every-hair-in-place Evan Wexley. The laptop screen-saver—a redheaded young man and a curvy brown-haired young woman—confirmed my assumption.

I eased my way out of the room and walked four paces to the sixth door on the right. By the flushness of the door to the wall, I could tell that Evan had installed a more secure lock than whatever was guarding Messy Redhead's quarters.

My credit card trick was useless, and all I did was bend the corner of my Amex.

I glanced back down the hallway. It was still empty. But that didn't mean there wasn't someone asleep in one of the surrounding rooms. Though, with tomorrow being Sunday—and no chance of someone cramming for a test—there was a good probability all the rooms were empty.

All I had to worry about were the fornicators in the communal bathroom. Hopefully, the shower and the moaning would drown out any sounds I made.

I took three steps back and braced myself against the opposite wall. The door was swimming in front of me. In fact, there were three doors.

Thanks, 151.

I stepped forward, raised my right foot, and smashed. I missed, hitting the doorframe. I took a step back and tried again. The door swung inward with a loud *crack*.

I waited for someone to appear from the stairway or for the fornicators to pop their heads out. There was an emergency exit stairwell at the end of the hall, and my plan was to race down the stairs, rip off my costume, and rejoin the fracas.

No one came.

I *hopped* into the room, then pushed the broken door shut. I flipped the lights. This room was spotless. Everything in its place. The bed was perfectly made, and a laptop was freakishly centered on the desk.

A picture of the entire Wexley clan hung on the wall above the desk—the five of them at a football game. They wore matching navy Penn shirts and were smiling widely. The three kids looked five years younger, and Brooke and her little sister both had half their faces painted a dark burgundy.

I put myself in Brooke's shoes. She had documents that she'd taken from Steven Eglund. Maybe she made copies and wanted to hide them. No one would connect her to her brother's frat. She came over, asked to see Evan's room, then locked him out. She had just a few minutes to hide them. She didn't need to hide them for long, they just needed to stay hidden for a couple days, until she bought her megaphone and informed the world of her father's misdeeds. She pulled the documents out of her backpack and . . .

I lifted Evan's mattress and looked underneath.

Nothing.

I opened his closet. His clothes were pressed and hanging. A lone cardboard box sat on the closet shelf, and I grabbed it. It was light, and when I opened it, I saw a small black jewelry box. I flipped it open, revealing a brilliant diamond ring I guessed to be at least four carats. Most likely an engagement ring for Bumblebee.

I spent another ten minutes going through his dresser, his book bag, his laundry hamper, anywhere and everywhere that Brooke might have hidden the documents.

But they weren't there, or maybe someone else had already come and taken them. Or, more likely, Brooke had come back for the documents.

I exited Evan's room, pulling his broken door shut as quietly as possible. In the hallway, I considered my next move.

Maybe she didn't hide the documents in Evan's room. Maybe she hid them downstairs somewhere. Or in someone else's room. I should have asked Evan if Brooke was with him every second while she was here. Or if she had gone into any of the other rooms.

"Hey!"

I shook from my daze.

The fornicators were both in the hallway. They were wrapped in towels. The young man shouted, "What are you doing up here?"

I turned and sprinted for the emergency stairwell. At the bottom, I kicked off my shoes and stepped out of the onesie. I was wearing basketball shorts and a T-shirt underneath. I rolled up the onesie, cramming it under the last stair. I burst through the side exit and into the chilly night air.

I was considering my next move, when I heard, "Ken Garoo!"

I turned.

Jennifer stood in a small group of smokers, everyone with a cigarette in their mouth but her. She held a party cup in each hand and wobbled toward me. As she got closer, I saw her mouth, nose, and teeth were stained red.

She let out a small burp. "I was just coming back inside to find you."

I took one cup from Jennifer and took a drink of the chunky, potent jungle juice. I covered my face with the red cup.

Two guys came barreling around the frat and into the court-yard. Both stopped and scanned the crowd back and forth.

Evidently, I wasn't wearing what the "lovers" had described, and their eyes swept over me like everyone else. A few moments later, the two frat guys gave up and headed back toward the entrance.

Jennifer held onto my shoulder for balance, and I asked, "Where's your cow friend?"

She pointed toward the half-moon high in the sky. "She's jumping over the moon."

"Okay," I said. "Time to get you home."

35

"BAXTERRRRR!" a voice shouted. "BAXTERRRR, WHERE ARRRRR-RRRE YOUUU?"

I cracked one eye open. Who in the hell was Baxter? And why had someone drilled several holes in my skull?

I rolled onto my back and opened my other eye. Bright lights swam above me. It took several seconds for everything to come into focus.

I was in the kitchen. More accurately, I was on the kitchen floor.

"BAXT—" My sister came into view. "Oh my God! What happened to you?"

"I'm not sure," I said with a groan. "I may have fallen out of an airplane." It was the only reasonable explanation for how much pain I was in. I let out a wincing exhale, then asked, "Who is Baxter?"

"My dog, Baxter."

"I forgot about him." I chuckled, sending a nail into my cerebellum. "Why *Baxter*?"

"I just thought it was cute. Have you seen him?"

"I have not."

"*Hmmm.*"

"I hope I didn't leave the door open last night and he got out."

"No, he was with me in bed twenty minutes ago. He has to be around here somewhere."

I pushed myself up onto my elbow.

"So, how did it go last night with Jennifer?" Lacy asked.

"She hasn't texted you yet?"

"Nope."

I wondered if she was on the kitchen floor in her apartment.

Anyhow, I remembered everything up to the point that I'd finished Jennifer's cup of jungle juice. She'd been annihilated, so I did the chivalrous thing and drank her cup so she couldn't. In hindsight, I should have done Future Thomas a favor and poured it out on the ground.

"I think it went pretty well."

"Did you get a goodnight kiss?"

I tried to recall how the night had ended. We'd gotten into a taxi, but I didn't remember any more than that. "I'm not sure. I know I kissed her once at the party."

"Nice!"

"Yeah, I'm a real Casanova." I sighed, then asked, "How are you feeling?"

"Dizzy, nauseous, and depressed."

"Welcome to the club."

She rolled her eyes.

I asked her if she'd seen my phone, and she picked it off the counter and handed it to me.

It was 11:15 a.m.

I groaned.

"What's wrong?" Lacy asked.

"I have to go play basketball." I'd never backed out of a bet in my life, and I wasn't going to start now.

Lacy snorted a laugh. "That's going to be miserable."

"Yes, it is."

She resumed her search for her dog, and with the help of the counter, I pushed myself to my feet. I had forty minutes to shake off this hangover and drive to Capitolo Playground. There was but one option: a peanut butter and Advil smoothie.

I grabbed the Costco jar of Skippy Extra Chunky, a carton of Lacy's almond milk, the protein powder, and the Extra Strength Advil.

We kept the blender in one of the low kitchen island cabinets, and I pulled the door open.

My eyes sprang open.

Next to the blender, lying on his back, his chest rising and falling, was the four-legged fugitive.

"Um, Lacy!" I shouted. "I found your dog."

≈

With the help of the PB&A smoothie, two blue Powerades, and a cold shower, I'd lessened one of the worst hangovers of my life by half. That said, my face was puffy, and my brain felt like it was filled with helium. So, it was no surprise when Gleason met me at my car in the parking lot and said, "You look like you just went ten rounds with a water buffalo."

As we walked to the courts, I gave Gleason a quick rundown on my previous night's festivities. When we reached the fencing gate, he placed one of his giant hands on my shoulder and said, "The next time you decide to go to a fraternity party—and I can't stress this enough—please, please, let me go with you."

I told him I would.

We joined the others on the court. I looked for Gallow but didn't see him.

I would have given this more thought had Puff not been striding toward me with a plastic bag in his hand and a shit-eating grin on his face. He had buzzed his hair away completely—taking all Tyrone's hard work with it—and he looked like he should be reporting for basic training.

He offered me the plastic bag. It was heavier than I would have predicted, and when I opened the bag, I realized why.

"You can't be serious," I said, pulling it out.

Gleason fingered one of the burnt-orange sleeves and asked, "Is that wool?"

It was.

I shoved the thick onesie—which was more of a full-body sweater—into Kip's chest. "I'm not wearing this."

"Ah, is Prescott a poor sport?" Kip asked in a high-pitched baby voice.

No, Prescott is super hungover and just happens to have sensitive skin.

Several of the other guys circled to watch the exchange. If I didn't put it on, I'd be forever marked a sore loser.

"Fine." I kicked off my shoes and then stepped into the onesie.

If Kip had smiled one more nanometer, his cheeks would have exploded.

I tugged at the neck, which after only fifteen seconds was already irritating my chin, and said, "Now, let's play ball."

≈

After fifteen minutes of running and jumping, my headache, which had dwindled to a dull throb, came back on steroids. My stomach felt like I'd eaten four Big Macs and washed them down with a carton of Pop Rocks. My neck, chin, arms, and legs were red and raw from the glorified scouring pad I was wearing. And to top it off, I missed all five shots I'd taken, I dribbled the ball off my foot three times, and I passed the ball to the other team twice.

"Get your shit together!" shouted a cop from the Fourteenth District—one of my extremely annoyed teammates. "You're embarrassing us!"

I clawed at my neck with my nails. "Sorry."

It was official.

I was the new Gallow.

I was Orange Shrek.

The other team brought the ball up the court. They were leading 7–4. I was guarding Hufflepuff, and he was posting me up, digging his butt into my stomach. He called for the ball with his hand, and his teammate passed it to him. He dribbled with his back to me, edging his way closer to the basket.

It took all my effort not to puke on his back.

He drained a fadeaway jumper, and then barked in my face, "Nothing but net, *sucka*."

If I hadn't been swallowing a mouthful of vomit, I might have slugged him.

Back on offense, I stayed on the perimeter. My goal was not to touch the ball for the rest of the game.

Gleason got the ball down low. Hufflepuff was playing loose defense on me, and Gleason kicked me the ball. I caught the ball and dribbled. Hufflepuff collapsed on me and knocked the ball away with his hand, or as they say "stripped me clean."

No one was near him, and he headed toward the opposite basket for an uncontested breakaway layup.

There are universal unwritten rules in pickup basketball. No cherry-picking. No blood, no foul. No fouls on game point, et cetera. But there are also unwritten rules on each individual court or within a group. It had long been decided within our group that if you steal the ball and have an uncontested path to the other hoop, no one will chase you down and try to block the ball. It's too wild, too unpredictable, and people end up getting hurt.

I'm not sure why I did it.

Maybe my judgment was still clouded by the alcohol. Or I was still upset about my baby sister getting diagnosed with MS. Or it was because Hufflepuff had forced me to wear a sweater made from poison ivy and he'd been talking shit all day.

After stealing the ball, Kip jogged nonchalantly toward the other hoop. I had a full head of steam when I caught up with him. As he went up for the layup, his head turned at the last moment as he noticed me in his peripheral vision.

He released the ball, which I swatted with my hand. The block was clean, and other than a little incidental contact, I didn't touch him. If it were an actual game on a real basketball court with referees, it wouldn't have been a foul. And if it had been a real court, with hoops that hang off the walls, Kip wouldn't have gotten hurt.

But at Capitolo, the hoops are attached to thick steel poles, and when I blocked the ball, it hit the steel pole and ricocheted right into Hufflepuff's face.

There was a *crack* as the ball flattened his nose.

He clapped his hands to his face, pulling off his sports goggles. A moment later, blood spurted through his fingers.

I stepped out of the orange onesie, scratched my neck a few times, then threw the foul garment to him. "You can use this to soak up the blood."

≈

There might not be a better hangover cure in the world than a twelve-inch cheesesteak and a double helping of fries.

It had been an hour since I'd unintentionally broken

Hufflepuff's nose, then abruptly walked off the court and crossed the street to Geno's. My phone blew up the entire time I was eating my sandwich, first with texts from Gleason updating me that Kip's nose now did a left turn at his cheek, then texts from Lacy that she thought maybe something was wrong with her new dog, then texts from Jennifer telling me she'd just woken up in her bathtub with a half-eaten Hot Pocket on her chest.

I dipped three french fries in my concoction of mayo and ketchup and tossed them in my mouth. Then I texted Jennifer back: "What kind of Hot Pocket?"

She replied a moment later: "Ham and Cheese."

ME: You do know that you're a college professor and
    not a student
JENNIFER: I'll be sure to write that on my hand
ME: Haha . . . what's the last thing you remember from
    last night?
JENNIFER: You abandoning me . . . just like my biological
    mother
ME: Please tell me you're kidding
JENNIFER: Jkjkjkjkjk . . . I remember everything . . .
ME: Did I get a goodnight kiss?
JENNIFER: You don't remember?
ME: No
JENNIFER: We made out like seventh graders in the back
    seat of the taxi . . . At one point the driver asked us
    politely to stop
ME: Nice
JENNIFER: Hahahahahaha

I was getting ready to text her back, when I received a series of text messages simultaneously.

The first one was an image. It was from Lacy. It was a
picture of Baxter with his head submerged in his water bowl.
The accompanying text read, "I found him asleep with his head
underwater????"

The next several were from Gallow.

The first two texts were images. The first was a shoe in a
clear plastic baggy. I recognized it as one of the shoes Brooke
had been wearing when she was killed. The left eyelets of the
shoe were numbered one to eight. The second image was also a
shoe. It must have come from the security camera on the bridge.
The shoe looked the same, but it wasn't. Again, the eyelets were
numbered—this time one to six.

Gallow's text spelled it out perfectly: "The girl in the surveillance footage isn't Brooke."

36

When I arrived at the Ninth District station, Gallow was in the detective bullpen, working at his computer. I dropped a to-go bag of Geno's on his lap and said, "Here you go, buddy."

He swiveled in his chair and smiled. "I don't care what everyone else says, you're the best."

"Gee, thanks."

He nodded at the desk next to him. "Grab Moore's chair."

As I pulled out Moore's chair, I noticed her desk was covered with gift baskets, flowers, and several cards.

Gallow was two bites into his sandwich when I slid next to him. "Shouldn't you drop all that stuff off at Moore's place?"

"I've already made three trips out there with Teddy bears and diaper boxes. Been meaning to get out there again, but I'm swamped."

"I can take it to her."

"Yeah?"

"Sure, I have to return Ms. Ruby's dream books anyhow." Plus, I hadn't talked to Moore since calling her a week earlier to update her on the Numbers case.

"Moore isn't staying at her mother's anymore," Gallow said.

"She moved to her brother Terrance's a few days ago. The stress was getting to her, and she almost had to go back to the hospital." He tossed back a handful of french fries. "Speaking of which, how's Lacy doing?"

"She's on day two of her meds, and she feels like crap. I was trying to cheer her up, and I bought her a puppy, but he might be defective."

"Defective?"

"Yeah, he keeps falling asleep in weird places." I recounted how I'd found him earlier that morning and then showed him the picture Lacy had texted me.

"He probably has narcolepsy."

"Dogs can get that?"

He swiveled to his computer. A moment later, he pulled up a video on YouTube called, "Pluto the Narcoleptic Dog."

He hit Play.

A man threw a blue Frisbee, and a golden retriever chased after it. After three seconds, the dog collapsed like a sniper had taken him out. The person filming ran toward the dog, and you see that the dog was fast asleep.

"Play it again."

He did. It was both funnier and sadder the second time. I texted Lacy that I'd come up with a possible diagnosis for her dog.

Gallow took the last bite of his sandwich, crumpled up his Geno's bag, and tossed it in the black trashcan under his desk. I noticed him staring at my neck, and he asked, "What's with the hickey?"

"It's not a hickey," I said, fingering the purple circle on my neck, which I'd covered up with makeup the night before. "It's a bruise from the paintball that your crackpot sister shot me with."

He laughed. And laughed some more.

I filled him in on everything that she'd done to me thus far.

"She just needs to meet another guy," Gallow said. "And then she'll leave you alone. That's usually how it works."

I nodded and then said, "So, Brooke's shoes?"

"Right." He wiped his fingers on his jeans, then handed me a piece of paper. It was a side-by-side comparison of the two shoe images. It was clearer than the pixelated images had been on my phone, the eyelets of each shoe easy to count.

"Have you told anyone else about this?" I asked.

"Just one of the tech guys. I wanted to run it by an unbiased third party before I pulled the pin on the grenade." He paused. "So, what do you think?"

"The shoes on the girl in the video are different from the shoes Brooke was wearing when she was killed. But that doesn't mean it isn't Brooke in the video. She could have had a change of shoes in her tent. Or the perp could have switched out the shoes?" I was playing devil's advocate. Both scenarios were unlikely.

"Well, let's assume that it isn't Brooke in the video," he said.

I rubbed my hands together. "Good, because it *isn't* her."

"I have my own theory, but I want to hear yours."

In the twenty minutes it had taken me to drive to the station, I'd come up with a couple different theories, but only one checked all the boxes.

"The catalyst is Occupy Wall Street in the middle of September," I said. "Maybe Brooke has buried these thoughts about her dad her entire life, and the Occupy protests get them bubbling to the surface. She knows her dad's firm is just as crooked as these other firms that took advantage of all these poor people in the financial crisis.

"She arranges to bump into Steven Eglund at a Smoothie King. If anyone has dirt on her father, it's going to be his partner of twenty-five years. Brooke gives him a burner phone under false pretenses, then starts a romantic relationship with him.

"Fast-forward to October fourteenth. Brooke has given Eglund a few hand jobs, and maybe he's let slip a couple secrets about her father. She discovers Eglund keeps a secret file on her father. They drive up to Eglund's cabin, and Brooke convinces him to try Ecstasy. Only it isn't Ecstasy, it's GHB—which at high doses makes the user highly impressionable. Brooke is able to coax Eglund into revealing the location of his hidden safe and the eight-digit combination. She texts herself the combination, so she won't forget—"

Gallow interrupted me: "Brooke gets into his safe and sees that Eglund has been paying someone to keep tabs on both his wife, Robin, and his longtime business partner—her dad."

"Right, and we can assume that the file Eglund kept on Nicholas Wexley was leverage for him—in case Eglund ever got busted by the FBI or dragged into an investigation by the SEC. Eglund would keep this info tucked away, so he had something to offer in exchange for immunity or a lesser sentence. I think we can assume that whatever was in that file would have ruined both of them."

Gallow said, "Because Brooke is dead?"

"Exactly." I paused a beat, then resumed the timeline. "So now it's October fifteenth, and Brooke has this highly incriminating evidence against her father. She's worried someone will come looking for the file, so she goes to her brother's fraternity and hides the documents there."

"What are you talking about?"

"Brooke went to Evan's frat three days before she was killed."

"Who told you this?"

"Her roommate Lauren."

"Why didn't you tell me?"

"I thought I'd have a better chance of getting Evan talking than you would."

"And did you?"

"Yeah, last night. After he beat me at beer pong."

Gallow stood and put his hands on his head. "Beer pong?"

I recounted my visit to the Monster Mash with Professor Jennifer Peppers.

"You broke his door down?" Mike shouted.

"I was seeing double by that point, and it took a couple kicks, but yeah, I kicked his door in."

I wasn't sure if Gallow was upset or jealous. Either way, I continued, "I didn't find the documents in his room, so either someone found them, or more likely, the day before she was killed, Brooke slipped back into the frat and retrieved them."

"Okay, so maybe Brooke hid the documents at Alpha Tau Omega and then goes back to get them. Or maybe she makes ten sets of copies. Or she scans them onto her laptop. Regardless, when she entered her tent the night of October seventeenth, she had a copy of the documents with her."

"Agreed."

"And she also had the megaphone that she bought at Target."

"Which she planned to use the next day to tell the world about her father's misdeeds."

Gallow had his own theory from this point forward, but he wanted to hear mine. "Then what happens?" he asked.

"Brooke is in her tent. It's now early on the eighteenth. She's got big plans for the next day: destroying her father's legacy. Maybe she's asleep, maybe she's too nervous to sleep. Then someone enters her tent."

"Who?"

I said, "Occam."

"I think so too."

Occam's razor is a principle that states that the simplest, most obvious explanation is usually the correct one.

I said, "Steven Eglund strangles Brooke, and his wife Robin impersonates her."

Gallow nodded at his computer screen. I leaned forward and scrutinized the Facebook post. It was a picture of Robin Eglund, Vera Wexley, and two other women. The four of them were holding apple martinis, and each was clad in a blond wig. A hashtag under the post read, "#BlondsHaveMoreFun."

"We know she has a blond wig," he said.

"And she's the right height." Based on the known height of the bridge railing and other constant factors, one of the Philly PD's resident tech wizards had calculated that the girl in the video was between five six and five seven, which was nearly the exact same height as Brooke, who was just over five six.

"How do you think it played out?" Gallow asked. "Give it your best shot."

"Steven Eglund figured out that Brooke had stolen his file on Nicholas Wexley. He tells his wife, Robin. Unlike her husband, Robin has only been living the life of the rich and famous for the past few years. She knows that whatever Brooke says on her soapbox the next day will ruin her husband's finances as well.

"After Eglund strangles Brooke, he takes Brooke's ID card and keys and gives them to Robin. Brooke had posted on Facebook earlier that night, so Robin knows how she's dressed. She stops by a store to buy a gray and blue Penn sweatshirt, or maybe she already owned one. They're similar in height, and with the blond wig and the hood of the sweatshirt up, it'd be nearly impossible to distinguish her from Brooke—at least on video, which is what they're banking on.

"Robin uses Brooke's ID and key to sneak into Brooke's dorm, and she takes her laptop, thinking Brooke might have scanned and uploaded the documents onto it. Robin walks back over the bridge with the laptop, so there's a false time stamp of Brooke coming back to her tent."

We looked at each other for a few seconds, then Gallow said, "It's time to run this up the chain."

≈

Captain Folch sat behind a large desk, digging into a Tupperware container filled with chicken, quinoa, and vegetables. Next to his healthy food was a green smoothie, which had separated into liquids and solids and resembled a fifth-grade science experiment.

"What can I do for you boys?" he said, setting his fork down.

Gallow turned and pulled the door shut. He spent the next ten minutes bringing Folch into the fold about what we knew and what we surmised. Folch was aware Steven Eglund had copped to having a relationship with Brooke, but the cabin in Harmony Lake, the hypothetical file, and the working theory that the girl in the bridge surveillance footage wasn't Brooke Wexley was all new information.

Folch said, "I would have preferred to be kept in the loop while all this was taking place, but if I was in your position, I can't say I wouldn't have played it any differently." He paused for a moment, then asked, "How many people know about Eglund's property near Harmony Lake?"

"Just me and Prescott," Gallow said, nodding at me.

I added, "Wade Gleason, the agent from Boston who is working the Numbers case, knows about it."

"We can't let any of this get out. Don't take this personally, Prescott, but you don't have the best track record. Even though you aren't officially involved in this case, if it gets out that you broke into Eglund's place, it could very well jeopardize any chance of putting them behind bars."

Gallow and I nodded.

Folch turned to Gallow. "Bring the Eglunds back in and see if you can get one of them to crack." He turned to me. "And Thomas, I know I shouldn't say it, but good work on locating the cabin and getting into the safe." He held up the text message record with the two codes. "No one working this case could figure out why Brooke texted herself those numbers." He dropped the paper. "But at any rate, we can't have you anywhere near this case going forward."

I put both hands up. "I'm done."

"Promise me."

"Scout's honor," I said, putting up my hand.

"Alright."

The three of us stood, and Captain Folch asked me, "Can you stick around for a second?"

I told him I would.

He said he had to take a leak, that the green stuff ran through him like a freight train, and he'd be back in a few minutes. He and Gallow exited the office, and I was left to twiddle my thumbs. After three twiddles, I stood and walked around the small room.

This was my first time in Folch's office. I picked up the heavy walnut and gold nameplate at the edge of his desk—*Capt. James Folch*—then set it down.

In the corner behind his desk, there was a giant water cooler—Folch bragged he drank a gallon of water a day—and his back wall was plastered with framed certificates. The right wall was covered in a series of busy bulletin boards. The left wall was taken up by shelving. Two of the shelves were packed with books, ranging from police procedure to triathlon training guides. Two framed pictures sat atop the bookshelf. One was an eight-by-ten photo of a much younger Folch going up for a layup. He was clad in a maroon and gold jersey that read "Boston College" on the front. Unlike the baggy college basketball clothes of the present day, his shorts were tight and rode high on his thighs. When I'd previously mentioned to him that Lacy was a collegiate swimmer, Folch had told me he'd played college ball from 1975 to 1978, but he'd either never told me or I'd forgotten where he played.

The second frame held two four-by-sixes, one on top of the other. The top photo was of two boys around ten or eleven years old. One was chubby; one was skin and bones. They had their arms around each other, and both were making goofy smiles. The bottom photo must have been taken thirty years later. The two were now standing in front of a golf cart, both doing precisely the same smile.

The chubby boy had turned into a fat man. He was easily recognizable: Mayor Bertram F. Stalnaker.

I picked the frame off the bookshelf and was attempting to read the inscription on the bottom photo when Folch returned.

"I've known Bertram since I was eight years old," Folch said, nodding at the photo. "Never in my wildest dreams did I think he would end up being the mayor."

"You guys grew up together?"

"Sure did. He lived three houses from me. He's still my closest friend."

I half expected him to tell an anecdote about him and Stalnaker growing up, but he cut to the chase. He said, "Nicholas Wexley."

I replaced the photos. "What about him?"

"Something tells me he's also involved in this."

"You think he was in on it with Steven and Robin?"

"That file would have endangered his empire."

I thought back on Wexley's alibi. It was too rock solid. No

one is on surveillance that much at two in the morning unless
they want to be.

"What do you want me to do?" I asked.

"Just see if you can rattle him." He added, "Unofficially,
of course."

"I thought you wanted me to steer clear of the case?"

"Forget what I said."

"Okey dokey."

I was getting ready to walk out the door, when I turned and
nodded at the framed picture of Folch and Mayor Stalnaker.

"What's written on the bottom of the photo?" I asked. The
inscription was in sloppy cursive, and I hadn't been able to
make out the words.

"To Lew," Folch said, pronouncing the last word as *Lev*. "It's
my nickname. It's Polish." He grinned. "It means *lion*."

37

"You wanted to see me," Jim Folch said, sticking his head into Coach Paduchowoski's office.

"Take a seat," Coach P replied, his heavy accent causing the words to come out, "Dake a zeat."

Jim sat and looked timidly across the desk. The Marston High School varsity basketball coach was in his early thirties, with blond hair, blue eyes, and a bulbous nose that had been broken more than once. His large hands were folded together, his knobby knuckles resembling two small mountain ranges.

This was Jim's second year under Coach P. Jim had made the varsity team as a sophomore, but he'd rode the bench. This year, as a junior, Coach had taken him under his wing, and he was starting at shooting guard. But Coach was constantly riding him, saying that he wasn't intense enough. That he passed too much. That he needed to toughen up.

"I'm sorry to hear about your dad," Coach P said. "It's a tragedy."

Inwardly, Jim scoffed. A tragedy is when a plane crashes or when there's an earthquake. A police officer killed for refusing to take a payoff wasn't a tragedy—it was premeditated murder.

"You know," Coach P said. "I lost my father when I was young."

"Really?"

"World War Two, when Germany invaded Poland. He was at work. The Nazis raided the place. Killed every worker there."

"How old were you?"

"Less than a year old." Coach P narrated how his mother had been forced to hide with him for three months, and then they were smuggled out of the country and into Latvia. It took another four years for them to find their way to the United States.

"When I started school here, I couldn't speak a word of English," Coach P said. "The kids were ruthless. They would beat me up every day. One day, when I came home from school, my mother saw that I had a black eye and a bloody lip. I will never forget what she said to me. She said, 'Ludwik, do you know what your father used to call you?' Of course, I didn't; I was too young. She said, 'He called you his little lion.' She said, 'I need you to be a lion.'"

"A lion?" Jim asked.

"Yes. And I became one. The next day, when the bullies surrounded me, I used a wrench to knock one of the kid's teeth out. No one ever touched me again."

Jim wasn't sure what this had to do with his dad's murder.

"Your father is dead," Coach P said. "He's not coming back. You are the man of the house now. You have to take care of your mother."

Jim's mother hadn't left the house since they'd identified the body at the morgue.

"I need you to become a lion. On the court. And off the court."

Jim had always been more of an Irish Setter—just happy to please everyone.

"Say it," Coach P coaxed him.

"Say what?"

"You're a lion."

"I'm, uh, a lion," Jim stammered.

"Say it like you mean it."

"I'm a lion!"

"Again! Louder!"

"I'M A LION!"

"Yes, you are," Coach P said, smiling. "When you step on the court tomorrow, you are no longer Jim. You are Lew." He pronounced the last word *Lev*. "That's *Lion* in Polish."

Jim walked out of the office. He would score thirty-seven points in the next day's game and go on to be named Second Team All-City. He would take care of his mother for the rest of her life.

And he would avenge his father's murder.

38

I spent Halloween morning with Lacy and then skipped the afternoon Numbers task force briefing in lieu of Operation Rattle.

Unlike last time, only one news van was parked in front of the Springlight Building. A lone reporter and camera operator sat on the small area of grass, tucking into hamburgers while they no doubt waited for one of the Wexleys to appear so they could bombard them with questions.

I walked up the steps toward the glistening front entrance. A doorman standing there appeared to be on high alert because of the reporters.

"Good afternoon, Donald," I said, reading the brass name-plate on his chest.

"Good afternoon," he replied sternly.

I pulled my FBI credentials out of my back pocket and flashed them. "I have a few questions about Nicholas Wexley."

He leaned in and scrutinized the card with my photo. Deciding it was authentic, his posture eased. "Happy to help, sir."

"Were you the doorman on duty when Nicholas Wexley returned home early on October eighteenth?"

"I was."

"Do you recall the exact time that Wexley arrived?"

"One thirteen a.m., if memory serves me correctly." He nodded at a video camera pointed toward the entrance. "Pretty sure the video surveillance confirmed it."

And according to Gallow, it had.

"Once anyone is inside, is there any way to leave the building without being seen?"

"There are two emergency exits, but they're wired to alert the fire department. We haven't had one of them tripped in over a year."

"Okay, but there must be a way to sneak out of this place." I lifted my eyebrows. "Or to sneak someone in."

"Not any way that I know of." If there was a way in, Donald was taking knowledge of it to his grave. Spilling tenants' secrets wouldn't do his job security any good.

"Alright," I said, "That's all for now."

As I pushed past him, I half expected Donald to dart a hand out and block me, but he didn't. I exited the revolving door and stepped into a wide foyer with elegant, light-blue tile.

I made my way to the elevator and stepped inside. I pushed the button for the penthouse—which is where I knew the Wexleys lived—but it didn't light up. There was a slit for a card beneath the button, and I figured you needed to slip in a keycard to access the top floor.

I rode the elevator to the twenty-first floor, stepped off, then walked to the stairwell and climbed up a flight. The door to the twenty-second floor was locked. It appeared there was no direct access to the penthouse.

I hustled down the stairs until I came to the emergency exit. I pushed the door open. The red light above the door flashed, and a klaxon alarm screamed.

The door opened to an alley, and I jogged from the exit for two hundred yards. Then I walked to the street and headed back toward the condos. Tenants were spilling out of the entrance, the fire alarm bellowing through open doors.

From across the street, I waited and watched for Nicholas Wexley to exit the building. He didn't. In fact, none of the Wexleys did. They were most likely at another one of their houses in town or even camped out at the place they had in the Hamptons.

The bored media representatives had scurried to their feet and one reporter was broadcasting live, detailing the building's evacuation as if it were a nuclear reactor meltdown.

Several teenagers had exited the building. Most of them had probably just returned home from school, and the vast majority looked supremely annoyed they had to leave their computers and televisions.

But one kid looked thrilled to be leaving. She held a skateboard under her arm, and after giving a half wave to her mother, she jumped on her board and took off.

I jogged behind her for a few blocks, but she was keeping a steady pace and I couldn't keep up. Thankfully, I knew where she was headed.

I cut through several alleys and then popped out on Market Street. She was skating in the bike lane on the street, and I stepped out in front of her. She skidded to a stop two feet in front of me, her long braid swishing out in front of her face.

"Get out of the way, assho—" She stopped mid-insult. "Oh, it's you—Hot Judge."

We both took a step to the safety of the sidewalk. "Hot Judge? Is that what you call me?"

"Some of the other girls do—and well, *Jeremy*." She cocked her head to the side. "I don't see it."

"I'm an acquired taste."

Braid laughed, then asked, "What's up?"

"You live in the Springlight, right?"

"Yeah."

"Can I ask you a few questions about the place?"

"I mean, I guess."

"You're in your unruly teen years. You probably want to sneak out of the condo every once in a while."

"Did Brian put you up to this?"

"Who's Brian?"

"My dipshit stepdad."

"I can assure you that your dipshit stepdad did not put me up to this."

"Then why do you want to know?"

"How about I give you a hundred dollars, and you don't ask any more questions?"

She agreed to $140.

I pulled out the dough and handed it over. She counted the money, then slipped it into her pocket.

I asked, "How do you sneak out of the condos without being seen?"

"Freight elevator."

"There are no video cameras?"

"Not on the elevator itself. There's a video camera in the basement, but it's easy to avoid."

"What's in the basement?"

"That's where they do the laundry, and the boiler room is down there."

"Where's the video camera, and how do you avoid it?"

"It's in the washroom. There are glass windows but if you crawl on the ground, it won't pick you up as you go to the boiler room."

"What's in the boiler room? An exit?"

"No, there's a door leading to another basement. I guess they used it when the place was a hotel."

"The condos used to be a hotel?"

"Yeah, it was built in like the 1920s. Then some big developers came around like twenty years ago and spent a bunch of money converting the place into luxury condos."

This wasn't unusual. A few years before the financial crisis, three different old hotels in New York City did the same thing. The profit margins for hotels are slim, whereas you could sell off condo units for big bucks.

"What's in this second basement?" I asked.

"Not a lot. It's mostly just storage. But there's a door that leads to a tunnel, and that *tunnel* leads to the subway."

"You're just messing with me here."

"No, I swear." She put her hand over her heart. "I've been down there a few times. It's super creepy."

I wasn't sure if I believed her. "What about the subway trains? How do you know when it's safe to go?"

"It's an old, abandoned line." She spent a few minutes explaining how the Spring Garden subway station had been shut down in the 1980s due to low ridership. "It's covered in a ton of graffiti, and there's a bunch of bums that live down there now."

"And you're telling me this is connected to the condo?"

"Yeah."

Braid could tell I was still on the fence about her veracity, and said, "My boyfriend uses the tunnel to sneak into the Springlight at least once a week."

"What for?"

She raised her eyebrows.

"Oh."

She laughed.

"Okay, I'm going to go check it out," I said.

"You need a key."

"A key?"

"Yeah, you need a key to access the sub-basement."

"Do you have one of these keys?"

"I gave mine to my boyfriend."

"And how did you get this key in the first place?"

"One of the old doormen gave it to one of the kids before he left. He used to sneak all sorts of people in and out of the hotel when he worked there. One of the kids made copies, and there are a few that are floating around. My older brother had one, and he gave it to me when he went off to college."

"And now your boyfriend has it?"

"Yeah."

"Can you text him and ask if I can borrow it?"

"I'm going to see him right now. In fact, I think you'll recognize him." She nodded at a kid on the other side of the street who was waiting for her. He was on crutches, and he had a big black boot on his left foot.

Ronnie.

≈

"You're back," the doorman, Donald, said.

I didn't reply.

"You know, it was the darndest thing," he continued, "but a couple minutes after you went inside the last time, the fire alarm went off. And then, strangely enough, I never did see you come out of the building."

"That wasn't me," I said. "That must have been my brother— Horace Prescott. He's always stealing my FBI badge and trying

to sneak past doormen and into condominiums. Then he likes
to pull fire alarms and not leave the building."

Donald stared at me vacantly.

I pushed past him and entered the lobby. I took the elevator to the basement and peeked through the glass window of
the laundry room. Several huge industrial-sized washers lined
the wall, and a maid was pulling sheets out of a large dryer and
folding them.

I continued down the hallway until I came to a door with a
loud buzzing emanating from behind it. I pulled open the door
and gazed at a series of large metal tanks that were connected
to steel plumbing: the boilers. The room was hot and muggy.
Behind the far-left boiler was a black door.

I pulled out the key Ronnie had given me and slipped it
into the lock. Even after everything that Braid had said, I was
still surprised when the door opened. I jogged down the stairwell, then entered the lower basement.

It was cleaner than expected with several large roll-up storage
doors, each secured by a padlock. I followed Braid's instructions,
going down the length of the hall and taking a hard right to
find yet another door.

This opened into a dark tunnel. I flipped on the mini flashlight on my keychain and illuminated a walkway about six feet
wide and eight feet tall. The concrete walls were covered in
graffiti and etchings. Most were hearts with initials inside, and
I guessed it was a rite of passage for Springlight teens to come
down here.

The tunnel ran a couple hundred yards. A rush of dank earth
odor overwhelmed me, and I pulled my chin into the neck of
my shirt. I coughed several times, then I stepped down onto a
narrow walkway.

It would have been easier to hop to the ground and walk

between the tracks, but no matter what Braid said, I wasn't risking getting run over by a train. Also, the third rail—the one that supplies the electrical current—could still be active.

No, thank you.

I walked for two football fields, then spotted a wide platform. I could see the outline of bodies in sleeping bags, and a few other people leaned against the wall.

As I neared, the silent faces of forgotten people appraised me. I wondered if any of them had seen Nicholas Wexley walk past two weeks earlier.

I approached one of them and asked, "Were you down here a couple weeks ago?"

"Give me twenty bucks."

I pulled out twenty dollars and handed it to him.

He put the money in his pocket and then said, "No."

We stared at each other for a moment, then I waved at his two friends who were asleep against the wall.

"What about them?" I asked.

"Give me fifty bucks."

I did.

This day was getting expensive.

"No," he said.

We had a three-second stare down and then I said, "Well, thanks so much."

I followed a staircase upward. According to Ronnie, the city had shuttered the Spring Garden Station exit with steel, but it wasn't flush. I pushed on a rusted steel panel with both hands, and it nudged forward, letting in eight inches of light. It bent forward another six inches. I wiggled my head and torso through the opening, then tumbled onto a sidewalk.

The subway exit was near Buttonwood and Twelfth—in front of a Korean restaurant. As I got to my feet, none of the pedestrians gave me a wayward glance. It must not be that uncommon to see someone exiting or entering the steel structure.

When I was ten feet away, I turned and looked back at the subway station entrance. Covered in corrugated steel, it resembled a shipping container half-sunk into the sidewalk.

I jog-walked to city hall, which I guessed to be just over a mile.

The day after Brooke's murder, the police had kicked the protesters off the marble walkway of city hall, but now they were back, and they had reproduced.

I weaved my way through the thicket of protesters and to the area where Brooke's tent had been erected. A makeshift memorial was set up with posters, flowers, candles, and stuffed animals.

I'd already done the math in my head but went over it a second time out loud, trying to put a dent in Wexley's alibi: "He checks for a package at the front desk at 1:17 a.m., then enters the fitness center at 1:38 a.m. That gives him twenty-one minutes to sneak out through the tunnel, get to city hall, strangle his daughter, then race back to the Springlight."

Wexley appeared to be in good physical shape. Could he do it?

There was only one way to find out.

I started the timer on my cell phone, then turned and ran, retracing my steps to the basement of the Springlight.

39

At fifty-eight floors of shimmering graphite and glass, for eleven years the Wexlund Tower held claim as the tallest building in Philadelphia. It wasn't until 2008—when the sixty-floor Comcast Center was built—that Wexlund lost that distinction.

Wexlund Capital occupied the fourth, twelfth, thirty-third, and fifty-eighth floors of its namesake. I expected Nicholas's office to be on the top floor and was surprised when the front desk attendant told me it was on the thirty-third.

"Do you have an appointment?" asked the attendant, Derrick. He was about my age, with spiky blond hair.

"I don't." I flashed my FBI credentials for the second time in the last two hours. "But I don't need one."

Derrick audibly gulped, and I said, "Don't even think about calling up there first."

He nodded and pushed a sign-in sheet toward me. I doubted he had time to read my name off my credentials, so I signed a name and slid the form back to him.

He filled out a visitor badge and handed it to me. "Here you go, Agent Yoon."

I clipped the badge to my shirt and headed to the elevator.

I exited on the thirty-third floor. The carpet was forest green, and the walls a beige stucco.

I pushed through a plate glass door and surveyed the young woman behind the desk. She was wearing cat ears. Her nose was painted red, and she had whiskers drawn on her cheeks. It was Halloween in corporate America too.

"Let me guess," I exclaimed. "You're a—*cat!*"

She didn't know whether to laugh or hit the panic button under her desk.

"Um," she muttered. "Yep, I'm a cat."

"I knew it," I said, snapping my fingers. "I've always been amazing at guessing costumes."

She smiled meekly and asked, "Can I help you with something?"

"I need to speak with Nicholas Wexley."

"He's in a meeting right now. Do you have an appointment?"

"I'll just go in and have a look around."

"No, you won't."

I flashed my badge. "I think I will."

Unlike Derrick who had cowered at the sight of the badge like a bowl of room temperature tapioca pudding, Cat wasn't easily intimidated.

Good hire.

She said, "Take a seat, and I'll see if Mr. Wexley will see you."

I continued standing.

She picked up the phone. A moment later, she set it back down and said, "I'm sorry, but Mr. Wexley is unavailable. He's directed you to call his lawyer." She rifled through the desk, then handed me a card.

I took it with a smile. "Thank *meow.*"

While she was dazed by my stupidly, I darted toward the door leading to the inner offices and ripped it open.

"You can't go in there!" Cat bellowed behind me.

I raced through the open hallway to a glass office at the back of the room, where I saw a meeting taking place. I jogged to the door, knocking loudly on the glass wall. Twelve heads swiveled to gaze at me.

Nicholas Wexley was at the head of the table, and I pointed at him. "You!" I shouted. "Now!"

Cat caught up with me and yanked on my shirt, trying to pull me back.

I hissed at her.

When I turned back around, Wexley had gotten to his feet. He rushed through the glass door and yelled, "What the hell is going on?"

"Agent Prescott," I said, flashing my credentials. "I need ten minutes of your time."

"Call security, Veronica."

"I already did."

As if on cue, three massive security guards came crashing through the doors. I didn't stand a chance. They grabbed me, and I went limp. They hauled me backward, my legs dragging on the lavish carpet, when I yelled, "Steven Eglund has been keeping a file on you!"

"What?" Wexley asked, striding forward.

"Eglund has been keeping a file on you for the past twenty years. It's leverage in case the SEC and Feds ever come knocking."

"Let him go," he instructed the three security guys.

They dropped me, and my upper body joined my legs on the fancy plush carpeting. I pushed myself up, dusted off my pants, and said, "Shall we?"

Nicholas Wexley directed me to his office.

We hadn't crossed the threshold, when he muttered, "What file are you talking about?"

"The file Steven Eglund has been keeping on you for the last twenty years."

"Steven wouldn't keep a file on me," he said, calmer now. "And so what if he did? I've never done anything illegal."

I ignored that, realizing why he wasn't as surprised. "So, Eglund told you about the file."

Wexley took a seat, spun in his fancy desk chair, and poured himself a whiskey from a decanter on the shelf. After facing me again with a drink in front of him, he made a circular motion with his index finger as if to say, "Let's hear the rest of this bullshit."

I took the seat opposite his desk and leaned forward. "You, Steven, and Robin Eglund all had a lot to lose if that file went public. You could not allow that to happen. So you came up with a plan. You knew Brooke was going to be in her tent at city hall, and you knew exactly what she was wearing because of the picture she posted on Facebook."

"I've never been on Facebook. Not once in my life."

"Sure, you haven't," I quipped.

He blew out a long breath.

"On the morning of the seventeenth, you get back to your condo at one in the morning," I said. I ran him through the timeline. "Then you go through the tunnel, empty out into the abandoned subway, exit on Buttonwood and Twelfth, and then sprint to city hall, and you strangle your daughter."

"Listen, asshole," he said, getting to his feet. "I didn't kill my daughter!"

I ignored him. "You take the documents, Brooke's student ID, and her keys. You hand off the ID and keys to Robin Eglund, then race back. I did the run from city hall to the subway and back to the condo in under eight minutes. Double that and leave time for strangling your daughter and cleaning up—maybe three minutes—and it took me under twenty." I nodded at him. "You're in good shape. I'm sure you could do the same."

He glared at me for a moment and then said, "Now remind me, where does Robin Eglund come into this?"

"She's the one impersonating your daughter."

"Impersonating my daughter. What the hell are you talking about?"

"Oh, cut the act."

"Seriously, what are you talking about?" He walked around his desk and sidled up an inch from my face. "What do you know?"

"We know that the girl on Market Street Bridge surveillance video is not Brooke. Robin Eglund wore the wrong shoes."

"Shoes? What shoes?"

I flipped open my phone and pulled up the picture. He stared at the picture for several seconds. "Why wasn't I told about this?" He picked up the phone, hit a button, and shouted, "Mark, get Rocklin on the phone. Now!"

Rocklin was the private investigator Wexley had hired.

"You guys almost got away with it," I said, not backing down. "At five foot seven, with her jeans, University of Pennsylvania hoodie, and blond wig, Robin was a perfect doppelgänger for Brooke. She used the ID card and the keys you gave her to slip into Brooke's dorm and take her laptop. You guys couldn't risk that Brooke had scanned and uploaded the file onto her computer."

"Listen, shithead, I have no idea what you're talking about. I didn't have anything to do with my daughter's death." He pulled up his left pant leg. "Not that I owe you anything, but I couldn't run a mile these days; I can barely even walk one."

His left knee had a puffy red scar running over the knee-cap. "That vacation I took to Saint Barts six weeks ago? I was down there getting my knee replaced. I didn't want anyone to know, so I didn't come back until I could walk without a limp."

If he was telling the truth, it would be another month or longer before he could run. He couldn't have done the round trip to city hall in under twenty minutes. Hell, he probably couldn't have done it in under an hour.

"That's why I was in the fitness center for almost two hours the night Brooke was killed. Doing my rehab." His phone rang and he snatched it up.

I guessed it was Rocklin.

"Why the hell didn't anyone tell me about the shoes?" Wexley said, slapping down the top of his laptop with a loud clap. I was guessing this was going to trace its way back to Gallow soon.

I stared at the laptop for a long second.

A loud *ping* went off in my head.

"I'm just going to let myself out," I said.

I raced past Cat.

The doors to the elevator swished closed.

How could I be so dumb?

Brooke didn't hide the documents in Evan's room.

She hid them on his *computer*.

40

It was Halloween night so I guessed that, at some point, most of the brothers of Alpha Tau Omega would hit the bars or maybe head over to one of the sororities.

I staked the frat out from my rented Camry a half block away. My own car was currently in the shop being "de-shithead-ed."

At nine thirty, a group of bros exited the frat. I saw a few costumes I didn't remember seeing two nights earlier, but most were repeat offenders. Evan Wexley was again unimaginatively outfitted as Hugh Hefner in a scarlet smoking jacket. The crucial difference was that tonight the male pledges were dressed in bikinis. Nine of them went around, passing out beers. The fraternity brothers did a big mass shotgun, then chucked their empty cans at the pledges.

College!

They departed a moment later, and once they rounded the corner of the next street, I jumped out of my car and headed to the side entrance that I'd fled from forty-six hours earlier.

The door was unlocked, and I climbed the three flights of stairs. Because it was a Monday, there was a solid chance that a few frat boys had stayed home to study. Thankfully, this time around I was sober and eased my way down the empty hall to Evan's door.

I hoped Evan hadn't been able to fix his door since I last kicked it in, but he had. The cracked door had been swapped out for a pristine one.

"Damn," I muttered.

I checked the door to make sure. Locked. There was only one other way inside: through the window.

I pulled out my wallet, and within ten seconds, I jimmied the lock on Messy Redhead's door. The room was still a disaster, and I plowed through the layer of clothes on the floor and to the window. His window, much like Evan's, gazed out on the fraternity's backyard. It was chilly, and I didn't see anyone out there, though I'm sure it was just a matter of time before someone popped outside to smoke a cigarette or a joint.

I slid the window up. A small concrete ledge ran the perimeter of the fraternity on the second and third stories. The ledge was narrow, less than four inches. I eased myself over the windowsill. I was comfortable with heights, but I still shouldn't have looked down. I was twenty feet up. If I fell, I might land in one of the bushes below, but I'd still break something. And if I missed the bushes, I'd be eating my next chocolate chip waffle through a tube.

The mortar had eroded from between the exterior bricks, and I found fingerholds at eye level. I shimmied two feet, five feet, eight feet, ten feet, twelve feet, then I reached Evan's window.

I was pushing the window up, when my right foot slipped. I caught myself, grabbing the windowsill with both hands and pulling my weight into the brick.

My heart fluttered.

I eased my foot back onto the ledge.

"Campus Blotter, October thirty-first, 2011," I muttered, "'Peeping Tom Falls to Death.'"

Literally.

I reminded myself why I was risking life and limb to solve this case. When I closed my eyes, it was no longer Brooke lying cold on the floor of that tent.

It was Lacy.

I shook my head clear and went back to work. Within a few seconds, I was folding myself through the window and then flopped onto the floor of his room. I pushed myself up, dusted off my pants, then sat at Evan's desk. His laptop was flipped up, and I pushed the space bar. If he had a passcode to get in, I was screwed.

He didn't.

I clicked open his document folder. It contained 457 files and ninety-one folders. The folders ranged from "English Lit" to "March Madness Research" and they were listed alphabetically.

The Mayan Apocalypse would come before I would get through all of them.

I moved to the back corner of the room, pulled out my phone, and dialed Lacy. She picked up on the third ring, and I explained the situation.

"Switch the sorting to Last Modified," she said.

She instructed me on how to change the sorting from Name (alphabetically) to Last Modified.

I hung up and then started in.

The top document was titled "Finance 203." It was last modified on October 16. I opened it. It was a four-page paper. I read the first paragraph, then closed the file. I verified the next three files were authentic, and then I came to the fifth folder down. Something had been modified in a folder titled "Freshman Orientation."

Why was a file in that folder modified recently?

I looked at the date: 10/15/2011.

Three days before Brooke was murdered. The day she came to the frat.

"Now we're getting somewhere."

I clicked the folder open.

Several documents were in the folder, but tucked in there was another folder titled "Completed Tasks." I clicked on it.

It contained a single document: a twenty-seven-page PDF. I clicked it open.

"Holy shit!" I whisper-shouted.

I tightened my hands into fists and squeezed.

≈

I checked the front pocket of my jacket. My face fell. The USB drive that I'd brought was gone.

Had it fallen out of my pocket somehow when I'd been out on the ledge? But how? Maybe it had tumbled out when I climbed through the window?

I shot out of the seat and scanned the floor for the drive. It was nowhere to be seen.

"Dammit," I muttered, though it wasn't that big of a deal. I would just email myself the file.

I sat back down and logged on to the internet. At least, I tried to. The page wouldn't load. I checked the internet connection.

There wasn't one.

I had no other option; I would have to print the file.

Hopefully, no one would hear the printer behind Evan's door and get curious. The printer located on a rolling shelf of the desk looked like it was top of the line. Hopefully, it was quiet.

I clicked the printer icon on the PDF. A screen popped up and showed the document had started to print. I glanced at the printer. The green light was on, but nothing was happening.

I leaned forward and read the print destination off the laptop screen—HP Envy #2.

Evan's printer was an Epson.

Uh-oh.

The document was printing somewhere else. But how was that possible without an internet connection? I looked at the back of the laptop and saw an Ethernet cable running into a plug in the wall. It must be connected to an industrial printer somewhere, which means there was likely a business center on one of the floors.

I thought about canceling the print job, but it had already finished.

I had to go.

Now.

I closed the file and then slapped the laptop shut. I was getting ready to open the door, when I heard voices in the hall.

The hallway wasn't an option. I had to go back the way I'd come.

I crawled out onto the window's ledge. There was enough of a gap between the bricks that I figured I could climb down. I eased my feet off the ledge, then lowered myself until I was hanging from the ledge with both hands. The drop was about fifteen feet.

I found a foothold on top of a row of bricks with the toe of my shoe, and a handhold on a brick three rows below the ledge. I added my second hand to the same row and then methodically began lowering myself a foot at a time. After a few minutes, I'd made it to the concrete ledge under the second-floor windows.

I was now only twelve feet up.

I'd just lowered my hands to the ledge when I heard a door open and a young man appeared below me. He gazed out on the back fence, then he pulled a pack of cigarettes from his pocket and lit one. He took a long drag and exhaled.

If he turned around or glanced up, he was going to see some imbecile doing his best Spider-Man impression six feet above him.

I could smell the smoke from his cigarette as I flattened myself to the brick. I could feel the smoke in my throat, tickling my lungs. I held back a cough, flexing against my body's natural programmed response to a pulmonary irritant.

After two seconds, I could fight no longer.

I coughed twice.

The kid glanced up.

"Hi," I said.

His eyes opened wide, and the cigarette dropped from his hand.

In this situation, there were two choices: fight or flight. Frat boy chose flight.

He was so frazzled that he had difficulty opening the back door, and after dropping to the ground, then springing to my feet—some might say like a jungle cat—I raced through the open door and grabbed him by the back of the shirt.

He let out half a scream before I clamped my hand over his mouth.

"Shut up, kid," I said. "I'm not going to hurt you."

The back door led to the fraternity kitchen, which was, luckily, empty. I dragged the kid to the prep area and into a big walk-in freezer.

I let him go, pushing him backward. He fell to the ground and back-pedaled eight feet until he ran into a shelf stacked high with frozen hamburger patties.

"Sorry I scared you, kid," I said.

"What do you want?" he mumbled, sinking to the floor, and crossing his arms over his knees.

"I just need something from the business center. Where is it?"

"I'm not saying anything," he said. Then, apparently noticing that he was twenty pounds bigger than me, he pushed up
to his feet. From the way he was positioning his feet, I could
tell he was considering rushing me.

"Don't do it, kid."

As I was backing toward the door, he charged.

I pulled an enormous bag of frozen corn dogs off the shelf
near me and brought it crashing down on the top of his head.

He crumpled to the cold floor.

I pulled him by his feet away from the door so it would
open, then speed-walked through the kitchen and into the living
area. Two guys were on the couch, fully absorbed in Monday
Night Football—which was blaring so loud it had masked their
brother's scream. They didn't give me a second glance as I walked
behind them.

I'd seen most of the first and third floors during the party,
and I guessed the business center was on the second floor. I
jogged up the steps and walked halfway down the hall to the
only room without a number. The door was unlocked and gave
way to several desktop computers and two industrial printers.

I went to the first one and grabbed the stack of pages.

The door opened, and I turned around.

A kid with shaggy brown hair strolled in. He wore sweatpants and a tank top. He held a beer in his hand.

I handed him the pages. "Here you go."

He eyed me skeptically as he took the documents. "Who
are you?"

"Gary." I stuck out my hand.

He shook it limply.

I said, "Chris said that I could sneak over and use your
guys' printer."

"Chris W. or Chris H.?"

"Chris H. I saw him over at the Zeta party and he reminded me we have this big paper due tomorrow. He gave me his keys and said I could print it out over here."

The kid took a drink of his beer. "Whatever." He turned and left.

The pages in the second printer tray were still warm and I hurriedly grabbed the thick stack, twisted them into a tight spiral, and jammed them into the front of my pants.

As I opened the door to leave, an exchange of loud voices erupted from the first floor. Freezer Guy must have recovered from getting corn-dogged and alerted the others to my presence.

Time to flee.

Luckily, I had practice.

I ran down the hall, went down the emergency exit stairs, burst through the side entrance, then ran to my car. I drove several blocks, then parked on a side street.

I picked up the file from the passenger seat. The top page read, "Troy Milligan, History 203, The Destruction of the Inca Empire."

Incas?

I groaned.

I grabbed some kid's homework instead of the Wexley file!

Or so I thought.

I picked up the large stack of pages, and on further inspection I realized it was the Wexley file. The kid's homework was only printed on the back of one of the pages of the file. The frat must recycle scratch paper back into the printer.

I flipped on the interior lights and spent the next few minutes poring over the printout.

It was worse than I ever imagined.

There were detailed records of more than two hundred deals ranging from insider trading to blatant fraud. The most damning evidence was a series of short sells that Wexlund Capital had made based on tip-offs from an FBI agent named Josh Chamberlain. Evidently, Nicholas Wexley had paid this Chamberlain hundreds of thousands of dollars for inside information on companies that were under federal investigation. If indictments or charges were likely coming against a public trading company, Wexley would short the companies' stocks. An Excel spreadsheet showed that from the years 1994 to 2006, Wexlund Capital had made roughly $235 million in profit off these shorts.

Brooke wanted this information to be made public.

She had wanted to destroy her father.

Now it was up to me.

41

When Gleason pulled over his sedan in front of my building, I ran from the entrance through the rain, covering my head with my hands as I ducked into the car.

"Where were you yesterday?" Gleason asked over the sound of the slapping windshield wipers.

"I had a few errands to run."

"Did these errands have to do with a Mr. Nicholas Wexley?"

"Perhaps."

I gave him a quick rundown on my visit to the Springlight and my field trip to Wexlund Capital. But I held off telling him about the documents. On that note, I'd nearly called Gallow to tell him what I'd found in the file, but he would have to follow procedure, sending them to the SEC and Feds. I didn't like the sound of that. I wanted to be in control of the carnage. It was like being the guy who carried the president's suitcase nuke. Then it was up to me to decide when and where to detonate it to inflict maximum damage.

Surprisingly, Gleason was more interested in the Springlight escape route than he was about my accosting the wealthiest man in Philadelphia.

"The condominiums are connected to an old train station?" he asked.

"I didn't believe it either at first. It's as creepy a place as I've ever been. I'm sure there are some dead bodies in those tunnels."

He asked a few more questions about the tunnels, and then I told him about my run-in with Wexley at his office.

"Was there any fallout?" Gleason asked.

"I haven't heard anything yet, though I have twenty-nine missed calls from Agent Joyce, so I'm guessing there might be."

"Good thing you don't have voicemail."

"A very good thing."

"Any texts?"

"Just that I needed to call him back ASAP."

"I'm going to walk fifty feet behind you when we go in."

"Smart."

≈

True to his word, Gleason lagged well behind me as I pushed through the doors of the FBI building.

I handed over my credentials to the security guard—a woman in her early fifties with blond hair going gray at the roots—and she scanned them into the computer. "Have a goo—" The computer made a beeping noise, which is rarely a good sign, and she said, "Looks like your card has been deactivated."

"Deactivated?" I asked.

"Yes," a booming voice shouted. It was Agent Joyce, striding toward the front entrance. "Deactivated!"

A body pushed through the front doors. I turned, expecting to see Gleason, but instead it was a man with two cascading black eyes and a splint on his nose.

Hufflepuff.

He must have been keeping watch in the parking lot and texted Joyce when he'd seen me approach.

"Nice face," I said.

He sneered—which likely caused him pain—and his hand went up to his nose.

I turned to Agent Joyce and asked, "Why the hell is my card deactivated? Are you kicking me off the Numbers task force?"

Gleason pushed through the front entrance. His eyes opened wide at the sight of Hufflepuff and Joyce.

"You're damned right you're off the task force," Joyce said, throwing his hands in the air. "You used your FBI creds to charge into the office of the most powerful man in Philadelphia. What did you think was going to happen?"

"Maybe a demerit."

"A demerit? This isn't boarding school, you idiot. This is the Federal Bureau of Investigation. You don't get demerits."

"Do whatever you have to do. But you guys need me."

"I am doing what I have to do. You're off the case. And, contrary to what you might think, we do not need you. We can and will catch this asshole without you."

It was quiet for a half second and Gleason said, "Um, I'm just going to sneak past here real quick." He gave his badge to the security guard, and she scanned it.

"Go on through," she said.

I wrapped my arms around him and hugged him from behind. "I'll never forget you." He squirmed out of my grip, and I added, "We'll always have the time we dug up that old lady together."

He was shaking his head and trying to hold back laughter as he hurried away through the metal detector. He grabbed his bag and headed for the elevators.

"Give me your creds," Joyce said, reaching out his hand.

I took my creds and Frisbee-tossed them through the large atrium. They landed on the tile and slid for another twenty feet. Then I walked out.

≈

This was the fourth time I'd been fired. The first time was when I was working at Baskin-Robbins in high school. Evidently, it goes against corporate policy to slip a piece of paper with your phone number into a cute girl's double scoop of mint chocolate chip. The second time was when I was working as a landscaper after dropping out of the University of Washington. Supposedly, I weedwacked a flower that only blooms every six years. Then, of course, there was the Seattle Police Department. And now the FBI.

"What do you think?" I asked Baxter, who was lying on my stomach in the living room. "Did I overreact?"

If I had a time machine, I would have responded more diplomatically, but alas, I could never muster the 1.21 gigawatts.

Baxter shook his little body back and forth and snorted.

"Yeah, I was out of line."

I picked up his favorite toy—a small stuffed green spider— and tossed it to the other side of the living room. He raced after it, grabbed it in his mouth, and darted back. He was a few feet from me when his body went limp and he somersaulted forward, landing a few inches from where I was leaning against the couch.

Lacy had taken him to the vet, but even with the pills they prescribed, he still crumpled asleep several times each hour.

Around 7:00 p.m. I went for a run.

I didn't know where I was headed when my feet first hit the pavement, but after five minutes, I'd unconsciously made my way toward city hall.

The crowd was enormous, Occupy Philadelphia having grown exponentially in the two weeks since Brooke Wexley's murder. The early hours of night were prime marching hours, and the streets and sidewalks were overflowing with young men and women holding signs.

I continued my jog until I found myself near the Rittenhouse Hotel, where I was surprised to see a large crowd gathered out front. Their collective breath fogged above their heads as they chanted, "*Hey Romney! Picture this! No more greedy politics!*"

Mitt Romney was projected to be the Republican nominee in the upcoming election, and I'd seen on the news that he was in town for a fundraiser at the Rittenhouse. It was a $10,000-a-plate affair, which wasn't going over too well with this liberal mob.

I made a U-turn and ran until I came to the Schuylkill River Trail. It would eventually lead to Paine's Park and the Philadelphia Museum of Art.

I'd cracked more than a few cases while running. The endorphin release helps to quiet all the white noise in my head, and small details that might have been lost bubble to the surface. But today I didn't want to think about the Numbers Killer or Brooke.

I just wanted to run.

I doubled my pace, and five minutes later I reached the sprawling Philadelphia Museum of Art, which was home to one of the most famous cinematic scenes in movie history. The seventy-two stone steps leading to its entrance are the steps that Rocky Balboa (Sylvester Stallone) triumphantly runs up in the movie and then raises his hands in victory.

I'd acted out the scene the day after Lacy and I first arrived in Philly three years earlier. And I'd done it another eighty-seven times since.

The limestone steps are five inches high and fifteen inches

deep. They are broken up into sections—separated by several wide landings—rising majestically to the museum, which is a towering Greek vestige modeled after the Parthenon.

I powered up the first two sections. Once I hit the third landing, I gritted my teeth, taking the remaining steps two at a time. When I reached the top, I turned around—just like Rocky—and raised my hands.

Something smashed into my left side.

I fell to the ground, hitting my right shoulder and rolling backward. My attacker was on top of me, and two heavy punches rained down on my face. The man was dressed similar to the man I'd seen on the SS *United States*. All black, gloves, ski mask. But it wasn't the Numbers Killer. Well, unless he'd grown seven inches and tacked on sixty pounds in the last week.

My attacker was huge. A giant.

After absorbing several more strikes, I grabbed the front of the man's jacket. I pulled him close so he didn't have any space to load his punches. With my left hand, I dug my thumb through the eyehole of his mask and an inch deep into his eye.

He screamed.

I slugged him in the face and then rolled to my left.

He dragged me back to him, then punched me hard in the side, sending the air out of my lungs. In my moment of weakness, he straddled me.

He pulled a yellow gun from his pocket. A Taser. I guess he didn't understand how currents work and I clamped my hands around both his wrists a millisecond before he pushed the trigger.

A shock of fifty thousand volts of electricity shot through my body. But it also shot through my attacker.

I'd been shocked before, so I knew what to expect. I doubted my attacker had any idea that for the next ten seconds he would be dipped in a volcano.

He screamed and attempted to roll off me, but our legs were intertwined, and his body took mine with it.

We rolled off the top step, then down another two. We picked up momentum as we went, a combined almost four hundred pounds of dead weight searching for a landing spot.

≈

When I came to, there was a teenage boy standing over me.

"Dude, you okay?" he asked.

"I'm not sure," I croaked.

I was lying in the middle of one of the landings. With one eye open, I gazed upward. "Did I fall down all those steps?" I asked, my breathing labored.

"Yeah. It was gnarly."

I thought back to my attacker. "What about the other guy?"

"He only fell down about ten of the stairs, then ran off."

Lucky bastard.

"Do you want me to call somebody?" the kid asked. "Like the police?"

I opened both eyes. Somehow my vision was clear. Evidently, my head had escaped major injury. My right side was stinging, but I would live.

"No, I'm good."

He helped me to my feet, stuck around for another minute to make sure I wasn't going to die, then went on his way.

I found the Taser hanging off one of the steps below me. I slipped it into my pocket, then limped toward home.

42

"I'm the one with MS, you know," Lacy said, tossing a plate of breakfast Eggos onto my stomach. "You should be the one taking care of me."

My abs instinctively contracted, sending blinding pain through my aching rib cage. "*Ahhhhhhhh!*" I yelped.

"Come on. It can't be that bad."

I set the plate of Eggos on the bed and gingerly lifted my shirt, exposing the ribs on my right side.

At the sight, Lacy's eyes widened in shock. "I stand corrected."

It hurt to move my head, and I didn't have a good viewing angle. "Is there a bruise?"

"Um, yeah—it looks like someone hit you with a cannon-ball." She shook her head. "I thought you said that you tripped and hit a stair."

"I may have simplified things."

"What really happened?"

"A guy attacked me, then tasered me, and then I fell and hit thirty-two stairs." I cocked my head to the side. "Though, there's a chance I may have skipped a couple stairs. We'll call it twenty-eight to be safe."

"You were attacked! Why didn't you say anything about this last night?"

"I didn't want to alarm you."

"Shit, Tommy, I think you need to go to the hospital. You're probably bleeding internally or something."

"Nah, I'm fine."

I attempted to reach over and grab one of the waffles, but it was too painful. I let out a groan.

Lacy shook her head, then sat on the edge of the bed. She cut my waffles and fed them to me.

"Does it hurt to chew?" she asked.

"Yes—and breathe."

After I finished eating and took a few sips of water, Lacy said, "Seriously, you need to go get checked out. You could have lacerated one of your kidneys or ruptured your spleen."

"Spleen? That's not a thing. What's it do?"

"I don't know, spleeny things. But it happened to one of the Drexel football players."

"I bet it was the kicker."

"Get up!" she barked. "We're going to the hospital."

≈

Dr. Garcia, the emergency room physician, pulled aside the hospital's privacy curtain and said, "The results from your CT scan came back and you have a ruptured spleen."

"*Ha!*" Lacy said. "I told you."

The doctor, a Hispanic woman with just the slightest hint of an accent, cut her eyes at Lacy.

"Sorry," Lacy said, shaking her head. "It's just—he didn't believe me that a spleen is a thing."

"It is very much a thing," Dr. Garcia said, regarding me sternly. "And yours has a small tear in it."

I asked, "Do you think it could have happened when I sneezed yesterday?"

The doctor knit her brows and appraised me for a beat, then patiently replied, "I think it's more likely your injury was sustained around the time you were tasered and fell down twenty-eight steps."

"Well, you're the doctor," I said, trying to sit up, then changing my mind.

Lacy pinched me on the shoulder, something she did when I was being a bit too Thomasy.

"*Ow!*" I shrieked.

Lacy pulled her top lip into her bottom lip and glared my way.

"Sorry, Doctor," I said. "Please continue."

Dr. Garcia said, "Thankfully, there's minimal internal bleeding, and I don't think surgery will be necessary."

"That's good," Lacy said.

"The injury should heal on its own over the next few weeks, but we're going to keep you overnight to monitor your blood pressure. And we'd like to have you here in the rare case that you should need an emergency blood transfusion."

"I've never had one of those," I said.

"That's certainly a good thing."

"The luck of the Irish."

Lacy shook her head. "We're not Irish."

Dr. Garcia looked like she was silently wishing for a "Code Blue" call to come over the intercom. She rattled off a few more logistics, then fled before I could hit her with another zinger.

"Why are you so annoying?" Lacy asked. "I know it can't be genetic."

"My spleen," I said, making a big frowny face.

Lacy fought down a smile, but she wasn't strong enough, and it flashed. "I'm going home now. Text me if you're bleeding to death."

"Will do."

"Do you need anything else?"

Lacy had brought her iPad, and she'd been playing internet doctor with it while we waited to be seen.

"Can I keep your iPad?"

She rocked her head from side to side.

"I want to play *Tetris*," I begged.

"Fine."

She pulled the iPad out of her enormous purse and handed it to me.

"Thanks, Lacy Marie."

It had been a while since I called her by her full name, and she let out a sigh, then gave me a kiss on the forehead.

"Bye, idiot."

≈

When there was a knock on the door to my hospital room, I glanced up and was surprised to see Gallow standing in the doorway, a paper bag in hand. "I snuck you in a little treat," he said with a giant smile.

I laughed, which didn't hurt too bad because of the two Percocet I'd taken an hour earlier, and said, "My guy!"

He came forward and gave one of my feet a slap. "Your sister texted me."

"What did she say?"

"That you were attacked, that you ruptured your spleen, and that it was entirely fine with her if I came to the hospital and smothered you with a pillow."

"That sounds like her."

"Where should I put this?" He waved the bag of Geno's at me.

I directed him to put it on the small side table. To be honest, the last thing I wanted to eat right now was a greasy cheesesteak, but I didn't want to seem ungrateful. Plus, there was a guy in the room across the hall who sounded like he didn't have much longer to live. Maybe it could be his last meal.

Gallow plopped onto one of the two cushioned chairs, and I detailed what had happened on the *Rocky* steps.

"Damn," he said. "Any idea who it was?"

"I'm guessing it was someone sent by Nicholas Wexley."

"But don't forget that you also beat up an old Mob boss in a nursing home."

"Oh yeah, that crossed my mind."

"Did you get any good licks in?"

"I stuck my thumb an inch deep into one of his eyes. He won't be passing the DMV eye exam anytime soon."

He laughed, and I asked, "So, what happened with the Eglunds? Did they crack and admit to killing Brooke?"

"Bad news. Their alibis held up."

"Their HBO marathon?"

"No, that was just a story they cooked up to cover for what they were really doing."

"And what was that?"

"Swinging."

"Bullshit."

"Seriously, they were with two other couples that night. All four of them vouched that the Eglunds were there until at least two in the morning."

"Damn."

"I know. Back to the drawing board."

≈

I woke from a nap around dinner time. The menu was turkey, green beans, mashed potatoes, and a fruit cup. I didn't have much of an appetite and after eating the peaches out of the fruit cup, I pushed the tray aside.

I picked up Lacy's iPad and logged into the hospital Wi-Fi. I'd just fizzled out on level 18 of *Tetris* and was preparing to start a fresh game, when a series of notifications came in from Facebook.

I clicked on the Facebook icon and found myself on Lacy's profile. Four minutes earlier, she'd posted a picture of Baxter asleep on the kitchen counter with the caption "I swear, I didn't put him up there!"

I was bored and decided to see if I could figure out who this Horse Doodle guy was, who she had a crush on. Lacy only had 293 friends, so it shouldn't be too hard.

I was scrolling through the thumbnails of all her friends, when I stopped cold. The thumbnail was tiny, but I recognized the smug smile and coiffed black hair.

I pulled out my cell phone and dialed Lacy.

"How much blood have you lost?" she answered. "It better be at least two pints."

"Why are you friends with Evan Wexley?" I asked.

"I'm not."

"He's your friend on Facebook."

"Oh, right. I friend-requested him a few days after his sister died. I wanted to send him a message to say that I was sorry."

"Did he reply?"

"No."

"You never pursued it any further."

"Pursued? No, I never pursued anything. He's got a super-serious girlfriend." She paused. "Make that *fiancée*."

"He's engaged?" I thought about the ring I'd seen in his room.

"Yeah, the post popped up in my feed a couple days ago. There was a pic of him proposing."

"How do I see that picture?"

"Are you in his profile?"

"Uh, hold on." I clicked on his picture and his profile came up. "Now I am."

"Scroll down."

I did.

The top post was a picture of Evan and the bumblebee I saw at the Monster Mash. She was holding her left hand out, the giant ring I'd seen in Evan's closet plastered on her finger. In the background of the photo were Evan's mother and younger sister. Both were smiling, and it must have been a respite, if brief, from the agony and sorrow of the past two weeks. From the water in the background, I guessed the picture had been taken at the Wexleys' Hamptons estate.

With her blond hair and brown eyes, I was again struck by Savannah's uncanny resemblance to Brooke. With a hooded sweatshirt, she could pass for her in person. Even more so on, say, a surveillance camera.

"I gotta go," I told Lacy, ending the call.

Evan had tagged Savannah Taggert in the post, and I clicked on her name. Her profile was public, and I spent half an hour scrolling through all her posts, photos, and workplace history.

Savannah wasn't a student at Penn or anywhere else. In fact, when Evan first came on the scene in the spring of 2009, she'd been a bartender at a local pub called Quiggley's.

Over the course of the next two years, you could see the trajectory of her life change. There was a clear demarcation between BE ("before Evan") and AE ("after Evan"). Her clothes

changed, her hair changed, her car changed. But most importantly, her job changed. She went from pouring drinks for drunk
college kids to working at one of the largest investment firms
in Philadelphia.

That's right: Wexlund Capital.

I hadn't seen her when I'd gone to interrogate Nicholas
Wexley at his office on Halloween, but more than likely, Savannah had been there. She was an assistant for one of Wexlund's
top executives. I'm sure the job came with a high salary and all
kinds of amazing perks.

Long story short, Savannah Taggert had a lot to lose if
Brooke had gone public with the documents exposing Nicholas Wexley's transgressions.

Motive? Check.

As for opportunity, the only things I could go on were her
Facebook posts. She was pretty active, posting several times a day.
She posted the lunch she ate on October 17, but her next post
wasn't until the afternoon of the next day, which was simply a
broken heart emoji. The time was listed as 3:21 p.m., which was
consistent with the time the news broke about Brooke's murder.

I was getting ready to call Gallow to have him check her
alibi, when I stopped. Something was nagging at me. Something
about the night I saw her at the Monster Mash.

I replayed the video in my head of walking into the room,
Evan and Savannah locked in a kiss. The video was grainy, shot
on an 8mm camera due to my intoxication. I closed my eyes
and rewound the video. I hit Play again. On the third viewing,
I saw it: Savannah's shoes—four-inch black pumps.

I scrolled back through her photos on Facebook. She was
in high heels in most of her pictures, but I found one of her in
sandals. She was standing next to Evan, who was a head taller
than her. I guessed her height to be around five foot two.

The girl in the surveillance footage was between five six and five seven.

It couldn't be her.

"Damn!" I shouted, sending a flash of pain through my side.

I clicked the button for the nurse. She entered a few seconds later, and I asked, "Can I get more pain medication?"

She loaded a syringe and shot the medicine into my IV port. "This should help you get some sleep."

I glanced down at the port, which was secured to the top of my forearm by a small piece of white medical tape.

My eyes sprang open.

The blue tape.

I thought back to the Target receipt they found in Brooke's pocket. Initially, I assumed Brooke bought the tape to fix a hole in her blue tent. Though, in hindsight, I didn't recall seeing any tape on the outside or inside of her tent. And according to the reports Gallow sent me, they hadn't found any blue tape on the tent. Nor was the tape found in her car or her apartment.

It's possible that Brooke had a blister on her foot or another injury, but they didn't find any blue tape or adhesive residue on Brooke's corpse.

So, then why did Brooke buy the tape? And, more importantly, what happened to it?

Brooke went shopping at Target at 6:35 p.m. on the night of the seventeenth, and she was in front of her tent at city hall less than an hour later. At some point in those sixty minutes, the blue sports tape went missing. Did Brooke throw it away? Did she use it for something? Did she give it to somebody?

The nurse told me to buzz if I needed her, and then she left. I only half listened, my brain whirring.

I picked up the iPad and navigated back to Evan and Savannah's engagement photo. But it wasn't them I was interested in.

I zoomed in.

A warm glow from the medicine washed over my body, and I fought to keep my focus. My brain was circling, a vulture hovering over its next meal.

"The blue tape," I muttered, my eyes half-closed. "The blond wig. The text messages."

The iPad slipped from my fingers and flopped onto my chest. The last image in my mind as I slipped into unconsciousness was the face of Brooke's killer.

43

Gallow's unmarked SUV pulled into the hospital entrance. I pushed up from the wheelchair, holding a slim plastic bag containing Lacy's iPad, a few days' worth of Tylenol with codeine, and instructions to take it easy for the next couple of weeks.

I pulled open the door and lowered myself gingerly into the passenger seat.

"This better be good," Gallow said. "I have ten more leads from the tip line to track down." I wasn't sure if he was referring to the Philly PD tip line or the Wexley line. Regardless, it didn't matter.

I hadn't told him much, only that I needed him to pick me up from the hospital ASAP.

"You won't have to track down those leads," I said. "I know who killed Brooke Wexley."

"Oh yeah? Who?"

"We have to make a pit stop first, and then I'll tell you." I needed to corroborate one last thing before I confided in Gallow.

"Fine." He sighed. "Where to?"

"The Springlight."

We drove in silence, then Gallow illegally parked on the street in front of the condo building. He flashed his badge to the doorman, and a minute later, we were riding the freight elevator to the basement.

"Where the hell are you taking me?" Gallow asked.

Gallow knew about my run-in with Nicholas Wexley at Wexlund Tower, but I'd never told him about the secret underground tunnel linking the condo to the abandoned train station.

I said, "In the 1920s and '30s, this place was a swanky hotel. There's a secret tunnel that connects to the old Spring Garden train station."

The elevator door opened, and we stepped into the basement. Gallow followed me to the boiler room, and I gave him a quick rundown on my fire alarm ruse and getting a key from Braid and her boyfriend.

I unlocked the door, and we walked down the steps to the sub-basement. I'd brought along the iPad, but the glow from its screen was too weak to see by, so I whipped out my keychain light. We walked the long corridor, stopping when we hit the first of the graffiti.

I scanned the walls.

"What are you looking for?" he asked.

I ignored him, continuing my scan.

"I know you're on here somewhere," I muttered under my breath. Finally, I found what I was looking for. "There!" I walked forward and knocked my knuckles against the initials.

"CW?" Gallow asked.

"Claire Wexley," I said. "Brooke's killer."

≈

"Her little sister?" Gallow said derisively. "Give me a break."

I stared at him. "You never found the blue sports tape Brooke bought from Target the night of her murder."

"No, we didn't."

"And you didn't find any tape on her tent or any blue tape anywhere else."

"That's right."

"That's because Brooke gave it to Claire. Sometime between going to Target and going to the protests at city hall, she met with Claire. I'm guessing it was at the rock-climbing gym they used to go to all the time."

"What gym?"

"It's called the Spot." Claire was wearing one of the gym's T-shirts in the background of Evan and Savannah's engagement photo. "According to her roommate, Brooke and Claire used to go indoor rock climbing together all the time."

"Why would Brooke give her a roll of blue sports tape?"

"I'm guessing it was a peace offering."

"A peace offering?"

"Yeah, I think Brooke met her at the gym and gave her the tape. Rock-climbers can't get enough of the stuff—they tape their fingers to prevent blisters." I'm guessing there was probably always blue tape lying around the Wexley condo, which is why Vera Wexley had blue tape around her wrist at the press conference. She must have taken a spill and used some of the tape to support her injured wrist.

I said, "That's probably when Brooke told Claire about the files she stole from Steven Eglund and her intention to reveal their father's corruption the following day."

"No one knows if that file really exists."

I'd scanned the paper file at a print shop and then emailed it to myself. I pulled up the PDF on the iPad and passed it to Gallow.

After a quick skim, he looked up. "Holy shit! Wexley was as dirty as they come." He licked his lips a few times, one of his idiosyncrasies, then said, "So, Claire kills Brooke to keep her from destroying their father."

"That's only part of it. Sure, the file would destroy their father, but I'm guessing Claire was more concerned with the fallout."

He scoffed. "College."

Gallow had obviously read the text messages between Brooke and Claire. For the past year and a half, almost every single conversation they had was about the University of Pennsylvania. Claire couldn't wait to follow in her dad, sister, and brother's footsteps. She was a legacy and she'd already been pre-accepted. In August, she'd thrown a massive Quaker-themed party.

"If that file got out," I said, "one of the very first things that would happen is Penn removing Nicholas Wexley's name from the conference center building. They would eliminate any trace that he ever went there, and I highly doubt they were going to allow Claire to attend next fall."

"I don't know," Gallow said. "Murdering your sister because she might ruin your chances of going to your dream college is a pretty big stretch."

"I agree. Which is why I don't think she ever *planned* on killing her."

"You think it was an accident?"

"I think Claire went down there to try to reason with her. When Brooke wouldn't listen, Claire snapped and wrapped her hands around Brooke's throat. She's been rock climbing most of her life. She probably has the finger strength of an offensive lineman in the NFL. Next thing she knows, Brooke is dead."

"That would explain the trauma to Brooke's neck."

"It would."

I could see that he was wavering. He no longer thought I was crazy.

"What'd she do after she killed her?" he asked.

"After Claire realized what she'd done, she took the file and slipped out of the tent. There were so many people protesting, and it was so loud she probably was pretty confident no one heard her strangle her sister. She ran back home and snuck in through this tunnel." I waved at the walls. "Which is the very same way she'd snuck out earlier that night.

"She knew what her sister was wearing, and she had the same sweatshirt," I continued. "She also had similar jeans, but she didn't have the same shoes. She found a pair that were similar, but of course, we know they had two extra sets of eyelets."

"But what about her hair?" Gallow asked. "She's a brunette." He snapped his fingers before I could reply. "The blond wig— the one her mom is wearing in the Facebook photo we saw."

"Exactly," I said, grinning. "After killing Brooke, then sneaking back into the Springlight, Claire went to her mom's room and grabbed the blond wig. Then she snuck out *again* and ran to city hall. She slipped into Brooke's tent and used the disinfectant wipes she brought to wipe Brooke's throat and any other surface she might have touched. She took Brooke's school ID card and her keys. After she left the tent, she took backstreets to Brooke's dorm.

"Claire used Brooke's ID card to get into her dorm, then she snuck into Brooke's room and grabbed her laptop, on which Brooke had scanned the documents. It was almost two in the morning by this point and all the roommates were asleep. She can't be positive that no one saw her sneak into her sister's tent earlier, so she walked back over the bridge, making certain the camera on the bridge records her with a time stamp so that it looks like Brooke is still alive at two in the morning. Claire is the same height as Brooke. With the wig on and the hood of the sweatshirt up, it's easy to pass for her. Even her own father couldn't tell the difference. Once Claire crosses the bridge, she hightails it back home."

Gallow nodded at the door that led to the train station. "Through there."

"Yep."

"What does she do with the documents and the laptop?"

I'd been racking my brain trying to think what she might've done with them, and I'd come up with one answer. "My best guess is that she burned them." It's what I would have done.

"Where?"

"Follow me."

I started toward the door. I used the key, then pulled it open. Gallow followed me into the abandoned tunnel. We didn't walk toward the platform. We jumped down onto the tracks and started following them away from the abandoned station.

Gallow said, "You're positive trains don't run here anymore?"

I shrugged. "I've never seen one."

"That's comforting."

We walked between the tracks for two hundred yards. Then three hundred. Between my keychain flashlight and Gallow's large halogen flashlight, we could see everything in front of us.

After another thirty feet, Gallow said, "Over there." He nodded at a large garbage drum, the kind bums burn fires in to keep warm.

Gallow shined his flashlight down into the drum. It was full of ash.

"Light a fire in a train tunnel," Gallow said. "Good way to get carbon monoxide poisoning."

There was a slight breeze in the tunnel, and I doubted the smoke could get thick enough. Still, it was possible. But I didn't think that's why the drum was here. Or why it was this far down the tunnel.

"You think she burned the documents and laptop in here?" Gallow asked.

I did.

Gallow leaned down and sifted through the charred refuse. He straightened a moment later, his mouth and eyes open wide.

It was badly burned and folded over on itself. The top was missing, and the small disk inside had been liquefied. But it was still recognizable.

It was a hard drive.

≈

Gallow pulled out his phone.

"What are you doing?" I asked.

"I'm calling to get a warrant to search the Wexley house."

I snatched the phone out of his hand.

"What the fuck?"

"You'll never be able to convict her," I said.

"You don't know that."

"There's zero forensic evidence, everything you have is circumstantial. Plus, she's only seventeen—she's a minor. Not to mention that she'll have the best legal team money can buy."

I watched as Gallow mulled this over. After a moment, he asked, "What are you thinking?"

"I'm going to get her to confess."

"How?"

I grinned. "With your sister's help."

≈

It was closing in on nine thirty at night when I stepped out of the cab. A line was coming out the door of the Pink Panther, and I found a spot at the back. Most of the people in line had dyed hair, lots of piercings, and torn clothing that wasn't nearly warm enough for a chilly November evening.

"Hey."

I turned.

Jennifer Peppers had her hair spiked in a mohawk, and she was wearing six dollars' worth of eyeliner. She was clad in black leather pants and a red tank top. White platform heels rounded out the ensemble.

"I thought we were dressing up," she said, her lips pouted.

"It took me almost twenty minutes just to put this shirt on." The Tylenol with codeine barely dented the pain in my side, and not wanting to wake up Lacy from her nap, I'd had to inchworm my way into my shirt.

Jennifer sidled up next to me and said, "So, remind me what we are doing here?"

"For our second date, I thought it would be fun to watch my ex-girlfriend's band play."

"You really know a way to a girl's heart."

I winked at her.

"Isn't there a part two?"

"Oh, yes. Since we're here, I thought we could set my ex-girlfriend up with a guy, so she'll forgive me for breaking up with her via text and stop hacking my life."

"Sounds like karma to me."

"I promise to break up with you in person."

She fanned herself with her hand. "I do declare, Mr. Prescott." We both laughed.

A few minutes later, the bouncer scanned our tickets, and we entered the dank confines of one of Philadelphia's best dive bars.

We ordered beers, then walked to the back of the bar, where the band was finishing setting up.

"That's her," I said, nodding at Carmen adjusting the height of one of her drums. Carmen was wearing a yellow sports bra and a pair of torn white jeans. Her hair was now dyed light blue.

"She looks friendly."

"That's what Roy said about Mantacore."

"Mantacore?"

"The tiger that bit his face off."

"Ah."

Carmen glanced up, her eyes locking on the two of us. She jumped off the stage, a drumstick in each of her hands, and yelled, "What are you doing here?"

"I just wanted to apologize one last time and introduce you to someone."

Carmen turned to Jennifer.

"Hi," Jennifer said. "I love your hair. Looks like a raspberry blow pop."

"Uh, thanks." Carmen turned to me. "Okay, I met her. You can leave now."

"That's not who I wanted to introduce you to."

I waved over Matthew Hutchings. He'd been standing in the back corner of the room. I'd texted him earlier that I needed him to meet me here at nine and that it was important.

Hutchings strode toward us. He tipped his beer bottle forward. "Hey, guys."

I introduced Carmen and Matthew and then said, "Something tells me that the two of you are going to hit it off."

Carmen ran her eyes up all six feet three inches of Mr. Hutchings's tall, rippled framed. She licked her lips and then said, "Yummy."

44

"*Please direct your attention to the jumbotron,*" the announcer's voice rang out over the loudspeaker, "*as we pay tribute to one of our own: Brooke Meredith Wexley.*"

It was fifteen minutes before kickoff for the Penn Quakers versus the Princeton Tigers football game. I'd bought tickets from a scalper, and Carmen and I were seated in the second level.

We looked up at the large screen just beneath the scoreboard. A quick two-minute video montage of Brooke Wexley played. When it finished, her name flashed, as well as the dates—June 27, 1991 to October 18, 2011—followed by a message: "If you have any information about her death, please go to Justice-ForBrooke.com."

"There they are," Carmen said. She held binoculars up to her eyes and pointed to the field. "By the forty-yard line."

She passed me the binoculars. After a few seconds, I located "them": Nicholas, Evan, and Claire Wexley. I wasn't surprised that Vera wasn't in attendance. According to a *TMZ* report, she hadn't left the Wexley compound in the Hamptons for weeks.

"Well, Claire is here," I said.

"When do you want me to do it?"

"Right before halftime."

"Alrighty."

Carmen had been incredibly amiable since I'd introduced her to Matthew Hutchings two days earlier. She'd removed the virus from my computer, somehow deposited a thousand dollars into my checking account to cover the cost of getting my car detailed, but most importantly, she'd agreed to help me with my ploy.

We watched football for the next hour. Well, I did. Carmen stuffed her face: two hotdogs, a plate of nachos, Dippin' Dots, a bag of Peanut M&M's, and two large Mountain Dews.

With two minutes left in the second quarter—Penn was leading, 21–3—I focused the binoculars on Claire. After the tribute had ended, she and Evan had made their way to seats in the Penn student section, and Nicholas had most likely gone to his executive suite on the second level.

"Do it now," I said.

Carmen tossed a last handful of M&M's into her mouth, then she pulled out her phone. After a few seconds, she turned the phone to me. "Done."

I watched Claire in the binoculars. She was talking animatedly to the person next to her. Two seconds later, she pulled her phone out of her back pocket. Her face fell as she read the text from an unknown sender: "I KNOW ABOUT BROOKE."

"Okay," I said. "Send the next one."

Carmen sent the follow-up message: "MEET ME AT GATE 326."

A moment later, Claire received it. She whipped her head back and forth. Then she began typing into her phone.

Carmen's phone pinged a few seconds later. She turned and showed it to me.

CLAIRE: Who is this?

"Send it again," I told Carmen.

She resent the second message.

After reading it, Claire went still. A moment later, she stood.

"She's on the move," I said.

Carmen and I both jumped up. As we climbed the stairs leading to level three, the horn sounded for the end of the first half. By the time we reached the third-level landing, fans were streaming into the corridor, headed for the bathrooms or to grab refreshments.

We passed 321.

322.

323.

324.

325.

We came to gate 326, which was home to a Starbucks and an Arby's. Not wanting to be seen with Carmen, I said, "Why don't you go stand in the Arby's line?"

She nodded and then strode off, her denim backpack swaying as she walked.

I leaned up against the wall, watching the thrum of people. Finally, Claire came into view. She glanced up at the gate sign and stopped walking. She scanned the masses.

I pushed off the wall and strode toward her.

Her back was to me when I approached. "Claire Wexley."

She turned. Unlike Brooke, her eyes were green, but that would have been impossible for the video cameras to catch.

Her gaze narrowed over her nose. "Do I know you?"

"No, you don't," I said, shaking my head. "But I know you. And I know you killed your sister."

≈

I waited for Claire Wexley to bolt, but she didn't. She stood there, staring back at me every bit as stoic as her father.

I pulled a roll of blue sports tape out of my pocket and flipped it to the silent Claire.

Instinctively, she caught it.

"Brooke met you at your rock-climbing gym," I said. "Probably right around seven o'clock that night, which is when you usually get there on Mondays. She gave you a roll of your favorite sports tape as a peace offering before she told you what she was going to do with the files she had on your dad."

"You're crazy!" Claire spat, tossing the tape into a half-filled garbage can nearby.

"You've dreamed about going to Penn your entire life. Both your siblings go there. Hell, your dad has a building named after him. It's all you've ever wanted. You knew if Brooke exposed your father's crimes, the Wexley name would become poison. They would rescind your acceptance, remove your father's name from the business school, and you would end up at some state college with the other peasants."

"I didn't kill my sister, you whack job."

"Then why haven't you walked away?"

It was because Claire Wexley wanted to know how much I knew.

So, I told her: "Brooke was waiting until the next morning to expose your father. You knew she'd be alone in her tent with those precious documents. Around midnight you snuck out of the Springlight, using one of the keys that open the door to the sub-basement."

She couldn't help her eyebrows rising a half centimeter.

"You ran from the abandoned station to city hall, then slipped into your sister's tent. You tried to reason with her one last time, but Brooke was stubborn and defiant. She was going through with it; she was going to destroy your father, his legacy, and your family. I don't know if you meant to kill her, but with the loud chanting going on outside the tent, no one heard you as you wrapped your hands around your sister's throat. But your hands and forearms are strong from your time in the rock-climbing gym, and next thing you know—Brooke is dead."

Claire tried to remain defiant, but the thought of what she'd done made its way into her upper lip.

"You don't panic, I'll give you that. I'm guessing you covered your sister's body with the sleeping bag so that if anybody ducked their head inside, they'd think she was asleep. Then you ran back to the Springlight. I've done it myself. It took me eight minutes.

"You sneak back up to your room. You know what your sister is wearing, and you have the exact same sweatshirt. In fact, I'm betting all five of you Wexleys have the same sweatshirt. Your dad is in the fitness room working out, and your mother, well, she's two Valiums deep and she'd be sound asleep at a Metallica concert. You grab a blond wig from her collection and a tub of disinfecting wipes, then you run back to city hall. You slip into your sister's tent, wipe down her neck and the tent, then grab Brooke's ID card and keys. If you haven't already taken the documents, you take them then.

"You leave her tent around one thirty, which we know because a witness saw you. Of course, he thought it was Brooke because of the wig. You run to her dorm, swipe her ID card, and go up to her room. You would have been screwed if any of Brooke's roommates were still awake, but they were asleep, and you sneak into Brooke's room to grab her laptop.

"Then you walk back over the bridge, making sure the cameras see the laptop in your hands. Then you sneak back into the Springlight for the second time."

The guilt Claire felt for killing her sister had evaporated, and the smug teenager had returned.

"I'm gonna go now," she said, feigning casualness as she walked away.

"Too bad about the mistakes you made," I said.

She stopped.

Opening my backpack, I pulled out the side-by-side comparison image of her shoes and Brooke's shoes. "You might have had the same sweatshirt and jeans, but you didn't have the same shoes as Brooke."

A vein near Claire's temple became visible under her skin.

"You had to dispose of the documents and your sister's laptop," I said. "So you walked deep into the train tunnel, where you've heard that sometimes the bum's burn fires to say warm."

I pulled a ziplock bag out of my pocket. Inside was a damaged and blackened hard drive.

"The hard drive survived," I lied.

I'd bought a MacBook, then run it over it a few times with my car, then set it on fire. Then I removed the hard drive.

"That hard drive could have come from any computer," she scoffed.

"This one came from Brooke's." I paused for a moment, then I said, "FBI Agent Josh Chamberlain."

Claire's knees buckled a few inches, and her face drained of color. She must have perused the file on her father before she'd destroyed the evidence, and she knew all about the FBI agent that her father had bribed for insider intel.

A woman bumped into Claire's shoulder. She was holding a Beef 'n Cheddar in one hand.

"Sorry about that," the woman apologized, then threw me the softest of winks before striding away.

Claire barely reacted, her brain a million miles away.

"The cops are going to arrest you in a few minutes," I told Claire.

She was frozen in place.

"Claire!"

She snapped out of it.

"Did you hear me?" I asked.

She nodded.

"You need to call your lawyer," I said, then turned and walked away.

If she called a lawyer, my plan was foiled. But I was banking on her doing what most seventeen-year-olds would do when they get into trouble.

She'd call her daddy.

45

I dipped into the men's bathroom, counted to twenty, then made my way back to the Starbucks.

"Do you think she bought it?" Carmen asked, taking a large bite of her sandwich.

"Hook, line, and sinker."

Carmen held out her fist, and I touched my knuckles to hers.

"What now?" I asked.

She crumpled up the Beef 'n Cheddar wrapper, tossed it in the trash, then pulled a sleek laptop out of her backpack. "Now we see if my friend Trevor screwed me."

"Trevor? The bass guitarist in your band?"

"He was the one who got me the microphone."

When Carmen had bumped into Claire, she'd dropped a tiny wireless microphone into the back of Claire's hooded sweatshirt.

"Trevor got the mic from a guy who used to work for the Department of Defense. It's top-of-the-line stuff. I could get a signal from a mile away when I tested it out, but with all these people and their cellphones, I'm worried about interference."

"How will you know if it works?"

She looked at me deadpan. "Um, we'll be able to hear her."

"Right."

Carmen opened her laptop and hit the keys for several seconds. "Okay, it's live."

I huddled up to her and the laptop. "I don't hear anything."

"It's too loud out here."

I thought she was going to suggest we find somewhere quieter, but she pulled a pair of earbuds out of her pocket and plugged them into the side of her laptop. She handed me one earbud, and I slid it into my right ear.

"All I've got is static." I leaned toward the computer, as if that might help the signal. "No, wait." I heard a muffled shout, though with only one earphone in it was hard to decipher if it was the ambient noise surrounding me or if it was coming from Claire's mic.

"It's working," Carmen said, "but we should head in the direction she went just in case."

I was 90 percent sure Claire was headed toward her father's VIP suite.

Several people gave us bewildered glances as Carmen and I moved briskly through the corridor with our shared earbuds connected to Carmen's laptop.

We took the stairs to the second level, then passed section 270—which was the highest number—then 201, 202, 203, 204, 205, 206, 207 . . .

Knock, knock, knock.

Carmen and I both stopped abruptly. We weren't far from the Wexley suite, and we leaned up against the inner concrete wall and waited.

We heard a door creak open.

"*I made everyone leave. What's going on?*"

I pumped my fist. "That's Nicholas Wexley's voice."

The second domino had fallen.

I assumed that in the three minutes since I'd left Claire standing in the middle of the corridor, she'd texted her father that she needed to talk to him. And him only.

Claire didn't respond to her dad, but you could hear the door shut behind her.

"*Are you hurt?*" Wexley said. "*Did someone hurt you?*"

Again, Claire didn't respond.

But then again, how do you begin to tell your father that you killed his oldest daughter?

"*What's going on, Claire? You can tell me. Did something happen with a boy? Are you pregnant?*"

I think Claire would have given her left ovary to be telling her father that she'd been knocked up by the high school quarterback. She didn't respond, but I could imagine the trembling of her body.

She said, "*It was an accident.*"

"*What was?*"

Carmen nudged me in the ribs and said, "It's now or never."

I almost forgot about the third domino.

Pennsylvania is a two-party consent state, meaning if you want to record a conversation, public or private, both parties have to consent to the recording. So even though the conversation was being recorded on Carmen's laptop, it wouldn't be admissible as legal evidence at any trial.

With zero forensic evidence and a slew of the best attorneys money could buy at her back, the only way Claire would be punished for her sister's murder was if she confessed.

Loudly and publicly.

I nodded at Carmen. "Do it."

She hit several keys, then she hovered her finger over the Enter key. After a light breath, she pushed the key down.

Originally, I'd asked Carmen if she could patch the signal to the main stadium speaker. She said it was an easy hack, but she pointed out that Claire and Nicholas Wexley would hear their own voices coming from the main speaker. If we only patched it through to the speakers in the corridors, there's a chance they wouldn't catch on.

A loud screech blared from the speaker attached high on the wall across from us, and Carmen and I both slipped the earbuds from our ears.

A moment later, Nicholas Wexley's voice crackled through the speaker: "*What was an accident?*"

"*Brooke*," whimpered Claire. "*She wasn't supposed to die.*"

≈

Several conversations around us in the corridor went silent at the sound of Claire's confession. Someone nearby tapped their friend on the shoulder and pointed to the speakers.

"*What in the hell are you talking about?*" Wexley asked.

"*She was going to destroy you.*"

"*Destroy me? Brooke? How?*"

"*Uncle Steven had a file on you. Going back to when you first started Wexlund. He had transcripts of all your deals. Brooke showed them to me.*"

"*Steven wouldn't.*"

"*Josh Chamberlain.*"

That Claire knew his darkest secret silenced Wexley.

"*I just went to go talk to her,*" Claire said, the shakiness in her voice gone for the time being. "*To talk some sense into her. She was going to destroy our family. You would go to jail, we would lose all our money, I would never get to go to Penn.*"

"*Keep your voice down.*"

Carmen and I traded a glance, and then both laughed.

If they only knew.

In a soft voice, Claire said, "*I was just going to steal the file she had on you, but then she told me it didn't matter. She'd scanned the file and uploaded it to her laptop. Then we started fighting in the tent and I, I, just—I don't know what happened. Next thing I knew, I was on top of her, and she wasn't breathing.*"

I gazed up and down the corridor. There must have been two hundred people in my line of sight, and nearly every one of them was frozen and staring upward at the closest speaker. Throughout the rest of the stadium's corridors, I'm certain several thousand others were doing precisely the same.

I'm sure a handful of people had recognized Nicholas Wexley's voice or had put together who the voices belonged to through context, and every one of them, including me, waited for—or, in my case, willed—Nicholas Wexley to burst into tears, to scream at his youngest daughter for the horrible thing that she'd done.

Instead, after a two-second pause, Wexley said, "*What did you do with the file and the laptop?*"

A swell of disgust blew through the corridors like a tidal wave.

To my right, Carmen said, "What a shithead."

"King Shithead," I said.

"He stole your throne," she quipped.

"*I burned them in the train tunnel,*" Claire's voice rang through the speaker.

"*Good girl.*"

I was tempted to pull the door open and smash my fist into his face until it was a pulpy mess of blood, bone, and cartilage.

Carmen sensed me pushing off the wall and said, "What's coming to him will be far more painful than any beating."

She was right.

"*But they found the laptop,*" Claire said. "*And somehow the hard disk survived.*"

"*How do you know?*"

"*Some guy just showed the hard drive to me.*"

"*What did he look like?*"

"*About your height, blue eyes. He knew about Josh Chamberlain.*"

"*Fuck.*"

Wexley's cell phone rang in the background. He answered it and a moment later he said, "*Hear us? What do you mean, you can hear us?*"

The door to the executive suite was pulled inward.

Nicholas Wexley and his daughter peered out at the small crowd that had formed.

"What's going on, Dad?" Claire said, her voice from the speaker booming over her voice from the doorway.

"Do not say another word," Nicholas Wexley said.

His eyes scanned the corridor, then found mine.

I waved.

I turned to Carmen and hit the enter key on her laptop, sending a copy of the file to over one thousand news outlets. A copy also went to Nicholas Wexley's private email address.

There was a chirp from Wexley's phone, and he glanced down.

I watched as he clicked open the email and realized that life, as he knew it, was over.

46

After I woke up, I went to the kitchen and found Lacy at the table, eating a bowl of cereal. She didn't mess around when it came to cereal: she was eating Apple Jacks out of a large Tupperware container and using an oversized cooking spoon. It was good to see her appetite had returned.

I gave the back of her head a kiss and said, "Somebody must be feeling better."

"A little," she said, gazing upward.

Lacy had been on her new meds for about ten days. The doctor told her it would take a couple weeks for the worst of the side effects—nausea, loss of appetite, depression, dry mouth, and countless others—to subside.

"That's good to hear."

I reached over her and attempted to pluck a Jack from her bowl. She smacked the top of my hand with her spoon. "Bad Thomas!"

I shook my hand out and laughed. "Where's Mr. Baxter?"

"Last I saw him, he was asleep in the bathtub."

"He certainly finds some interesting places to conk out. Thank God, I noticed him in the washing machine before I started my last load."

Her eyes opened wide. "He was in the washing machine!?"

"Well, I think he fell asleep in my laundry basket, and I dumped him in. But I didn't notice him until I poured half a cup of Tide on his head."

She laughed, then took a heaping spoonful of soggy Apple Jacks and crammed them into her mouth.

I made myself a quick smoothie, then joined Lacy at the table.

Lacy's iPad was on the table in front of her. I hopped on the internet and spent the next ten minutes learning about the fallout from Claire's public confession two days earlier and the document dump Carmen had sent.

Not wanting to stay overnight at the jail, Claire had waited until this morning to turn herself in for her sister's murder. No doubt, she had a team of Wexley's best lawyers by her side, and according to the latest article by the Associated Press, she'd pleaded not guilty to second-degree murder at this morning's arraignment, then posted the half-million-dollar bond.

Most likely, in the coming days, the DA, knowing what they were up against with the Wexley lawyers, would offer a plea. Probably manslaughter. As a minor, she would get less than five years, and I'd be surprised if she served more than two.

As for the Wexley file, it had been even more explosive than I could have predicted. The SEC had filed an emergency injunction, and starting this morning, Wexlund Capital was unable to trade. The firm's assets were frozen, as were both Nicholas Wexley's and Steven Eglund's personal bank accounts.

It would take a while for the FBI and the SEC to comb through the documents and verify their authenticity. As of now, Nicholas Wexley—who had to stay local for his daughter's hearing—was holed up at the Springlight. I could only imagine the number of news vans parked outside right now.

Steven Eglund, on the other hand, had decided on a different tactic: flight. He and Robin had driven to the Delaware Coastal Airport, intending to board a flight bound for Panama. Unfortunately for them, an employee at the airport recognized the pair and summoned authorities. They were arrested for trying to flee while under investigation and forced to turn over their passports. They were currently under house arrest.

FBI Agent Chamberlain, who worked out of the New York office, had been put on leave pending investigation.

I finished my smoothie and made my way to the carpet in the living room to play with Baxter, who had just awoken from one of his many slumbers.

"Look who's awake," I said.

Baxter got a quick case of the zoomies, zipping through the living room at Mach 3, then he climbed up onto my stomach, panted twice, and conked out.

"Your dog is weird," I said to Lacy.

"You picked him out, dummy."

I'd yet to tell her that when I picked him out, he'd been lying on his back fast asleep—a harbinger of things to come. "He was the most active of the whole bunch," I lied. "He was doing cartwheels."

I was watching Baxter's small chest rise and fall, when Lacy erupted in laughter.

I glanced backward at her and asked, "What's so funny?"

"Oh, you know, just watching my big brother beat the shit out of a bunch of old people on YouTube."

I sighed. "How many hits does it have now?"

"Over three hundred thousand."

"Shouldn't I have gotten a call to go on *Ellen* by now?"

She ignored me and said, "There's one thing you were right about."

"What's that?"

"Her tree did suck."

My laugh stirred Baxter back to life, and he darted forward and began licking my face.

"*Groooosssss*," I said.

I stood up, cradled Baxter, then plopped him on Lacy's lap.

Lacy was scrolling through the comment thread below the video. "Not a whole lot of people taking your side on this one."

"I wouldn't imagine."

She cleared her throat and then read, "If some asshole stiff-armed *my* grandma, I'd kill that sumbitch."

"Yikes."

"You're lucky they haven't tracked you down yet."

Thankfully, I didn't have any social media for these trolls to find. And if they called the nursing home and got the visitors' log, the only thing they would find out about Ernest Worrell is that he *Went to Camp, Saved Christmas,* and *Went to Jail.*

Lacy continued scrolling through the comments.

"Wait," I said. "Go back up."

She did.

I read a comment off the screen: "Why is this crazy old man shouting out six-eight-three over and over in Italian?"

Lacy and I locked eyes. She reloaded the clip, and we both watched it. Sure enough, while I'm twisting and thrashing about, trying to get Angelo Capetta off my back, he was muttering something over and over. I suppose at the time I'd been too preoccupied to notice.

Lacy looked up the numbers in Italian: six (*sei*), eight (*otto*), three (*tre*), and that was precisely what Angelo was screaming: *Sei-otto-tre! Sei-otto-tre!*

I raced to my bedroom and grabbed my copy of *The E.K.*

Dream Book. There was only one entry for 683. It brought everything full circle.

Revenge.

≈

It'd been five days since I was discharged from the hospital. My side was still tender, and after jogging half a mile, I had to stop. The Schuylkill River was nearby, and I found a seat on a bench under a bare oak tree.

I watched the water for a few minutes, emptied my brain of thoughts, and then went back over the Numbers Killer timeline, all fifteen murders.

Murder 1: July 1973, Philly—Dominic "the Soldier" DeSipio.

Murders 2, 3, 4, and 5: August 1973, Philly—the Queen's number runners (Maurice Jackson, Lenny Jackson, and Maxwell Yates) and an unidentified John Doe.

Murders 6 and 7: July 1976, Boston—Jessie Dalwood and Clyde Landis.

"Nothing happens for the next thirty-five years," I said out loud. "Then Murder Number Eight takes place in fall of 2011."

Murder 8: October 3, Philly—Eugene Kirovec.

Murder 9: October 8, Philly—Constance Yul.

Murder 10: October 17, Camden—Peter Boland.

Murder 11: October 21, Philly—Marty Inaba.

A perfect image of Marty Inaba's long, bloody hair splayed out on the bottom of the SS *United States*' pool played over my eyes. I thought back to chasing the killer, running through the ship, and then standing next to the giant propeller, gazing over the railing at the water below, the ripples churning outward from where the killer had entered the water.

Something about the chase nagged at me, but after going back over it several times, nothing jumped out.

"Murder Number Twelve," I said, moving on.

Murder 12: October 24, Philly—Officer Clement.

I couldn't shake the image of the bag of chips between his legs. He'd known the killer.

Murders 13, 14, 15: October 24, Philly—Loretta Carroll, Jumpy, and Palmer.

It'd been nearly two weeks since those last murders, which led me to believe our killer was done. He'd finished telling his story.

I separated the murders into two groups: targets and pawns.

There were five pawns. Murders of opportunity, necessary to move the killer's story forward: Eugene Kirovec, Constance Yul, Peter Boland, Marty Inaba, and Officer Clement.

There were ten actual targets: Dominic DeSipio, the five number runners, the John Doe, Queen Loretta Carroll, Jumpy, and Palmer.

All the targets had one thing in common: *Numbers.*

The killer had to be someone who wanted revenge against both the Mafia and Queen Loretta.

But who?

While I'd been playing Batman, most of the task force had been hitting the streets, finding out who had possible vendettas against the Capettas and the Queen. I'm sure they had a long list of names. There's a chance Gleason had access to the list, but I'd already done enough to the poor guy. He had my stench all over him. In fact, he was no longer in Philadelphia. He'd been sent back up to Boston a day earlier.

Still, it was worth a try.

I pulled out my phone and called him. It went to voice-mail. I told him to call me back when he got a chance and that it was important.

I turned my attention back to the river. There were a few rocks nearby, and I picked one up and chucked it into the river. The ripples flashed for a quick second, then receded to the current.

"You bonehead!" I shouted.

On the SS *United States*, it never occurred to me that the killer might not have jumped. He could have thrown something overboard to make a splash. Yes, it needed to be something heavy, something that would make a sound and significant ripples, but it wasn't impossible.

And if he didn't jump, it made more sense why he'd had time to carve the numbers under the propeller. That would have been no simple task, facing upside down and etching the numbers into the underside of one of the blades. The numbers were clean and crisp. He'd had plenty of time after I left. He was in no rush.

The killer played me.

"You were hiding inside the door and watched me leave," I said.

It took another moment for the significance of my insight to wash over me. If the killer didn't jump off the boat, he must have walked off.

And there were cameras.

≈

"Do you want one?" Carmen asked, shaking a Monster energy drink at me.

"I'm good," I said. "I like to keep my heart rate below three hundred."

"Suit yourself." She plopped into the expensive-looking black gamer chair facing four large computer monitors.

I thought about inquiring how it was going with Matthew Hutchings, but the tattoo on her shoulder spoke volumes. "Nice ink," I said, nodding at the still-healing image of a human heart with MH carved into the left ventricle.

"Thanks. If you ever want to get one, I've got a great girl."

"Good to know."

She took a long swig of her drink and crushed the can in her hand. "So, the Port of Philadelphia, huh?"

I nodded. "Do you think you can hack into their servers and pull up a video?"

"Piece of cake."

It took her just fifteen minutes to hack through the Port of Philadelphia's firewalls and into their surveillance footage.

"Pier Eighty-Two," I said. "The morning of October nineteenth."

She clicked around, then said, "Got it."

I'd already seen the footage detailing Marty Inaba's arrival, then Gleason and me coming onto the scene. "Fast-forward to 9:20."

She did.

Gleason could be seen on his phone, calling in the cavalry. In the next few minutes, he was joined by several port authority cops. One of them headed toward the ship and out of view. This was Officer Billups, who I'd run into as I'd returned to the pool.

Throngs of people entered the screen over the next twenty minutes, crime scene techs, Philly PD, more port authority folks, detectives, plus Agent Joyce and a few other task force members.

By 9:43 a.m., it was a full-blown circus.

I continued watching.

At 10:12 a.m., when most people were still walking toward the ship, one person could be seen walking away.

"Zoom in on that guy." He was dressed in black pants and a dark T-shirt. He held a jacket under his arm.

Carmen made a square around the guy on-screen and the image enlarged.

I sucked in a breath.

It made sense. It explained why Officer Clement had his guard down when he was killed. Why the killer was always just a few hours ahead of the task force. And why the killer strolled off the SS *United States* without anyone batting an eye.

I thought back to the jersey hanging in his office: *Boston College*. He'd played there from 1975 to 1978. He was in Boston when the two number runners were killed.

"Do you recognize him?" Carmen asked.

"No," I lied. I couldn't risk her telling her brother.

The man was Gallow's boss: Captain James Folch.

47

"With three districts yet to report," the News 4 anchor said on TV, "it's still too close to call."

A blue banner under the anchor read *Philadelphia Mayoral Election 2011*. There were three candidates: Hank Ridenour, Independent; Karen Turnquist, Republican; and Bertram F. Stalnaker, Democrat. Ridenour had carried 3 percent of the vote, and the rest was split evenly between Turnquist and Stalnaker, 48.2 and 48.3, respectively.

"Come on, Bertram," I said. "Pull it out."

My only rooting interest was that if Stalnaker won, I'd know exactly where Captain Folch—one of his closest friends and my prime suspect in the Numbers murders—would be for the next few hours. The victory party.

Ten minutes later, the largest district reported their numbers, and they officially called the race for Stalnaker.

I grabbed my backpack, ran to my restored Range Rover—which I'd picked up from the detail shop three days earlier—and pulled out of the underground parking lot.

Evening traffic was light, which is the only reason I noticed the silver Nissan five cars back.

I had a tail.

Logically, I surmised the man behind the wheel was the same dude who'd caved in my ribs on the *Rocky* steps a week earlier. That he was back told me he had a job to finish. I guessed that after reporting Nicholas Wexley—who I was fairly confident was picking up the hit man's tab—to the SEC, he might want this guy to rough me up even more.

Maybe even kill me.

The Nissan had a New Jersey front license plate, and after memorizing it, I stepped on the gas and zipped through a green light. The next light wasn't for two blocks, and I tried to time the algorithm in my head. I slowed, and by the time I reached the light, it had just turned red. The Nissan was now four cars back. I could just make out the occupant in the rearview mirror, but with his hat pulled down low and night-driving glasses on, I wouldn't have been able to pick him out of a line-up.

I waited for two cars to cross in front of me, then gunned the engine, running the red light. After a left, then another left, I took the on-ramp to the freeway. I sped past two exits, then pulled off.

Satisfied I'd lost my tail for the time being, I wound my way twenty-three city blocks until I came to the street where Folch lived. His house was in a middle-class neighborhood with a Stalnaker campaign sign in his front yard.

I drove past his house and parked on a side street a block away. The lights in his house were off, and there was no car in the driveway. Folch was ten years divorced and lived alone.

I checked the time on my phone. It was 9:41 p.m. I wasn't sure how long Mr. Health Freak would stay at the victory party. He seemed like the type of guy who would already be fast asleep by now.

I grabbed my backpack, which was packed with a drill

wrapped in a towel—in case I had to remove a window or a door—and exited the car.

If you act like you're supposed to be somewhere, most people won't give you a second glance. I confidently walked up the sidewalk, holding the phone to my ear, feigning a call for anyone who might gaze out their window. I went directly to the gate on the side of Folch's house and pulled it open.

I leaned against the gate for ten minutes. If any of the neighbors had seen me and called 911, the cops would have arrived by now.

I crept onto the deck and tried the back door.

Locked.

Although I'd brought the drill, I doubted I could use it without alerting the neighbors. I was considering heading home, when I noticed that one of the back windows was cracked open half an inch. Folch must like a breeze running through his house and forgotten to close and lock the window.

I eased the window upward five inches, then a foot. It didn't make a sound, and I slid it up the rest of the way.

I pulled off my backpack and set it inside the house.

Bark, bark, bark.

WTF!

I dove through the window and inside the house, landing in a small guest room. I closed the window, then grabbed my backpack and unzipped it. Baxter's little face stared back at me, his tongue darting in and out.

"How in the hell did you get in there?"

I'd left the backpack on the ground after I'd stuffed it with the drill and towel. I must have left it partially unzipped, and Baxter must have wiggled his way in and then fallen asleep. Thinking back on it, I'd wondered why the drill was so heavy, but I was in such a rush that I hadn't given it much thought.

I pulled out Baxter and set him on the ground. I said, "You can't pant, you can't snort, and no barking."

He fell over sideways.

Even better.

I picked him up and set him on the bed, which was a foot higher than my sister's and would hopefully deter him from jumping off.

I pulled the small flashlight from my pocket and turned it on. There wasn't much in the guest room other than a relatively empty bookcase and an old ski coat in the closet. I closed the door behind me, then continued through the rest of the house.

I checked the garage to make sure Folch's car was gone, then did a quick recon of the downstairs. Finding nothing of consequence, I made my way up the stairs. The door to the master bedroom was open, and I wasn't surprised to see the bed perfectly made and the room spotless.

I checked his dresser and found an alarming amount of Spandex. I moved to the walk-in closet. Half of it was filled with Folch's suits and dress shirts. Orange New Balance shoe boxes were stacked against the far wall, and I checked each one. They each contained an identical pair of shoes.

Several more shoeboxes were stacked on a shelf in the closet. They were older, and the logos faded. I grabbed the top one and pulled it down. It was full of old basketball cards. The second and third ones were full of newspaper clippings.

I pulled a few of the articles out. They were articles about Folch's high school basketball career. Most were from the *Philadelphia Tribune*, but a few were from the *North Philly Gazette*. I knew Folch had been a star player, but I didn't know he'd been Second Team All-City his junior season and First Team All-State his senior season.

One article covered a game in his junior year when he scored thirty-seven points. I skimmed through the article, stopping abruptly when I read the line, ". . . was an emotional week for Folch whose father was tragically murdered three days earlier."

His father was murdered.

I opened the last and final shoebox, and I wasn't surprised to see the box was filled with newspaper articles covering the murder of his father, Lieutenant Ralph Folch. His father's body had been found stuffed in a sewer drain by a construction worker. He'd been shot in the forehead.

No suspects were ever apprehended, but according to the article, it was rumored Lieutenant Folch had refused a payoff from the Capetta crime family.

"There's your motive," I said out loud.

I couldn't believe I hadn't heard this before. Certainly, if Gallow or Moore had been aware of this, they would have told me.

There was a loud grinding sound, and I froze.

It was the garage door opening.

"Shit!"

I shoved everything back into the boxes. I was putting the lid on the box full of basketball cards when I noticed the light-blue edge of a booklet poking out.

Could it be?

I dug my hand into the madness of cards and pulled it out. In different circumstances, I would take a moment to celebrate the find, but I had to move.

And fast.

I shoved the dream book in my pocket, replaced the shoe-boxes on the shelf, then darted out of the room. The sound of the garage door opening ceased as I was halfway down the stairs.

I darted to the guest bedroom and opened the door.

Baxter wasn't on the bed.

"Baxter," I whispered. "Where are you, you little turd?"

I ducked and looked under the bed.

He wasn't there.

I poked my head out of the room and scanned the living room. He was nowhere in sight.

I felt a soft tug on my right shoe and glanced down. Baxter was yanking on my shoelace.

Where did he come from?

The door to the house opened.

I pried Baxter from my shoe and clamped my hand over his mouth. "Shhhh."

After grabbing my backpack from beneath the windowsill, I smoothed out the comforter where Baxter had been asleep on the bed, then slipped into the open closet. I eased the door closed, leaving it a half inch open.

A cabinet opened and shut. Folch was in the kitchen.

Baxter licked the inside of my hand like it was covered in peanut butter.

"Stop," I whispered. "Go to sleep."

He bit the inside of my hand with his razor-sharp daggers.

I grimaced.

Folch was on the move. A moment later, a shadow flitted across the guest room carpet. The shadow disappeared, and then a moment later it returned.

Folch entered the room. I could see the back of his "Stalnaker '11" T-shirt. He glanced at the window.

I silently cursed. In my rush, I forgot to crack the window open.

Folch's head tilted an inch to the side, and I could almost see the thought bubble above his head: *I could have sworn I left that window open.*

He stared at the window for a moment, and then he pushed it up. He turned around, then his eyes found the bed. I'd done a good job of smoothing the comforter out, but there were still a few wrinkles. Folch pulled the comforter taut, then he turned around. His eyes flitted to the closet.

I held my breath.

He moved his head forward.

Did he see me?

No, it was too dark.

His mustache lifted just faintly.

Then he was gone.

I held my breath for another thirty seconds, half of me expecting Folch to come back into the room with a shotgun.

The refrigerator opened and closed, then Folch started up the stairs. A minute later, I heard the shower start running. There's a chance he was toying with me, that he had seen an intruder in the closet and that he was baiting me, but that was a risk I had to take.

I waited another minute, then eased open the closet door. I opened the backpack and dropped the now asleep Baxter back in.

Thirty seconds later, I was back outside. I slunk my way out the gate and then calmly walked the three blocks to my car.

Just as I was getting settled into the car, my cell phone buzzed.

It was Lacy.

"I can't find Baxter!" she shouted.

I pulled him out of the backpack and plopped him on my lap. "I have him." I gave her a quick recount of what happened.

She thought it was hilarious. I told her I would be back to the house soon, then ended the call.

With Baxter between my legs, I pulled Folch's copy of *The E.K. Dream Book* out of my jacket pocket. I turned on the overhead light and cracked the book open.

503, 914, 386, 772, 415, 623 . . .

They were all there.

Every single number the Numbers Killer had left. Every one of them circled in red ink.

My suspicions had been verified: Folch *was* the Numbers Killer.

I was getting ready to call Mike Gallow and tell him what I found, when I slapped my phone shut.

"The Ironman," I muttered.

On October 8, around 8:00 p.m. Philly time, when Constance Yul was being brutally murdered, Jim Folch had been in Hawaii, about halfway through a twelve-hour race.

He couldn't have killed Constance. And the details of Eugene Kirovec's death hadn't been reported so it couldn't have been a copycat.

There was only one explanation.

Folch had a partner.

48

Marston High School was smack-dab in the middle of North Philly. Just over two thousand students were enrolled there, and I was shocked to learn that at the age of seventy-two, Ludwik Paduchowoski was still coaching men's varsity basketball. He'd started working at the school in 1968, and over the course of forty-three seasons "Coach P" racked up an astonishing 547 wins, making him the sixth winningest coach in the history of Philadelphia high school basketball.

I found a parking spot in the crowded lot outside the red brick building. Three minutes later, school let out and kids started spilling through the doors. I waited for the sea to dissipate, then entered. The last time I was inside a high school had been three years earlier during Lacy's high school graduation ceremony.

Two security guards were inside the front entrance, but they were preoccupied separating two arguing boys. I waltzed past unnoticed.

Coach P's office was near the gymnasium; its door was closed.

I knocked twice.

"Come in," a voice bellowed.

From my research, I knew Coach P was first-generation Polish American. He was light skinned with white hair and he had a sheen of sweat running down his cheeks and leaking into the collar of his blue tracksuit.

"What can I do for you?" Coach P asked, motioning at the seat across from his desk. Even after seventy-plus years in the US, his words came out pickled.

"I'm doing a story for *Philadelphia Magazine* about local heroes turned police officers. It's a profile of Captain Jim Folch, and I wanted to ask you some questions about him if that's okay."

"Of course, of course. I'm so proud of that boy. What would you like to know?"

"How many years did you coach him?"

"Three. He made varsity as a sophomore, but he didn't get many minutes that year. He really came out of his shell the second half of junior year and then his senior year, well, he still holds the Marston scoring record—he averaged over twenty-nine points per game."

"I read that something happened to his father his junior year."

"Yes, a tragedy." His eyes were downcast for a quick moment, then sprang back to life. "But he took his anger and channeled it onto the court. From that point on, he was a force to be reckoned with."

Jim Folch didn't just channel that anger on the basketball court. He channeled his rage into the murders of Dominic DeSipio, three of the Queen's number runners, and a fourth unidentified victim.

But he couldn't have done it alone.

"Who did Jim hang out with back in those days?" I asked. "Was it mostly Stalnaker?"

"Bertram?" Coach P said with a laugh. "That little fatso

tried out for the team every year. But he could hardly dribble. Good thing he went into politics!"

Bertram F. Stalnaker was my leading suspect to be Folch's partner. The two men had known each other since they were eight years old, attended third grade through high school together, and Folch had stated that Stalnaker was his closest friend.

"Did you see Folch and Stalnaker together a lot?" I asked.

"Not really," Coach P said, shaking his head. "Lew—that was Jim's nickname—mostly hung out with the other players. And he was always with Allen."

"Allen?"

"Allen Collier."

It took a moment for me to place the name. Then it came rushing back. Folch's friend who played pickup ball. The sickly Black guy who taught criminology at Drexel. The one who I owed a phone call about guest lecturing.

"They were close?"

"They were buddies before it happened. But afterward, they were attached at the hip. And I can see why: no one else could understand what they'd been through."

"What do you mean?"

"Collier's mother committed suicide a few months after Lew's father was murdered."

"Damn."

"So sad. In many ways it was sadder than what Lew had to deal with."

"What happened?"

"It wasn't a great home life for Allen. A single mother, she'd lost her job, started drinking. She also had a gambling problem. It all got to be too much for her."

"A gambling problem?"

"Yeah, those Numbers."

It took every ounce of my will not to jump up from my seat.

"And she was abusive," Coach P said. "Not so much on Allen, but I think she roughed up his little sisters a few times. I know at one point Child Protective Services almost took the kids away."

"How did Collier's mom kill herself?"

"Slit her wrists. Poor Allen was the one who found her."

"That's terrible," I said, then asked, "Did Collier and his sisters have to go into foster care?"

"Thankfully, no. Collier had been held back a year in elementary school, and he'd turned eighteen a few weeks before his mother's death. He became legal guardian of his two younger sisters." He paused. "Such a shame—he had a full-ride scholarship lined up to play at a Division Two school in Florida."

"He didn't go?"

"Nope. He already had a part-time job trying to make ends meet, and after his mom died, he started working full time. School, basketball, working forty hours a week. After graduating, he took another part-time job. Worked his tail to the bone until his little sisters got old enough to take care of themselves. He started going to night school, got his degree. I went to his graduation in eighty-six."

"Do you have any pictures of Folch and Collier from back then?" I asked.

He placed his large, liver-spotted hands on the desk and pushed himself up with a grunt. "Follow me."

We walked down the hallway to the gymnasium. A glass display case against the wall was filled with trophies and team photos.

"We were league champions their junior year," Coach P said, wiggling a massive finger at one photo.

Allen Collier and Jim Folch stood next to each other in the

back row. Folch was a couple inches taller than his counterpart. Both boys were smiling.

"Their senior year, in seventy-four, we won the state championship. Best team I ever coached."

I squinted at the team photo from that year. Collier and Folch were once again standing beside each other. Collier had grown a couple inches, and now he and Folch were almost the same height. But unlike the photo from a year earlier, neither boy was smiling. They stared ahead, mouths limp, eyes vacant.

A lot had happened between those two photos. Both boys' worlds had been turned upside down. I glanced at the one from 1973, then back to the one from 1974.

"Please don't touch the glass," Coach P said.

Unconsciously, I'd put both hands on the glass as I scrutinized the photos.

"They changed their numbers," I said.

In 1973 Collier was number 34, and Folch was 21. But in 1974 Collier had changed his number to 35, and Folch had changed his to 6.

"That's right," Coach P said. "If I remember correctly, they said they wanted to change their numbers to honor their deceased parents. One of the other kids was already number six, and Lew ended up paying him for the number."

He must have wanted that number pretty badly.

I think I knew why.

I thanked Coach P for his time, we shook hands, and I left, ducking out the first exit I could find and calling Lacy. She picked up on the first ring.

I'd left both my and Folch's copy of *The E.K. Dream Book* at the condo and I told her what to do.

"Okay, I've got the dream book open," she said, a moment later.

"Look for number 3-5-6." It could also have been 6-3-5, but I guessed Collier and Folch would want it to read correctly in the photo from left to right. So it was there in plain sight. Their little secret.

She put the phone on speaker, and I could hear her flipping through the pages.

"I found it!" she said. "3-5-6 . . ."

I mouthed the word as she said the entry: *"Murder."*

49

Jim stuck his hand into the twelve-pack and pulled out a can. He'd only drunk a few times previously. He'd have been grounded for a month if his old man had caught him drinking, but now it didn't matter; Dad wasn't around anymore.

It was easy getting beer. An amendment had been passed a few years earlier, and several states had lowered the legal drinking age from twenty-one to eighteen. Apparently, if an eighteen-year-old could be drafted into the Vietnam War, he should also be able to legally imbibe some suds. New Jersey was one of these states, which is where Allen, who'd turned eighteen in February, had bought their Schmidt's.

"Pass me one," Allen said, turning down the volume of the car stereo, blasting the Billboard number one song, *Killing Me Softly with His Song* by Roberta Flack.

Allen was in the passenger seat of Jim's orange 1967 Dodge Polara. It had been Jim's father's car. On his off days, Lieutenant Ralph Folch would always be tinkering with the car in their driveway.

Jim passed Allen a beer. They cracked the fresh cans open,

sucked the foam, then took long swigs. It was a warm night, and the beer went down easy.

"We have to do something," Allen said.

It was a Friday night, and they'd been parked near a vacant playground in North Philly for the past hour.

"We could go by Bertram's," Jim said. "See what he's up to."

"He'll just want to make prank calls or something else really stupid. Plus, that's not what I'm talking about."

Jim set his beer on the center console and looked at his best friend.

"We need to do something *to them*," Allen said.

"Who?"

"The Capettas. Queen Loretta. The runners. All of 'em."

Allen blamed Queen Loretta for his mother's death. His mom had bet with the Queen, and she'd hit big. But then the Queen stiffed her, refused to pay her out her winnings. Allen's mother was never the same. She started drinking, doing drugs, stealing from Allen, and she even started hitting his two little sisters.

And then there was Jim's father. Murdered for refusing a payoff from the Capetta crime family.

"What would Coach P say?" Collier asked. "What would he say, Lew?"

Pretty much everyone on the team called him Lew since Coach P had given him the nickname several months earlier.

Jim thought about it and said, "Coach would tell us to get off our asses and do something."

"Exactly."

Allen said, "I happen to know that the Capettas hang out at this Italian restaurant in South Philly—Villa di Parma."

Jim had heard of it. His dad had told him to steer clear of the place.

Before he could second-guess himself, Jim chugged the rest of his beer. He tossed it over his shoulder, cranked the stereo up—now playing, "Superstition" by Stevie Wonder—then slammed the car into drive.

≈

Jim parked the Dodge Polara across the street from Villa di Parma. For the past several hours they'd watched patrons come and go. The Italian restaurant was packed until ten, then the place emptied out.

But after closing, a different type of character started showing up: young men, mostly clad in black, their hair slicked back. They congregated outside the restaurant's entrance, smoking cigarettes and shooting the shit.

Mobsters.

"What about him?" Allen pointed at a guy exiting the restaurant who had a noticeable limp. "He's got Capetta written all over him."

Jim watched as the guy yanked open the driver's-side door to a green Nova, then slid behind the wheel.

"Follow him," Allen said.

Jim stayed several cars back as they drove a few miles. *They were really going to do this! No more sitting on the sidelines!*

Eventually, the Nova took a left onto a narrow street that fed into FDR Park. The park was vast, over 120,000 acres, and there was a golf course, tennis courts, soccer field, as well as a boathouse and gazebo beside a small lake.

The parking lot was a popular meetup spot for teenagers, and a car full of guys was parked next to a car full of girls. Several were leaning up against their cars, swigging beers and smoking.

"Go to the next parking lot," Allen instructed.

Jim continued another fifty yards, then pulled the vehicle into the deserted lot. He flicked off the lights. In the distance, they saw a shadow walking toward the center of the park.

"He's headed to the boathouse," Jim said.

"Follow him," Allen said again, steel in his voice.

Jim reached into the glove compartment and pulled out a six-inch switchblade. The handle was imitation ivory, though it looked just as good as the real thing. His dad had given it to him on his fourteenth birthday. He'd last used it a couple years earlier to whittle a stick while camping.

The two boys exited the car, then started across a wide expanse of unlit park. After Jim's eyes adjusted to the dark, he saw the trees, playground, and the lone figure about fifty yards in front of them.

They went around the quarter-mile-wide lake the opposite way. A few minutes later, they saw a lighter flicker under the boathouse roof.

"He's alone," Jim said.

They nodded at one another before starting their approach. When they got about ten feet from the boathouse, Jim called out, "Hey! Can we bum a smoke?"

The man sat on a bench. He swept his hair back with one hand, then took a last pull on his cigarette. "I'll give *you* one," he said to Jim. "You can share it with Darky."

Jim glanced at Allen. This wasn't the first time he'd heard his best friend called a racial slur. In fact, he'd heard worse.

"Yeah, okay," Jim replied.

The guy pulled a pack of cigarettes from his pocket and reached it out to him.

Allen scanned the area for anyone approaching, then gave Jim a quick nod.

Jim pulled the switchblade from his pocket and flicked it out.

As he extended his shaking arm, pointing the blade at the mobster, he thought back to that day at the morgue. He and his mom having to identify his dad's dead body. The coroner pulling the sheet back. Seeing his father, a bullet hole in his forehead. His dad's body had been stuffed down into the sewer, and Jim could see where rats had chewed away most of his right ear and his fingers had been nibbled down to the bone.

"Get down on the ground!" Jim barked.

Instead, the youthful mobster laughed. "You got any idea who I am, kid? Do you got any idea who you're messin' with? I'm Dominic 'the Soldier' DeSipio, dumbshit. I'm untouchable."

"Do it!" Jim shouted. "Get down on the ground."

DeSipio stood up. "I'm gonna give you one chance. Beat it, and I won't kill you and everyone you've ever loved."

Jim's hand was trembling. What had he gotten himself into?

"You know what happens when I tell Don Angelo—who is on his way to meet me this very second—that you threatened his nephew." DeSipio let out a whoop. "He's gonna make you eat your own dick, buddy." He gazed around, looking for Allen. "Where's your nigger friend?"

DeSipio lurched forward, his eyes open wide.

Allen had snuck up behind him, plunging the filet knife he'd taken from Jim's house into the mobster's back. Jim heard the gruesome sounds of the knife sinking into flesh a second, third, fourth, fifth time.

DeSipio fell to his knees, his mouth gaping. He collapsed forward onto his face.

"Help me roll him over," Allen said calmly.

Jim snapped out of his daze. He squatted and helped Allen get DeSipio onto his back. Allen climbed on top of the mobster, then used his knife to begin carving into the dead man's forehead.

"What the hell are you doing?" Jim asked. This hadn't been part of their plan.

"I want the Capettas to think the Queen is responsible, so I'm carving a number in his head from the dream book that my mom always used."

"Why do that?"

"So these assholes will all kill each other and we won't even have to do it."

"What's the number?"

"6-8-3." He added, *"Revenge."*

"How are they gonna know that?"

After finishing his work on DeSipio's forehead, Allen pulled a small blue booklet from his pocket and stuffed it in DeSipio's jacket pocket.

Then they ran back across the park to Jim's Polara.

50

"How's the sandwich?" Ms. Ruby asked.

My mouth was full, and I gave her two big thumbs up. She smiled, then topped off my iced tea with a large pitcher.

Thankfully, Moore was still at her brother's house. This worked in my favor, as I didn't particularly want the house-bound detective privy to what I had to say to her mom. This way there was no chance that Moore might relay the information to Gallow—or worse yet, Captain Folch.

I peeled the bread back on the second half of the turkey sandwich and placed several Lay's potato chips inside. Then I crunched the bread back down.

Ms. Ruby chuckled. "My Clarence used to do that very same thing." Her eyes danced for a few seconds as a memory of her late husband floated past, then she took the seat next to me at the kitchen table.

I finished the sandwich, took a swig of iced tea, then said, "Last time I was here, you mentioned that some of the Numbers bankers were *rotten* and that they wouldn't pay on a big hit or that they would skip town after a heavy day."

"I did."

"Was one of those bankers Queen Loretta?"

"Sure was," she said, nodding. "She was notorious for not paying out big hits."

"But you never did bet with her?"

She shook her head. "She was the biggest banker in North Philly, one of the only bankers who would take a bet over a few dollars. My bets were rarely more than a dollar, and my neighbor was a runner for a guy named Jesse Malcom, so it was easier to bet with him."

"When you moved from your North Philly apartment to here, did you keep in touch with any of your friends up there?"

"Oh, yes. My dearest friend, Fannie, still lives in North Philly."

"So, you would have known if someone hit it big with the Queen or if the Queen didn't pay out on a big hit?"

"I would."

"Did you ever know a woman named Tina Collier?"

"Tina?" Ms. Ruby's face fell. "Of course I remember *her*."

Allen Collier and his two sisters had lived in a small apartment in North Philly. My working theory rested on Ms. Ruby's answer to my next question. "Did Tina play the Numbers with the Queen?"

"She sure did. And she hit big."

I knew it.

"But the Queen didn't pay her," I said—not a question.

As the mother of a detective, Ms. Ruby knew where I was headed. She tightened her top lip against her gums—something I'd seen her daughter do on several occasions—and said, "Tina bet ten dollars on a number. The Queen stiffed her out of six thousand dollars."

I had thought it had to be a decent amount of money. Six

thousand dollars was a lot of dough back then, an amount that could have been life-changing for a struggling single mother of three.

"Do you remember what year that was?"

"Well, let's see here." She looked up at the ceiling. "I hit just a few weeks after that . . ." She looked at the dining room table, the one I recalled her saying that she'd bought with the winnings. "Let's see, we bought this in—yeah, 1972."

Another piece fell into place.

"Tina Collier had a dream, didn't she?" I asked. "And she played a number from her dream?"

"It must have been so. A powerful dream. That's the only reason she'd bet that much money."

My next question was a stretch, but Ms. Ruby's memory had proven razor sharp, so it was worth asking. "You don't by chance remember the number that she played?"

"Oh, heavens no. That was forty years ago."

"Well, it was worth a try—"

She interrupted me, clapping her hands together loudly. "I used to mark up my dream books!"

I wasn't sure what she was getting at and asked, "What do you mean?"

She pushed up from the table and hurried into the living room.

I followed.

She pulled a stack of *Three Wise Men* dream books from the shelf and began sifting through them, looking at the year on each cover, then tossing them aside.

She explained, "Back then, whenever someone hit big, I'd record it in my dream book. Lots of people did it, to keep track of the numbers that were hot."

My eyebrows jumped.

A moment later, Ms. Ruby found the *Three Wise Men* from 1972. She slapped the book with her palm, flipped the back cover open, and handed it to me.

In neat print was a list of two dozen numbers and their payouts:

560—$400
328—$795
104—$1,200 . . .

I moved my finger down halfway until I came to *258—$6,000.* A small asterisk was next to the payout, and I asked, "What's the asterisk mean?"

"That it wasn't paid," Ms. Ruby replied.

It was the one number we could never fit. The one that had been carved into Loretta Carroll's forehead.

258.

We couldn't figure it out because the entries were so vague: *Carriage* or *Whooping Cough.*

That's because one of them was a dream.

≈

"After that, Tina was never the same," Ms. Ruby said from where she sat on the couch. "I think she was fired from her job, started drinking."

I was back on the Barcalounger and asked, "How did you hear about what happened?"

According to the death certificate I'd found at the records office, Tina Collier died on March 11, 1973.

"Fannie called me. She'd heard it from someone else." She shook her head. "Her poor son Allen found her body." She stared at the ground for a few seconds, then looked up at me. "You think that Allen Collier is the Numbers Killer?"

I didn't think it.

I knew it.

He and Jim Folch.

"You have to admit, that's quite the motive," I said. "Collier's mother was stiffed by the Queen, then ends up killing herself. He'd want payback."

"I suppose." She didn't look convinced. Or more likely, she didn't want to be convinced.

There was one last piece of the puzzle, so I asked, "What I don't understand is, why wait thirty-five years and then kill again? Why now?"

Ms. Ruby stood and walked behind the couch. She paced for thirty seconds. It was clear she was wrestling with something. I didn't want to coax it out of her. Whatever it was, it would have to come from her voluntarily.

"My son CJ ran into Allen back in July," she said, turning toward me. "He's dying."

51

With my purple JanSport on my back and my navy-blue Drexel hat pulled down low, I looked like just another student attending Wednesday morning classes.

I pushed through the doors of the McNeil Criminology Building and found room 203. It was a large auditorium, and I found a seat on the aisle in the second to last row. Allen Collier and Jim Folch were conversing near the whiteboard. Allen was dressed in a collared shirt and a sports coat. I half expected Folch to be dressed in his full uniform, but I was pleasantly surprised that he had dressed casually.

When I'd been first plotting how to confront the two Numbers Killers, I recalled that when I first met Collier at the pickup game, he'd mentioned that Folch would be guest lecturing in his class sometime in mid-November. Lacy had tracked someone down who was in the class and had them send her the syllabus. We lucked out and had almost an entire week to prepare.

Collier pulled the lower door closed, then raised his hand, hushing seventy-five conversations.

"Welcome, class," he said, his voice bellowing through several speakers in the ceiling. "It is my great pleasure to introduce you to our guest lecturer, Philadelphia Police Captain Jim Folch."

I joined in the applause, and when it died down, Collier said, "Captain Folch has been with the Philadelphia Police Department for thirty-two years, the last seven as acting captain of the Ninth District." He spent another thirty seconds expounding on Folch's history and accolades and then closed with, "I'll let him take over now."

Collier made his way to the third stair on the opposite side of the room and leaned against the wall.

I listened halfheartedly as Folch spoke, and the students surrounding me typed notes into their laptops. I checked my phone at 10:31 a.m.

What was Lacy doing? She should have called one minute ago. I'm sure Baxter was responsible for the delay. Knowing him, he probably . . .

My phone rang.

Justin Bieber's voice—"*Baby, baby, baby oooh, like baby, baby, baby nooo*"—echoed through the classroom.

Folch stopped midsentence, and a hundred and fifty necks craned in my direction.

From across the room, Professor Collier snapped, "Please turn off your phone."

I silenced the call, took a deep breath, and stood.

Go time.

I took off my hat and glared at Allen Collier. If I had any doubt of his guilt, it was erased when he stumbled backward a step. The last time he'd seen me was at the pickup basketball game, a meeting that in hindsight didn't seem all that serendipitous. No, he had been there specifically to meet me, to get a look at an unknown third player in the game he was playing with Captain Folch.

"Prescott?" Captain Folch shouted from the front. "Is that you?" His face quivered for a half second, then he started laughing. Now, with permission to laugh, all the students joined in.

Folch waved me to the front. "Come on down here."

I grabbed my backpack and walked down to the front.

Folch clapped me on the shoulder and said, "That was great. Hilarious!" He turned to the class. "Let me introduce you all to this jokester and one of the best detectives to ever grace this good earth: Thomas Prescott."

There were a few claps and even one catcall.

I kept Allen Collier in my peripherals, making sure he wasn't preparing a dash for the exit.

"Thomas here," Folch said, giving me another clap on the shoulder, "has been part of a task force investigating the Numbers Killer."

A few days after the story broke, more and more details were leaked to the public, and the media, too, began referring to the man as the Numbers Killer.

Folch turned to me. "Can you give the class any updates on the investigation?"

He was goading me, seeing how I wanted to play this out.

"Actually, I was kicked off the task force."

"That's right," he said. "I'd forgotten."

We both knew that I'd been kicked off the task force because Folch had asked me to rattle Nicholas Wexley.

I said, "But I can still give an update on the investigation."

Folch and I locked eyes. He was daring me to press forward.

"It all started in 1972—" I said, my voice not nearly as booming as Folch's had been on the microphone that was attached to his dress shirt, but loud enough to carry to the top seats. I pulled a laser pointer out of my pocket and shined the red laser on Collier's chest forty feet away. "—when your professor's mother, Tina Collier, wagered with a Numbers banker named Loretta Carroll."

The students in attendance looked confused, though I'm guessing most of them thought this was a skit, something they might get quizzed on later.

Sadly, I was on a strict schedule, and I didn't want to waste valuable time explaining the Numbers lottery to a bunch of twenty-year-olds.

"Carriage," I said, locking eyes with Collier. "Your mother had a dream about a *carriage*." It was an educated guess. But just like the monster rolling pin from my dream, a carriage showing up in a dream was mighty specific.

"She used *The E.K. Dream Book*, and *Carriage* was 2-5-8. She played it for ten dollars. And guess what, she hit!" I kept my eyes trained on Collier.

"What in the hell do you think you're doing?" Folch's voice rang through the speakers. "This isn't funny."

I ignored him, watching Collier. His tongue moved around on the inside of his lips as he considered his next move.

"Come on," I said to Collier. "You've wanted this to come out. You've been waiting forty years for this."

The criminology professor stared at me.

"Come on," I said. "Don't make me do all the work."

One second passed.

Two.

Three.

"She won six thousand dollars!" Collier said, his voice loud over the speakers. "I'd never seen her so happy. She'd been play-ing the Numbers her entire life, and she'd never won more than a hundred. With that six thousand dollars, she was going to move us out of North Philly. She was going to buy a house."

"But Queen Loretta didn't pay."

He shook his head. "The Queen said my mom had played a different number and refused to pay out. My mom would call in her numbers over the phone, so there was no receipt. It was just her word against Queen Loretta's." He gritted his teeth. "I never saw my mother smile again."

The class was now invested. Whatever this was, they now realized it wasn't a joke.

"You wanted revenge," I said.

"Of course I did!" he shouted. "Queen Loretta killed my mother!"

There was a collective gasp from the students.

"But you didn't do it alone." I whipped the red laser pointer around and focused it on Captain Jim Folch. I said, "You enlisted the help of your best friend, whose father—a Philadelphia police lieutenant—had just been killed by the Mob for refusing to take a bribe."

"What are you doing, Prescott?" Folch said, his face stiffening.

I set my purple JanSport on the ground and unzipped the top. I pulled the large stack of eight-page packets out, then walked to the first row. There were fifteen seats across—one empty seat—and I counted out fourteen packets, then handed the stack to a young woman in the aisle seat and said, "Take one, and pass it down."

I continued this for all twenty rows, then I returned to the front. I handed Folch a packet. "Here you go."

As he read "The Numbers Murders" at the top of the first page, I thought I saw him squint, but otherwise, he remained stoic.

I approached Allen Collier, handing him a packet. "Here's one just for you."

Up close he looked like an old bike tire. Pancreatic cancer will do that.

I needed to make sure he didn't flee, so I walked down to the lower door and stood guard. Many of the students had flipped through the packet, which had taken Lacy and me three days to perfect.

I overheard one young man say, "Do you think this is going to be on the test?"

"Okay, students," I said, "Please follow along with me on page one."

I had everything in the packet memorized, and I'd be lying if I said I hadn't given a practice lecture to Lacy, Baxter, and three stuffed flamingos.

"July twentieth, 1973, eighteen-year-old Allen Collier and seventeen-year-old Jim Folch murdered Capetta family enforcer Dominic DeSipio. They carved 6-8-3 in his forehead, which they hoped the Mafia would realize is *Revenge* from *The E.K. Dream Book* and that this revelation would trigger a war between the Capetta Mafia family and the high-profile Numbers banker Queen Loretta Carroll." Turning to Folch, I said, "You hoped the Capettas would strike back at the Queen, but instead, they hit back at another Mafia family. You guys inadvertently started the Mob war of 1973.

"A month later, you made another run at the Queen. She was too heavily protected, so you couldn't get to her, but you found an opportunity to kill three of her number runners. You carved *Queen* into each of their foreheads. Then you freaked out—I mean, you're still just kids—and you guys buried the bodies at the edge of an empty lot attached to a church."

I left out the part about the fourth unidentified victim. I still had no idea where he factored into things.

"You don't want to brag about it," I said, "but you both decide to change your jersey numbers before your senior basket-ball season. You make it so your numbers arranged in the team picture, read 3-5-6, which only has one entry in *The E.K. Dream Book*: . . . *Murder!*"

I turned and looked at Folch. He seemed surprised that I'd figured this out. Underestimate me at your peril.

"Folch heads to Boston College to play ball. Collier—who is working two full-time jobs and trying to support his sisters—decides to visit you in 1976. You guys get the itch. Maybe it was a murder of convenience—you just happened to see two number runners. And you both remember how much the Numbers had taken from you. You kill these two guys, then hide their bodies somewhere.

"Nothing happens for thirty-five years, but then Professor Collier," I swiveled the laser pointed back to the professor, "is diagnosed with stage-four cancer." I added, "Go ahead, tell them how long you have to live, Allen."

He inhaled through his nose. "Three months."

I resumed my lecture: "Professor Collier wants people to know what Queen Loretta did to his mother before he dies." I turned back to Collier. "That's what spurs you on to contact your old friend, now *Captain* Jim Folch, and threaten him: if he doesn't help you with the murders, you're going to spill the beans on what you guys did when you were kids. He knows you hold the keys to ruining his life, so Captain Folch agrees to help.

"You guys kill Eugene Kirovec, Constance Yul, and Peter Boland. They're pawns in your game. You don't want to make it too easy to figure out the clues, so you find victims that were born in the area code that correlates with the three clues you need to send investigators to the Bunker Hill Burying Ground."

In the packet, I'd spelled it out in a chart—how each clue (e.g., *Hill*) corresponded to a specific area code.

"After the third murder, a task force is formed." I turned to Folch and swirled the laser on his face. "You know that, at some point, someone is going to figure it all out. That's what Allen wants: he wants the world to know what the Queen did to his mom."

Folch had been quiet, but I sensed he was getting antsy. He was definitely eyeing the door.

I reached my hand into the JanSport and pulled out a gun.

Well, a Taser gun. The one I'd picked up on the *Rocky* steps.

I had just pointed it in Folch's direction when I heard the door open behind me. I half expected to see the backside of Professor Collier as he made a dash for it, but instead, I saw the front side of Hufflepuff.

"About time," I said.

I'd texted him twenty minutes earlier that I needed him to meet me here. What I didn't expect was for him to pull his gun up from his waist and point it at my chest.

"Drop it, Prescott!" Hufflepuff yelled. "You're under arrest."

52

"Calm down," I said to Hufflepuff. "Don't do anything rash."

"I mean it, Prescott!" he shouted. "Drop the gun."

"It's a Taser. I'll drop it but hear me out."

Folch grinned as I set the Taser on the ground.

"Turn around!" Hufflepuff yelled. "And put your hands behind your back!"

"Collier and Folch are the Numbers Killers."

He stared at me.

"That's right. The two of them. They've been friends since they were kids."

Puff cocked his head to the side. "What the hell are you talking about?"

I hadn't told him anything in my text message. Only that it was an emergency and to come alone. I couldn't risk involving Gallow, and with the slim amount of evidence I had—every drop circumstantial—there was no way I was going to trust anyone else with the information at the Philly PD. And as far as Agent Joyce and the FBI went, they could go fuck themselves.

This was my bust.

I snatched the packet from one student in the front row

and offered it to Kip. "Look this over. It's all there." I spent the next two minutes giving him a condensed version of the events.

"That's crazy," Kip said when I finished.

"Collier just about admitted it. Ask any of these students."

Kip glanced up at the 150 students gazing down at him, many of whom were filming the action on their phones.

"It's bullshit," Folch said. "Prescott has lost his fucking mind." He waved at Kip, then pointed to me. "Arrest him!"

Kip stepped toward me, and I said, "Isn't it a funny coincidence that Folch asked you to follow me?"

He stiffened.

"Let me guess. You had orders to report all of my movements back to Folch. To track me. That's why you were in front of Frank Capetta's restaurant that day, and it's why you were tailing me in your mom's Nissan on election night." The car tailing me had been easy enough to confirm with someone at the New Jersey DMV for a $200 bribe. From the look on Kip's face, I knew my theory was correct.

"That's why Folch recommended you for the task force. Think about how thin the department was spread with the Occupy Protests and the Wexley murder. They couldn't spare you, but somehow, they did. And no offense, but you were the only police officer on the task force. Everyone else was a detective or higher. Why you?" I added, "Plus, I bet Folch made certain you had free rein to do as you pleased with the task force, which I'm guessing for the most part was to follow me."

With Kip weighing my words, I continued, "Folch played you. But don't feel bad, he played me ten times worse." I turned to Folch. "You needed to find someone who would sabotage the investigation, make it so none of the evidence would be admissible in court. Ensure that no matter what happened, you would never see the inside of a jail cell." I unconsciously shook my head at how obvious it all was in hindsight. "That's where I come in. You knew I have a history of crippling investigations. That's why you recommended me for the task force."

It hadn't dawned on me until a few days later, but there was no doubt in my mind that there were video cameras set up in Folch's house that recorded my breaking and entering. That alone would disqualify any evidence I'd touched.

"You wanted me to go to your house on election night. You wanted me to know you were friends with the mayor. You even left a window partially open to make it all that much easier." I was kicking myself for not realizing this sooner.

"I have no idea what you're talking about, Prescott," Folch said. He turned to Kip and said, "If you don't arrest this idiot right this second, I'll make sure you never become a detective for as long as I live!"

Kip glanced from Folch to me to Collier, up at the many students, then back to me. He pulled handcuffs from behind his back and stepped toward me.

"I'm sorry I broke your nose," I said. "I'm sorry I had Tyrone cut *pizazz* into the back of your head. I'm sorry I've been such an asshole to you. But you have to believe me, Kip, I'm telling the truth. I'll wear that wool onesie every day for the rest of my life if I'm wrong. Every day until I stop breathing."

Kip's gun was pointed at my chest. He raised it until it was pointed at my eyes.

"Prescott, Prescott, Prescott," he said, shaking his head.

A half second later, he swiveled around, pointing the gun at Captain Folch. He said, "Put your hands behind your back."

"You're making a big mistake," Folch said incredulously.

Folch reached his hand into his briefcase and Kip shouted, "Don't even think about it."

"Relax. I'm just getting my phone so I can call my lawyer."

I could tell by the shape of his hand that whatever he was grabbing in his briefcase wasn't a phone. No, it was round.

"Everybody, get down!" I screamed.

Kip should have plugged him two in the chest, but he froze.

Folch pulled out his hand. He was holding a six-inch cylindrical canister in one hand and a long pin in the other. He tossed the canister near my feet, then darted toward the door.

I shouted, "Cover your ears and close your—"

The flash-bang grenade exploded, the detonation of ammonium nitrate filling the auditorium with an ear-splitting 170 decibels and twelve million lumens.

I fell to my knees and covered my eyes. Even with my palms dug into my eye sockets, it was as if a supernova had exploded behind each of my corneas. All I could see was a ball of white.

I pushed up to my feet, struggling to walk. An explosion can mess with the inner ear fluid, and I felt like I'd just chugged a liter of moonshine.

"You stay here and get Collier!" I shouted in the direction I'd last seen Kip, though it was futile. No one in the auditorium would be able to hear anything for at least another few minutes.

I edged forward until I felt the wall and started toward the door. I was guessing that at least one of my eardrums was ruptured, but after five seconds the white tunnel of light was starting to dissipate.

It sounded like there was a jet engine inside my ears as I crashed through the doors and outside. My vision had cleared by half, and I spied Folch fifty yards ahead, speed-walking up a flight of stairs.

He must have recovered from the effects of the flash-bang faster than I had, but I could catch him. I *would* catch him. I reached the stairs five seconds later, just in time to see Folch weaving through a parking lot that led to Market Street.

Folch probably wasn't familiar with the Drexel campus and was unaware there was a path leading to Market Street that was much faster. I raced down a flight of stairs, knocking aside a young woman holding a large textbook before finding the path. I tried to keep Folch in sight as I ran, but I lost him.

If he was smart, he'd head for city hall and get lost in the Occupy Wall Street protests that were still going on.

The path popped me out onto Market, and lo and behold, Folch was thirty yards ahead of me, running on the sidewalk, headed for the bridge.

I don't know if he sensed my presence, but just before reaching the bridge, he stopped and turned. I'd closed the gap between us to twenty-five yards, and his eyes widened at the sight of me. He turned and resumed sprinting.

I pumped my legs harder, making up another five yards. I'd catch him before he reached city hall. He knew this too, which is why he stopped. I might not be able to run fifty miles, but I was faster at a short distance.

He turned and gazed at my approach. For a split second, I expected him to put his hands in the air and give up.

He didn't.

He ambled up the bridge railing and, without hesitating, jumped twenty-five feet into the river below. I gazed over the railing and watched him disappear into the black water, then emerge a moment later, and begin swimming.

"Dammit!" I hated cold water.

I climbed up the railing and jumped, plunging into water so frigid it pulled the breath from my lungs. I kicked to the surface, then shook the water from my eyes. Folch was fifty feet in front of me.

I put my head down and started after him.

In my head, Lacy was coaching me.

Reach, pull, push.

Reach, pull, push.

Every ten strokes, I lifted my head to triangulate Folch's location. After about a hundred strokes, I was catching up. Folch might be a seasoned triathlete, but I was younger, fitter, and totally pissed off.

I was a fucking dolphin.

Ninety seconds later, Folch was only four body lengths ahead of me. Water from his kicking feet splashed me. I gritted my teeth and dug for five strokes, then ten, then twenty.

I shot out my arm and grabbed his ankle. He tried to kick my hand off, but he failed, and I pulled him backward. I wrapped my arms around his waist and pulled him underwater. He whipped back and forth in my grip. I slugged him in the side, stunning him for a moment.

He kicked to the surface, and I followed.

I broke the surface and pulled in a breath. Folch's fist crashed into my jaw. I dipped underwater to escape a second punch, and once again I grabbed for his legs. Pulling him back under, I slammed him in the face with my elbow. His body went limp, and he slipped downward.

I'd knocked him out.

I grabbed him under the arms and swam to the surface. Holding his body against my chest, I began side-stroking toward the shore. After several strokes, Folch coughed. He wriggled out of my grasp, turned, and then I felt it. I'm not sure if it was a punch or a kick, but something hit me hard in my abdomen.

Directly in my spleen.

It was the single worst pain I'd ever experienced. A stick of TNT exploding in my side.

My body shut down.

I watched Folch swim away, but I couldn't get my arms to move. I began sinking in freezing water.

I looked up at the shimmering surface as it slowly moved farther away.

I was going to drown.

If it weren't for Lacy, I would have. But I needed to be there for her.

I screamed, but no one heard me.

My right foot kicked. Then my left.

I kicked, kicked, kicked.

My fingers broke the surface, then my elbows, then my head. I sputtered for air, gulping in and out. My arms splashed frantically, just barely keeping me afloat. I slapped at the water, edging closer to shore until I finally grabbed some weeds.

After three attempts, I pulled myself onto the bank.

Then I collapsed.

53

APRIL 25, 2012
9:18 A.M.

A cold front hit eastern Pennsylvania the third week of April, snapping a series of record-breaking high temperatures, and as I stepped out of the car, I could see the vapors of my breath in the frigid mountain air.

It had been five months since Jim Folch had wrestled out of my grasp in the Schuylkill River and I'd dragged myself to shore. After lying there for several minutes, I'd pushed to my feet and hobbled back to the Drexel campus.

When I arrived, there were dozens of police cars and the entire campus had been evacuated. Kip had arrested Professor Allen Collier, who was immediately sent to the Ninth District for processing.

Agent Joyce was there, and I half expected him to have me arrested as well, but he congratulated me on cracking the case, giving me a solemn nod. He informed me he'd put out an APB for Jim Folch.

Folch was never found.

There was an ambulance at the scene, and I asked for a ride to the ER. I suspected that Folch's underwater strike had caused my still-healing spleen to rupture. Turned out I was right. I had emergency surgery that night and spent the next three days in the ICU.

Kip Hufley—yes, Mr. Hufflepuff himself—visited me on my third day there, updating me that Allen Collier had admitted to fourteen of the fifteen Numbers murders. He wouldn't cop to the murder of the John Doe buried with the number runners. Professor Collier refused to implicate Folch. He was insistent that Folch hadn't been part of the killings in the 1970s or any of the present-day murders.

I wasn't surprised. That might have been part of the deal he struck with Folch. If Folch helped Collier with his plot— helping him kill Eugene Kirovec, Constance Yul, Peter Boland, Marty Inaba, Officer Clement, the Queen, Jumpy, and Palmer— Collier would keep his name out of it.

The case had dominated the local news for six weeks, reaching a fever pitch on January 27, 2012, when Allen Collier plead guilty to fourteen counts of first-degree murder. He was sentenced to life without parole.

But Collier never saw the inside of a jail cell. He had no reason left to live, and his cancer quickly advanced. After the trial, he was admitted to the hospital, and three weeks later, he was dead.

With no forensic evidence tying Folch to any of the crimes and the only witness now in the grave, the search lost momentum. Even if Folch were found, it would be nearly impossible to bring a case against him.

His insurance policy worked. I'd sabotaged any hope of ever convicting him of the murders. But that didn't mean I couldn't find him and beat the living shit out of him.

Lacy's MS went into remission at the beginning of January, and she returned to school. However, with limits on how much strenuous activity she could undergo, she lost her position on the swim team and ultimately her scholarship. She'd been upset, but with Baxter at her side and a renewed passion for painting, she was handling it better than I'd expected. The apartment complex where she'd been living didn't allow pets, so the three of us were roomies for the time being.

By the end of January, I felt comfortable leaving Lacy alone for a few days at a time, and that's when Kip—who was determined to capture the man who'd sullied the PPD—and I resumed our manhunt for Jim Folch.

Throughout February and March, we followed several leads, but none panned out. At the end of March, Kip took the detective exam for the fifth time, and—surprise, surprise—the guy passed. With a full plate of fresh cases, he could no longer play Robin to my Batman, and then it was just me.

It was up to me to find Folch.

And now I had.

$$\approx$$

I slipped the purple JanSport over my shoulder, and with the sun cresting over the top of the mountains, I ducked behind a series of large fir trees and jogged toward Steven Eglund's cabin.

The cabin hadn't been on my radar until three days earlier, when I was reading an article in the newspaper about Eglund cutting a plea deal with the FBI. He'd been under house arrest since his attempt to flee the country with his wife, and I realized that this entire time his cabin had sat empty. And it was stocked with several years' worth of food.

Only four other people on the planet knew of the cabin's existence, and one of them was Jim Folch. Plus, Folch had access to Brooke's text message files. He had the code to gain entry.

After a quick detour, I beelined to the house and climbed the stairs to the front door.

I tapped in the code, and the light flashed green. While pushing the door inward, I pulled a newly licensed Glock 19 from my waistband. The interior lights were out, and I flipped a switch.

"Hey, Jim!" I shouted, sweeping the gun through the living room. "That was pretty crafty slugging me in my spleen." I cleared the kitchen, then headed into the guest room. "It wasn't nearly as painful as what's in store for you, but it hurt like hell."

I continued to goad him as I cleared the master bedroom and the master bath. Finally, I made my way to the guest room and slid the closet panel to the side.

"I know you're in the bunker, Jimbo!" I yelled, pushing the hidden door open and stepping to the side. "Or do you prefer Lew? Or maybe, Mr. Lion?" I laughed at my own joke. "You must be sick and tired of canned food. That's probably been the hardest part of this whole thing for you. Not having access to your quinoa and disgusting shakes—all that rabbit food you love."

I waited for Folch to unload ten rounds from the AR-15 that Eglund kept down there, but nothing came.

I took a deep breath, then stuck half my head into view. "Come out, come out, wherever you are!"

There was a deafening blast, and I pulled my head back.

The good news was that I escaped the onslaught of shotgun pellets. The bad news was that my left eardrum—still not fully recovered from Folch's flash-bang grenade—began ringing. A wave of nausea rolled over me.

No more shots came, and the nausea passed, though I was still unsteady on my feet.

I would be a sitting duck going down the stairs, but that wasn't my plan.

I pulled off the backpack and set it on the ground. The bag rustled.

Both Gallow and Moore had been beyond shocked when I explained what their captain had done. Neither had much time to commit to the hunt for Folch, but they had tagged along on a few of Kip's and my road trips. One small piece of information had come up: Folch had a phobia of rats.

I unzipped the backpack halfway, then tossed it down the stairs. Hopefully, the eight rats inside were unharmed and would find their way out.

Within seconds, I heard a scream. Then a barrage of gunfire as Folch must have taken aim at the advancing rodents.

I took several steps back into the kitchen and leveled my gun at the opening.

After ten seconds, he still hadn't appeared.

I hadn't expected him to.

He'd use the trapdoor exit that I was sure he'd discovered in his months hiding out.

Sure enough, twenty seconds later, the sensor alarm I'd placed near the hatch in the woods started shrieking. I was unsteady on my feet, and it took me ten seconds to make it to the front door and around the side of the house. By the time I reached the trail, Folch was fifty yards ahead.

"Folch!" I shouted, leveling my gun at his back. "Stop!"

I was surprised when he stopped and turned. Gray hair flared out over his ears. He had a bushy beard to match. "You're right about one thing," he called out. "The food was the worst!" He smiled, then took off down the trail.

I casually walked in the direction he'd run.

A few moments later, a loud *whomp* echoed through the forest.

I continued down the trail for another hundred yards, then came to Folch on the ground, writhing in pain.

Wade Gleason stood over him, still holding the heavy stick he'd used to hit Folch in the chest.

"It went just how you said it would," Gleason said, flashing his brilliant smile. "I'm pretty sure he shit himself when I jumped out from behind the tree."

I put my foot on Folch's chest and pushed down. It had the desired effect, and he glared up at me. I thought back to when he'd slugged my spleen in the Schuylkill River and left me to die.

I dropped to my knees and slammed my fist into his face.

≈

After navigating to the highway, I glanced in the rearview mirror. Folch was in the back seat, on the passenger side. He hadn't resisted when Gleason—who had already headed back up to Boston—and I handcuffed him, then shoved him into my car. Folch's left eye was starting to swell where I'd punched him and blood dripped from his nose, coloring his beard.

"I thought Professor Collier blackmailed you into committing the murders with him," I said. "But I had it all wrong. It was *you* calling the shots. You blackmailed Collier into helping you with the murders and then taking the rap."

He didn't respond.

"At first, I couldn't figure it out. What possible leverage could you have on Collier that was worse than him taking the rap for fourteen counts of first-degree murder?"

I kept coming back to how Tina was gambling all their money away, trying to hit that elusive number a second time and get the payday that she deserved. Eventually, she lost her job. She fell into a well of depression. She drank. She did drugs. She became abusive.

According to records, social services had been called twice

in 1972. The two little Collier girls never admitted the bruises on their bodies were from their mom, but investigators knew otherwise. Sadly, they couldn't prove it. And Allen, who was still only seventeen, kept his mouth shut.

I'd talked to the social worker in charge of the Collier case, who said the state was getting close to taking the three kids away from Tina. With no direct family in the area and Allen still just seventeen years old, the three kids would be put in foster care.

On March 11, 1973, three weeks after Allen Collier turned eighteen, Tina Collier was found dead.

"Then I realized what you had over him," I said. "Allen Collier killed his mother."

54

"One more game?" Jim asked Allen.

It was a cold March evening, and they'd been playing ball under the streetlights for the past couple of hours. Their high school basketball season had ended a few days earlier. They'd advanced to the Sweet Sixteen of the state playoffs but lost on a last-second jumper to a rival school. Allen had played well, but Jim had his worst game of the season. After the loss, Jim made a vow that he would lead his team to a state championship his senior year.

"I have to get home," Allen replied. "And pick up my sisters from the Johnsons."

For the past year, Allen's mother had been a mess, had even started stealing money from Allen to feed her gambling addiction. His sisters had been staying at the neighbor's apartment across the hall more and more lately.

Jim and Allen headed home. As they walked, they chatted about their two favorite NBA players. For Allen, it was Pete Maravich; for Jim, Oscar Robertson.

"Maravich is too flashy," Jim said, nearing the rundown apartment building where Allen lived.

"That's why he's so great!" Allen said, pulling open the flimsy door.

Jim asked for a glass of water before he headed the half mile home and followed Allen into the building. They reached apartment 4D and Allen unlocked the door. He always checked how drunk his mother was before he grabbed his sisters from the Johnsons.

Jim followed Allen inside.

"Mom!" Allen called.

No response.

Jim grabbed a glass out of a cabinet and filled it with water as Allen made his way into his mother's room.

"Wake up, Mom!" Allen's voice rang through the thin walls.

A moment later, Allen stormed into his room and Jim followed. There were two twin beds, and the room was tidy. Allen fell to his knees and rifled under his bed for a shoe-box. He flipped it open and then shook his head from side to side.

"She took it all," he muttered.

Jim knew it was grocery money. Money to feed Allen and his sisters.

Allen made his way over to his closet. A moment later, he turned, his eyes blurry with tears.

"What?" Jim asked.

"My Nikes are gone." Knowing how tough Allen's home life had become, Coach P had bought Allen a pair of the popular sneakers a few weeks earlier to replace his worn Chuck Taylors. "She must have pawned them."

Allen turned around and made his way to the kitchen. He pulled open a drawer and removed a knife. Jim followed behind him as Allen made his way into his mother's room.

Tina Collier was lying on the carpet. She was clad in a

tank top and stained gray sweatpants. An empty bottle of gin lay beside her.

Allen hovered over his mother, the tip of the knife pointed at his mother's chest.

"What are you doing?" Jim asked.

"What I should have done a long time ago."

Allen knelt and then ran the blade of the knife over his mother's left wrist. He did the same to her right wrist. He dropped the knife near his mother and then stood.

Jim and Allen watched for the next several minutes as the life drained from Tina Collier and onto the carpet.

"This is how we found her when we came in," Allen said.

Jim nodded. "Got it."

55

According to the police report, when Tina Collier was found in her bedroom with her wrists slit, Folch had been at the Collier residence. Collier's two sisters had been eating dinner at a neighbor's house, which they often did because their mother rarely cooked.

"You were over at the apartment that day," I said, flicking my eyes to the rearview mirror. "When you and Collier got back from playing basketball, you went inside. You guys found Collier's mother on the floor. But she wasn't dead. She was drunk. Collier was furious, and he slit his mother's wrists. The coroner didn't bat an eye, calling it a suicide. And Collier, who had turned eighteen three weeks earlier, became his sisters' guardian."

Folch remained stoic, but somewhere underneath his Unabomber disguise, I knew he must have been impressed.

"Forty years later, when Collier called and told you he was dying, that he only had a few months to live, you decided you wanted to finish what you'd started. I'm guessing Collier wanted no part of it. He'd built a great life for himself. He didn't want to spend the last days of it dredging up old memories, and he certainly wanted no part in any more killings.

"I'd gotten it all wrong. It wasn't Collier calling the shots. It was you who wanted the story to come out. It was you who wanted the world to know what the Capettas did to your father. You couldn't imagine the story staying buried. That's when you used your leverage on Allen. You threatened that if he didn't help you with the new murders and take the rap for everything, you would tell his sisters that he'd killed their mother."

Collier would rather his sisters—and now seven nieces and nephews—think he was a serial killer than know he'd killed their mother and grandmother.

"That's an interesting theory," Folch said, the first words out of his mouth since we started driving. "Good luck making it stick."

He was right. There was no forensic evidence tying Folch to any of the murders. There were no witnesses. A dead man had already taken the rap for the murders. Not to mention that the mayor of Philadelphia was Folch's closest friend.

He was Teflon.

The only thing going against him was that he'd gone into hiding after I'd confronted him in the classroom. But he could just whip out the video of my breaking into his home and say that he was scared for his life. He could say that he thought I was a lunatic stalking him, so he fled, and that's why he'd been sheltering in Eglund's bunker.

"You're right," I said. "It won't stick."

When I dropped him off at the police station, they might take him into custody, but I had little doubt he'd be free within the day.

That was why I wasn't taking him to the police station.

It was silent for the next hour, then I exited the freeway.

"Where are we going?" Folch asked, fidgeting.

I drove another mile, entering an industrial area of Philly: three city blocks of warehouses, junkyards, car repair shops, and factories. One warehouse had a roll-up door, open just high enough for the Range Rover to slip beneath. I pulled into the dusty confines of the abandoned building and put the car in park. I flipped on the headlights, illuminating three men.

Frank Capetta and two of his goons.

One goon had a patch over his left eye. Evidently, during our melee atop the *Rocky* steps, I'd done permanent damage by digging my thumb into his eye.

I turned and glanced over my shoulder.

"Don't do it, Prescott!" Folch said, whipping his body from side to side. "Don't give me to them!

"I'll admit it all!" he shouted. "I planned it! It was all me! I blackmailed Allen into it!" He pushed forward against the seat belt restraints. "I took pictures. I can prove it was me! Come on, you'll be famous. You figured it all out. Come on, please!"

I said, "Shut up."

He did.

"I have questions," I said.

"Yeah," he sputtered. "Anything!"

I glanced at the Capettas, who were awaiting my thumbs-up signal, then turned back to Folch.

I said, "That day I made my presentation in the classroom. Why didn't you just let it all play out? Like you said, you never would have been convicted. There was no evidence against you. You would have walked away with a full pension."

"I panicked," Folch said, his chest heaving. "I couldn't be sure Allen would take the rap. I thought maybe he'd get cold feet and tell them that it was all me. That I'd forced his hand."

"Okay, I get that. But why not come forward after he does take the rap, then dies?"

"You never know what's going to happen. There's always that slim chance I overlooked something. Cops don't do well in jail. And the food—I can't even imagine."

Yeah, he wouldn't last long on bologna sandwiches.

"One other thing," I said. "Who is the fourth body that you buried with the three number runners at the church?"

"That was Ugly Marky."

"What?"

"When we killed the three number runners, we found him in the back of their car. He had a bullet hole in his head."

So, Jumpy hadn't been the one to kill Ugly Marky after all.

I said, "Okay, great."

I waved at Capetta and the goons, then put the car in reverse.

Folch let out a sigh of relief from the back seat.

I reversed a foot, then put the car back into Park.

I hit the Unlock button, then flashed a thumbs-up.

"No!" Folch screamed. "I answered all your questions."

The door opened, and a large pair of hands unbuckled Folch and began pulling him out. I watched as the two goons dragged him to the back of the warehouse and through a swinging door.

I rolled down the window.

Frank Capetta leaned down a few inches.

"Are we even?" I asked him.

"You mean, for you clobbering my papa?"

That was the deal. I deliver the guy who killed his cousin Dominic DeSipio in 1973, and he forgets I swung his ninety-four-year-old dementia-ridden father around by his arms and then tossed him on the ground.

He stuck out his hand. "Yeah, we're even."

≈

I was about to jump on the highway and head home, when I decided to drive back to Eglund's cabin. One thing had been bugging me for the past few months, and I wanted to check it out.

No longer needing to be inconspicuous, I parked in Eglund's driveway. I made my way back through the house and downstairs to his bunker. A few rats scurried around, but I didn't mind. I found the safe and plugged in the combo from memory. The lock whirred, then opened.

Eglund's bugout bag was missing. That means that at some point before he and Robin had hired a private jet to fly them to Panama, Eglund had driven up here and grabbed the Dopp kit with his fake passport, money, and diamonds.

However, that wasn't the reason I'd driven back here.

I pulled out the two files, which I supposed hadn't been important enough for Eglund to take with him, and set them on the small desk. I flipped open the file on Robin, then set it aside. I picked up the Wexley file and opened it.

Here's what kept nagging at me: Brooke had first met up with Eglund on September 14, three days before Occupy Wall Street first started in New York City.

There were rumblings of the movement as early as August, but at least from what Brooke's roommate had said, it wasn't on Brooke's radar until it started to crescendo the third week of September.

So then, what was the catalyst to meet up with Eglund? Did she already know that he had a file on her father? Was she already disgusted with her father's business practices?

The timing of it was strange.

Was it just a crazy coincidence that right when Brooke tried to find this file on her father Occupy Wall Street happened?

I glanced at the glossy photo of Nicholas Wexley stepping out of his Rolls Royce, the picture Brooke had left when she stole the file so that if Eglund ever gave the folder a quick glance, he wouldn't suspect the rest of the pages were blank.

I picked up the picture, then dropped it.

"How in the hell?"

I picked up the stack of pages underneath the photo and thumbed through them. It was there. All twenty-seven pages of the file.

Someone had come here after I'd been here on October 26 and returned the file. And it certainly wasn't Brooke.

56

I pushed through the heavy front doors of the Van Pelt-Dietrich Library and into the main foyer. It was the Saturday before finals week, and most of the tables were full. I walked around the library for twenty minutes before I found him. He was tucked away in the fiction section, sunken deep into a blue beanbag chair.

He glanced up as I approached.

I reached out a single printed page to Evan Wexley.

"What's this?" he said, taking it with a sneer.

"It was in the file. The one you replaced in Steven Eglund's safe."

Similar to when I'd printed the file at his fraternity, one page here had been printed on the back of scratch paper from someone's homework.

"Why didn't you use the printer in your room?" I asked.

He didn't answer and I could tell he was trying to place me. He could have been too blotto to remember our meeting at the Monster Mash.

"Kangaroo Boy," I reminded him.

"Right," he said, with a nod.

I repeated my question. "Why didn't you use the printer in your room?"

He knew the jig was up. "I ran out of ink. I went to buy some at the store, but you have to special order it for that stupid printer." He paused, then asked, "How much do you know?"

"I know you were the one who stole the file from Eglund's safe." It was the only logical explanation for the timeline. "And when Brooke was up there, she was supposed to put it back."

He nodded.

"But she didn't. And that's why Brooke came over to your frat three days before she was killed."

Again, he nodded.

"How did you find out about the file?" I asked.

He pushed himself up from the beanbag, then cracked his neck on both sides. "Steven is my godfather. We go on a fishing trip each summer." He pulled a book off the shelf, stared at the cover for a moment, and then slipped it back into its spot. "Over the years, Steven hinted there had been some shady stuff going on behind the scenes at Wexlund Capital when they'd first started out. He never got into specifics, but after a few drinks he'd always say, 'I've got my ass covered if shit hits the fan.'"

"We went on our fishing trip the last week of August this year," he said. "We'd always go to the same place."

"Harmony Lake?"

"Yeah."

"Where would you stay?"

"A hotel right there on the lake. Anyhow, the second day out on the boat, Steven was just downing them. After a few hours, he couldn't even tie his flies on anymore. I had to do it for him. That's when he started going on about this file he's been keeping on my dad for the past twenty years. He said he had all this evidence: names, transactions, short sells, bribing this FBI agent, all this stuff that he's going to use as leverage against my father when the FBI eventually comes calling.

"The next day, I don't think he remembered telling me about it. He acted like everything was hunky-dory. But then, on our way out of town, he said he wanted to show me something and started driving deeper into the mountains. I had no idea what he was up to, but then, after fifteen minutes, he pulls up to this beautiful house hidden in the middle of nowhere. I think he called it 'Safehaven.'

"He said that a few years earlier, he'd bought the house through a dummy corporation that he'd set up in the Philippines. He said he only came out there a few times a year. But he was super paranoid that something terrible was going to happen, an EMP or super virus, and he'd turned the basement into this crazy doomsday bunker.

"He took me down there and showed me all his stuff and how he could live there for like five years if he had to. That's when I saw the safe. I knew that if the file he had on my dad was real, that's where it would be."

"When did you steal it?"

"Three days later. I'd watched him enter the code on the front door when we'd been there. I've always been good with numbers and filed that code away. The safe was a different story. I would have to guess the code. But it turned out that wasn't hard. These old guys use the same password for all their stuff. I'd once had to help Steven get back into his iPhone account. He was obsessed with that show *Survivor*, and his code was 'Survivor 1.' The pad on the safe was alphanumeric, so I tapped in SURVIVOR1, and it worked. I found the file he had on my dad and swapped it out with a bunch of blank computer paper he had in his office."

"But you left the top page of the file, just in case he gave it a quick glance."

He shrugged as if to say, "Of course."

"Then what?"

"I drove home, scanned the file, and uploaded it onto my laptop."

"What were your plans for the file at that point? Did you steal the file to save your father's ass or to destroy him?"

"I wanted to ruin him," he said. "All our money is dirty. He deserves to be in prison. But, I mean, there would have been a lot of collateral damage."

And there had been. Nicholas Wexley was looking at twenty-five years behind bars, Penn had publicly condemned him and removed all trace of any affiliation, and the FBI had frozen all of his assets. The Wexley name had become arsenic.

"So, why involve Brooke?" I asked.

"After a week, I told Savannah my intentions to leak the file anonymously, but she talked me out of it. I decided it would be best if I put the file back. It was only a matter of time before Steven would notice it was gone. And since I was the only person he'd ever told about the cabin, he'd know it was me.

"I drove back up there and tried to open the safe, but Steven had changed the code." He shook his head. "I still don't know why. It was one thing if he'd figured out that I'd taken the file and then changed the code, but I'm positive he didn't know what I'd done."

"I think I know why he changed the code."

"Why?"

"Was there a black Dopp kit in the safe when you first took the file?"

"No. It was just the two files. One on my dad and one on Aunt Robin."

"He added a bugout bag at some point. A fake passport, a few hundred thousand in cash, and a bag of diamonds that

were probably worth a couple million. He probably got paranoid and changed the password." Eglund must have retrieved
the bag sometime between the time I'd come up to the cabin
and before Evan replaced the file.

"That makes sense," Evan said.

I thought I'd figured out how Brooke first got involved and
said, "You needed Brooke to seduce him to get the new code to
the safe and then put the file back."

"If I'd just left her out of it," he said, his bottom lip quivering, "she'd still be alive."

Maybe.

Maybe not.

I'd played this same game myself a million times. If only. If
only I'd called my parents that one last time. If only I'd noticed
something going on with Lacy sooner.

"You can't think like that," I said.

He nodded.

I asked, "Was it Brooke's idea to seduce Steven?"

"Yeah. I never would have suggested it. Makes me sick just
thinking about it. All I did was tell her about what I'd done and
showed her the file."

"When did you do this?"

"On our monthly hike."

This was news to me. "In the Poconos?"

He nodded.

Evan read my expression. "Everyone thought Brooke and I
hated each other, but the truth is, we were close friends. We've
been sneaking off to go hiking in the mountains since high
school."

"Let me guess, you had burner phones that you used to
talk to each other."

"We had to. Our dad reads our text messages. If we wanted

to talk about him, or any family stuff, we had to do it on one of our hikes or use a burner phone."

Brooke must have had a different burner phone that was never found which she used to communicate with her brother.

Evan continued, "Even if we just talked about our plans for the future, what we wanted to do with our lives, our dad would lose it if it wasn't part of his plan. He's a control freak." He made a circular motion with his hand. "You think I wanted to come here? To this school? Hell, no. I wanted to go out west to Cali or down to Florida. But Czar Nicholas said otherwise. You're going to go to Penn, you're going to join Alpha Tau Omega just like I did, you're going to be treasurer. You're going to marry this girl. You're going to give her this ring."

He turned around, and I could see his arm move up toward his face as he wiped tears from his eyes. When he turned back around, I said, "Okay, back to Brooke."

"Right. When I told Brooke everything, she told me Steven had made a pass at her a couple years earlier at her high school graduation. He said something like, 'Now that you're eighteen and about to start college . . .'" He made a gagging noise. "I told her not to, that I'd find a different way to get the file back into the safe. But she was determined. She didn't want me to get in trouble."

I knew what happened next. Brooke spent the next month seducing Eglund and getting him to take her up to Safehaven.

"You gave her the GHB, didn't you?"

He nodded. "I got some from one of the creeps in my frat."

Brooke dosed Eglund with GHB, which he thought was Ecstasy, and she was easily able to coax the new password out of him. But she didn't put the file back.

"Brooke never returned the file," I said, "And then three days before she was murdered, she came over to the frat and told you her plan."

He nodded. "Occupy Wall Street had opened her eyes to how crooked some of these big financial institutions are, and she said that the truth about Dad had to come out. I was worried it would all fall back on me, but she said she would fess up and say that she took the file from Eglund. I would be in the clear."

Sometime during this chat, Brooke must have told Evan the new code to the safe.

"Did you try to talk her out of it?" I asked.

"At first I did. But I was just being selfish, thinking about how it would affect me."

"So, you knew what Brooke was planning to do the next day?"

"Yeah."

"But you guys decided not to tell Claire?"

"Right. We couldn't. Claire was Daddy's little angel. There's no way she would have gone along with it."

"But then Brooke decided to tell her the night before."

"I guess she decided Claire deserved to know what was coming." He leaned his head back, tears now streaming down his cheeks. "I can't believe Claire killed her."

Evan began weeping. He fell into me, and after an awkward second, I gave his back a few rubs. He was still just a kid. A broken kid.

After a few seconds, we separated.

"What now?" I asked.

I knew from his Facebook profile that he'd called off the engagement with Savannah.

"Now?" he asked, which I think was a hypothetical directed at himself. "Get through finals. Graduate. Pack up my life. Head to San Diego or South America. Go someplace where the name Wexley doesn't mean shit."

I gave him one last pat on the shoulder. "It gets better."

He nodded, and then I walked away.

57

"How about here?" Lacy asked.

"Oh, that's perfect!" Sheila Gallow replied.

The Gallows had settled into their new home, and they were having a combination housewarming/Memorial Day barbecue. Lacy had given them her latest painting as a housewarming gift. She'd really found her niche with landscapes. After much discussion, it was decided the painting would hang in their living room.

Mike Gallow pounded a nail into the wall and expertly hung the framed oil painting of the Turtle Rock lighthouse.

Jennifer leaned in and whispered, "I don't know whether to be proud of my star pupil or jealous."

"You can be both," I whispered back. *"Prolous."*

She shook her head. I think she may still be regretting her decision to go steady with me.

Anyhow, after our small group admired the painting for a few more silent seconds, Lacy said, "Alright, enough of this. I'm starving." She looked from side to side. "And I have no idea where my dog went."

Today was Baxter's "nine-month birthday." In the half hour

since we'd arrived, he'd fallen asleep three times. Once on the sidewalk. Again, attempting to go up the stairs. And then a third time, going down the stairs—which hadn't sounded much different from a Slinky. Thankfully, the little guy—now tipping the scales at an impressive seven pounds—appeared to be made of gelatin and, thus far, had escaped serious injury.

The five of us exited the living room and made our way through the sliding glass door and into a modest backyard. Twenty-five guests were spread out on the small porch and a perfectly manicured lawn, where a game of cornhole had been set up. There was also a wooden swing set and princess castle.

Carmen Gallow and her new husband—she and Matthew Hutchings had eloped in Vegas six weeks after I first introduced the pair—were manning the grill on the far side of the porch. They wore matching aprons that read, "Shut Up and Eat My Meat."

Twenty bucks says those two will end up on a *Dateline* special at some point.

After grabbing a beer from the cooler, I walked over to the swing set, where Desiree Moore and Ms. Ruby were playing with Moore's twins. One of the girls, Max, was in the rubber swing bucket, and Moore was lightly pushing her. Ms. Ruby held Lou and was feeding her a bottle.

I said, "Well, both my goddaughters look happy and healthy."

"For the last time," Moore said, rolling her eyes, "You aren't their godfather." She added, "Gallow is going to be."

"But I named them." I turned and nodded at Gallow, who was dressed in the same Eagles jersey as when I'd first seen him, though it was much tighter these days. "Plus, at the pace Gallow is consuming cheesesteaks, he's going to have a massive coronary before the girls' christening."

Both women laughed, and I asked Moore, "Have you given any thought about when you're going back to work?"

"I have another month of maternity leave, then I'll probably start back in July."

Ms. Ruby said, "Which means, I get plenty of time with my science babies."

"If you keep calling them that," Moore said, "I'm going to track down the donor and let *his* mother watch them."

I said, "Grandma Number 1085342."

They laughed. I was on a roll.

"Speaking of numbers," I said to Ms. Ruby, "I can't believe you hit on Thursday."

I'd kept in touch with Ms. Ruby through text and we shared the numbers we played each week. That's right, the Numbers had become part of my life. In addition to playing my pet number, 517 (Lacy's birthday), I'd had several dreams and played the corresponding numbers. I used *The E.K. Dream Book*. Not Ms. Ruby's copy. I'd given that back. No, I used Folch's book, the one with all the numbers he'd used in his killing spree circled in red.

"I couldn't believe I hit either," Ms. Ruby said. "Fifth time!"

"What are you going to buy with your winnings?"

"College funds for these precious little babies."

"Really?" Moore asked, her eyes instantly getting watery. "Okay, I changed my mind. You can call them *science babies* all you want."

"Oh, Ken Garoo!"

I turned my head to see Jennifer waving a plate of food at me. I excused myself, joining Jennifer and Lacy at one of the plastic picnic tables set up on the porch.

I hadn't expected Jennifer to get me a plate, and I thanked her profusely.

"How did I do?" she asked.

I took a look: a fully dressed hamburger, corn on the cob, potato salad, baked beans, and a slice of watermelon. "I'll give you a C."

"Barely a passing grade?" she said. "And why is that?"

I lifted the top bun and pulled out the two sautéed mushrooms that Jennifer had hidden under the tomato. "I present you with exhibit A and exhibit B."

She made a frowny face, then she took the mushrooms and ate them.

I said, "You do know that I'm a detective." Which wasn't exactly true, as once again I found myself gainfully unemployed.

"To Jennifer's credit," Lacy said, swallowing down her lunch regimen of pills with a swig of root beer, "you act like such a moron most of the time, it's easy to forget."

"It must be our silly Scandinavian bloodline."

"I didn't know you guys were Scandinavian," Jennifer said.

Lacy sighed. "We're not."

I laughed, then asked her, "Did you find Baxter?"

"He was asleep in one of the bushes," said Lacy. "Last I saw him, he was in the princess castle with Ainsley. He's protecting the kingdom."

After we finished eating and I'd cleared everybody's plates, I noticed a man playing cornhole by himself. I dropped off fresh drinks for Jennifer and Lacy, then said, "If you ladies will excuse me, I have to go redeem myself."

The man eyed me as I approached, then broke into a wide grin. "Hey, Prescott."

"Hey, Kippy." It was a new nickname for him, which he didn't seem to mind. But I suppose it was quite the upgrade from Puff. "How's detective life?"

"I'm still getting the hang of things, but I think I'm going to be pretty good at it."

I didn't doubt that he'd be an above-average detective. If nothing else, he was persistent.

"Let's play," I said, nodding at the Philadelphia Eagles–themed cornhole setup.

"Alright," he said, leaning down to pick up several small green sandbags with an Eagles logo.

I asked, "Care to make it interesting?" I was still bitter about losing the onesie bet. Partly because I hated losing at anything, and partly because seven months later, I still had a rash under my armpits.

After a moment of mulling, Kip said, "Loser has to get their hair cut at Tyrone's." In an odd twist of fate, Kip had gone back to Tyrone's after his hair had finally grown back out. Evidently, aside from the "pizazz" haircut he'd first received, Kip had thoroughly enjoyed the Black barbershop experience. Now he went to Tyrone's once a week for a trim. He added, "Winner picks the haircut."

"You're on," I said.

Kip said that I could start, and I tossed my first bag. The board was ten feet away and my bag hit the left side, then slid off into the grass.

After Kip's throw, which landed just to the right edge of the hole, he asked, "Are you still looking for Folch?"

"No," I said, shaking my head. "He's in the wind. Probably on a different continent by now."

I'd never told Kip what happened. I don't know how he would have felt about my playing judge, jury, and executioner. Though I didn't know for sure, I assumed that after handing him over to the Capettas, Folch became part of the Delaware River ecosystem.

I hadn't told Gallow anything about Folch either—at least not explicitly.

It had happened three Sundays earlier, while Gallow and I were shooting around before the first game. He leaned over and asked, "How crazy would it be if Captain Folch just showed up here one of these Sundays?"

To which I replied, "Not gonna happen."

Gallow had simply nodded and made no further inquiries.

Kip and I continued to play. Cornhole scoring is similar to shuffleboard (you play to 21), and by the fourth round, Kip called out, "I'm up, twelve-seven."

"Are you sure?" I asked. "I thought I was up, nineteen to three."

He smirked. "Asshole."

I tossed my next throw, which landed on the board and then slid into the hole.

"Nice shot," Kip said, then asked, "So, what's next for you?"

I wasn't sure. My phone wasn't exactly ringing with offers. There wasn't much demand for a thirty-year-old ex–homicide detective who had been described by his SAC as "like a pimple the size of Jupiter" on his ass. Even though I'd cracked the Numbers case, I was persona non grata in the world of law enforcement.

At least for now.

I said, "Actually, after my shakedown lecture in Collier's classroom, I'm considering going into teaching."

Kip laughed. "You—a teacher?"

"It's a possibility." Something about holding that red laser pointer had really invigorated me. Plus, just like Brooke's handsome professor had done to me, I would get to embarrass kids daily.

Kip threw his last sandbag directly in the hole.

There were two soft barks, and a moment later, Baxter wiggled his little head out through the opening. He panted, his tongue darting in and out, doing his best groundhog impression.

"What in the hell?" Kip asked. "Has he been in there the whole time?"

"It's a long story," I said, walking forward and prying Baxter from the hole.

I set him on the grass, and he bounded toward the princess castle.

Once we'd resumed the game, Kip asked, "Are you planning on staying in Philadelphia?"

Lacy and I had talked, and if she wasn't able to swim for Drexel, there was nothing tying her to Philly. Of course, I would have to take my relationship with Jennifer into account. But wherever Lacy went, I would follow.

I gazed over at her at the picnic table. She was laughing. Today was one of her good days.

There was only one thing I knew for certain.

Our future was *unforeseen*.

AUTHOR'S NOTE

My first introduction to the Numbers was the podcast *Criminal*. Episode 108, "The Numbers," was an interview with Bridgett M. Davis, author of *The World According to Fannie Davis: My Mother's Life in the Detroit Numbers*.

I was fascinated.

A three-number illegal lottery!

Dream books!

Numbers Kings and Queens!

By the midway point of the episode, I knew the Numbers would be the backbone of my sixth Thomas Prescott thriller.

I'd pushed Thomas to his brink in the fifth book (*Jungle Up*), which is why I decided on a prequel. *The Numbers* would be Thomas's origin story: how he ended up in Philadelphia, how Lacy was diagnosed with MS, how Baxter entered the picture, and when and where Thomas met Jennifer Peppers.

I wanted Thomas involved in a second investigation, and I started looking into events that occurred in Philadelphia in the 2010s. I came across an article about the Occupy Wall Street (Occupy Philly) protests taking place near city hall in the fall of 2011.

My own experience with the Occupy movement was limited. I was still living in Colorado at the time, and I vaguely remembered going to watch a movie in downtown Denver and seeing a parade of protestors chanting and holding signs.

I never saw one of the tent villages that had popped up in many big cities throughout the United States, but I imagined that these young protestors (mostly high school and college-aged kids) would be especially vulnerable in their tents.

What if one of them were murdered?

≈

I took substantial literary license with the city of Philadelphia, the FBI, the Philadelphia Police Department, forensics, dream books, collegiate swimming, multiple sclerosis, and countless other story elements. Any errors or omissions in the story are mine alone.

≈

I could never have written this book or reached the finish line without the help of an extraordinary group of people.

Special thanks to author Bridgett M. Davis, whose remarkable memoir *The World According to Fannie Davis* was my main reference material for the book. It is sensational and everyone should go read it immediately!

A heartfelt thanks to all my beta readers, Nelda Hirsh, Kari Miller, Karen Mize, Laura Schile, Jeff Ward, Mike Tarter, Shannon Grosso, Michelle Ann Kelly, Andrew Linden, Tom Reid, and Ellen Reid, who each made invaluable contributions to the story.

Massive, warm thanks to my first reader, my mom, who

read the book countless times and provided invaluable insights and recommendations with each draft.

Big thanks to my dad for his keen eye and meaningful advisement.

Huge thanks to my developmental editor, Dana Isaacson, for his expertise and the *many* hours he put into shaping this story.

My sincere thanks to my literary team, Danny Baror and Heather Baror, for their incredible support, guidance, and friendship.

Enormous thanks to the team at Blackstone Publishing for their support and patience as I got this story just right, including Rick Bleiweiss, Megan Bixler, Josie Woodbridge, Alex Cruz, Michael Krohn, Jeffrey Yamaguchi, Brandon Bobkowski, Laura Skulman, and Sarah Bonamino.

My forever thanks to my person, my best friend, and my greatest supporter—Stephy. I never want to write a single word without you by my side. I love, adore, and cherish you. I can't wait to see where we go!

A tearful thanks to my sweet little thirteen-year-old shih-poo, Penny, who became a star in January 2022. She was only nine pounds, but she was fearless. When I moved to San Diego in 2012, I took her (and my other dog, Potter) to the beach for the first time. I knew both dogs were comfortable in the water, but nothing could prepare me for Penny darting into the ocean, swimming through the waves, and dive-bombing for seaweed. She was epic. Thank you for bringing me so much joy!

And to you, my readers, my deepest thanks for turning the pages and letting me live out my dreams.

God is love.
Nick
December 2022

ABOUT THE AUTHOR

Nick Pirog is the bestselling author of the Thomas Prescott series, the 3:00 a.m. series, and *The Speed of Souls*. A Colorado native, he now lives in South Lake Tahoe with his other half, Stephy, and their pup, Potter.